AN APPALACHIAN SUMMER

ANN H. GABHART

Revell

a division of Baker Publishing Group
Grand Rapids, Michigan

Published by Revell
a division of Baker Publishing Group
PO Box 6287, Grand Rapids, MI 49516-6287
www.revellbooks.com

Printed in the United States of America

Library of Congress Cataloging-in-Publication Data
Names: Gabhart, Ann H., 1947– author.
Title: An Appalachian summer / Ann H. Gabhart.
Description: Grand Rapids, Michigan : Revell, a division of Baker Publishing Group, 2020.
Identifiers: LCCN 2019039573 | ISBN 9780800729288 (paperback)
Classification: LCC PS3607.A23 A87 2020 | DDC 813/.6—dc23
LC record available at https://lccn.loc.gov/2019039573

ISBN 978-0-8007-3860-0 (casebound)

Scripture used in this book, whether quoted or paraphrased by the characters, is taken from the King James Version of the Bible.

This book is a work of fiction. Where real people, events, establishments, organizations, or locales appear, they are used fictitiously. All other elements of the novel are drawn from the author's imagination.

The author is represented by the literary agency of Books & Such Literary Management.

20 21 22 23 24 25 26   7 6 5 4 3 2 1

Praise for *River to Redemption*

"Sometimes a story is almost too wonderful to be true. Thankfully, the bit of history at the heart of Gabhart's latest novel is absolutely true, providing the perfect platform for a tale of love and generosity that will restore the reader's faith in mankind. From the deeply compelling opening pages to the satisfying ending, readers will be inspired to examine their own lives and whether or not they 'pray believing.'"

Sarah Loudin Thomas, author
of the Appalachian Blessings series

"Ann H. Gabhart's *River to Redemption* will both capture your heart and bolster your spirits. Each of the well-drawn characters stepped off the pages and into my heart. This story will remain with you long after you've read the last page. A genuinely wonderful book."

Judith Miller, award-winning author of *The Chapel Car Bride*

"Ann Gabhart weaves a sympathetic tale set in pre–Civil War Kentucky. Rich in historical detail, *River of Redemption* reveals the heartbreaking reality of slavery in the first half of the nineteenth century, one young girl's dangerous quest to end it, and a slave's strong faith in God's timing and providence. You will fall in love with these unforgettable characters."

Jan Drexler, award-winning author of The Journey
to Pleasant Prairie series

Praise for *These Healing Hills*

"Gabhart paints an endearing portrait of WWII Appalachia in this enjoyable tale about two people trying to find their place in the world and discern what it means to truly be home. . . . Gabhart handles the Appalachian landscape and culture with skill, bringing them to vibrant life."

Publishers Weekly

Books by Ann H. Gabhart

An Appalachian Summer
River to Redemption
These Healing Hills
Words Spoken True
The Outsider
The Believer
The Seeker
The Blessed
The Gifted
Christmas at Harmony Hill
The Innocent
The Refuge

Heart of Hollyhill

Scent of Lilacs
Orchard of Hope
Summer of Joy

Rosey Corner

Angel Sister
Small Town Girl
Love Comes Home

Hidden Springs Mystery as A. H. Gabhart

Murder at the Courthouse
Murder Comes by Mail
Murder Is No Accident

To my beautiful granddaughters—
Sarah, Fiona, Ashley, Katie, Jillian, and Raegan

And my handsome grandsons—
Austin, John, and Matt

CHAPTER
ONE

May 20, 1933

Piper Danson's cheeks hurt from smiling for what seemed like hours with no relief in sight. More people waited in line to take their turn in front of her and pretend happiness over her debut into society. Then again, their smiles might be sincere. Piper was the one feigning excitement as she repeated socially appropriate words of welcome.

Her ridiculous gauzy white dress looked made for a sixteen-year-old instead of a woman with two years of advanced studies at Brawner Women's College. If only she could fiddle with the neckline where it chafed her skin, but a debutante didn't adjust her clothing in public. She pretended everything was wonderful and that she loved all the flowers presented to her in celebration of her coming-out party. But the cloying odor of so many flower arrangements made her feel as if she were at a wake. Perhaps she was. The funeral of her freedom. Time to pick a man and marry.

That wasn't exactly right. More like time to accept the man her parents had chosen for her and settle down into a proper life, the way her sister Leona had done after her debutante season four years prior.

Where was Jamie Russell when she needed him? She quickly scanned the room before the next person stepped in front of her. Jamie was nowhere to be seen. His absence was disappointing, but hardly surprising. Not now. Not after his family had lost everything in the stock market crash. While debutante balls had surely waned in importance for him in the face of such misfortune, she still expected him to come to hers. If only someone would open the ballroom's balcony doors to let in some air. She considered fainting simply for the novelty of it, but her mother would never forgive her. Besides, fainting was for fragile girls. Piper was anything but fragile. Tall, willowy for sure, but strong enough to rein in the most fractious of horses.

"How beautiful you look." One of her mother's friends took Piper's hand.

Piper held on to her smile and tried to remember the woman's name.

"You are so lucky to have this lovely ball with so many families struggling right now."

Piper didn't know whether to keep smiling or look sad. Perhaps this woman's family had fallen on hard times. Her dress did look like last year's fashion. Piper glanced over at her mother for a clue. Not only had her mother's smile not wavered, it looked genuine, as if produced specifically for this very woman.

Piper murmured something polite and continued to smile too, although she thought having such an elaborate event at a time when men stood in soup lines out on the streets of Louisville was reprehensible. Were it not for her mother, Piper would have flouted Emily Post's guide to proper etiquette for a debutante and escaped to somewhere. Anywhere away from this receiving line.

But she couldn't disappoint her mother, who had worked tirelessly to organize this ball as though Piper's future depended

ANN H. GABHART

entirely upon a successful debut. Piper had managed to put her
off for two years, until now at twenty she was a bit old for a first-
time debutante. She told her mother that, but she would have
none of it.

"We may have been wise to wait a few years in between Leona's
and your debuts. Especially with the situation as it is," her mother
had said.

That was the closest her mother ever came to speaking about
the depressed economic state of the country. She chose to sail
above it, as though money were the least of her worries. She had
been a debutante in better financial times and married the man
her parents thought she should.

When Piper had asked if she loved her father when they married, her mother avoided a straight answer. "My parents had my
best interests in mind. Love grows with time."

Whether love had grown or not, her parents were comfortable with their union. Her mother maintained appearances and
ensured their two daughters and son had the advantages of an
upper-society life. Her father supplied the necessary funds to make
that possible through his partnership in a prestigious law firm,
although the family had made some adjustments due to a reduc-
tion in clients able to pay the firm's fees.

The guest list was shorter than when Leona had her debutante
ball, the hotel ballroom smaller. Piper didn't care. She had tried
to convince her mother to simply have a tea and forget the ball.
Her mother was aghast.

"What would people think?" She had actually turned pale at
the thought. "Appearances are important. Vitally important for
your father's firm. If clients thought we were affected by the situation, then they might fear bringing their concerns to Danson
and Harbridge."

"But a tea would be so much more sensible." Piper paused and
then added, "Considering the situation." When her mother's eyes

9

narrowed on Piper, she knew she had made a mistake using her mother's word for the depression.

While her mother, who had the look of a hothouse lily, might be several inches shorter than Piper, she could be hard as nails when crossed. "That's enough, Piper. You will have a ball. Leona had a ball. A very successful one where she captured a perfect husband in Thomas Harper. Now it is your turn."

When Piper opened her mouth to continue her protest, her mother held her palm out toward her. "Not another word."

Now Piper looked out to where Leona sat with her perfect husband. She looked absolutely miserable, but that could be because she was well along with her first baby. Leona was petite like their mother, and no matter how flowing her dress, her condition couldn't be hidden. Some of the ladies were no doubt whispering behind their hands that Leona should have stayed home, started her confinement. A proper lady didn't parade her expectant body around for the whole world to see.

From the look on Leona's perfect husband's face, he wished they were both home. Or at least, Leona at home and he in his accounting office making sums add up. The man was ten years older than Leona and continually looked as though his cheeks might crack if he smiled.

Piper again resisted the urge to massage her own cheeks before they did crack. After tonight, she was not going to smile for a week. Maybe two. What was there to smile about anyway, with Jamie not showing up at this mockery of a party? He had to know about it, even if he had moved to Danville with his mother after his father's fatal heart attack. Brought on by the collapse of the Russell fortunes. Or so people said when they weren't gossiping that perhaps he hadn't had a heart attack at all but had taken an overdose of some sort.

People did like to gossip in the social arena. As if they had little else to do but find fault with one another. Piper held in a sigh.

She was definitely fodder for the gossips with her late debut. A girl of twenty should already be married or at least promised to someone. Piper could almost hear the whispers. *If that girl doesn't watch out, she'll end up the same as Truda Danson.* Alone. With no prospects.

As if she'd beckoned her with the thought, her aunt Truda stepped in front of her.

"You look like you just swallowed a raw fish, my dear." Truda took both Piper's hands in hers and gave them a shake. "A very slimy one at that."

Fortunately, Piper's mother had turned to signal the musicians since all the guests had been greeted. She either didn't hear Truda or chose to pretend she hadn't. Piper's mother often turned a deaf ear to her sister-in-law. That made for a more peaceful family life.

On the other hand, Piper's father failed to follow her mother's example. He and Truda often had very animated discussions about matters of politics or money. Truda, who held a position in the bank their father had founded, was the main reason Piper's family hadn't lost everything in the slump. She feared a crash was coming and talked her brother into selling the family stocks that were next to worthless a mere month later.

Millions of dollars of investments disappeared into thin air. But Truda wisely socked away the Danson money in a fail-proof account. Piper's mother wasn't at all sure she hadn't stuffed her mattress with it, but wherever it was, they had avoided ruin.

"I'm smiling." For the first time that evening, a real smile sneaked out on her face.

"That's better." Truda gave Piper's hands another shake before she turned them loose. She lowered her voice. "I know you would rather be jumping your horse recklessly across fences or curled in a corner with a book, as would I. The book for me, not the horses. But instead, here we are, making your mother happy. A daughter has to do that at times."

"Did you?" When Truda gave her a puzzled look, Piper went on. "Make your mother happy."

"Oh heavens, no. Poor dear had to give up on me." Truda laughed. "Although I did indeed wear the white dress that looked as atrocious on me as this one does on you. Green is your color. No pale sickly green either. Vibrant green to make your eyes shine like the emeralds they are." She winked. "That would have set those Emily Post readers on their ears. Who decided Post was the expert on everything anyway? Why not Truda Danson's Rules of Etiquette?"

Piper's mother gave Truda a strained smile. "Really, Truda, you promised not to upset Piper's evening."

"Not to worry, Wanda Mae." Truda's face went solemn, but her eyes continued to sparkle with amusement. "I will refrain from speaking any more truth the entire evening and speak only words that will tickle my listeners' ears."

"Piper and I will appreciate your restraint." Her mother motioned Piper toward the dance floor. "Now, go. Braxton is waiting to usher you out for the first dance. I hear he is an excellent dancer. Do try not to step on his toes."

"But he has such big feet, Mother dear." Truda whispered the words near Piper's ear as they moved away from her mother.

Piper stifled a laugh.

"Does the young man indeed have big feet?" Truda peered out at the guests as though checking shoe sizes.

"Braxton's feet are fine. My feet are the clumsy ones." Piper sighed, her giggle gone. She'd taken dancing lessons. Her mother insisted on it, but though she learned the steps, the smoothness of their movement escaped her.

"Then you should do something else. Something better." Truda turned her gaze back to Piper.

"But a debutante must dance to the tune played for her."

"Perhaps for this evening, but come tomorrow you can pick

your own tune. It is 1933, dear girl. We are no longer in the dark ages where a woman has no say in the choices she makes." Truda gave Piper's arm a squeeze. "Marry if you must, but only do so for love."

"Mother says love will grow."

"So it can. Properly nourished." Truda raised her eyebrows. "But a good seed well planted in the rich loamy soil of romance puts down the strongest roots and grows best."

"Did you ever plant such seeds?" Piper had never heard of Truda having a suitor.

Truda shook her head without losing her smile. "I was born before my time. Independence in a woman was not admired twenty years ago. Nor was I beautiful enough to encourage young men to court me in spite of that stubborn lack of coyness. Or perhaps I never met the right man to tempt me to court him."

"They say I look more like your daughter than my mother's." Piper smiled. "So perhaps I will be in the same situation."

"Come now, child. You are much lovelier than I ever hoped to be. Didn't your mother just say this Braxton was waiting to sweep you off your feet? One of the Crandalls, isn't he?"

"Yes."

"Your excitement at the prospect sounds a bit lacking. I can't remember which one he is. Point him out." Truda looked out at the guests again.

"He's beside Thomas." Piper didn't look his way. She could feel him waiting for her. A nice man. Already established in his family's business. Something to do with railroads. Her father claimed him a good match. Love would grow.

"Hmm. A pleasant-looking fellow. Tall enough so you won't have to worry about towering over him if you wear a shoe with a heel. That's good. Men don't like to feel short. That's why they sometimes prefer those petite girls, but I say be glad you're tall enough to reach the high shelves in a cabinet. A useful ability."

Truda let her gaze wander around the rest of the room. "But where is that curly headed boy with the burnished brown eyes who was always trailing you around before you went off to college? Jamie Russell, wasn't it?"

"He must be otherwise occupied this evening." Piper pretended she didn't care.

"Or uninvited. We do close ranks against the less fortunate, don't we? Such a shame about his father. I hear his brother is trying to revive their business. Manufacturing washing machines, I think. Or was it stoves? Either way, no one can afford new things right now."

"Yes." Piper looked around at the ornate room, the flowers, the plates of food. "Unless one is a debutante."

"Try not to sound so thrilled." Truda laughed softly. "Or so much like me." She gave Piper a little shove. "Go. Dance with Braxton of the Crandall railroad fortune. Tomorrow you can take a vow of poverty and walk a different path. But for tonight, be your mother's daughter. A blushing debutante."

A flush did climb up into Piper's cheeks as she turned toward Braxton but stayed where she was. Surely a blushing debutante should wait for the man to approach her.

She scarcely knew him. Since he was five years older than her, he'd been away at Harvard while she and her friends first tasted the freedom of stepping out. Then she'd been away at school except for holidays or summers when she spent every moment possible with Jamie.

She wanted to glance around again to see if perhaps, invitation or no invitation, Jamie had come. But instead, she kept her gaze on Braxton Crandall. One might consider him handsome. A strong chin line, a nose not too big, neatly coiffed brown hair parted on the side. He excused himself from the group around him and came toward her. She had to wait until he stepped nearer to see that his eyes were a grayish blue. He was clean-shaven. That was a plus. Piper had never cared for mustaches.

She almost laughed aloud as she imagined Truda's voice in her head. *"Well, I should say not. A mustache never looks good on a lady. That's why some wise person invented tweezers."*

The nonsensical thought did help. Her smile was genuine and whether it was meant for Braxton Crandall or not little mattered. His own smile got wider.

"Miss Danson." He reached for her hand. "I do think you, as the lovely lady of the hour, are expected to lead off the dancing. Would you grant me the pleasure?"

Piper inclined her head and let him take her hand. As they walked toward the dance area, she hoped for a slow waltz where she could count her steps, even as she remembered the last time she had danced with Jamie. A fast Charleston that had them laughing and leaning on one another in exhaustion when the music stopped.

With Jamie, she never had to count steps.

A balcony door opened and music floated out to where Jamie Russell leaned against the brick wall around the Grand Hotel's prized rose garden. The hotel's brochures spoke glowingly of the beauty and peace it afforded all their guests.

Jamie felt none of that peace. He shouldn't be here. He had told himself not to come. Better to stay in Danville where his mother had found refuge on her brother's estate.

Uncle Wyatt was a physician. While well respected in his town, he was not rich. He claimed any doctor worth his salt could never get rich. Too many needed his services without the coin to pay. Especially now. But he was thrifty and had preserved his inheritance from his much more ambitious father. Part of that inheritance was the family house and acreage in Danville. Jamie's mother had inherited a like amount of money, along with a second house in Louisville.

All was lost when Jamie's father's loans were called in after the crash. He had so wanted to be rich. None of them knew how deeply he went into debt to buy stocks. It seemed a failsafe prospect, with how the market kept booming. For a while it had worked. Profits mushroomed. His father bragged about doubling his money. He repaid the loans but turned around and borrowed more. The gains were there to be grabbed by those brave enough to play the market or foolhardy enough to think stocks would continue rising instead of the bottom dropping out. The crash took it all.

Not only from his father. Others ended up in the same sorrowful position after the ticking of the stock market tape on Black Tuesday.

Jamie had never cared much for numbers. He liked words. Hated the hours he spent in the family business, figuring supply and demand. Supply had overwhelmed demand and now nothing was worth anything. Certainly not Jamie himself, if money were the measure of worth.

Money did seem to be the measure at events like the one playing out in the ballroom above him. He could go in. He was appropriately dressed. The creditors hadn't taken their clothes. Only their self-respect. And his father.

Financial ruin had been more than his father's heart could stand. A stronger man might have fought through. Come back from nothing. Jamie's older brother was that kind of man. Simon was working to revive the family fortune by finding investors to finance a new manufacturing venture. He claimed the economy had to improve and people would again want to spend money.

Perhaps they would, but now all commerce moved at a snail's pace. Still, a new president seemed ready to bring the country out of the depression. President Roosevelt's fireside chat had come through the radio to bolster the courage of men like Simon. So much so that Simon was thinking of changing from manufacturing washing machines to making radios. Even during this downturn in fortunes, people still wanted their radios. That was the future. Simon was every bit as ambitious as their father had been but with a more conservative bent. No loans to gamble on the market. Only on his business future.

Jamie, at twenty-two, was five years younger than Simon and five years older than their baby sister, Marianne, who would never have an elaborate debut party like the one going on in the hotel. That worried their mother, who feared their loss of fortune would keep Marianne and Jamie from finding a good match. Simon was already married with two children. Fortunately, he had made a good match, a lovely lady. An inheritance from her grandmother kept them from losing their house.

Simon and Estelle could have been on the guest list for Piper's party. If so, Piper's parents probably hoped Jamie wouldn't ride Simon's coattails through the door and mess up their plans to match Piper with a more likely husband candidate.

Not that Jamie and Piper had ever mentioned marriage back when they were forever together. Before the crash changed everything. Jamie had been able to continue his education. Uncle Wyatt made sure of that. Jamie had just graduated from Centre College in Danville. A fine college that had tried to prepare him for the future, if he only knew what that future was.

Simon said he could work for him as soon as he got the new business up and going, but Jamie hated the thought of being stuck behind a desk, adding up figures. Uncle Wyatt said he could consider medicine, but the sight of blood made Jamie queasy. Teaching was a possibility, although the idea didn't excite him. Nor would it excite a debutante's parents.

He looked toward the balcony and wished Piper would step outside. He hadn't seen her for months, but at one time they could almost converse without words. Guessing each other's thoughts had been a game they played. She was better at it than him, always knowing when he was thinking blue instead of red or yellow. At church, sitting on opposite sides of the aisle, if he looked toward her, she was always turning to look at him at the same time.

He wondered now why he had never told her he loved her. Why he hadn't made her promise to marry him when they came of age. She would have kept her promise whether her parents thought she should or not.

Perhaps he should climb up the trellis to the balcony. Be a Romeo to his Juliet. But then that story hadn't ended so well for Romeo or Juliet.

That didn't mean he couldn't still ask. Step up to her and ask for a dance. Any dance she wanted to do. A waltz. A Charleston. A dance for life.

Piper, I am here. In the rose garden. He pushed the thought toward her and stepped out of the shadows. He felt foolish, but he couldn't tamp down the hope, making his heart beat faster. If she came outside, that would mean their special connection hadn't been broken by his change in fortune.

The music stopped. The balcony doors opened, and Piper stepped out. Jamie's smile faded when a man followed her. They were obviously together. He recognized the man. Braxton Crandall. The son of the man Simon hoped would invest in his radio factory. The Crandalls' railroad money hadn't disappeared in the crash.

Jamie moved back into the shadows. Money did matter. In so many ways. Perhaps not for love but for all those practical things a person needed. Love wasn't practical.

What if the two had slipped out on the balcony for a kiss? Jamie could not bear watching that. Better to leave without anyone knowing he was there. He pulled in a quick breath when he brushed against a bush. If they heard the rattle of leaves, he hoped they would think it was the wind.

He resisted the urge to look back toward the balcony as he went out the gate. Nor did he think *goodbye*. Instead he thought the words he should have said when he was sixteen or nineteen or twenty. *I love you, Piper Danson.*

Piper was sorry she suggested stepping out on the balcony to Braxton. She should have sent him for a drink and then slipped out alone for a breath of fresh air. His hand was on the small of her back as though they were still dancing. A possessive touch. She eased away from him.

Her cheeks warmed as she realized Braxton might think she hoped for a kiss. That was often the purpose of a couple escaping a dance floor onto a balcony. She remembered a few such times with Jamie. Before the crash changed everything.

Yet, she had still expected him to be here. She almost felt as though he was there somewhere, thinking about her. She bit back a smile as she remembered how they used to see if they could guess each other's thoughts. Perhaps she should have sent thought messages to ask him to come. She didn't care that his family no longer had money. He was young. She was young. Opportunities would surface. But then, what if she was wrong about Jamie caring for her? He had never told her he loved her. They had never talked of marrying someday. She had assumed it, but she might have assumed too much. She stared up at the sky where a few stars were showing up. *Jamie, why aren't you here?*

A rustle of brush in the rose garden grabbed her attention away from the stars. "Someone is in the garden."

Braxton had his hand on her back again. "Perhaps a young man went out to steal a rose for his sweetheart."

Piper looked up at him with an easier smile. "What a romantic thing to say." She had no reason to hold him at arm's length simply because she was pining after Jamie. She had promised her parents to at least get to know Braxton, whether any sparks ignited between them or not.

The polite lines on Braxton's face melted away as he smiled back. Piper hadn't considered that he might find their association tonight every bit as awkward as she did. Had he agreed to be her escort because he was attracted to her, or was it nothing more than a match of fortunes made on a bank floor?

"Roses are the language of love, are they not?" he said.

She would have preferred he had stayed with romance instead of bringing the word *love* out between them, but it was simply a word. She was being too sensitive. Neither of them was ready to think love. She didn't expect to ever be ready. Not with Braxton Crandall, no matter how nice he turned out to be.

If only he'd quit touching her back, herding her this way or that. But that was how dancing was supposed to be. The man leading. The woman following. Her mother said that was the way a woman's life was as well. A good wife following her husband's lead.

Piper supposed her mother was right. Women needed to be wives and mothers to keep things in balance. To keep the world spinning on its axis. The Lord said to go forth and be fruitful. There was Adam and there was Eve. Abraham and Sarah. Isaac and Rebekah. Jacob and Rachel. Well, Leah in that story did complicate matters a bit.

Love could complicate matters. Or the lack of love.

Another rustle in the garden below drew her attention and she moved closer to the railing to look down. A man slipped through the gate to the street. Shadows hid his face, but something about him was so familiar she had to bite her lip to keep from calling out Jamie's name.

She wanted to race back through the ballroom, down the stairs, and outside to run after the man. She hadn't seen Jamie since his father's funeral at the end of summer. Months ago. They had held hands under a tree near the family burial plot and promised to write. Both clinging to a past forever lost and avoiding the very real future that would never be the same.

Jamie moved with his mother to his uncle's house. Piper went back east to school. The holidays when she'd come home, he was in Danville. Not an impossible drive to Louisville, but he hadn't come to see her.

They exchanged a few letters. His oddly stiff and impersonal. *How are you? I'm fine.* But of course he wasn't fine. It didn't take much reading between the lines to know that. Perhaps he had found a girl closer to home. One who wasn't hundreds of miles away at college. It seemed a reasonable assumption for the change in his correspondence. She may have been the only one thinking they were more than friends.

The person in the garden couldn't have been Jamie. He wouldn't have lurked there in the shadows. He would have come in. Thinking it might be him was merely a result of her wishing him there. Not there. Here. Beside her. His hand on her back guiding her to step nearer to him, to share a life with him.

He did love her. At least he had loved her once upon a time. But "once upon a times" were only in fairy tales. That echo of Jamie's voice in her head telling her he loved her was no more than her own desire to hear the words.

She straightened up. Time to stop imagining things, finish out the night, and somehow endure the irritation of the gauzy dress and this man's hand on her back. Better to dance away the hours until the party would finally be over.

As she turned to go back inside, Braxton stepped closer. But one of the things she had learned at college was how to avoid an unwanted kiss at the many dances with the men's college across town. A slide to the side, a smile, and a quick word to dispel any romantic ideas.

"Oh, listen. The music has started up again."

"Then the dance floor awaiteth." Braxton smiled, obviously very aware of her escape tactics. After all, he wasn't a kid. He'd no doubt stepped out on plenty of balconies where kisses were exchanged or refused. But now he offered her his arm, and she slid her hand around his elbow.

She gathered a debutante persona around her and chattered on about nothing that mattered as they went back inside. The band. Or the extravagant bouquet of pink roses he had sent that now graced one of the tables and practically demanded attention.

Just as Braxton Crandall had a way of demanding attention. Were this not Piper's night, other debutantes would be pushing her out of the way in hopes of getting his attention. They would get their chance. After she and Braxton had this next dance together, then the two of them could dance with others. It wasn't as if they were yoked in any way. At least not yet.

When they came back into the ballroom, Piper's mother sent a radiant smile her way, as though Piper were following the proper debutante script. Perhaps she was. At least on the surface, while inside she wished the evening over. More debutante events would follow. Other girls, younger than her, would have their debut balls. Engagements would be announced. Volunteer activities for the betterment of the community would be required. And unavoidable evenings with Braxton Crandall, unless he decided on a more appealing debutante than Piper.

Truda also smiled Piper's way with her eyebrows raised a bit. Piper smiled back at them both. Let the masquerade continue.

CHAPTER
THREE

Truda watched Piper playing the debutante role. That smile didn't mean anything. Girls were taught to smile and follow the rules. Ignore personal wants and wishes and behave as expected. Keep up the show. Piper was doing that. Truda was surprised when Piper stepped out on the balcony with the young man of favor. Perhaps the smile wasn't all a pretense. If so, that should make her father happy.

Braxton Crandall had waltzed Piper around the dance floor and was the excellent dancer Wanda Mae had said. Pluses in a ballroom, but one wasn't in a ballroom often. Looks could be deceiving, as could smiles. But since Truda barely knew him, she couldn't tell if he was acting his part the same as Piper or if he was truly attracted to the young woman.

Dear Piper. She was entirely too much like Truda herself. Poor girl. Not something Truda would wish on Piper even if, at the same time, it made her smile. She did love her niece. Had a special place for her in her heart ever since she'd been by Wanda Mae's bedside when Piper was born. Erwin was off on a trip somewhere, hunting tigers or fishing for sharks or, more likely, trying to make his first million with some business finagling. Who knew what? Whatever it was, he should have stayed home with his wife.

To give him fair credit, he had planned to be home before the birth, but Piper made her appearance sooner than expected. The girl's impulsiveness had started early.

Circumstances conspired to have Truda there. Winter. Snow. Erwin asking her to check on Wanda Mae while he was gone. And so, she happened to be there when Wanda Mae's labor pains began. What a gift that was to Truda. To be present for the miracle of birth.

When the doctor announced a second daughter, Wanda Mae had said, "Oh dear. We were so hoping for a boy that Erwin and I haven't considered girl names."

"Time to consider some now," the doctor said.

The doctor cut the cord and handed the baby to Truda as she made an angry cry of protest against this bright world she'd entered. A maid stood ready to bathe the baby, but Truda waved her away and bathed the newborn herself with great care before wrapping her in a soft blanket.

"She's beautiful," Truda said as she laid the baby in Wanda Mae's arms.

Wanda Mae had smiled down at her baby and kissed the soft fluff of dark hair sticking up in points from her bath. "She is." A worried look pushed aside some of the new-mother joy. "I do hope Erwin won't be too disappointed that I didn't have a boy."

"He'll be ecstatic with such a fine daughter. I do think she has his chin."

"Or yours." Wanda Mae looked up at Truda. "What would you name her, Truda?"

"Piper."

Heaven only knew where Truda came up with that name. She had often wondered about it, amazed that Wanda Mae allowed the baby to keep it. Wanda Mae surprised her by going a step further

25

and adding Jayne, Truda's middle name, as though she were giving Truda a gift. And she had.

A week passed before Erwin managed to make it through the snow and get home. Truda was still there. With the snow as a feeble excuse, she had not gone home or to her job at the bank since the birth. Instead, she changed Piper, rocked her, walked the floor with her, and did everything except nurse her. Even now, twenty years later, she could remember the feel of Piper's soft baby hair against her cheek. And each time she had held her, she thanked the Lord for a baby girl named Piper Jayne.

Erwin had looked down at his new daughter, peacefully sleeping in her cradle. "What kind of name is Piper? I've never heard you mention that as a family name, Wanda Mae."

Wanda Mae, still resting in bed from the birth, had smiled over at Truda. "Perhaps it is a name from your side of the family. Your sister named her."

Erwin turned to Truda with a frown. "My soul, Truda, why would you pick such a name? That's worse than Mother naming you Truda."

When Truda admitted having no reason for the name, Erwin said, "Then we'll change it. Shouldn't be a problem with her only a week old. I'll tell Dr. Hastings we've picked something more sensible."

Truda wanted to defend her choice of the name that, odd or not, had felt right for this child. But she kept quiet. The baby was Erwin and Wanda Mae's, not hers.

That was when Wanda Mae surprised Truda yet again. She had looked up at Erwin. "No. Piper Jayne is her name."

Whether keeping the name was Wanda Mae's way of punishing Erwin for not being at her side when the baby was born didn't really matter. Piper stayed Piper Jayne.

Truda hoped she'd always stay Piper Jayne, an independent thinker in this new age of more opportunities for women. A suitable marriage was not the only path for young women these days. Not that Truda didn't hope Piper found love. Nothing would give her more joy than to see Piper happily married.

While few might believe it of Truda, she was a true romantic. Wanda Mae was right when she told Piper love would grow. Or might grow. But what Truda had always wanted was for love to explode, leaving a coating of joyful happiness on every surface.

Perhaps that could happen with this man of Erwin's choosing. After all, Piper had not seemed reluctant to accompany him out on the balcony where romance had a way of blooming in the moonlight. But something about the set to her shoulders when Piper stepped back onto the dance floor with the young man made Truda believe nothing had been decided yet. Truda couldn't keep from smiling.

Of course she could smile. She was long past those awkward times when a girl had to stand along the wall and hope someone would ask her to dance. Piper didn't have to worry about being a wallflower. Plenty of young men would line up to whirl her around the dance floor, even if their toes were in danger, as Piper claimed. She was a beautiful girl, with a heart and spirit as lovely as her face. While she did look like Truda, she was a softer, lovelier version. Truda's jaw was too square, her hazel eyes too intense, and her nose a fraction too large for beauty.

She had accepted her God-given looks years ago. Rarely worried about what others thought about her at all. But those debutante years had been a trial, as every man her father introduced into her life found another more to his liking. It wasn't all her looks. Her father's money would have been enough to cover that. Not that she was completely unattractive. Besides, ugly girls got married all the time. Truda's problem was her romantic insistence on love growing like a magic vine long before a wedding date was set. She lacked confidence in that idea of love growing after the vows were spoken.

She hadn't been exactly honest when Piper asked about her

debutante days. There was one man. Not a candidate for Truda's hand in her father's eyes, but Truda had felt an immediate attraction to him when he showed up as an unexpected guest at a friend's debutante ball. A cousin from out of town, they said. His suit had been a little shiny on the elbows. His hair looked ready to spring away from the lines he'd forced it into with pomade. He was skinny to the point of hunger. But his light blue eyes seemed to see everything and sparkle with ideas. Ideas he was eager to share with her. At the same time, he listened every bit as eagerly to what she had to say.

Truda thought she'd stepped right into heaven as they sat in a corner of the ballroom and ignored the music while everyone else danced. Jackson was a medical student, just passing through Louisville on his way home somewhere in the eastern part of the state.

When he left, she gave him her address. He promised to write. He couldn't give her an address since he didn't yet know which hospital he would be assigned to in order to continue his training. When she didn't hear from him, she decided he must have lost her address. Not one to give up easily, she contacted his cousin, who promised to find a way to send Jackson her address. But more weeks, then months went by. Eventually she had to accept that she would never get that hoped-for letter from Jackson.

Only later, after her father died, did her mother confess that he had intercepted Jackson's letter to her and ordered him not to write her again.

Truda didn't dwell on it. Not then or not now. Some things weren't meant to be. She did sometimes wonder if that chance encounter with Jackson had perhaps ruined her prospects for a good marriage. Not because she fell in love with a man she'd met only once. She was much too sensible to believe in such nonsense as love at first sight. But that night with Jackson raised her expectations. Made her aware there were men who believed a woman had thoughts worth hearing.

A few other suitors came courting at her door. Truda could have made a match, but never with anyone she thought she could learn to love.

Better to take the path she'd taken. A position in her father's bank, where it turned out she had an aptitude for figures and an instinct about investments. And good she did, or Wanda Mae could have never thrown this lavish party so unappreciated by Piper.

Perhaps Braxton Crandall would be a man such as the long-ago-but-never-quite-forgotten Jackson. Somehow Truda doubted it. Now if that curly headed Russell boy with the smile that could light up a room had been the man of choice, romance might have danced into this party.

It was a shame about Lawrence Russell. She'd known the man was on a path to destruction, but he hadn't wanted to see the warnings. So many hadn't wanted to see the warnings. They wanted to believe the good times would continue to roll. But panic had rolled instead, picking up steam with every dire headline in the newspapers until now commerce was practically at a standstill.

We have nothing to fear but fear itself. Perhaps the new president could convince the people that was true. Franklin Delano Roosevelt's voice on the radio seemed to spread a blanket of comfort over the country, in spite of how banks continued to fail and factories kept shutting down. Her father's bank wasn't in danger of failing since her father had used good sense in picking capable men to lead the bank after his death. Men willing to sometimes pay mind to the investing instincts she must have inherited from her father. While she might only fill a bookkeeping role and never be recognized as a vice president or any other officer of the bank, she did know numbers and risks.

Fortunately for all of them, Erwin had gone into law instead of following their father into the banking industry. Else their bank might be one of those shuttering their doors.

She watched Piper dance again with Braxton Crandall and then the two paired off with others. Older couples joined the younger dancers. She could too. Many here would waltz her around the dance floor, but while being a wallflower had once been painful for a young Truda, now it was preferred.

Not that she didn't still have the physique for dancing. She had stayed slim. Taller than most women, just as Piper was, but graceful on her feet. After all, she was only forty-five. Not exactly ready for the rocking chair. Some of those new opportunities and freedoms had expanded horizons and ways of thinking for a woman her age as well as for younger ones.

Tomorrow she would host a tea for a woman who proved that true. Mary Breckinridge had started a nurse midwifery program for the betterment of mothers and children in the Appalachian Mountains, where poverty was rampant and proper medical care rare.

There would always be those less fortunate. The Bible said so, even as it commanded those with the means to reach a hand out to the needy. But lack of money wasn't the only way to be poor. Being poor in spirit was surely worse. A person should have the courage to go after what he or she wanted. That was why Jamie Russell not showing up tonight to give Piper the choice of choosing love over money disappointed Truda. She had thought the young man had more spunk. Just as years ago Jackson's choice to heed her father's warning and not write her still rankled.

Truda pushed that out of her mind. A person couldn't control everything. Sometimes one had to turn things over to fate or, better yet, to the Lord. She had heard it said that unanswered prayers could turn out to be a blessing. Then again, who said they were unanswered? No was an answer.

Or not yet.

That was the answer she hoped for when it came to Piper marrying. Not yet. Experience life first. Tomorrow's tea might be the very thing to open some new doors.

FOUR

The room buzzed with conversation as ladies arrived for Truda's tea. Piper caught a word here and there as she helped everyone find seats in the parlor. She was amazed Truda had talked her mother into hosting this tea.

"For a worthy cause," Truda had said.

"But I couldn't possibly manage it, Truda. Not the day after Piper's debut." Piper's mother sounded flustered. "I'll gladly host it another time."

"Mary Breckinridge will only be here in Louisville that one day before she continues on to Chicago. To raise money for her work in the mountains."

"What work did you say that was?"

"The Frontier Nursing Service. Nurse midwives in the Appalachian Mountains. She is one of the Breckinridges, you know. Very socially prominent."

"They have society in the mountains?"

Piper, eavesdropping from the next room, smiled at the surprised tone of her mother's voice and moved closer to the door to not miss Truda's answer. She admired her aunt's persuasive skills. Piper could rarely talk her mother into anything.

"No, no. Mary Breckinridge is the socially connected one," Truda said. "The people in the mountains, well, I'm sure they have social connections. Just nothing like what you are thinking. They depend on their extended families, or so I've heard."

"I've heard the families are forever feuding with one another. That they might shoot you with very little provocation."

"You can't believe everything you hear."

"Are you saying they don't carry guns as the pictures depict? Or make moonshine?" Piper had no trouble imagining her mother peering at Truda with raised eyebrows.

"I'm sure they do have guns for hunting, and I won't say moonshine isn't made. Life is hard on those hillside farms without any conveniences. No electricity or running water in their drafty cabins."

"That does sound dreadful."

"Yes, well, they do lack much we take for granted, including access to medical care. That's why Mary Breckinridge started her Frontier Nursing Service in Hyden. But with so much poverty in that area, she depends on donations to support her nurses who ride horses up into the hills to help mothers have babies in their homes."

"Nurses on horseback. How peculiar. Why don't they use motorcars?"

"No proper roads. But doesn't it grab your imagination to think about nurses on horseback? They carry their nursing supplies in saddlebags."

"I suppose." Piper's mother sounded far from convinced. "Perhaps we can send a donation."

"She would really like to talk to several ladies." Truda kept pushing her. "It's only a little tea. I'll hire the pastries made. We won't put that on your Della. All she will need to do is heat water for the tea and make coffee. That's hardly anything."

"Sunday is Della's day off."

"Then I'll heat the water and make coffee." Truda sounded as if she was struggling to stay patient. "Piper can serve, and I'll recruit a daughter of one of the other ladies to help. Another debutante. It can count on their community service."

That, of course, was Truda's telling blow. A debutante was required to do volunteer work.

"Oh, very well." Piper's mother had given in. "I can never say no to you, but if I am too exhausted to attend after Piper's debut, as I may very well be, then you will just have to assume the hostess duties."

But exhausted or not, her mother was not going to miss being in the midst of all these ladies to hear what they had to say about her party. More hers than Piper's. So now she was basking in the praise the others showered on her.

Piper received her own share of compliments as some of the ladies went on and on about her dress.

She smiled as if she agreed, but said dress was in a heap on a chair in her room. She would have stuffed it in the trash bin, except that seemed such a waste of material. No way would she ever wear it again. She much preferred the white blouse and dark blue skirt Truda had asked her to wear today.

Lynette, the other girl Truda recruited, wore a similar outfit. "We look like maids," she complained. "All we lack is aprons."

"We are acting as maids," Piper said.

"I am not a maid." Lynette sniffed. "You can hire people for events like this, you know."

Piper simply smiled at the girl. She was younger than Piper. Barely eighteen. In ten years she would be married to a suitable husband, dressed to the nines, and perched on a chair at a social event somewhere, waiting to be served. Piper shivered at the thought of sitting beside her. She wanted more out of life than an endless round of teas and parties, but she could feel the push to conform to expectations.

She looked across at Truda talking with the guest of honor, Mary Breckinridge. As they stood together, the other women in the room kept glancing toward them. Both were impressive women. No one would call Truda pretty, but she had an air about her. Mrs. Breckinridge lacked Truda's height, but she had the same commanding presence.

Neither of them had conformed to anything. Truda had little patience for the niceties of social conversation. If she had something to say, she said it with no concern about the gentle ears around her.

While Mrs. Breckinridge appeared to possess some of the same directness, she had a certain grace and charm that had the ladies anxious to hear what she had come to share with them. She was smiling, self-possessed, and seemingly without the least concern about what she or anyone else in the room was wearing. At the same time, she appeared to be aware of everything. Piper had the feeling that if Mrs. Breckinridge were to raise her hand, those in the room would fall silent for her to speak.

"She's sort of frumpy looking, don't you think?" Lynette whispered.

"Who?" Piper was puzzled. Frumpy didn't fit anyone in the room in their colorful afternoon dresses and hats.

"That woman. Mrs. Breckinridge. In a plain navy suit, and look at her shoes with hardly a heel."

Piper glanced at Mrs. Breckinridge's shoes. "They look very comfortable."

"What does comfort have to do with anything? A person has to keep up appearances. Just as you did last night in that beautiful dress. You looked as though you were floating on air." Lynette sighed. "And why not? Dancing with the gorgeous Braxton Crandall. We all should be that lucky."

"You'll have your debut ball soon."

"Oh yes. Next month. Mother wanted to have it in June, the

height of the season." The girl did have the grace to look a bit flustered when she realized how her words sounded. "Not that May isn't a wonderful time for a debut. Your ball was a fabulous start to the season."

"Yes, and I am very glad to have it over with."

"Really?" Lynette's eyes widened.

"Really." Piper pointed to the tray of strawberry-and-chocolate truffles and the teapot. "Which would you like to serve?"

"No way am I pouring tea." Lynette reached for the truffles. "I'd be sure to spill it on somebody and never hear the end of it forever after."

"Right. There would go your chances of getting a position as a maid." Piper picked up the teapot and a napkin. That sounded entirely too much like Truda. Her mother would be mortified, but sometimes a person just had to say something.

She didn't want to go to Lynette's debut anyway. She didn't care if she went to any more parties. That included this tea. She hadn't been riding for weeks, with all the preparations for her debutante ball. But the same as her mother, she could never say no to Truda.

"Meeting Mary Breckinridge will be well worth one more day indoors," Truda had said when she arrived at the house that morning and noted Piper longingly looking out at the sunshine. "She's a horsewoman too. She rode up and down every hill in Eastern Kentucky searching for the right location for her Frontier Nursing venture."

Now Piper carefully filled Mrs. Breckinridge's china cup.

"Thank you, my dear. I am so pleased that someone here does know how to brew a proper cup of tea." Mrs. Breckinridge raised her cup to breathe in the aroma before she took a sip. "I do love my tea."

Piper smiled. "Mother and my aunt Truda are delighted you could come today."

"Oh? I feared it might be a tad inconvenient for your mother.

After your debut ball last night. I am aware of how involved such events can be." Mrs. Breckinridge peered over her cup as she took another sip.

"Mother has been very busy, but she's always ready to help others."

"Indeed. That is very good to hear since I must depend on the kindness of those like your mother and aunt to keep my nurses' horses in oats." A smile turned up the woman's lips.

Piper didn't know whether she was serious or joking. "I suppose so."

The woman's smile got bigger. "I can tell by your face that I should perhaps speak about needing oats for my nurses instead of the horses if I have any hope of gaining donors today. But the horses do carry the nurses up the mountains to their patients." She held out her cup for a refill. "Do you ride?"

"Every chance I get."

"Excellent. You must come to the mountains and be one of our couriers."

"Couriers? You mean someone who delivers messages?"

"Much more than that. Our girls take care of the horses. Assist the nurses with whatever is needed. At times they accompany the nurses on calls." Mrs. Breckinridge set her teacup down on a table and turned her piercing blue eyes on Piper. "Have you ever seen a baby come into the world?" She didn't wait for Piper to answer. "But of course you haven't. Young women such as you are shielded from the natural events of birth and death."

"My sister is in the family way."

"A blessing for her, but what way are you in, Piper Danson? An endless round of parties as you seek a husband? Or perhaps you already have someone in mind." Mrs. Breckinridge raised her eyebrows as her gaze pinned Piper in place.

"No." Jamie popped into her mind, but Piper pushed him aside. "No one at all."

Mrs. Breckinridge smiled. "Do I hear a little doubt in those words? Even more reason to come spend a summer in the mountains. I promise it will be an experience that will change your life. For the better."

"My mother would never agree to that."

The woman gave Piper a considering look. "And how old are you, my dear?" Again she didn't wait for an answer. "Truda told me twenty. I would think that is surely old enough to make some decisions on your own."

"Well . . . y-yes." Piper stumbled over the words.

Mrs. Breckinridge patted her arm. "Don't let me fret you. Just give it some thought. You have the rest of your life to wear fine clothes and gossip with your friends. But first, do something. You won't regret it."

Do something. Those words echoed in Piper's head as she continued around the room, filling teacups. Serving. Not being served. But this was only one afternoon of her life. Could she find other ways to serve, to be more than a privileged young woman ready to be forever served by others? What would it be like to step into a completely different world?

Piper stood in the back of the room and listened to the stories Mrs. Breckinridge shared about the different worlds she'd seen and the work of her frontier nurses.

"In France after the Great War, I witnessed how the nurse midwives there helped the families devastated by the war. But one doesn't have to go overseas to find need. Many families in our beautiful Appalachian mountains lack basic medical care. I determined to make it my life's work to help such mothers and children."

Piper was spellbound by Mary Breckinridge's voice as she talked about the nurse midwives. They always found a way to reach their patients in spite of storms that brought high water in the spring and summer or snow and ice in the winter.

Mary Breckinridge looked around the room, letting her gaze

touch on each woman there. "Some of you are mothers. Think of how it would have been when you were in the midst of the birthing pains to be alone in a remote cabin with no one to help you other than a neighbor, if that. Think then of how happy you would be to have a trained nurse midwife by your bedside to deliver that sweet baby you were so anticipating. This nurse would bring a sense of calm and control to the birthing experience. The mountain men love their wives, but they are often next to useless when it's time for their babies to be born." Mary Breckinridge raised her eyebrows a bit. "Didn't you find it so with your own husbands?"

Laughter rippled through the room. A few of the women touched their midsections as if remembering the pain of child-birth. Piper looked at her mother. She had always seemed delicate, almost fragile to Piper, and yet she had borne three babies. Piper could hardly imagine her looking the way Leona did now. Off balance by the baby's weight and with swollen feet and an aching back. Piper wanted to go right then to hug her mother.

Mrs. Breckinridge went on. "But while we are blessed with wonderful donors, we continue to have many needs. Medicines and supplies, not to mention horses and the oats they eat." She glanced at Piper with a wink. "And if you have daughters in their late teens or early twenties, let them come to the mountains to take care of the horses and help my nurses for a few weeks. I promise they will come back to you stronger and more inspired to live a full life."

Lynette leaned close to Piper to whisper. "Give up my debut season to clean horse stalls? Can you imagine?"

Piper didn't answer, but she could imagine the mountains Mrs. Breckinridge described and the nurses riding their horses along the trails and through the creeks. The clip-clop of horses' hooves and the cries of newborns sounded in her head. She did want to do something different. Something that mattered. Maybe this was it.

In the past, when Piper had wondered about her future, her mother always said doors of opportunity would open. While her mother wouldn't be expecting Piper to go through these doors that Mrs. Breckinridge was opening, she had watched her go through others. Off to boarding school. Off to college. Now she was ready to see her at a wedding altar, but what was the hurry? Who knew if she and Braxton Crandall would even like each other enough to hope for more?

A few weeks away from all this debutante nonsense might clear Piper's head, and the mountains could be the very cure for pining after Jamie. A sudden pang of sadness made her heart feel heavy. She had been so sure she would someday marry him. A teenage girl's dream. She was no longer a teenager. Time to move on and dare to do something different. Shrug off the debutante title and ride off to the mountains.

The ladies collected their purses and stepped up to speak to Mrs. Breckinridge before Piper's mother and Truda ushered them to the door. Lynette left with her mother, declaring she'd never play a maid's role again.

Piper picked that time to approach Mrs. Breckinridge, who studied her with intense blue eyes. "Did I entice you into coming to the mountains?"

Piper saw no reason to beat around the bush. "Yes. What do I need to do next?"

"Get a train ticket. You need a sponsor, but I'm sure your aunt will be glad to do that. She's spoken about coming to visit herself sometime this summer. How delightful it would be if you were the one to escort her around to the various centers." Mrs. Breckinridge smiled. "Can your aunt ride?"

"If the horse is gentle enough."

She laughed. "That is true of many of our guests. Our couriers sometimes have to be riding instructors."

"When should I come?" Piper asked.

"Tomorrow is good. I will let them know to expect you so somebody can meet you."

"I might need longer than that to convince Mother."

"Don't be so timid, my dear. Try your wings." When Piper didn't say anything, Mrs. Breckinridge gave her arm a little shake. "Very well. Take a few days. That's all. The train only goes to Hazard. If our car isn't available—and something always seems to be wrong with that vehicle—one of the girls will meet you there with a horse for the trip to Wendover."

"Okay." Piper tried not to sound uncertain.

"Thursday. That should give you plenty of time. You won't need much. Riding boots. Jeans and shirts. Preferably white. I like my girls to look uniform. Helps the mountain people know who you are." She patted Piper on the cheek. "You will love this, Piper." She smiled and headed toward the hallway where one of the ladies waited to drive her to the train station for the next leg of her fundraising trip.

Piper's head was spinning as though she'd just survived a whirlwind. She did want to go to the mountains and try her wings. But Thursday? This was Sunday. What was her mother going to say?

"Who put these crazy ideas in your head?" Piper's father paced back and forth, the way he might in front of a jury. "That Jamie Russell hasn't been sneaking by to see you, has he?"

Standing in the middle of the room, Piper did feel as though she were on trial. Her mother sat on the edge of what could be the witness seat as she twisted her handkerchief into a tight spiral.

"I haven't seen Jamie since his father died." Piper had no idea why her father had brought up Jamie.

Her father stopped pacing to point his finger at Piper. "I'm glad to hear it. He has nothing to offer a girl like you now. But Braxton Crandall does, and if you persist in this idiotic notion to go ride horses in the mountains, you may very well miss your chance with him."

"My chance? I scarcely know the man." Piper had never seen her father in such a state of agitation.

"You can get to know him. Don't you have a dinner engagement with him this evening?" He looked from Piper to her mother with exasperation. "Isn't that how these debutante things work? Girl and boy meet and nature takes its course?"

"Sometimes." Her mother shook out her handkerchief and smoothed it flat on her lap. "Please calm yourself, Erwin. You're getting overwrought."

"Overwrought! My daughter is throwing away her future. Don't you think that is reason to be upset?" Piper's father flung out his hands in irritation.

While his age showed in the gray streaking his hair and his thickening waistline, he prided himself on being in control of every situation. He did not like the peace of his home life disturbed by a contrary child, no matter how old she was.

Piper's mother stood and stepped in front of him. She put her hand flat against his chest to make him stop pacing. She looked so slight in front of his strength, but looks could be deceiving.

That was what Truda had told Piper after the tea. She'd been excited when Piper asked for her courier sponsorship.

"Of course I will. If only I were a bit younger, I'd go with you. But I'm too old."

"You're not old." Piper and Truda were washing the china cups.

Piper's mother had told them to leave the dishes for Della, but Truda waved away the suggestion. "Poor woman would hardly have a day off if you simply saved all Sunday's work for her to do on Monday. But you go rest. Leave it to Piper and me."

"Very well, but keep in mind those are your mother's china dishes."

Truda held up the cup to the late-afternoon light streaming in the window. "Indeed. She was always so proud of these. Said you could almost see through them. Never could figure why that was good, but Mother knew her niceties." She smiled at Piper's mother. "Go. We will tiptoe to the kitchen, carrying each cup one at a time. No stacking these delicates on a tray."

Piper's mother shook her head. "For mercy's sake, Truda. I know you. As soon as I turn my back, you'll have those cups stacked ten high simply to prove you can."

"Never over five high. And I haven't broken a cup since I was sixteen."

Piper's mother laughed then and left them to the cleanup.

That had given Piper the perfect opportunity to tell Truda about her rash promise to Mrs. Breckinridge. Thursday. It would take her that long to figure out how to break the news to her mother. Piper carefully ran the dishcloth around one of the cups.

"You're worried about telling your mother." Truda didn't make it a question. Nor did she wait for an answer as she dried a saucer. "You underestimate her. Just as this china is sturdier than it looks, your mother is tougher than she looks. She will not fall apart over you wanting to do this any more than this saucer will break all that easily." She tapped it on the sink to prove her point.

Piper held her breath, expecting it to shatter. "Don't do that."

"It's only a saucer, dear. If it breaks, we'll sweep up the pieces and pitch them in the trash."

"But it belonged to Grandmother."

"It is a dish. We can get more dishes. You are what cannot be replaced. And it's the same with the opportunities that come to us. We must grab them while we can. Or lose them."

"You sound sad." Piper glanced at her aunt.

"Oh, I doubt anyone can get to my age without a few regrets, but this, going to the mountains, will not be a regret for you. It will be an adventure. The Lord's presenting you with a wonderful opportunity to expand your horizons."

"If Mother doesn't forbid me to go."

"Your mother had some of her own adventures before she married. She's probably never told you, but she marched with the suffragettes. Not once or twice, but many times. Wore the white dresses and carried signs demanding the vote."

"My mother?" Piper looked over at Truda, not sure she could believe her words.

"Oh yes, your mother. Thank goodness she never went on any

of the hunger strikes. As tiny as she is, she might have melted away. Now me, I could have done those hunger strikes except for that hunger part. I do like food on my plate or saucer." She set the saucer down on the cabinet and gave it a twirl.

Piper eyed the spinning saucer and was relieved it didn't end up on the floor as she handed Truda another cup to dry. "What did Father think about that? Mother being a suffragette."

"He didn't march with her. That's for sure." Truda laughed. "Let's just say that he married your mother in spite of her activist ways. And once Leona came along, your mother settled into a wife-and-mother role. But you can believe that when the vote for women was finally won in 1920, she was there voting alongside me. Whatever your father thought."

"Was he against you voting?"

"He is a bit old fashioned in his thinking, but Wanda Mae has a way of changing that sometimes. So it could be she will surprise you about this courier business. Just as it is remarkable this delicate china has survived me." Truda pretended to take a drink out of the cup she had just dried before she set it down in the saucer with the greatest of care.

She had been right about Piper's mother. While Piper had been braced for screams, a lecture, and maybe tears, her mother had merely sighed after Piper told her she wanted to volunteer as a frontier nurse courier.

When Piper couldn't hide her astonishment, her mother smiled. "I'm your mother. I know you better than you know yourself. I saw you talking to Mrs. Breckinridge." She touched Piper's cheek with affection.

"So you're not upset?"

"I can't say that I'm not disappointed you are giving up your debut season." She shook her head a little. "You will miss so many wonderful events. And your father will not be happy. He worries about your future."

44

She said they should wait until Monday morning to break the news to him.

"That way he can go on to the office, where he can grumble about females who don't know what's best for them," her mother said. "By the time he comes home, he may have considered the pluses of the situation. No need for more new dresses to wear to debutante affairs, for one." Piper's mother gave her a look. "Like your ball dress."

"You do know I hated that dress."

"No matter what Truda said, the dress was lovely. A debutante must look like a debutante."

"Then praise the saints I am through being a debutante. Mrs. Breckinridge says I only need jeans and boots."

"You have always wanted to walk a different path than Leona. She loved everything about her debut season. And happily married the man your father wanted her to choose."

"She doesn't seem very happy now."

"That's simply her condition. Once the baby gets here, things will be better. She'll make a wonderful mother."

"Like you, Mother."

Her mother flushed with pleasure. "Thank you, Piper. You children have been the sweetest blessings. I hope that someday you will know this same blessing."

"I do want to marry and have a family. But first let me do something."

"Trust me, sweetheart. Being a mother gives you plenty to do." Her smile faded. "Even when that something is packing a child up to head out on trails where you can't follow. You will be careful in the mountains, won't you, Piper?"

Without hesitation, Piper had promised she would. A promise she had no idea if she could keep or not, since she had little idea of what she might be called upon to do once in the mountains. Whatever it was, she couldn't wait.

Now her mother's very touch seemed to defuse her father's anger. She looked up at him. "Our daughter is twenty, Erwin. Old enough to try her wings."

"She's liable to get them broken down there in the mountains." He looked over her mother's head at Piper. "I simply want you to marry well and have a good life."

Piper bit back the words that she could take care of herself. Her father was in no mood to hear about a woman's new freedoms. Instead she said, "It's only for a summer, Father. Not forever."

"But Braxton Crandall may not wait for you."

"Braxton seems very nice, but we are a long way from any kind of commitments."

"Don't be so sure," he said. "I think he's had his eye on you for a while, simply biding his time to push his case."

Piper's mother spoke up. "Then perhaps it will yet work out. Just as our marriage did." She smiled up at him. A private smile that made Piper turn her gaze away. "You do remember that it took a while for our parents to convince us to marry."

"I don't remember that at all. What I remember is thinking I would never give up until you said yes."

"But I needed a little time and so does Piper. She may not look like me, but she is my daughter. She has her own mind, and she wants to do this. As she said, only for a summer."

"These girls today. Thinking they need to do something more. As if finding a husband isn't enough." Her father shot another look over at Piper, but his face had gone back to its normal color. He almost smiled as he turned back to Piper's mother. "Very well. You've always known best with the children. So I'll leave it to you." He checked his watch. "I must go. I have an appointment at ten."

"Of course, dear." Piper's mother tiptoed up to kiss his cheek. "Will you be here for dinner?"

"I'm entertaining a potential client at the club tonight." As though that made him remember Piper's date with Braxton, he gave Piper a stern look. "I expect you to keep your date with young Crandall this evening and assure him that you won't be in the mountains forever. I daresay you will be glad enough to come home to comfort after a few days of roughing it there."

Piper started to deny his words, but her mother caught her eye with a look. So Piper let her father have the last word before he rushed out.

Her mother blew out a breath. "Well, that's done. Your father will continue to grumble, but he won't try to stop you now. He merely needed to blow off a little steam."

Piper looked toward the door, then back at her mother. "Do you think he will be upset with Truda for sponsoring me?"

"She may hear about it, but no worry there. Truda hasn't let what anybody says bother her since she was twenty-one and refused to go to any more debutante parties. She hated being there with those younger girls and feeling passed over."

"Like me."

Her mother laughed. "You may be older than some of the other girls, but you're certainly not passed over. Not with Braxton Crandall, the catch of the season, ready to camp on your doorstep."

"Father is probably right that if I go to the mountains—"

"If? Are you not sure about this?"

Piper changed her words. "*When* I go to the mountains, he will visit some other doorstep."

"Does that bother you?" Her mother peered at her.

"No."

"Then all is well." She came across the room to put her hand on Piper's arm. "Your father really does want what's best for you. As do I. But I know you better than he does. He sees you as a taller, younger Leona, but the two of you are nothing alike."

Her mother studied Piper's face a moment before she went on. "Leona knew what she wanted early on. A good marriage. A place in society and a secure future. You . . ." She hesitated as though considering her next words. "You? I really don't think you know what you want yet. You're always searching."

"Is that so bad?"

"I suppose not." A slight frown wrinkled her mother's brow. "As long as you don't forever search without finding what you are looking for."

"But what if I don't know what I'm looking for?"

Her mother laughed again. "It's love, sweetheart. Always love." As quickly as her laughter came, it disappeared. "But I don't think you've been in love since you spent all your time with Jamie."

"We were young." Piper tried to sound as though she hadn't given Jamie a thought for a long time. Her mother knew better.

"It is a sorrow about his family, but I want you to know we did not forbid him to come to your debut. I sent an invitation to his brother. He could have come with Simon. We would have received him with grace."

"Simon and his wife didn't come either."

Her mother sighed. "This situation with the economy makes everything difficult." She hugged Piper. "But your father is right about one thing. The Crandalls' fortune is secure. I doubt whoever Braxton Crandall chooses for a bride will ever have to be concerned about buying buttons and bows."

"I've never particularly liked buttons and bows."

That brought back her mother's laughter. "Well, then horses and saddles."

CHAPTER
SIX

Any woman should be thrilled to see a man like Braxton Crandall sitting across the table from her. Not just for a dinner engagement such as this, but every day. The thought brought a stain of heat to Piper's cheeks. She glanced down in hopes Braxton wouldn't notice.

He had been a perfect gentleman since he came for her in his roadster. A sleek car with leather seats and a top that folded down. She liked the wind in her hair. Made her remember finally getting to the stables to ride earlier that day. Not for long, since she had to be ready for her meeting with Braxton.

She didn't call it a date. She didn't want to think of it as a date, but Braxton obviously did. He had brought flowers to her door. More roses. Red this time, instead of pink. As if their house wasn't already glutted with flowers from the debutante ball. Piper wished them gone. And now she had more to wish gone. She should send the roses over to Leona's house. After all, Piper wouldn't be at the house to see them. She would be on the train to the mountains.

In three days she would be in Hyden, Kentucky, where the flowers would be blooming on the mountains instead of on every table in the house. Then again, Mary Breckinridge might have a fondness for cut flowers. Piper had before they became a symbol of her loss of freedom. She was circumventing that now. Grabbing a whole summer of freedom. A smile slipped across her face.

A smile Braxton returned. He must have thought she was smiling at something he said when, in fact, she had been woolgathering instead of giving his words about the menu's fancy desserts much attention. He reached across the table to put his hand over hers. She didn't guess his intent soon enough to slip her hands out of reach.

Not that she minded him touching her hand. That was casual enough. But she didn't want to lead him on when she was leaving for the summer. So never mind the flowers and dinners. But a person couldn't brush off a potential suitor that way. Especially a suitor so favored by her father. Besides, she wasn't sure she wanted to completely sever their ties. When she came back from the mountains, she might be ready to settle down. And why not with someone like Braxton Crandall?

An image of Jamie Russell with his curly black hair and warm brown eyes peeked over Braxton's shoulder. She should have delayed her mountain adventure and instead taken the train to Danville. There she could brazenly knock on his uncle's door and confront Jamie.

Do you think I'm so shallow that the only thing that concerns me is money? The words blew through her head.

"Is something wrong?" Braxton squeezed her hand. "If you don't like your entrée, you can order something different."

"No, no. It's delicious." Piper glanced down at her plate where her chicken parmesan was untouched.

Braxton laughed. "I don't know how you would know unless it's from the memory of a previous dinner with a different guy."

The smile lurking in his eyes made her feel too young and a little foolish. Plus, what he said was true. She had eaten here with Jamie a few years ago. An easy time, with laughter on both sides of the table. Had Jamie held her hand? She couldn't remember.

He had probably been too busy gesturing while telling some crazy story. His big dream was to be a writer.

"I might work in my father's factory, but that doesn't mean I can't write stories in between selling washing machines," he'd told her once. She wondered if he was writing stories now that his family's business was gone.

She pushed the memory aside. Jamie was not here. Braxton was, and the food on her plate gave a perfect excuse to slip her hand away from Braxton's and pick up her fork.

"It's been forever since I've come here with anybody." She forked a bite of the chicken. "I've been away to college."

"Did you leave a brokenhearted suitor behind in the East?"

Piper swallowed and dabbed her lips with her napkin. "Dozens of them, I'm sure."

That made him laugh again, but this time he seemed to be laughing with her instead of at her. "That wouldn't surprise me."

Whether that surprised him or not, what she was ready to tell him next surely would. She had no idea what his response might be. Anger? More laughter? Disbelief? Probably disbelief. For what girl would give up a potential future with a man like him?

She searched for the right words as she took a sip of tea.

He spoke first. "Your father tells me your schooling is finished."

"Yes. It was a two-year course."

"What did you study?"

"Literature and English. I could get a teaching position."

"Is that what you want? I hear the pay is dreadfully low."

"Everything isn't about money." She folded her napkin once and then again.

"Not everything," he said. "But money does make life easier. Gives one the opportunity to take a beautiful woman out to dinner."

She wondered how many beautiful women he had taken out to dinner. She certainly wasn't going to ask. "I do appreciate the dinner and you being my escort at my debut."

51

"Kindness had nothing to do with it." He stared at her as if probing behind her polite words. "I'm not one to beat around the bush, Piper. I know you are aware of your father encouraging our match, but whether he had or not, I would still want to get to know you better."

A blush warmed her cheeks again. As she sipped her tea, she felt like a silly schoolgirl. She put the glass down. "Again, I do appreciate that."

"Oh dear." He looked more amused than upset. "This sounds like the beginning of a 'thanks, but no thanks' speech."

"Not at all. I've enjoyed the time we've been together, but I'm going away for the summer."

He frowned a little. "Your father didn't tell me that."

"He didn't know until this morning. An opportunity to do some charitable work with the frontier nurses in the Appalachian Mountains suddenly presented itself on Sunday at a tea my aunt hosted for Mary Breckinridge. Your sister was there."

"Oh? She's not heading to the mountains too, is she?"

"I don't know. You'd have to ask her that."

He leaned back in his chair and studied Piper as though she had changed into someone different right in front of his eyes. "So what will you do in the mountains?"

"Mrs. Breckinridge said I would be assisting the nurse midwives in myriad ways, such as taking care of their horses. The nurses ride up into the mountains to treat the mothers and children."

"It does sound amazing."

His voice lacked so much as a hint of amazement. At the same time, she didn't hear any timbre of disappointment either. That seemed to indicate her father was exaggerating Braxton's interest. She met his gaze. "Yes, doesn't it? I had thought I'd have longer to prepare to go, but Mrs. Breckinridge is a woman of action. She said Thursday and I couldn't say no."

"Really? You seem fine at saying no."

"I can't recall a question you asked where I answered in the negative." Piper pushed her plate away. Truda's rooms weren't far from the hotel. She could walk there. She picked up her gloves.

Braxton leaned across the table to once more put his hand over hers to keep her from putting on the gloves. "Forgive me if I upset you, Piper. I'm simply blindsided by this."

Piper slid her hands away from his and clutched them together in her lap. "I fear my father has encouraged you to consider a potential arrangement between us more seriously than I am prepared to do at this time. I barely know you, Braxton."

"That is true." He pulled his hand back and picked up his knife to tap against the edge of his plate. "But it is also true that I had hoped to spend the summer getting to know you better to see if we might establish the proper connections between us."

Proper connections? She must be sitting in on one of her father's business meetings. She pushed aside her schoolgirl embarrassment. If he was going to speak plainly, then so would she. "Are you saying you are in love with me?"

He stopped tapping on the plate. A bemused smile turned up his lips. "You are direct, aren't you? Did you learn that in the East?"

She ignored his question. "When you start talking about connections"—she paused a moment on that word before she went on—"it seems time to be direct."

"All right then. While I can't say I am in love with you, I can imagine loving you and the two of us sharing a good life together." His gaze on her was steady. "All this type of considering would surely have been better spread across a summer of dates, but with only one night to declare my interest, things have to be rushed up a bit."

"Too rushed."

"Perhaps so. But I can't promise to wait until fall to pursue my case again." He paused a moment before continuing. "There are many attractive debutantes."

"So there are. I may be the least attractive of the season, since I delayed my debut until I am older than most."

"That actually made you more attractive to me. A mature woman not full of teenage giggles."

"Mature woman." Piper couldn't keep from laughing. Not giggling, however. "You make me sound like my mother."

"I like your mother."

"So do I." Piper let her smile slip away. This time she reached across to touch Braxton's hand. "Look, Braxton, we haven't signed any kind of contract." She purposely used a word her father might use. "I have no hold on you. If you fall in love with the woman of your dreams before the summer is over, then I wish you nothing but happiness."

"Should that happen, what will that leave for you?"

"An adventure." Excitement bubbled up inside Piper at the thought. "I'll have the experience of doing something. Something different."

"But you may be passing up your chance for a secure future."

"That could be." Piper pulled her hand back and picked up her gloves. "But you can be assured that if I do marry, it will be for love and not simply security."

"Have you noticed the newspaper pictures of soup lines and hungry children?" He didn't wait for her to answer. "A secure income that ensures a roof over one's head and food on the table is not a bad thing." His eyes went to her plate of food only half eaten.

"I can't argue that, and seeing those pictures in the news does make me sad for our country." She pushed back from the table. "Would you be so kind as to escort me home?"

He stood as well. "Again, I must ask you to forgive me. I have been less than gentlemanly in my conversation tonight. Won't you sit back down so we can have dessert and end our evening on a sweeter note? The chocolate éclairs here are excellent."

"Very well." Piper sat back down. Her father would never forgive her if she stormed out of the hotel in a huff. Already the people at the tables around them were giving her looks. Looks that would turn into gossip on the morrow.

They chatted about books while they ate their desserts. Braxton described a play he'd recently seen in New York City. None of the words in the air between them mattered. But after he drove her home and walked her to the door, he departed from their meaningless chatter.

He took her hands and smiled down at her. "May I ask a special favor?"

"Certainly." She was positive he was going to ask for a kiss, and what would it hurt to let him kiss her cheek? In a gentlemanly way. That kind of kiss never meant anything.

But he surprised her. "Will you write me?"

When she didn't answer right away, he went on. "Only if you have the time and inclination."

"I don't know if I'll be doing anything very interesting."

"Let me be the judge of that." He pulled a card out of his pocket. "My address."

She stared at it, as though hoping to see what she should say next written there. "All right, but only if you'll write back." She smiled up at him. "Unless you are too busy going to debutante balls."

He returned her smile. "I'll scribble a few lines between dances."

"Then I'll scribble lines back between feeding horses."

"You are a delightful girl." He leaned down then and brushed his lips across hers. In a gentlemanly way.

He was an interesting man. It wouldn't hurt to write him. At least once. When he didn't write back between those dances, she could go on with her life and he with his.

Once inside, she started to peek out the window at him, but she pushed aside the urge and ran up the stairs to her room. Time to pack for her trip. No looking back now.

CHAPTER
SEVEN

When she took Piper to catch her train Thursday morning, Truda wasn't sure which of them was more excited—Piper or her. If only she'd done something like this when she was younger. She had broken from tradition and stayed single instead of settling for a man she didn't love. She had kept hoping for that man when she was Piper's age, until it became apparent she was dreaming of a man who didn't live in her world.

She wanted Piper to marry and be happy, but the girl had plenty of time. A horizon-expanding experience with Mary Breckinridge's nurses was not to be missed, even if her father was frantic with worry she was throwing away her chance to capture Braxton Crandall.

He blamed Truda for that. He had pounded on her door Monday night, his face red, his hands clenched, ready to fight. She loved her brother, but sometimes he lacked vision. He wanted everything to stay the way it had always been, but one sure thing in life was that everything changed. Except the Lord. He didn't, but people and situations did. Those who accepted such changes were more likely to find happiness. She'd told him as much.

"A daughter listening and abiding by her father's wishes shouldn't change." He had paced back and forth in her small sitting room, on each round barely avoiding banging into the wingback chair where she sat. But if he bumped into the chair, on purpose or not, he would be the one with a bruised leg.

His words echoed his thoughts of how a sister should listen to her brother. Especially a spinster sister with no man to take care of her. She chose to go for peace rather than telling him she had quite capably taken care of herself for years.

"I'm sure Piper listens to you, Erwin. Just because she wants to do something out of the ordinary doesn't mean she won't come back after the summer and be more than ready to marry and settle down."

"Braxton Crandall may not wait. I do think he was ready to ask for her hand in marriage."

"You're rushing Piper. She isn't going to agree to a business arrangement between you and the Crandalls. She wants to marry for love."

"Bah. You're talking romantic nonsense. You make a good match and do what you should for the marriage to work. The way Wanda Mae and I did. We listened to our parents and everything has been wonderful."

"Do you love Wanda Mae?"

He stopped pacing and frowned at Truda. "What kind of question is that? Of course I do. She's my wife. And Braxton Crandall will love Piper in the same way if she's not so foolish as to throw away her chances with him."

"If it's meant to be, it will happen."

"Balderdash. Things happen because people make them happen." He glared at Truda and pointed his finger at her. "This is your fault. Piper has always admired you." He looked around. "Why, I have no idea. Living here all alone in these little rooms with no children."

Truda pulled in a breath to hide how his words hurt her. "I realize you are upset, so I'm going to pretend you didn't say that. I had nothing to do with Piper deciding to go to the mountains. All I did was host a tea for Mary Breckinridge. How could I know Piper would hear her talk and then choose to spend her summer in a charitable endeavor there? I'm proud of her. You should be too."

Erwin stopped pacing and stared down at the floor. "I am proud of her. Of course I am. I just want what's best for her."

Truda stood up and took his hand in hers. "I know you do. But she's twenty years old. Being away to school gave her a taste of independence and now she wants to think for herself." She squeezed his hand lightly and turned it loose.

"But all this debutante stuff was supposed to signal her readiness to marry."

"You know she only went through that ordeal to please Wanda Mae."

"The same as you did for our mother."

"Yes, but times were different then. Had I found the right man, I would have married. I would have loved having children of my own, but such didn't happen."

"There was one man, wasn't there? One who didn't work out."

"Not really." There was no reason to look back at something so long ago with regrets.

But Erwin didn't let it go. "He was going to be a doctor, I think." Erwin's face tightened with concentration. "Yes, that was it, but Father claimed he wasn't a suitable match and nixed the relationship."

"There was never a relationship." Truda shrugged off his words. "Only a dream."

"And now you've passed along that dream to Piper."

"I have not. Piper has her own dreams. Be glad she can chase one of them this summer."

So this morning Truda was taking Piper to do that very thing.

Piper had thrown her case packed with jeans and shirts in Truda's back seat. One dress just in case, Piper said. "I don't know in case what, but Mother insisted. She can't imagine not needing a dress for something."

"Perhaps for church. She wants you to be prepared."

"Oh, I am, Truda. Prepared for something different." Piper practically bounced on the car seat. "I can hardly imagine how different."

"You will write, won't you?" Truda parked at the train station and climbed out of the car to walk with Piper to get her ticket.

"Of course. I hope I have time to write all the letters I've promised to everyone. To you. To Mother. To Leona. Even Braxton Crandall wants me to write."

"That should make your father happy."

"I didn't tell him and don't you either. I wouldn't want to raise Father's hopes. Braxton is nice. Who knows? Given time, we might make a perfect couple, but I don't like feeling as though I'm just another name on a business agreement."

"Stick to your guns on that. Hold out for love. Not a business contract."

"I suppose it would be possible to have both. If I weren't heading to the mountains." Piper's face lit up and she looked ready to dance right there on the train platform. She was wearing riding pants in case she had to make the final leg of her journey to Mary Breckinridge's house at Wendover by horse. "Love is officially postponed until further notice."

"Are you going to write to that Jamie boy too?" A shadow fell over Piper's face and Truda rushed out more words. "I'm sorry. I shouldn't have asked that."

"That's all right. And who knows? Maybe I will write to him. What's one more letter?" Piper laughed. "I hope they sell ink in Hyden."

"Worry not. I'll send you some."

Worry not. Her aunt's words echoed in Piper's head after she climbed aboard the train. She wasn't worried. Not exactly. She wanted to think she was nothing but excited, but she couldn't deny the apprehension tickling through her. She knew nothing about the mountains or the people there. Nothing for certain anyway. She'd heard the stories about feuds and shootings. Her father warned her that mountaineers didn't like strangers. But Mrs. Breckinridge said they welcomed her nurses. That had to include her couriers too.

Piper found a seat by an open window and watched the people milling around the platform, either arriving in Louisville or leaving the way she was. She didn't see Truda. She must have already gone back to her car.

A man walking away from the train station made her think of Jamie. Truda mentioning him must have her dreaming him up. But when the man glanced back, Piper's heart leaped up in her chest. It was Jamie.

She stuck her head out the window to wave. "Jamie."

"Jamie."

At first she thought her shout might be echoing off the station walls, but no, someone else was calling him. A girl in a blue dress and heels ran across the platform. "Wait up, Jamie."

Jamie stopped and turned around. A smile lit up his face. A smile Piper remembered well from other times but then for her.

The girl's blonde curls bounced on her shoulders as she caught up with him and grabbed his hands. Piper didn't know the girl.

"Miss, please sit down in your seat." The conductor stood in the aisle by Piper.

Piper pulled her head back inside the window, but she could still see Jamie and the girl. They were obviously happy to see one another. As happy as Piper would be if she were the one holding Jamie's hands.

She turned to properly sit in her seat. "Oh, sorry. I just saw somebody I hadn't seen for a while."

"An old boyfriend, eh?" The conductor grinned. "You'll have to see him another time. This train is on the way and trains don't stop for nothing. That's why they've got cowcatchers on the front of them." He chuckled and headed on down the aisle to make sure no passsengers risked arms and heads by leaning out the windows.

Piper didn't see any reason to laugh. She stared down at her hands clutched in her lap. Obviously, Jamie had moved on, found another girl. Tears popped up in her eyes as she took a shaky breath. She couldn't stop imagining his brown eyes full of light, looking at her as if she were the only girl in the world. Turns out she wasn't. Those eyes had been smiling at the blonde in the blue dress and not at Piper.

He didn't see you. The words ran through her head. *But he did see her*, she argued back. The beautiful girl in the blue dress. And was very happy about it. Piper didn't know if the girl was truly beautiful. She hadn't seen her face. Only her back as she ran toward Jamie, with the golden curls bouncing with each step. She had seen Jamie's face. The smile. The welcome.

He looked fine. Not at all miserable, as she'd been imagining him. She should have known better. Jamie couldn't be miserable. Not for long. It wasn't in his makeup. That was one of the things she liked best about him. How he could always find a reason to laugh and make her laugh too.

But she hadn't seen him for months. A person could change. He could leave behind old friends and forget promises made. But then, they had never made any promises. Not for the future. Not for now. She had no claim on him. A guy could find another girl. He had no claim on her. A girl could decide to do something different.

Piper swiped away her tears, relieved nobody was sitting in the seat beside her to notice. She lifted her chin and stared out the window. They'd left town and were rolling through the country-side. Wind blew in the open window to tousle her hair, and some ash from the steam engine smoke dotted her arm. She pushed the window partly closed, but the breeze still ruffled her hair. The day was warm. The air felt good.

She would keep her eyes and thoughts forward and not look back. She would push the sight of Jamie and the blonde girl clear out of her mind. Soon she'd be riding horses up into the mountains with no time for romance anyway. Not until after summer.

Then if Braxton Crandall kept his promise to write to her and he didn't find a more amenable bride this summer, maybe she would entertain his attentions.

Still, she wished she had been out on the depot platform to see Jamie and find out how he was doing. He could have introduced her to his new girlfriend. Maybe she would write to him after all. Simply as one old friend to another.

CHAPTER
EIGHT

For a crazy second or two, Jamie was sure he heard Piper calling his name. But then Victoria Smothers was running between people and yelling at him to wait. It must have been wishful thinking to imagine Piper's voice instead of Victoria's. Piper wouldn't have any reason to be at the train station. Unless she was going to the big city to shop for a wedding dress. He felt a little better when he remembered the train schedule he'd just read. That train pulling out of the station was headed southeast. Destination towns in the Appalachian Mountains.

Not that he wasn't happy to see Victoria. She was one of his sister's best friends, or had been before they moved to his uncle's house. A cute girl that Marianne claimed had a crush on him. He certainly didn't want to encourage that, but he could hardly ignore her either.

She grabbed his hands the way a schoolgirl might. She probably was still a schoolgirl, although he seemed to remember she was a year older than Marianne, who was seventeen.

"Jamie." After her dash across the platform, Victoria had to get her breath before she could go on. "I was afraid I wasn't going to catch you."

"Hello, Victoria. Marianne will be excited when I tell her I ran into you. Catching a train somewhere?"

"No. Seeing my father off to Boston. Mother is talking to someone over there. So we have time to chat." She gave his hands a squeeze. "What brings you to Louisville?"

"I came to see Simon." He eased his hands away from hers.

"Oh, your brother." She gave him a coy look. "I thought maybe you came to see that girl Marianne says you're carrying a torch for." A little frown wrinkled the skin between her eyes. "The one with the funny name."

Jamie kept his smile bland. He and Marianne were going to have a talk when he got back to Danville.

"Piper. That's it." Victoria's frown disappeared. "Piper Danson. She had her debut last weekend. I wasn't invited. I suppose my family isn't high enough on the social ladder." She raised her eyebrows a bit. "I heard her escort was the one and only Braxton Crandall. Girls have been trying to catch him for years, but he's a slippery fellow."

He didn't want to talk about Braxton Crandall. He looked over Victoria's head, hoping to spot her mother looking for her, but she was nowhere in sight. "Would you like me to walk you back to your mother?"

She laughed. "That's so sweet of you, but terribly old fashioned. A girl doesn't have to be escorted everywhere anymore." Then as if realizing she'd given him a chance to leave, she slipped her hand around his elbow. "But I like old-fashioned guys. Besides, Mother would never forgive me if I didn't give her a chance to say hello and ask about your mother and Marianne. I do miss Marianne."

"Why don't you write her? She'd like that." Where was the girl's mother? They had walked halfway across the platform.

"I'm terrible at writing letters." She hugged his arm close to her. "Maybe Mother will let me visit instead. I could take the train down. That would be so exciting. I've never ridden on a train, but we do plan to go to Boston to shop for my debutante dress next year." She looked up at Jamie. "You will come to my debut, won't you? Please."

"If I can." Who knew what another year would bring? He hoped it wouldn't be as bad as last year. In fact, things could start getting better today. When he saw Piper. But he'd promised his mother he would do it the proper way and ask her father permission to call on her. They were no longer kids. Now was the time to be serious.

At least he could tell Piper's father he had a job. Not anything that would impress Erwin Danson. A teaching position at the local high school. Jamie wasn't that excited about it either. He'd never thought about teaching, but a man had to take what he could find. Perhaps he could pass on his passion for words and books to his students. And teaching didn't mean he couldn't still pen some stories. Writing was what he really wanted to do.

The Danville newspaper published one of his articles last week. Better than that, he'd sold a story to a Chicago magazine for enough to buy a new camera. He couldn't wait to tell Piper.

Seeing his byline excited Jamie, but it wouldn't impress Piper's father or Simon either. That didn't matter. Jamie couldn't walk their paths. He had to find his own. While not having money could be inconvenient, at the same time not chasing after ways to line his pockets gave him a certain freedom.

They finally spotted Victoria's mother. After a few pleasant-ries about his mother and Marianne, he escaped to find a bus downtown to Mr. Danson's office. He wished he hadn't made that promise to his mother so he could go straight to Piper's house.

Just thinking about seeing Piper made his heart skip a beat. He loved Piper. He'd loved her since they were kids, but this last year of not seeing her made him realize just how much he needed her in his life.

She was going to ask why he had stopped writing to her while she was away at school. She would want to know why he hadn't come to her debutante ball. He didn't have good answers, but he hoped she'd forgive him anyway.

Of course, he could be too late. Piper might have decided on Braxton Crandall. With his family's railroad money behind him, she would lack for nothing. Jamie mentally shook away the thought. While he didn't have much to offer in the way of things, he had everything to offer in the way of love.

But would that be enough? He kept seeing Piper on the hotel balcony with Braxton Crandall's arm around her. Jamie should have gone inside that night. Asked for a dance. Instead he'd slunk away into the night without even letting Piper know he loved her. Still, was it right to ask her to give up the kind of life she was accustomed to for him?

So the arguments had spun around in his head ever since last weekend. Actually for weeks before that. He was the one who had abandoned their friendship. Not her. But he had his reasons. Or maybe *insecurities* was a better word.

At the offices of Danson and Harbridge, Mr. Danson's secretary asked if he had an appointment.

"I'm a friend of the family," Jamie said.

When she gave him a doubting look, he turned on his best smile. Piper used to say he could charm a bird out of a tree with his smile. It worked on the secretary too.

"Jamie Russell, right?" She picked up the phone. "Let me see if Mr. Danson can squeeze out a few minutes for you."

Mr. Danson came out of his office right away, smiling, with his hand outstretched to shake Jamie's. "Jamie, my boy, good to see you. Come on in." He put his arm around Jamie's shoulders to usher him into his office.

Jamie didn't remember the man ever being that friendly. But then, since his father died, several of his old business acquaintances made an extra show of chumminess when they saw Jamie. As if they needed to exaggerate the goodwill to avoid mention of the bad times.

"What brings you to Louisville?" Mr. Danson motioned him toward a chair while he sat down behind the polished oak desk. A ledger was open in front of him. Mr. Danson pulled an envelope out of a drawer to stick in the book before he closed it. Then he leaned forward on his elbows and didn't wait for Jamie's answer. "If you're looking for a position, I'm afraid we don't have any openings right now."

"I'm not here for a job, sir. I've found a teaching position in Danville."

"Teaching. Ahh." Mr. Danson sat back. "A noble profession, but I hear there's not much money in it."

"Teachers get by." This was starting out on a wrong note.

"Yes, yes. Of course they do. Get by."

An uncomfortable silence fell between them as Mr. Danson waited for him to say why he was there. The words Jamie had practiced on the way to Louisville flew clear out of his head now.

He pulled in a breath. "I'm here about Piper."

"Oh?" Mr. Danson picked up a pencil and rolled it between his fingers. "What about Piper?" His smile was gone.

No need putting it off. Just be out with it. Keep his word to his mother and then deal with whatever happened next. "I came to ask your permission to call upon her."

Mr. Danson's face didn't change as he drummed the pencil on his desk a moment before speaking. "You do know Piper had her debut last week."

"I was sorry to miss it." Jamie looked straight at Mr. Danson, the fact that he wasn't invited hanging in the air between them.

"Yes, well." The man hesitated and stared at the pencil in his hands. He blew out a breath and looked back up at Jamie. "The two of us have no reason to play games, Jamie. I realize you and

Piper have been friends for years. But things change. Opportunities change. It's not that I don't like you. I think you are a wonderful young man in control of your destiny. But I have to look out for my daughter. I'm not sure what kind of future she might have with you."

"A very loving one, sir."

"Hmm." Mr. Danson dropped the pencil and laid his hands flat on his desk to lean forward and pin Jamie with his stare. "I can see you are very sincere, Jamie, and I do understand your feelings. Honestly, I do. But love is not the only consideration when I think of what's best for my daughter. I want her to have love. Of course. But I would not want her to ever have to worry about where her next meal is coming from or if she could afford a new dress or be able to obtain proper care for the grandchildren I hope she will give her mother and me."

Jamie started to speak, but Mr. Danson held up his hand to stop him. "Wait. I'm not through. How old are you? Twenty?"

"I'm twenty-two, sir. I just graduated from Centre College. With honors." He didn't know why he bothered to mention that last. The man in front of him wasn't going to be impressed by anything except money in the bank.

"That's good to know." Mr. Danson smiled. "And because I know you care about my daughter, I'm sure you won't want to stand in the way of her happiness. She has the opportunity to make an advantageous match with a man who can give Piper the life she deserves. A life you haven't the resources to provide her." He almost looked sorry. "You know that and I know that."

"Don't you think Piper should be the one to make that decision? Not you."

"Young people can be foolish. They think they can overcome even the harshest difficulties, but it's up to those of us with more experience to guide them away from the pitfalls of life. Were he here, your father would tell you the same thing."

"My father fell into some of those pitfalls. Of his own making." Jamie couldn't keep the bitterness out of his voice. But he wasn't angry at his father. The poor man had simply been trying to keep up with men like this one in front of him. He had never felt good enough or rich enough.

Mr. Danson looked embarrassed by Jamie's words as he stared down at his desk. "Black Tuesday destroyed many good men."

"It did my father and our family's fortunes, but it didn't destroy me." Jamie stood up. "Thank you very much for your time, sir." He managed a smile before he turned toward the door.

Mr. Danson's words stopped him. "I won't forbid you to see Piper, but I hope you will weigh what is truly best for her. If you do love her as you say, you will want her to have a good life."

"A good life." Jamie echoed the man's words as he looked back at him. "But what is life without love?"

"Braxton Crandall is prepared to love Piper."

"Prepared to? How do you prepare to love someone?"

"You give love a chance."

"Is Piper prepared to love him?" The words almost choked him, but they had to be spoken.

"She is."

His answer was a knife in Jamie's heart. Perhaps he had waited too long to gather his courage to state his case to Piper. She used to love him. He was sure of that. When they were kids, but they weren't kids now.

"Good day, sir." They had nothing more to say, but he wouldn't give up. Not yet. Not until Piper told him there was no hope. Her father might not realize it, but they had entered a different era, one where girls didn't always have to do what their fathers said. At least he could hope Piper had entered that era.

He caught the bus to Piper's house. The day was nice, so he started to go to the stables where she liked to ride. Where he had once ridden with her. He remembered the last time. They'd stopped at a creek and sat in the shade while their horses munched on the grass. When a breeze blew a strand of hair into Piper's face, he'd reached over to loop it behind her ear. He loved her so much, but just as he worked up the nerve to tell her that, she'd yanked off her riding boots and waded out in the creek. He waded in after her. They'd both ended up soaking wet and laughing, but the moment had vanished for declaring his love.

Then she'd gone away to school. His family situation became direr. The factory had failed. They had no money for the bills that came to the house in piles. The bank foreclosed on the house. His father died. Not by suicide as rumor had it, but shame had played a part.

Shame played a part in Jamie not answering Piper's letters. In not going to see her. The very things her father had just said to him had been in his mind for months. She did deserve better. More than he could give. Even now.

His mother was the one who had convinced him to lay his heart on the line. She was tired of the way he kept moping around after he came back from Piper's debut. He had admitted not going inside that night, but he hadn't told her about seeing Piper with Braxton Crandall. On the balcony. When he should have been the one on the balcony with her.

"Go see her." His mother had used her sternest voice, the one that meant he was in trouble.

"She might not want to see me. She hasn't written in months."

"How long since you wrote to her?" She didn't wait for an answer. "More than months, I'll wager. You're the one at fault there. Not Piper. If I know Piper, she still claims you as a friend."

"I want to be more than friends."

His mother's voice softened then as she put her hand on his cheek. "I know that, son. But does she know it?"

Jamie always assumed Piper did, but the words had never been out there between them. Those words were going to be spoken today.

He knocked on Piper's front door, then knocked again. Just as he was about to knock yet again, Della came to the door with a dish towel draped over her shoulder.

Her face lit up. "Mr. Jamie, if it's not the nicest thing to see you standing there. How have you been? I've missed you being in and out around here."

"I've missed you too and those delicious cinnamon cookies you make." That made the housekeeper smile. "Is Miss Piper here?"

Della frowned a little. "I'm sorry as I can be, but you just missed her."

"Do you know when she'll be back?"

Della shook her head. "She's gone for the summer. Won't be back till August. Maybe September."

"September?" Surely he heard wrong. That was months from now.

"That's what she told me. She's up and gone to the mountains to help some nurses down there. Charity work, Mrs. Danson says. I wish the missus was here to tell you exactly what, but she was so upset by Miss Piper leaving this morning that she had to get out of the house. Meeting a friend for lunch would be my guess. That's fine with me. I've got plenty to do keeping all the petals and leaves cleaned up from all these flowers." She waved at a vase of red roses in the hallway behind her. "Miss Piper got that one the other day from that Crandall man, but I guess he couldn't talk her out of going to the mountains either."

Jamie stared at the roses and didn't know what to say. He hadn't considered Piper not being home. Gone out of town. He'd been ready to fight Crandall for her attentions, but the mountains?

"You want to come in and wait for Mrs. Danson? She can tell you where Miss Piper went. They said some town, but I didn't keep it in my head. And then Miss Piper kept talking about frontier nurses. But we don't have frontiers in Kentucky these days, do we?" Della frowned again.

"Maybe frontiers in the world of medicine. I don't know."

"That could be." Della's smile came back. "I do know there are mountains to the east. Never been there, but I wouldn't mind seeing them. I told Miss Piper to be sure to send us some pictures."

"Did she leave an address?"

"No, sir. She aims to send that once she gets there. Wish I knew more to tell you." A sympathetic look settled on her face. "Why don't you come on inside and wait for Miss Wanda? I don't have any of those cinnamon cookies, but I've got a chocolate cake back there in the kitchen."

"That sounds good, Della, but I better head on over to my brother's house." He turned to leave.

"I'm sorry you didn't get here yesterday," she called after him. "Miss Piper would have been happy to see you. I'm sure of that."

Jamie forced himself to smile and wave. His feet felt like they each weighed a hundred pounds as he walked away. But once he was back out on the sidewalk, his step lightened a little. At least, Piper wasn't out of town shopping for a wedding dress.

CHAPTER
NINE

The rumble of the train wheels awoke a new feeling inside Piper. She had escaped the debutante expectations. Instead, she was doing something worthwhile with her life, at least for this one summer. A swell of excitement rose within her as if she'd never been on a train although she had many times. But those trains to Boston where she went to school were different. Sleeker. Smoother. The wheels on this old train as it headed southeast played a song in her ears. New. Freedom. Adventure.

Outside the window the landscape changed. She'd never traveled out into the state. Louisville had everything she needed. At least until Jamie moved to Danville.

She wondered if the train would pass through Danville. She should have traced the route on a map. Not that it mattered. She was going to Hazard, not Danville. Besides, by some quirk of fortune, Jamie was in Louisville. She'd just seen him there. Meeting that pretty blonde.

She pushed that thought away and stared out at wide-open fields with herds of cows. Then on down the track, trees pushed in on the train from both sides. Now and again the train stopped in small towns to let passengers disembark and others climb on.

At one of the stops, an older woman came aboard and settled in the seat beside Piper. She gave Piper's riding pants a curious look as she adjusted her skirt and stowed her bundle under the seat. Piper smiled and turned back to the window, but the woman didn't take the hint. She was ready to talk and Piper was a captive audience.

"I always get nervous catching these trains. Afraid the thing will go off without me." She wiped her face with a large white handkerchief. Her printed cotton dress made Piper wonder if it was made of flour sacks. She'd heard farm wives used the material to make ends meet. "Where you headed, honey?"

"Hazard and then from there to Hyden."

"Oh really? Have they got tracks to Hyden now?"

"I don't think so. Someone is meeting me in Hazard. Maybe with a car. Maybe with a horse."

"Well, what about that? Guess that explains the britches," the woman said. "You must be headed down there to work with those frontier nurses."

"Are you from there?"

"My ma grew up in the mountains, but she married a flatlander and moved to a farm outside of Elizabethtown. That's where I still live to this day. My husband took over the farm after Pa died. We've spent some happy years there. Before Ma passed on, we did go back to the mountains now and again. Not Hazard or Hyden. Pineville. I've run all over those mountains with my kinfolk." She chuckled at the memory. "Couldn't do that now." She peered over at Piper. "But you won't have any trouble going up and down those hills. Look at the size of you. Slim as a reed in a pond. And pretty too."

"Thank you," Piper mumbled, a little discomfited by the woman's scrutiny.

"Aww, don't mind me, honey. I wasn't aiming to get you bothered. Slim is good. Me, I could carve off some inches, but seems like when you add on the years, a body has a way of packing on the pounds in places you'd rather wasn't packed so heavy. And goodness gracious, I haven't even given you my name. Chattering away like a magpie. I'm Maxine Crutcher. Was Maxine Parker before I married, but that's been so long ago, I can't hardly remember it." She paused, obviously waiting for a name in return.

"Piper. Piper Danson."

"Well, isn't that an interesting name? Piper. But names generally end up suiting a person once you get used to them. My daughter, she just had a baby. Her first. A girl. That's where I've been. Seeing to her, but I'm headed home now. My Harold don't like me being gone overlong. Misses my cooking."

"What did your daughter name her baby?" Piper asked to be polite.

"Harriet. After her grandmother. Harriet Sue. The Sue is after her mother-in-law. I thought that was extra nice of my girl since the woman is a pill to be around. Could be the baby will soften her up." Maxine paused for breath and looked Piper up and down again. "So was I right that you're a nurse headed down to help that Mary Breckinridge out? She's turned a trick down there in Leslie County."

"Not a nurse. I'm going to be one of the couriers."

"Couriers. That's Mrs. Breckinridge for you. She likes those fancy-sounding words. She come to the mountains from the city, you know. But they say she does right by the mountain folk."

"That's good to know," Piper murmured.

"I suspect you're fixing to have some eye-opening times down there with those nurse midwives. They go right to the houses to help those mamas have babies, you know. Best way, if you ask me. My daughter, she went to a hospital. Waste of money. I had her right in the same bed where my man and me did what has to be done to make her. Worked fine." The woman reached over and touched Piper's arm. "Now I've done gone and made your cheeks bloom again. You'll see plenty down there in Leslie County to make you blush, but it'll all be good. As long as you step where the Lord wants you to step."

"How can you know that? Where he wants you to go. What he wants you to do." Piper was curious about what the woman would say. She seemed free and easy with advice.

"That can be a puzzler sometimes, but you can figure it out if you listen and watch. The mountains are a good place for doing that. You get up high in those hills and the Lord just seems nearer. That was where he first spoke to my heart. Out on a mountainside. Been right here with me ever since." She put her hand over her heart.

When Piper didn't say anything, Maxine peered over at her. "You have him in your heart, honey?"

"I go to church."

Maxine smiled a little. "Going to church is mighty fine, but it don't mean you know the Lord here." She tapped her chest again before she gave Piper a look. "I'm guessing things has always been easy for you. That can make it harder to recognize what the Lord does for you. You can think maybe you've done it all yourself and don't need him none. But you walk down some rocky trails with troubles on every side, and you'll be wanting the Lord right there with you."

"I believe in God."

"'Course you do. Folks have to be half blind not to see the hand of God in this world." She patted Piper's arm again. "And don't you worry. You'll have plenty of chances to step closer to the Lord whilst you are in the hills. While I don't know much, I do know that."

Piper wasn't sure what to say. She'd never had anybody actually question her faith. At the appropriate age and with the urging of her mother, she'd joined church. She attended every Sunday with her parents. She said her prayers at night. For Leona and her baby on the way. For Jamie. For the poor men out of work. Of course she believed. She had no reason for this woman's words to make her feel as though somebody were scratching around inside her to find something wrong.

"I'm looking forward to being in the mountains," she finally said.

"I sure wish I could go down there with you. It's been years since my feet touched those hills. But I'd best head on home to see to Harold." She fished under the seat for her bundle. "My stop is coming up." She leaned over to give Piper a hug. "It's been fine passing the time with you. If you ever need anything, you hunt me up. Maxine Crutcher in Waynesburg. For sure I'll remember your name. Piper Danson. Sounds like a movie star. You look like you could be one too."

Out the window, Piper watched Maxine's husband take her bundle. Maxine gave him a hug. He didn't hug her back, but he did smile before they headed off. Piper wondered how many years they'd been together. But however many years they'd shared, some of them might have been along those rocky trails Maxine talked about where they had to depend on the Lord.

Piper looked around at the people in the other seats. Some were talking. Others were sleeping. A few were staring straight ahead as though only interested in their destinations and nothing about the road on the way.

Could that be how she was? Only worried about her own journey without being concerned with those she met on the way? She gave her head a mental shake. She had no reason to let Maxine Crutcher's words settle uncomfortably in her mind. Living a comfortable life wasn't a sin. Her father would say it was a blessing. A blessing he wanted to continue for her with Braxton Crandall.

But she wasn't going to think about the future. At least not past today and the idea of going to Wendover. Tomorrow she would find out what was next.

Wendover. The very name suggested something out of the ordinary. Piper's fingers itched to pull a pencil out of her case and write a letter about what might lie ahead of her. But who would she write to? Jamie immediately popped into her mind. Then the sight of the pretty blonde running toward him and the way he had smiled at her was there too.

Piper pulled in a deep breath and let it out. She was going to block all thoughts of men from her mind. No need to think about who might or might not love her. Not for months. The summer was hers.

The farther east the train went, the more the landscape changed outside the window. More trees. Lots more trees. Fewer towns. Hills. At last they pulled into the station at Hazard. Two-story brick-façade buildings lined the street where cars and trucks shared the road with some horses and wagons. A train sat on a side track with boxcar after boxcar filled with coal.

Piper picked up her case and stepped off the train. Nobody came forward to meet her. The train took on new passengers and chugged out of the station, belching smoke. Piper walked from one end of the platform to the other and then retraced her steps. Just as she was about to find someone to ask about a bus to Hyden, a girl about her age came around the depot. No horses in tow, but she wore riding pants and boots.

"Oh good. You're still here. I saw the train was gone and was afraid you might have given up on me and gone into town. I'm sorry I'm late. Don't tell Mrs. Breckinridge. She hates people being late. For anything!" The girl's light-blue eyes widened. "But that horse I brought for you is a slowpoke. Took me forever to get him across the river." She stuck out her bottom lip to puff a breath that ruffled her light brown bangs.

When Piper didn't speak up right away, the girl rushed on. "You are the new courier, aren't you?"

"Yes. Piper Danson."

"Right." The girl wiped her hand off on her pants and held it out to shake Piper's. "Marlene Preston here, but everybody calls me Marlie. We all have nicknames. It's a thing with the frontier nurses." She gave Piper a questioning look. "Anybody ever call you Pip?"

"Pip." Piper frowned. "Not sure I'd like that."

Marlie shrugged. "Won't matter. Nicknames just happen. Pip might be better than Thumper, and that's what we call Mrs. Breckinridge's secretary. I don't know that I've ever heard her first name. Oh well, like I said, everybody has a nickname. That is, except for Mrs. Breckinridge. No Miss Mary or Mrs. B for her. They say she recruited you in Louisville. I'm from Chicago myself."

The girl talked so fast Piper could barely keep up. She was very petite and almost delicate looking. Piper could imagine her on a dance floor. Not on a horse.

"How long have you been here?" Piper asked. "I mean as a courier."

"A month. And don't worry. I felt as green as you when I got here. I was lucky. They did come for me in the car. But something's wrong with the brakes right now. So it's horses for us." She gave Piper another look. "You do ride, don't you?"

"Yes, but I've never ridden a horse across a river."

"That's a piece of cake compared to some things you'll have to do. It's a challenge a minute around here, but you'll love it. I promise."

When Piper must have still looked unsure, Marlie laughed. "No backing out now. Well, some do, but not many. Besides, you don't look like the kind to give up on something without at least giving it a try. Where's the old college spirit?"

"This isn't college."

"Not officially, but there's plenty to learn. Just call it the College of Life."

Marlie led the way back to the horses, where she gave Piper's case a look. "Glad you didn't bring a trunk of stuff, but that case might be a problem."

With dismay, Piper looked at her case. Why hadn't she thought about bringing something easier to carry on a horse? "I guess I should have found a soft-sided one."

"Or saddlebags, but a girl can't think of everything." Marlie shrugged. "You'll just have to hold it in front of you. Think you can manage that?"

"I'll give it a try." What other choice did she have? Because Marlie was right. She wasn't a quitter.

"That's the spirit." She untied one of the horses and pulled him forward. "This is Puddin. We use him for first timers. I'm not saying you did, but some of the girls have been known to exaggerate their horsemanship. Riding on park trails is a little different from riding up here in the hills." Marlie stroked the big horse's neck before she handed Piper the reins. "But if you had never ridden a day in your life, you'd be okay on Puddin. It would take a direct hit from a lightning bolt to get him to run off with anybody. So you'll be fine."

Marlie held the case while Piper mounted Puddin. Then she handed it up. "We could try tying it on the back, but it might unbalance the load or rub a sore on Puddin's rump. Should that happen, we'd never hear the end of it. Wouldn't be good at all." She shook her head.

"I can hang on to it." Piper tried to sound surer than she felt. She propped the case in front of her and clutched the reins on either side of it. "You've got a nice-looking mare." Piper nodded toward the other horse.

"Fancy is top-notch. A sweet little mare with enough spirit to make riding interesting." Marlie swung up into the saddle. "We better get going. It's a good ways. About eleven miles."

Plodding along behind Marlie, Piper might have dozed off if not for the need to hang on to her case. Marlie had to hold Fancy back to stay with Piper. Sometimes when the road was wide enough, they rode two abreast and Marlie pointed out landmarks.

"Try to keep them in mind," she said. "You might have to fetch the next person home to Wendover."

Piper didn't say anything, but she'd be lost in a minute out here alone.

Marlie chattered on about Chicago and her boyfriend. "Ray wasn't happy about me coming down here. Not at all. He threatened to go looking for a new girl." She laughed. "But he won't. He's got it bad for me."

"Do you have it bad for him?" Piper asked.

"That's the question, isn't it?" Marlie sighed. "I do like him. I figure we'll get married next year. A girl can't wait forever. If you get too long in the tooth, nobody will want to marry you."

She grinned and let her mare prance ahead as thick bushes covered with buds pushed in on the road.

When Marlie rode back to her, Piper asked what they were.

"Rhododendron. The mountains are ready to explode in beauty, or so Nurse Robbins tells me. She's been here working with Mrs. Breckinridge for a while now. Long enough to know the mountains." Marlie looked around. "I can't wait."

They turned off the road into a creek bed.

"A shortcut," Marlie said. "Besides, the creeks make better riding than the roads around here. They have neat names too. Like Cut Shin Creek or Greasy Creek. And then there's Hell-for-Sartin Creek. You have to wonder about that name."

When they got to the Middle Fork River, Puddin stepped into the water behind Fancy like a man condemned to hard labor, but the water wasn't deep at the ford. Piper had no problem keeping her boots dry.

Once across, Marlie pointed up the hill to a log house. "Wendover. That's where Mrs. Breckinridge lives and where we eat our meals. That is, if we're not at the hospital or out at one of the centers." The two-story log house seemed to belong there on the hillside.

"Where do we sleep?"

"The Garden House." This time Marlie pointed to a two-story building down a narrow roadway. "It's not bad. No electricity, but we do have a shower. And that's a rarity around here."

The hillside was dotted with structures. One that might be a henhouse. A smaller cabin up above Mrs. Breckinridge's house. A log barn next to the road.

"I'll show you around after we see to the horses." She slid off Fancy and headed toward the barn. "Puddin and Fancy have earned their supper."

As Piper followed Marlie, she had no doubt the adventure had begun. She had come to a different world.

CHAPTER
TEN

Thursday, May 25, 1933

Dear Mother,

I promised to write right away when I got to Wendover. I'm keeping my promise, but it may take a while for the letter to make its way back to you. There is a post office here, but they say the mail is often slow. Sometimes still delivered by mule up in the hills. Can you believe that?

I made the trip without problem. Met an interesting woman on the train who told me about the mountains. What she said has me believing the summer here is going to be great although, of course, I'll miss you and everybody there at home.

You can't believe how beautiful it is here with the lush green of the trees and wildflowers everywhere you look. The rhododendron will be blooming soon and they promise to be gorgeous.

Father was right about me having to rough it. Wendover doesn't have electricity yet and I'm not exactly at the

Waldorf Hotel. But I have a bed in a room with another courier. Marlie is from Chicago. I've met another girl too. Suze all the way from New York City. Compared to them, I'm almost at home. Suze was here last summer so she can show me the ropes.

I'll be working with the horses. Feeding and watering them and cleaning their stalls. You know that fun shoveling manure. I can see you frowning at that indelicate word. Sorry. I should have said used straw. Suze assures me I'll get a chance to do a little of everything, maybe even accompany the nurse midwives on calls. Can you imagine me helping a midwife when a baby is born? I can't either.

I'll write more soon, but I better blow out the oil lamp and get some sleep. Tomorrow I have to be ready for whatever jobs they give me. Next week I get to go on a round of the outlying centers with Marlie. I have to know where they are in case I need to take something to the nurses there. I hope I can keep the directions straight. We'll be riding horses and Marlie says it'll take several days. I do hope I get a more spirited horse than Puddin, the one I rode from Hazard. He was a slow slog in the sand. No sand really, but you know what I mean.

Tell Truda I'll write her soon.

Love to all,
Piper

Piper folded the letter and stuck it in an envelope. She looked around the small room with the two beds, a small desk, and a bureau she and Marlie shared. The oil lamp barely gave enough light to write by. A bathroom down the hall served for everybody.

Suze said that before they built the Garden House, the couriers slept in what wasn't much more than a shed with a pitcher and a bowl for washing up. Compared to then, things were easy now, but Piper's mother would still think they were roughing it.

Even so, sleeping on the side of a mountain without many of the conveniences she'd thought necessities last week was somehow refreshing. A breeze came in the open window and brought a bird's call.

"What's that?" Piper asked.

"Whippoorwill." Suze, who was hanging out in their room, whistled the sound, then grabbed Piper's hand to pull her toward the door. "Come on outside where you can hear it better. And you have to look at the stars. You've never seen stars like you can here."

Marlie groaned and sat up in her bed to warn Piper. "Don't let her keep you out there all night. Suze goes all poetic on you about stars and nature."

"Don't mind her." Suze waved her hand at Marlie, but she was smiling. "She thinks the only animal worth seeing is a horse."

"Horses are why we're here." Marlie yawned. "And I was on one of those horses for miles and miles today. Time for me to dream about handsome guys in roadsters. One of them shows up, let me know. I might be ready to share some starlight with him." With a sigh, she settled back down on her pillow.

The stars were amazing. Since the new moon was not up, the sky was a dark canvas sparkling with a million stars. Maybe two million. The sight took Piper's breath.

"See." Beside her, Suze stared up at the sky. "That sight is worth some lost sleep and a crick in your neck."

Suze was nearly as tall as Piper but built sturdy. That was how Piper's mother would describe her. She looked ready and able to handle anything that came her way.

Suddenly from out of the woods came a sound almost like a woman screaming. Chills ran down Piper's back. "What's that?"

Suze laughed. "Don't panic. Just a screech owl."

"Oh." Piper blew out a breath. "It's aptly named. How do you know all this? Didn't you say you were from New York?"

"I was as ignorant to the natural world as you when I came last summer, but a person doesn't have to stay ignorant. Being ignorant is different than being dumb. Ignorant simply means you haven't learned it yet. So I listened and asked questions. The mountain people don't mind questions if asked the right way."

"What's the right way?"

"With respect for how they live and for these mountains they call home. While we might think they are backward in ways, they think something the same about us. And they're right. We wouldn't have a clue about how to survive on a mountainside with nothing but a gun and a hoe. These people live with nature on their doorsteps and sometimes right through their doors or the cracks between the logs of their houses. But the beauty of the hills is in their souls."

"That does sound poetic," Piper said.

"Oh, you can't pay any attention to Marlie. She's a sweet kid, but this is just a fun little adventure for her. A little detour in the smooth sailing of her life. She'll go home and marry that great-looking guy in the roadster, have her three kids. Two sons and a daughter. Join all the socially correct clubs and live happily ever after." Suze stared up at the stars for a long moment before she went on. "And nothing is wrong with that, but it's not right for everyone."

"How is it for you?" Piper kept her eyes on the sky too.

"I like it here. I like feeling as though I'm doing something important. Experiencing life."

"Don't you want to get married? Have those three kids of your own?"

Suze didn't answer for a moment. "Sure. Probably. Maybe." She looked from the sky to Piper. "Is that what you want?"

Piper continued to stare up at the stars. "Someday. I'm not in any hurry."

"Someday is good because right now we're here. And I get the feeling you're a little like me in wanting to find out more about this place where you've landed."

Piper listened to the whippoorwill a moment before she said, "It sounds lonesome."

"Maybe he is, and he's singing to invite a girl bird over. Or he could be letting his sweetie know he's keeping watch while she sits on their eggs. They don't make nests. Just lay their eggs on the ground."

"They don't get broken?"

"I guess not. At least not all of them or we wouldn't have whip-poorwills." Suze shrugged. "I've never seen one. Birds or eggs. The people around here tell me you have to know what you're looking for. That's what it said when I looked up about them too. The birds blend right in with the ground leaves or the low branches where they sleep during the day. You might step right beside one and never see it if it didn't get scared by your big foot and fly up."

The bird repeated its call over and over. "It keeps on singing its song."

"Not a bad thing. To keep on singing. Sometimes we need to do that too."

"I'm not much of a singer," Piper said.

"You don't have to be a great vocalist to sing. I admit it helps those listening if you can carry a tune, but the joy of the song can be in you whether it tickles the ears or not." Suze sang the last few words. She had a pretty voice. "I like to sing. It's up to those around me to decide whether to listen or not. And out on the trails, it's not a bad idea to sing as you ride."

"Why is that?" Piper looked at Suze. "Does that make the horses calmer?"

"That could be, but mostly it's an easy way to let the mountain people know you're out there in their territory. You don't have to worry about anybody bothering you as long as they know you're one of Mrs. Breckinridge's girls, but sneaking up on anybody in the woods isn't smart, intentional or not. If you don't want to sing, talk to your horse or to God or to yourself. Whatever, as long as you make a little noise to let whoever is out there know you're coming."

"They wouldn't shoot me, would they?" Piper remembered her mother telling Truda that all mountaineers had guns.

"No." Suze sounded very sure of that, and Piper breathed a little easier. At least until Suze went on. "Definitely not on purpose. But shot on purpose or by accident can lead to the same unfortunate outcome."

Singing to keep from getting shot? What kind of place had she come to? Something cold nudged her leg. Piper let out a little shriek.

Suze laughed. "I've got you spooked. Sorry about that, but you can relax. That's just Ginger wanting to make friends. She loves everybody." She patted the dog's head.

"Oh." The dog flapped its tail back and forth to brush against Piper's leg. Her light-colored fur showed up in the dark. "She just surprised me." Piper stroked the dog's back. "Is she a Golden Retriever?"

"I suppose. She looks the part anyway. Miss Aileen—she's the one in charge of us couriers—she says one of the girls brought Ginger down here a few years ago as a pup. When the girl went home, she left Ginger. Said it wouldn't be fair to take her back to the city after she'd had a taste of mountain freedom." Suze knelt down in front of the dog. "Isn't that right, Ginger? You're a mountain dog."

"Is that different than a regular dog?"

"Definitely. Everything is different here in the mountains." Suze looked up at her. "But you'll love Ginger. She sleeps in Marlie's room most nights." Suze stood up. "That may prove interesting after she has her pups."

"Pups?" Piper ran her hand along the dog's side. "Feels like she might be having a bunch."

"Goldens can have big litters. Nobody's sure about the father, but there is a male Golden around here too. So maybe we'll luck out and have a whole slew of Golden puppies. They are such sweet dogs. The nurses love them, although the favorite breed for going along with them on the trails are collie or shepherd mixes. Those dogs are extra smart and will fight rattlesnakes for you, or so some of the nurses have told me."

"Rattlesnakes?"

Suze laughed again and put an arm around Piper's waist to turn her back toward the Garden House. "It's okay. They always rattle to warn you. You'll be fine. As long as you wear your boots."

The dog followed them in and curled up beside Piper's cot. "Rest easy." Suze kept her voice low, since Marlie was already asleep. "Ginger will protect you from any rattlesnakes that show up." With a grin, she waved and left.

As Piper settled into bed, her thoughts kept whirling. Everything was so different. Birds singing their name. Owls sounding like women screaming. Singing to keep from sneaking up on anybody. Stars so thick that some places in the sky looked like streaks of glowing silver. A dog by her bed to keep away the snakes. Piper trailed her hand over the side of the bed to touch the dog's back. Having her there did make Piper feel better. More at home. Welcomed.

That was how she continued to feel the next day as she cleaned the horses' stalls, picked their hooves, and combed burrs out of their tails. Needed and welcomed when she gathered with the others at the big wooden table in the dining room of Mrs. Breckinridge's log house.

Marlie said whoever was at Wendover always ate their meals together. "Good food too, whether Mrs. Breckinridge is here at the Big House or not. Sometimes we help in the kitchen if Rayma needs us. That's the cook. And we always do tea at four in the afternoon when Mrs. Breckinridge is home. I do hope you know how to brew tea. Mrs. Breckinridge is very particular about her tea."

"I can't cook, but I can make tea."

"I can't cook either, but anybody can peel potatoes and apples or chop up greens. My mother would be amazed to see me in the kitchen. Suze says we sometimes have to cook for the nurse midwives out at the centers. All I have to say is they better have detailed recipes." She laughed as she opened the door to go inside.

The dining room windows gave a view of the Middle Fork River flowing by at the bottom of the hill. While it wasn't dark out yet, candles flickered down the middle of the long table where Suze and four others were already seated.

"Sit here, Piper." Miss Aileen patted the chair beside her, then looked around at the others. "Meet Piper Danson, our new courier. She got here late yesterday from Louisville. Tell us what brought you here."

"I met Mrs. Breckinridge at a tea my aunt had for her last Sunday. She made being a courier sound like a wonderful experience. So I got on a train and here I am."

Marlie spoke up. "And she can ride."

"If you can call poking along on Puddin riding," Piper said.

"Oh no. You poor thing." A young woman, obviously another courier, spoke up. She looked at Marlie. "I can't believe you made her ride Puddin all the way from Hazard."

"My orders, Nan. Better safe than sorry, and Puddin is our safest horse," Miss Aileen said. "We've had some exaggerate their riding ability." She gave the girl beside Nan a look. "Right, Jessie?"

Jessie held up her hands. "I got better." The girl smiled at Piper. "But I will admit that Puddin is my favorite ride."

Everybody laughed.

"So that's Nan and Jessie, also couriers, but going home this weekend. We'll miss them," Miss Aileen said. "And Nurse Robbins is down at the end."

The nurse smiled and lifted her hand in greeting.

Miss Aileen went on. "We're a family here. All of the frontier nurses and couriers. So if you need anything, you can ask any of us." With the introductions done, she gave Piper a considering look. "So, Piper Danson, shall we call you Pip?"

"I'm not sure I like that."

Everybody laughed again while Miss Aileen patted her hand. "Nicknames make you belong. So what do the rest of you think?" She looked around the table.

"Pippay. What about that?" The nurse midwife spoke up from the end of the table. She had a strong English accent.

Piper bit back a protest since she had a feeling that would saddle her with the name for sure.

Marlie came to her rescue. "No, Pippay doesn't sound much like Piper. Danson, hmm. How about Dancer? Piper said she had her debut dance last weekend. So Dancer might fit."

Piper saw no need in mentioning that she wasn't much of a dancer. Being nicknamed Dancer didn't sound bad. Sort of fun.

Miss Aileen frowned slightly as she studied Piper. "Dancer sounds odd."

"No odder than Pippay." Marlie defended her choice. "Sorry, Nurse Robbins."

Suze spoke up. "We could call her Louie since she's from Louis-ville."

"Oh, please." Piper held up her hands as though to ward off that suggestion. "Pip is sounding better and better."

"She's too tall for Pip," Jessie said. "What about Danny?"

"I like it. Danny, it is." Miss Aileen hit the table with her hand like a judge pounding his gavel.

Almost in unison, they all said, "Hello, Danny."

Piper sighed and managed a smile.

Miss Aileen laughed. "It's not so bad. You don't have to take the name home with you, but while you're here you can be a different person. Someone new. You might be surprised at how a name change can open up new vistas for you."

"I thought just coming here opened up the new vistas."

"True. The mountains. The people. The animals. All that is new, but what will be the finest new thing is you yourself." The woman patted her hand again. "Trust me on that." She paused and looked amused as she added, "Danny."

CHAPTER
ELEVEN

Saturday morning Miss Aileen gave Piper messages to take to the Hyden Hospital. "It's only a few miles, Danny. A nice walk on a pleasant day like today. So no need bothering with a horse."

"I don't know how to get there." Piper could imagine wandering around the hills all day, totally lost.

"Ask Marlie. She'll tell you." Miss Aileen waved Piper out the door and turned her attention back to the papers on her desk.

"She gave you the easy job." Marlie came out of the barn and stuck her pitchfork in the dirt.

"I'll switch. I know how to clean stalls. I don't know how to get to the hospital."

"No, no. You need to learn your way around, and it's easy peasy getting there. Just over the swinging bridge and straight across to the hospital. Easy trail all the way. Nobody can get lost between here and there." Marlie pointed the direction. "Walking will help you get a feel for the lay of the land before we head off to the centers next week. Later, you can copy some of my maps so you'll know how to get places."

Piper had seen one of those maps with squiggly lines, circles, and squares that meant nothing at all to her. But Marlie claimed it was plain as day. Creeks, boulders, trees, trails, and springs.

"It's good to know where these springs are in case the creeks dry up and your horse needs a drink." Marlie had pointed to wavy lines. "At least that's what they told me. But right now there's plenty of water in the creeks."

Piper stared at the paper while Marlie explained the markings. Some of the little squares had names scribbled beside them. Houses, Marlie said. Piper couldn't imagine finding anywhere by looking at those maps, but Marlie and Suze both claimed she'd figure it out in no time and find her way around with no problem.

"Honest. We've not lost a courier yet." Suze had squeezed Piper's shoulder. "And if you do go missing, we'll send Ginger to track you down."

Now, as Piper listened to Marlie repeat the directions, she did wish Ginger could go along. But the poor dog was too heavy with pups to go out on the trails. However, a beagle mix called Rusty came out of the barn and leaned against Piper's leg.

"I think Rusty likes you," Marlie said. "That's the way it is around here. The dogs pick their favorites. Well, except for Ginger and everybody is her favorite, but especially whoever is sleeping in our room."

"Do you think Rusty will go with me over to the hospital now?" Piper leaned down to scratch behind his ears.

"Possibly. He seems to want to be your buddy." Marlie looked down at the spotted brown-and-white dog.

"So if I get confused about the trail, I can follow him." Piper straightened up and stared toward the river.

"You won't get confused about the trail."

"Maybe not this one, but maybe another one sometime." Rusty jumped up on Piper to get another head rub.

"Rusty knows where his food dish is." Marlie smiled. "So he might get you home. Unless he sees a rabbit. Then he'd be gone to who knows where, and you might end up in the middle of a blackberry patch. Not a place you want to be. Trust me. You'd come out looking like you'd had a fight with a dozen mad cats."

"Not to mention that snakes might be hiding out there." Piper pushed Rusty down.

"Don't talk about snakes." Marlie shivered. "I hate them. Absolutely 'Garden of Eden' hate them. I don't care what Suze says about how they are an integral part of nature's plan by eating mice and such. They can participate in the plan somewhere far from me."

"Have you seen any since you've been here?"

"Oh yeah. This time of the year, the creatures love to crawl out on a warm rock to soak up sunshine, or so Suze says. She's a veritable walking encyclopedia about the mountain flora and fauna." Marlie looked around as though worried a snake might be slithering up beside them right then.

"Where is Suze?" Piper peered past Marlie at the barn.

"While you helped clear away breakfast, Nurse Robbins came for her to go on a call. A man showed up to say his wife was punishing bad."

"Punishing?" Piper frowned.

"That's what the men say when their wives are in labor. The local people have plenty of odd sayings, but you get so you know what they mean. At least the nurses generally do. Even those from England. Come to think of it, you might have to listen to the nurses twice too, to get what they say. They put the prettiest lilt to their words. Well, you heard Nurse Robbins last night." Marlie pulled some coins out of her pocket and handed them to Piper. "After you're through at the hospital, go down to Hyden and buy some candy bars. Always good to have a snack when you're out on rounds in case we miss a meal."

Piper stuffed the coins in her pocket. "You're sure I won't get lost?"

"I'm sure. Over the bridge." She pointed toward the river. "Then follow the path. Hyden is just down the mountain from the hospital. Mercers is a good place to buy things. If you get back in time, you can help me give the horses a bath down at the river. And then Miss A wants us to work up a row in the garden. Mrs. Miller is coming by later to plant more beans. You'll like her. She's full of mountain sayings."

Marlie pulled the pitchfork out of the dirt and headed back to the barn. At the door she turned and pointed her finger at Piper. "Next time I get to go to town and you get to clean stalls."

"Fine with me," Piper said, but Marlie had already disappeared into the barn. She muttered the rest of her words. "I know horses. I don't know hills."

Yet. That was the key word. Yet. And the same as a person couldn't learn to ride without getting on a horse, she wasn't going to learn the hills without stepping out on their paths.

She reached down and fondled Rusty's ears again. "You going with me? You might be good company if you don't see a rabbit."

She went by the Garden House to get some money of her own. If she was going to a store, she might as well look through their offerings. Marlie was right. A person could get hungry out on the trail. Piper did know that much.

Rusty lay down in the road as though not at all interested in wherever Piper was going. She didn't know if she should call him, but a click of her tongue didn't seem wrong. He lifted his head, stood up, and stretched. Then as though deciding he didn't have anything better to do, the dog trotted after her.

"Good dog," Piper said. Maybe the dog would scare away any snakes along the way.

Marlie was right. The path was plain, and by the time Piper got to the swinging bridge, her step was light. She wasn't going to lose her way on her first solo assignment, and so far no snakes had slithered into sight. Rusty ran this way and that on the trail, sniffing bushes, clumps of grass, and sticks. She wondered what his nose was telling him about whatever had passed this way before them. Must not have been rabbits since he didn't chase off through the bushes.

At the bridge, she wished for the camera back in her room. She had promised Della some pictures, but their cook wouldn't expect a picture like this. The narrow plank walkway floated out in the air over the river. Cables attached to wooden post structures on opposite sides of the river held it up.

When Piper stepped gingerly out on the first planks, the bridge swayed as though she were standing in a swing. But with the sides fenced up to her waist, she couldn't fall off. She moved farther out on the bridge and stopped, suspended in air. Definitely an adventure.

She thought of Jamie then. He wouldn't be standing still. He'd be running across the bridge, shaking the cables to make her scream or maybe laugh.

Yes, laugh. Jamie could always make her laugh because he had a way of always seeing the fun in something. That might not be true anymore. His father's death could have changed him. Must have changed him or he wouldn't have stopped writing her. He would have found a way to come see her. Then maybe the other girl was what had changed him.

Ahead of her on the bridge, Rusty stopped and looked back. When she didn't move, the dog barked as if to say, *Come on. Not going to find any rabbits out here.*

Piper shoved thoughts of Jamie aside. "I'm coming," she called, as though the dog would understand.

Rusty turned and plodded on across the bridge. So maybe he did. Piper held on to the cables and stepped lightly, but the bridge still bounced and swayed under her feet. Not a bad feeling, and by the time she was halfway across, she had adjusted to the cadence of the bridge and walking was easy.

She had to write to someone about this bridge. But who? She

had promised to write to Braxton Crandall, but she couldn't imagine him being interested in how being on the bridge made her want to shout into the wind or throw a rock into the water below just to hear it splash. She had no idea what he might be interested in. A wife, he'd said. She certainly didn't want to write to him about that. She might stick with rhododendrons or maybe the whippoorwill. He might like birds. Who didn't like birds?

Jamie. That's who she wanted to tell about the bridge. Maybe she'd forget about that pretty blonde holding his hands and write him anyway. They could surely still be friends. No wife talk with him either. Wasn't her plan to completely forget thoughts of a future husband this summer and think horses and mountains? And dogs, she added when Rusty barked at her as though to hurry her up again.

When she stepped off the bridge, the ground felt too solid. Sometimes she had that same feeling after dismounting from a horse. Back to earth. But she wouldn't stay forever tied to the ground. She'd be riding all over these hills this summer, and who knew how many times she might walk across this swinging bridge.

At the hospital, she left Rusty to chase his rabbits while she went inside to deliver Miss Aileen's messages.

"You must be the new courier." A nurse came up to Piper in the hallway. "Good. We can use some extra help."

Piper held out the bundle of messages. "Miss Aileen wanted me to give these to Nurse Thompson."

"That's me." She took the bundle and stuffed it into the generous pocket of her uniform without the first glance at them. Instead she peered at Piper's shirtsleeve. "Where are your initials?"

Piper looked down at her arm. "Initials?"

"FNS. Didn't you get patches to sew on your sleeve?"

"Oh. Yes, but I haven't sewn them on yet."

The nurse gave her a disapproving look. "I'm guessing you haven't the first idea of how to thread a needle." She sighed. "Tell

Suze to help you. I showed her how to sew on her patches last year when she was here. I am amazed at the basic skills you girls come here not knowing. Everybody should know how to sew on a button. Or a patch."

"I'll sew it on tonight."

"Yes, you will." The woman tapped the spot on Piper's sleeve below her shoulder. "And don't go out in the hills without it. It's pretty evident you're an outlier. A pretty one at that, but you won't have the first problem with any of the mountain men with that patch. They respect Mrs. Breckinridge's people. And you, as one of her people, need to respect them."

"Yes, ma'am." Piper was ready to agree with anything this woman said.

The nurse turned and started down the hall. When Piper didn't follow her, she frowned over her shoulder at her. "Well, don't just stand there. We've got things to do."

"Yes, ma'am," Piper said again.

"What's your name, anyway?"

"Piper Danson." She didn't see any reason to introduce herself as Danny.

"Right, Danny." The woman smiled at Piper's face. "We do have telephones. Aileen told me you were on the way over. And your nickname. The other nurses call me Tommy. I'm not so crazy about that either, but I put up with it. You'll have to do the same, but keep in mind the couriers need to be more formal with the midwives. So Nurse Thompson to you."

"Yes, ma'am." Piper didn't think anything else was safe to say.

"You do sound rather like a parrot." Nurse Thompson peered over at Piper. "My fault, I suppose. I have been told I come on a bit strong. So forgive me for that. As for the name Danny, you'll get used to it. Count your blessings. It could have been Pip."

"Or Pippay," Piper muttered as she hurried to keep up with the nurse.

The nurse actually laughed. "That has a bit of a French flair. Pip-*pay*." Without slowing her steps, she made a flourish in the air with one hand. She looked over at Piper. "Do you like babies?"

"I . . ." Piper wasn't sure what to answer. She had never been around babies. At least not since her brother was born and she was only six then. Maybe she should just stick with "yes, ma'am," but Nurse Thompson didn't wait for an answer.

"Who doesn't like babies? And children too. They are so brave when they are sick or must get a shot. Poor little tykes."

She started to push open a door, but then stopped. "I had thought to let you rock the babies, but maybe I'll let you spend some time with Billy. The poor kid spilled lye water from his mother's soap-making on his leg and arm. By the time his father brought him in, the burns were infected. Worried for a while he might lose his leg, but we got past that."

"That sounds awful," Piper said.

"You'll see plenty of awful while you're here." Nurse Thompson's voice was grim. "Billy's mother can't come down to stay with him. Not with two other children at home. Billy is six, hardly a baby, but he's homesick." She gave Piper another look and nodded. "You might be just what he needs to cheer him up."

"What will I do?" Piper could work with horses. She could dig in gardens. She had no idea how to entertain a child.

"Whatever you want. Tell him stories. Read him a book. Draw pictures. Just don't let him bother his bandages. I have the feeling he thinks if he can get rid of those pesky things, he can go home. Little rascal."

"All right. I'll give it a try."

"Of course you will, but wash your hands first." She pointed toward a restroom. "And do a proper job. Under the fingernails too. Cleanliness is vital in a hospital. I do hope you are aware of that, Danny."

"Yes, ma'am." Piper hurried to do as she was told. She could almost hear Nurse Thompson tapping her foot impatiently and counting to be sure Piper was taking enough time to scrub her hands properly.

When Piper went back out into the hallway, she resisted the urge to hold up her hands for the nurse's inspection while at the same time half expecting the woman to demand she do so.

CHAPTER
TWELVE

As Nurse Thompson led the way into the children's ward, her stern face melted into a smile. She stroked a baby's face as she passed her crib, perhaps only a comforting touch or a quick check for fever. In a different crib, she tucked a blanket around a sleeping child. The little boy's bed was in the back of the room beside a window.

"Hello, Billy," Nurse Thompson said. "Somebody's here to see you."

"Ma?" The child pushed up in bed to look toward the door.

"No, but I'm sure you'll see her soon. This is Danny." The little boy's face fell as Nurse Thompson gestured toward Piper.

Piper pushed a big smile out on her face as she pulled a chair over beside the bed. "Hi, Billy. You care if I sit with you awhile?"

"I reckon you can sit wherever you want. They ain't my chairs."

"Be nice, Billy. Danny just got here from the city and she doesn't know a thing about the mountains. She needs you to help her." Nurse Thompson tapped Piper's shoulder. "Somebody will be around if you need anything."

Piper kept smiling as the little boy's bright blue eyes zeroed in on her with some suspicion. His light brown hair lapped over his forehead to tickle his eyebrows. He seemed small for six, but kids came in all sizes. A bandage covered his left leg below the knee. On his arm, ridges of puckered red skin looked as if they might still be tender.

"I'm Danny." She might as well get used to the name.

He didn't smile. "The nurse done told me that. Where you from?"

"Louisville. I had to ride a train to get here."

"I ain't never been on a train, but I saw one once in a picture. I ain't never been nowhere but here and where I live up in the hills." He scooted back in his bed until he was leaning against the metal headboard. He grimaced but didn't cry out when he shifted his leg. After he got settled, he asked, "You ever been up high on a hill?"

"Not until I got here. I rode a horse over some hills between here and Hazard."

"Pa's been to Hazard. Didn't like it. Said it was too crowded with people practically pushing against one another. 'Bout like in here." Billy looked over at the cribs where one little child still slept and the other kicked her feet and made the crib rattle. "Said he'd rather be up on our hill."

"Must be a good place." Piper smiled. "That hill. Why don't you tell me what to expect when I go up in the mountains?"

"They's steep. That's what a feller needs to remember. My grandpa says sometimes they is so steep that if'n you aren't careful, you can fall right off a path and roll clear back down to the holler, where you'll have to start up the hill all over again. I ain't never had that happen to me. I make sure to hug the ground."

"That sounds like a good idea. I'll hope my horse is sure-footed when I come up your way."

That caught his interest. "If'n you go anytime soon, will you come get me? I wouldn't mind going up home on a horse. My pa brought me down on his mule. Spec, he's a right nice mule, but you can't hurry him up. Not like some horses I've seen out the window here that flat-out run. That must be a fine way to get somewhere."

"You've seen cars too, haven't you?" The road came up to the hospital.

"I seen them, but ain't no way they is ever going to make it up the hill to my house. Pa says they can run in creeks, but not straight up hills. Too many trees in the way. But a horse could make it."

"I suppose you're right about that."

"Right as rain. 'Course some of the time we just have to shank's-mare it if'n we want to go somewhere. Like to Grandpa's house over the way."

"Shank's-mare?"

"You don't know what shank's-mare means?" A little smile sneaked out on Billy's face as if he'd gotten something over on her.

Piper shook her head. "Afraid not. But I hope you'll tell me."

Billy actually laughed. A sweet little-boy giggle. "It means you ain't got no horse and you're gonna have to get wherever you go by walking on your own two feet. That's how my grandpa goes everywhere. Says the good Lord give him feet, and a horse would just eat him out of house and home. He needs a mule, he borrows Spec."

"Your grandpa sounds like a smart guy." Piper smiled. "I hope I get to meet him someday."

Billy's face lit up even more. "You can."

"Oh?"

"When you take me home on your horse. We can go by Grandpa's house first."

"Well, I might not be here when you're ready to go home." The little boy's bottom lip jutted out a bit, so Piper hurried on. What difference did it make to let the boy have fun thinking about it? "You wouldn't want to have to wait on me. But if I am around, we can see what the doctor says. Okay?"

"I reckon." He pushed at his bandage.

"Nurse says not to bother that." Piper gently touched his arm. "Might hurt if you do."

"Did hurt. I was kilt. Not kilt dead, but 'bout that way. That's why Pa brought me down here and said I had to be big and do whatever the doctor said. Dr. Jack, he gives me some sucking candy when he changes the bandage. Don't hurt like it did, but I frown some anyhow so's he'll still give me the candy." Billy suddenly looked a little worried. "You won't tell him that, will you?"

Piper pulled her finger over her lips like she was zipping them. "My lips are sealed."

That brought back Billy's smile as he took his hand away from his bandage to make the same gesture across his lips. "Mine too."

He was quiet a minute. "Does that mean we can't never say nothing ever again?"

Piper laughed. "That would be too hard for me. I like to talk to people, don't you?"

The little boy nodded. "Especially to my grandpa."

"So, we can talk, but just not about that certain thing you want to keep secret. Have you ever kept a secret?"

Billy scrunched up his shoulders and squinted his eyes. "I can't tell you."

"That's the perfect way to keep a secret." Piper kept her face serious.

"I told you a secret." He gave her a curious look. "You oughta tell me one."

"Hmm. That does sound only fair. Let's see." Piper thought a minute. "Don't tell anybody, but the first time I got on a horse, I was really, really scared."

"Did you fall off?"

"I hung on to the reins and the horse's mane and pretended I wasn't afraid. Nobody knew. Well, except the horse. Horses always know, but this was a nice horse and he just kept walking the way he was supposed to, like I was guiding him instead of being petrified."

"Pet-tri-fide?" Billy said the word slowly and frowned. "What's that mean?"

"So scared you can't move." Piper held out her arms and froze them in place.

"But the horse moved."

"He wasn't scared. He was probably laughing inside at the silly person on his back."

"You reckon horses can laugh?" Billy wrinkled his brow thinking about that.

"Sure. They curl their lips back, show their teeth, and shake their heads at you. But this horse didn't do that. Good thing too. If he'd shaken his head, I might have fallen off."

"You ever really fall off a horse?"

"A time or two. It happens, but that was after I wasn't scared anymore."

"How did you get over being skeered?"

"I just kept getting on horses until I wasn't scared anymore. But I wouldn't want anybody to know what a scaredy-cat I used to be."

"Can you ride good now?"

"Pretty good. But you will keep my secret, won't you?"

Billy ran his finger over his lips. "I ain't telling nobody."

"Telling anybody what?"

Piper had been so intent on talking to Billy she hadn't noticed the doctor coming into the room. She looked up at him. "Billy and I were just talking about secrets. Nothing important, right, Billy?"

"Nope." Billy put his hand over his mouth, but his eyes were smiling.

"I see." The doctor smiled too. "So who's your friend here?"

Billy took his hand away from his mouth and peeked at Piper. "I don't reckon that's a secret, is it?"

"Not at all. I'm a new courier. Piper Danson, but they're all calling me Danny." Piper stood up to face the doctor. He was a few inches taller than her and slim. His brown hair was going gray at his temples and a few wrinkles gathered around his blue eyes. He had a pair of glasses propped on top of his head. "Nurse Thompson said I could talk to Billy for a while."

"Well, it appears the two of you had plenty to talk about. I'm Dr. Jack." The doctor smiled at Piper and then looked back at Billy. "Time to make sure your leg is doing all right, Billy. You ready?"

Billy flashed a look at Piper before he pulled a sad face. "I don't know, Dr. Jack. I'm skeered it'll kill me."

The doctor reached in his pocket. "Maybe something sweet will help." He held out a piece of candy.

"I'm thinking it might." Billy took the candy and popped it into his mouth. He looked as pleased as the cat that swallowed the canary.

"Tell you what," the doctor said. "Since Danny is here, why don't you let her hold your hands while I give your leg a look?"

The doctor nodded at Piper, and she took the little boy's hands. The doctor gently cut the bandage and lifted it away. Piper managed not to shudder at the sight of the wound. A nurse came up beside the bed with a pan of water and new gauze. She smiled over at Piper.

"You must be the new courier, Danny. I'm Nurse Greene. I see you've met our Billy. He's quite the brave little guy, aren't you, Billy?"

The doctor took a cloth and gently bathed Billy's leg. This time his grimace didn't look at all pretend as he gripped Piper's hands tighter.

"Almost through, Billy." The doctor patted the leg dry and spread a salve over it.

"Can I go home now?" Billy asked.

"Not yet. But maybe soon."

"Can Danny take me on her horse?" Billy looked from Piper to the doctor.

Piper shrugged a little when the doctor looked at her. "He asked a while ago. I told him I might not be around at the right time, but if I was, he could ask the doctor. I guess he's ready to ask now."

Dr. Jack laughed. "Seems like he might be. Well, Billy, we'll have to wait and see about that. Danny might be off at Redbird Creek when you get ready to go home." He glanced back at Piper. "What did you say your last name was?"

"Danson. That's why they're calling me Danny."

"I met a girl named Danson once. In Louisville a long time ago." He began carefully wrapping Billy's leg. "I just happened to be visiting my cousin, and he wanted to go to this party. So I tagged along. I met the most remarkable girl that night." He got a soft smile on his face.

Could he be talking about Truda? Or perhaps some other girl named Danson. Did she dare ask?

He went on. "It was something like that fairy tale 'Cinderella.' We were at the ball and saw nobody but each other. But we didn't dance and she didn't run away and lose her glass slipper."

"That's a dumb story," Billy spoke up. "You'd be plain stupid to wear glass shoes."

Dr. Jack smiled. "Doesn't sound too practical with the trails we have to travel, does it, Billy boy?"

"Or doing jigs," Billy said.

"We didn't do any jigging. Just sat and talked. Can't remember a time I felt that good talking to a girl. I was always backward with girls."

"Come now, Dr. Jack," Nurse Greene said. "We all love you."

"But none of you ever wanted to marry me."

"Did this girl?" the nurse asked.

"We only met that one time, but I liked to imagine she would have."

"She must have kept you imagining about her since you never found another girl." The nurse teased him.

"You all keep me too busy to go courting." He fastened the last end of the bandage. "Folks getting sick. Boys like Billy having accidents and wanting to ride a horse with a pretty girl." He lowered his voice to a pretend whisper. "You might be too old for her, Billy."

"Oh, Doc." Billy yanked his hands away from Piper's. "I ain't wantin' no girlfriend. I jest want to ride a horse."

"That's good thinking, Billy." Piper winked at Billy, then looked at Dr. Jack. Her curiosity got the best of her. She had to ask. "What was that girl's first name? Do you remember?"

"Oh yes, I remember." He stared out the window and smiled as if seeing something none of the rest of them could see. "Truda. Truda Danson."

CHAPTER
THIRTEEN

Jamie knew something was up when Simon and family drove all the way from Louisville on Sunday. They were long overdue for a visit, but the way Simon twitched all through dinner as though his chair had barbs suggested something more than a pleasant afternoon with Mother. While Jamie didn't know why, he had no doubt he was the reason for Simon's agitation.

After their mother cleared the dessert dishes away, Simon nodded toward his wife. With a sympathetic glance at Jamie, Estelle suggested taking the children outside for some sunshine. "You can help me keep an eye on them, Mother Bianca, and you too, Marianne."

His mother knew something was up too, but nothing trumped time with her grandchildren. So whatever the reason for Simon's visit, she was simply glad they were there.

She did direct a look at Simon before she picked up little Keith to follow Estelle outside. "I expect you boys not to fight."

"We're not children, Mother." Simon didn't bother hiding the irritation in his voice.

"You'll always be my children and you haven't outgrown listening to me. Not now. Not ever." Mother wagged her finger at Simon.

Uncle Wyatt spoke up before Simon could say anything else. "Now, Simon, one must never ignore the wise counsel of one's mother no matter one's age." He pushed back from the table and stood up. "I think it's time for my Sunday nap. Jamie, if the phone rings, I'm not home." Then he shrugged. "Unless I am."

Jamie knew what that meant. Uncle Wyatt never refused to go when he got a call. "Maybe nobody will get sick."

"We can only hope, but it's not likely. Some foolhardy child will climb a tree and fall out or something of that sort." Uncle Wyatt smiled. "So good to see you, Simon. Glad you took time to come see your mother. She misses Louisville."

Mother stopped before she went out the door and looked back at Wyatt. "That's not true, Wyatt. I'm perfectly content here in Danville. It's a lovely town with lovely people. Nobody acts as if they need to see one's bank statement before they invite you to tea." She smiled toward Simon. "Of course, everyone loves your uncle Wyatt."

"No need to butter me up, Bianca. You know you have a home here as long as you need one." He looked from her to Jamie. "You and your children."

Simon waited until Wyatt was out of the room before he muttered, "He's always throwing it up at me that I didn't open my house to all of you. But I had to consider Estelle in her delicate condition with a baby on the way."

Jamie frowned. "I don't think Uncle Wyatt meant that at all. He likes having Mother here."

"I'm sure." Simon sounded as if that were the last thing he could believe. "You know an old bachelor like Wyatt is simply thrilled to have three people move in to upset his routine."

"So it seems."

"Don't be so dense." Simon scowled at Jamie. "You heard what he said about Mother missing Louisville. That was a definite jab at me."

"If he's upset about us being here, he hides it well." Jamie rattled the ice in his tea and tried to shift the conversation. "Would you like some more tea?"

"No."

Jamie studied the ice melting into the amber tea. He liked the way the condensation formed on the outside of the glass. If film wasn't so expensive, he'd take a picture, maybe several pictures, to capture that look of refreshment. Maybe he should go into advertisement. That sounded better than teaching.

With each day that passed, the dread of being shut up in a schoolhouse all day grew. He had little trouble imagining a roomful of young people with no interest in learning to conjugate sentences. But a job was a job, and a man had to have a job.

"Shall we move into the parlor?" Simon asked.

Jamie sat back in his chair and propped the glass on his thigh. "We're fine here. You might as well be out with whatever it is you've come to say."

"You're right." Simon leaned forward in his chair. "It's my duty as your older brother to keep you from doing something foolish."

"And what is that, brother dear? Teaching? While I can't say that has been my lifelong dream, it is a paying position."

"This has nothing to do with you taking a teaching position but sounds as though you should develop a better attitude before school starts. You've always been a dreamer. But you're not a kid now. You're what?"

Jamie didn't bother answering. Simon knew how old he was.

"Twenty-two? By the time I was your age I was already married and supporting a family. While the current economic crisis has hindered my earning ability, I am still finding a way to support said family. A growing family, I might add."

Jamie could have mentioned Estelle's family money, but he

didn't. Instead he rubbed his thumb through the condensation on his glass to make a *P*. It didn't have to be *P* for Piper. It could be *P* for pray that Simon would get whatever he wanted to say said without Jamie wanting to punch him. Another thing *P* could stand for. Punch.

But his mother had asked them not to fight. Not that he ever started any fights with Simon. He grew up wanting to be like his big brother. His father said be like Simon. So did his teachers. But he wasn't Simon. Instead he was pathetic. Another *P* word.

The *P* could stand for those other words, but it didn't. Piper had danced through his thoughts continually since he'd missed seeing her by mere hours. *Not expected back until the end of summer.* He'd spent months trying to push her completely out of his mind rather than risk rejection.

Now he couldn't imagine what he had been thinking. He could blame his father's death. He could blame the loss of their home and everything that had once defined the Russell family, but the person really to blame was him. He'd been the one not to answer Piper's letters. He was the one who had stood in that hotel garden too cowardly to go inside and demand a dance with Piper. He had been the one to watch Braxton Crandall put his arm around Piper as though she belonged to him and had made no move to prove it not true.

He should push Piper out of his thoughts again. She hadn't promised him anything. He hadn't promised her anything. Her father was right. He had nothing to promise her. Nothing but his love.

Simon was still talking about his work and how he had held on through these hard times and managed to make progress. Jamie nodded and muttered something now and again to make Simon think he was paying attention.

"Are you listening to me?" Simon raised his voice. "I come all the way to Danville to talk sense into you and you're daydreaming. Are you ever going to grow up, Jamie?"

"I heard you. You've worked hard. You have opportunities." Jamie rubbed what was left of the *P* off his glass and looked straight at Simon. Time to act serious or contrite or whatever it was Simon wanted. He did love his big brother, but he couldn't turn into the person Simon wanted him to be.

He'd tried that when he was nineteen, before their father died. He'd sat at a desk, added up numbers, and died a little inside every day. It was a terrible thing, but he was almost glad for the economic crash that took their factory. While it had destroyed his father, the crash freed Jamie from the dreary accounting desk.

Even while grieving his father and helping his mother move out of the house she loved, he couldn't quite lose the grateful feeling of not having to go back to that desk and try to make numbers add up right. That was shameful, but no use lying to himself. Sometimes a person had to look the truth in the face and pray for forgiveness and mercy.

From the look on Simon's face, no mercy was forthcoming from him. "I will not let you spoil my chances to get financing for my new factory." Simon glared at Jamie. "Not over some juvenile idea about love."

So that was it. Simon must have found out about his visit to Piper's father. Probably from Mr. Danson himself. A man like Danson wasn't one to leave things to chance. That was what Jamie did. He'd left too much to chance. That may have cost him Piper, while pursuing her might cost him his brother.

"I've done nothing to harm your venture, Simon. A radio factory is a wonderful idea and I hope you get it off the ground."

"I will get it off the ground and it will be a success."

Simon sounded as though he was not only trying to convince Jamie but also himself. He must be running into some difficulties, but Jamie didn't ask. He simply needed to deny being a difficulty himself. With Jamie here in Danville and Piper off somewhere in Eastern Kentucky, that seemed to eliminate any problems for Simon. Whatever problems he might be imagining.

"Good." Jamie set his tea glass back on the table and stood up. As far as he was concerned, they had said all they needed to say.

"I'm not through with you." Simon jumped up and stepped closer to Jamie.

"What do you want from me, Simon?" Jamie faced him.

"I want you to stay away from Piper Danson. Her father says she's been promised to Braxton Crandall."

"Been promised? By who?" Jamie fought the sick feeling rising inside him. It couldn't be true. He couldn't lose Piper. "We don't live in the Dark Ages. A woman can make her own choices."

"What makes you think she hasn't made her choice? She'd be crazy not to jump at the chance to marry Crandall. With him, she will never have to worry about lacking money for a new dress."

"There's more to life than new dresses." Jamie wanted to believe that was true. Desperately.

"Yes. There's food on the table. Money for the right schools for your children. A comfortable life. All things you have no way of giving Piper or any other girl." Simon's eyes narrowed as he went on. "And don't bother mentioning love. Love is a poor substitute for security. Especially with the way things are now. You're witness of that with Mother."

"I'll keep what you say in mind."

It was useless to argue with Simon. Anyway, he was right. Jamie couldn't offer Piper that security Simon mentioned. Plus, he couldn't be sure she hadn't already chosen Braxton Crandall. The two had seemed very chummy the night of her debut. That didn't mean Jamie had to let her step to the marriage altar with Crandall without first hearing him tell her he loved her. If she then said she wanted to marry Crandall, he'd wish her well.

Simon poked his finger into Jamie's chest. "Do more than keep it in mind. Stay away from her and from all the Dansons. I won't have you ruining my chances of getting financial backing from the Crandalls. Do you understand?"

Jamie knocked Simon's hand away and stepped back. "I under-stand perfectly, but I doubt the Crandalls make financial decisions based on romantic arrangements."

"Don't be naïve. Everything is based on connections in the busi-ness world." Simon scowled at Jamie.

"Then it's good I don't plan to be part of that world. I'll just putter along teaching school." *And dream of making money with my words and pictures*, he added silently.

As though the confrontation was over and he'd won, Simon threw an arm around Jamie's shoulders. "You'll be a great teacher. Teaching English, did you say?"

"English." Jamie didn't move away from Simon. That was just how his brother was. Once he thought he'd brought Jamie in line, he was ready to be best buddies again. It used to work when Jamie was a kid. But he wasn't a kid now. He was his own person, and whether Simon realized it or not, he hadn't promised anything. He wouldn't promise anything. He wasn't sure when he might see Piper again, but he would before she made the mistake of walking down the aisle with Braxton Crandall.

CHAPTER

FOURTEEN

Dear Truda,

I'm having a wonderful time. This week I went on a circuit of some of the outlying centers. Confluence, Red Bird, Brutus, Wilder Ridge, Beech Creek. Don't you love the names? There's even a creek named Hell-for-Sartin. And one named Hurricane. Not the way we say it, but Hurri-kin. You have to say things the way the mountain people say them or you just know they're trying not to laugh at you.

But the people are great. I met this cute little six-year-old boy at the hospital. I was told to entertain him for a while, but Billy was the one who entertained me. He had some bad chemical burns where he'd spilled lye on his legs when his mother was making soap. Poor little guy.

I also met someone else at the hospital. Dr. Jack Booker. He says he met you once a long time ago. He remembers you very fondly.

Truda read the name and then read it again before she looked up from Piper's letter and stared out her front window. Could it really be that young medical student from so long ago? They had had such a brief time together. Only a few hours out of a lifetime. How many years ago now? Over twenty. When she did the math, more like twenty-five.

And yet when she thought of that night, something still went soft inside her. She gave herself a shake. Where she was soft must be in the head to feel that way. She had built that night up until there was no way reality could match what she remembered. A young girl's foolishness. She wasn't young now. Into her forties. Sometimes she almost had to do the math to remember how many years she'd added on.

But what had Piper written? That the doctor, this doctor she'd met, remembered Truda fondly? She looked back down at the letter. Very fondly. How did Piper know he remembered Truda fondly? What exactly had he said? And what did he look like now?

She stared at his name while an image rose in her mind. A tall, very slim young man with blue eyes and straw-colored hair that needed a trim. He'd had the faint shadow of a beard and a nose that was a shade crooked. She remembered wondering if he'd broken it when he was a kid. His suit jacket had looked well worn, but in spite of the awkwardness of coming into a party where he knew no one, he'd had an air about him. Not exactly confidence. Rather a sureness of knowing his path in life and what he was meant to do.

Truda wondered what he might remember about her, for she'd felt sure of nothing at the time as she floated along waiting for some man to choose her as a wife. That seemed the only path open to her. But as it turned out, she had not married. Had instead stepped out into a different life. She had few regrets about that, but she did have that niggle of wondering what might have happened if her father hadn't ordered the young medical student not to write to her.

At the very least, they might have exchanged some interesting letters and then still gone about their lives in the same way. He as a doctor. She as a bookkeeper in an investment bank. He was no doubt married with a houseful of children. But there was that word "fondly." "Very fondly."

Truda started reading Piper's letter again, but she wrote no more about this Dr. Booker. Truda had no trouble imagining Piper's teasing smile as she'd written those "very fondly" words. She would guess her words would incite Truda's curiosity. Truda wouldn't rise to the bait when she wrote back. She'd pretend scant interest with a carefully worded comment. At her age, she wasn't about to act like a silly debutante. She was long past searching for a husband.

Piper went on about her new friends Suze and Marlie. She said everybody had nicknames and that they were calling her Danny. Truda hoped that didn't stick as she read the end of the letter.

I want to thank you again for sponsoring me as a courier. It is so nice here. You can't imagine how lovely the rhododendrons are. Words simply can't describe how the hills are in bloom. I'm not sure how long they last, but I hope some will still be blooming when you come to the mountains. You are planning to come this summer, aren't you?

Mrs. Breckinridge said if you came, I could be the one to fetch you in Hazard. There is a bus of sorts that comes from there to Hyden, but I know you'd rather get the full experience of riding in on horseback. You would, wouldn't you? We can hope it's not raining. Riding is more pleasant when it's not raining.

Love you always,
Piper

Truda folded the letter and slid it back into the envelope. She tapped the envelope on her chin. Mary Breckinridge had encouraged her to come to Hyden. In hopes of getting a bigger contribution, of course. Truda did have some money set aside for charitable causes.

Erwin might tell her charity began at home and that if she had money to spare, she should help her family. Business was slow for his law firm in the current economic downturn. Spending so much on Piper's debut hadn't been the wisest financial decision, although Erwin would think it money well spent if Piper entertained young Crandall's interest.

But the money was hers, not Erwin's. She could spend it however she wanted. If that was supporting Mary Breckinridge's work in the Appalachian Mountains, then so be it.

She'd always heard June was a beautiful month to travel. Something she'd done little of in her life. Always tied to a desk and a mountain of figures. But a mountain of flowers sounded more enticing right now. The truth was, she wasn't getting any younger and she needed a holiday.

She sat down at her writing desk and pulled out a piece of stationery. She wouldn't tell Piper she was coming. Not yet. Just that she was considering it. Truda had to make arrangements. A person couldn't simply throw aside all responsibilities and take off for the mountains. No matter how alluring the idea was.

She would see Wendover. She'd see those rhododendrons and the creeks with the interesting names. She would even ride that horse, though riding was not her favorite thing.

It would be interesting to see how this Dr. Booker had turned out. To find out if he'd married. He'd probably thickened around the middle, as men sometimes did as they got older. He could be bald by now. He wouldn't look anything like the young man she remembered. She would meet him and they would no longer have a thing in common. Not a thing. Simply saying hello might turn out to be an awkward social nicety.

That Piper. Trying to fire up her curiosity. Truda wasn't about to admit how well it worked.

CHAPTER
FIFTEEN

Dear Braxton,

Piper stared at the words she'd written what seemed like a half hour ago. *Dear Braxton.* Nothing more. The lamplight flickered and made shadows on her stationery. She shifted her gaze from Braxton's name to the oil lamp on the small writing desk between the beds. Suze, visiting from her room as she did every evening, was at the desk, sketching a flower she'd discovered that day. Márlie lounged on her bed and leafed through a tattered *Saturday Evening Post.*

"Only a year old." Marlie held up the cover with a Norman Rockwell illustration of a little boy going fishing. "These covers make you smile every time you see them. But a movie mag would be more fun. Gosh, I miss going to the movies."

Suze spoke without looking around. "They have movies in Hazard."

"Yeah, movies I probably saw two years ago."

"That could be." Suze erased something on her drawing. "I wish I could draw like Norman Rockwell." She held her sketch up to the light and sighed. "I just can't get this right."

Marlie pitched the magazine on the floor and stood up to look over Suze's shoulder. "Looks pretty good to me."

"But it doesn't look that much like the flower I saw. Oh well, I should have taken a picture." Suze put the drawing in a folder and looked at Piper. "So do you miss going to the movies too?"

"Not that much." Piper looked at the blank paper. Maybe she could ask Braxton what movies he'd seen. It would be something to write. "I was ready for something different."

"Bet you weren't expecting this different." Marlie bounced up on her toes and stretched. She was barefoot and in her nightgown. "Neither was I when my mother decided I needed to expand my horizons after she heard Mrs. Breckinridge talk. I wasn't all that keen for it, but once my mother gets an idea, you might as well go along. No changing her mind. I had to pack my bags, but I'm not sorry I came. Are you?"

"Not at all, but I'm doing things I would have never imagined doing three weeks ago. Hauling water. Giving horses baths in the river. Trying to keep geese from nipping me."

"Oh yeah." Marlie laughed. "What about dressing Puddin's sore leg? Eww. Nothing fun about that."

"But it's helping, isn't it?" Maybe she could tell Braxton about spending most of the night in Puddin's stall to tend his leg. The old horse might be slow, but he was sweet.

"I don't want to think about it. I'm not into pus unless I have to be." Marlie shivered and made a face. "So let's come up with something happier to talk about." She peeked at Piper's letter. "Like who is Braxton? Your sweetheart?"

"I wouldn't say that. Exactly." Piper looked down at her pen. The ink had dried on the nib. She should have put the cap back on it, but she did need to write something. She'd promised Braxton a letter. And a promise was a promise.

"What would you say?" Marlie teased. "Exactly?"

"My father wants me to like him."

"And you don't?" Suze asked. "If you don't mind me asking. If you do, then just tell us both to hush and go to bed."

"I don't mind." It might be good to talk about it. "Braxton was my chosen escort for my debut."

"But not your choice." Marlie plopped down on the floor and leaned back against her bed. She grabbed a pillow to stuff behind her back.

When Piper didn't answer right away, Marlie went on. "Braxton is a great name. Sounds handsome."

"He is nice looking."

"With money?" Marlie raised her eyebrows.

"Money isn't everything," Suze said.

"But it helps everything," Marlie said.

Piper sighed. "Yes, he has money. His family is in railroads."

"Oh my." Marlie whistled softly. "That could mean lots of money. Lucky you."

"What's his last name?" Suze asked. "I know a Braxton whose family had something to do with railroads. His name was Crandall."

"You're joking." Piper stared at her. "You know Braxton Crandall?"

"I do. We used to talk whenever we were at the same social events in New York. Seems like back then there was some kind of party or dinner every day. Before the crash. His father or maybe his grandfather and my father had some kind of business connection. I don't know what." Suze shrugged. "I was younger then, with little interest in commerce."

"You have interest in commerce now?" Marlie sounded as though that would be the very last thing that might catch her interest.

"Sure." Suze gave her a "why not" look. "I'm interested in everything that makes the world go around."

"I thought you were just rewriting the nature encyclopedia," Marlie said.

Suze laughed. "I think that task is beyond me, but I do like noticing whatever is growing around me. Or happening. Don't you want to know what's going on?"

Marlie waved her hand. "I take things as they come. What can I do about it anyway? Except maybe help out by going to shows or buying a new dress." She grinned at Suze before she looked over at Piper. "You're awfully quiet. Forget commerce and tell us about this Braxton. Sounds like our Suze was impressed by him, and not much impresses Suze unless it's blooming or sprouting money now, I guess."

"I barely know him. We danced at my debut. Then we went out to dinner where I told him I was coming here."

"Ooh." Marlie grinned. "Playing hard to get. How did he take that?"

"Not too well. I think he thought he and my father had already worked out an arrangement, but I'm not something to be auctioned off to the highest bidder."

"Sounds like he could bid pretty high," Marlie said.

"Come on, Marlie," Suze said. "The girl is right. Women have made some strides. We don't have to simper and coo and hope for a man to rescue us."

"No, we can come to Wendover and brush horses and scoop up their Easter eggs." Marlie laughed.

Suze frowned at her. "You know what I mean."

"Yeah, I'm sorry. But what about it, Danny? You must not have rejected him outright." She pointed toward the letter. "You are writing him a letter."

"I know." Piper sighed and stared down to the page. "He asked me to write him and I told him I would. But I figure by now he's already been captured by a more-eager-to-be-married girl than me. He told me straight out he was ready to get married."

"Wow! You really did turn down the jackpot. Good-looking. Money. Ready to settle down and have babies. Well, you'd have the babies." Marlie got an odd look on her face. "You know, I'm down here where babies are being born right and left. I was with one of the nurses a couple of weeks ago and she delivered the baby of a sixteen-year-old. Sixteen. Said she got married when she was fourteen. I'm almost twenty and I can't imagine having a baby yet. I want to someday, but not tomorrow or anytime soon."

"That's good," Suze said dryly. "Mrs. Breckinridge would be very upset if that kind of thing was going on among her couriers. We aren't supposed to think about boys while we're here. Only work."

Marlie yanked the pillow out from behind her head and slung it at Suze. "You know what I mean."

Suze caught it and pitched it back. "Just how many boys did you leave on a string back in Chicago?"

Marlie stuffed the pillow behind her head and then held up her hand with all fingers up. "Not more than five." She curled her fingers to stare at her nails. "I could use a manicure." She looked back at Suze. "That is, five if I don't count Ray."

"I thought Ray was the one who counted most," Suze said.

"He's okay." Marlie shrugged a little. "But he better not be running around with other girls back there in Chicago or he'll be history. A girl has her pride."

"'Pride goeth before a fall,'" Suze said.

Marlie groaned. "Now you're quoting the Bible at me. Do you give lovelorn advice too?"

"As if you would listen." Suze made a face.

"So what about you, Suze?" Piper asked. "Do you have some fellow waiting for you in New York?"

"I'm no Marlie with her dozen guys on a string."

"I said five. Not a dozen." Marlie held up her hand again and wiggled her fingers. "Five."

"Okay, five plus Ray." Suze looked from Marlie to Piper. "And I'm no Danny with guys asking me to write them letters." Suze shook her head and sighed dramatically. "Guys like petite and cute or willowy and beautiful like the Gibson Girl."

"Don't talk about that Gibson Girl," Marlie said. "Whatever magazine came up with her did all us not-so-tall girls a major disservice."

"True enough, but that Gibson Girl seems to be one guys want. Not someone like me, a little too stout through the middle. But worse than that, a girl who is way too ready to tell guys when they're wrong. But only when they're stupidly wrong."

"Oh, come on, Suze," Marlie said. "Nothing at all wrong with how you look. A little lipstick and rouge and you'll knock their socks off."

"Yeah. That's me." Suze threw out her arms wide. "The next Miss America."

Marlie giggled. "I'm not tall enough to be Miss America. But Danny here might fit the bill. Tall and beautiful."

"That's funny," Piper said. "I lack a lot being beautiful."

Marlie frowned. "No boy ever told you you're pretty? Made you feel beautiful?"

"See, there you go again. Thinking we can't feel pretty unless some guy thinks it for us," Suze said.

"Didn't you just say the same thing?" Marlie's frown got deeper. "About yourself."

"I guess I did," Suze admitted. "But we're not letting Danny say anything. Come on, girl. Surely something makes you feel pretty. Gosh, I can feel almost pretty when I first get up in the morning and splash some cold water on my face and then look outside.

Everything is so fresh then, with the promise of something good about to happen."

"What do you expect to happen?" Marlie asked. "Cleaning out more stalls? Weeding gardens? Cleaning tack?"

"Watching a baby come into the world. Finding a new flower," Suze said. "That's just it. I don't know what might happen, but I know something will. So why not expect something that's going to make me feel good? Works for me. So what do you say, Danny girl?"

They both looked at Piper.

"What makes me feel good?" Piper ran her hand across the paper in her lap to give herself a moment to think. "Maybe riding into the wind. You don't have to worry about your hair or what you look like. It's just you and the horse."

And the guy on the horse beside her. She left that out. No need getting the girls curious about Jamie too. But back when they spent every weekend riding, he had a way of making Piper feel pretty. When they dismounted, he would snatch up a daisy or some other handy flower to present to her with a smile that wrapped around her like a hug.

"That's a pretty dreamy look if you're only thinking about a horse," Marlie said.

Piper lifted her chin a little. "A girl can love her horse, can't she?"

"Spoken like a true horse lover," Suze said. "Me, a horse just gets me there faster than on foot. I always seem to get the pesky ones that want to nip you when you're saddling them. Give me a faithful dog companion any day."

Piper looked toward their door. "So where is our faithful dog buddy? Ginger is usually settled down on the rug in here by now."

"She is missing." Marlie jumped up, grabbed her jeans, and jerked them on under her nightgown. "Come on. I'll bet she's having her pups out in the barn. She was curled up in one of the empty stalls earlier today."

Piper stuffed her feet in her shoes and grabbed her flashlight.

The three of them tiptoed out into the hallway but not quietly enough.

Miss Aileen stuck her head out her door. "Where are you going?"

"We think Ginger is having her pups. She didn't come inside," Marlie said.

"Oh. Well, check on Puddin while you're out there. But if nothing's wrong, I can wait until morning to know how many new mouths we have to feed." She shut her door.

Puddin nickered when they went in the barn.

"Spoiled baby." Marlie gave his nose a touch on the way past his stall.

Ginger looked up at them and flapped her tail when Piper shined the light on her. Little golden pups wriggled in the straw next to her.

"How many did you have, girl?" Suze reached for the flashlight and then knelt down to count the pups. "Looks like several sets of triplets."

Piper leaned over to caress Ginger's head. "Way to go, girl."

The dog scooted one of the pups closer with her nose.

"Ten," Suze announced.

"Aren't they the cutest things?" Marlie gently picked up one of them. It fit in her hand. "This one's a boy."

Ginger whined as she watched Marlie.

"Maybe we should leave them alone. We don't want to get Ginger agitated." Suze stroked Ginger from head to tail. "What a good girl."

"Here he is, sweetie." Marlie placed the pup right beside Ginger.

When they went out of the barn, the moon was so bright, Suze turned off the flashlight. Down below the river rushed by. The whippoorwills and tree frogs competed to see which could be loudest. Crickets played their songs too. Piper didn't know whether it was the moonlight or seeing those puppies, but she felt like dancing.

Suddenly there was a splash down at the river and a shout of "Halloo" came ringing up the hill to them.

CHAPTER
SIXTEEN

"Somebody must need a nurse." Suze looked at Piper. "You ready to take your turn with Nurse Robbins? At night, nobody goes out alone."

Piper froze, wanting to go but scared at the same time. "Will I know what to do?"

"Sure. Whatever the nurse tells you to do," Marlie said. "No way to know what to expect when you head out with a nurse."

"Don't worry. Nurse Robbins has the patience of a saint." Suze turned to Marlie. "You get Nurse Robbins. I'll saddle the horses."

"Right." Marlie gave Piper a little push. "Hustle up and get your boots on, Danny. Better grab a candy bar too."

"Good idea. The nurses stay till the baby comes, no matter how long it takes." Suze headed to the barn.

Back in her room, Piper's heart pounded as she pulled on her boots with shaky hands. "Calm down, silly," she muttered. "You aren't the one delivering the baby."

Her gaze caught on the unwritten letter to Braxton. She could write about this, going with a nurse midwife to see a baby being born. Then again, with the way he'd frowned when she told him about being a courier, she probably should stick to describing rhododendrons or telling him about Suze actually knowing him. That should work.

But wouldn't Jamie love hearing about her riding off on an adventure? He could make up a whole story about that. If things were the way they used to be between them, she could write him every detail. If. So many ifs.

She pushed those thoughts aside. She needed to live in the moment and not be trying to step back into the past. She grabbed a candy bar out of their stash and hurried outside. Nurse Robbins was coming down the steps from the Big House with her saddlebags slung over her shoulder.

Piper ran over to offer to carry the saddlebags.

"No need, Pippay. I'm accustomed to them slung on my shoulder." The nurse hadn't accepted the rejection of her nickname for Piper. "Are you ready for a midnight ride? A full moon does bring the babies, but at least we'll be able to see where we're going. It's practically as light as day out here."

"True. We can see our shadows." Piper kept pace with her.

"So we can. Both of us are tall and lanky, aren't we, Pippay?"

The nurse didn't wait for an answer as she stepped over to where the man still on his mule waited in the roadway. "Is it your wife's time, Mr. Whitton?"

"She's punishing bad, Nurse."

"How long?" The nurse adjusted the saddlebags on her shoulder and peered up at him.

"She didn't start with the punishing pains until right before I came down after you, but I ain't lying when I say she's punishing bad." His voice rose a little.

"There, there, Father. I'm sure we'll be in plenty of time to help the little one come into the world." The nurse sounded calm, as if nothing more exciting was happening than a pleasurable walk in the moonlight. "You head on back. We'll be right behind you."

"You will come on in a hurry?"

"Yes, of course. I promise."

The man kicked his mule to start back toward the river.

Suze had the horses waiting. Nurse Robbins adjusted her saddlebags across Fancy's rump. Suze handed Piper the reins to Dickens, the gelding she'd ridden on the tour of the outlying centers.

"If you feel a little woozy," Suze said, "take a deep breath and try not to faint."

Nurse Robbins laughed. "She wouldn't be the first. Babies don't come wrapped in soft cotton blankets, all neat and rosy. But rosy soon enough." She mounted the horse in a quick movement. "Come along, Pippay. The two of us will have a lovely time."

They could hear the man already crossing the river.

Nurse Robbins turned the mare in that direction and called over her shoulder. "Do keep up."

A new worry reared up inside Piper. Losing sight of the nurse. Piper swallowed hard and flicked the reins to urge Dickens forward. That wasn't really necessary. The horse trotted after Fancy. He knew more what to do than she did.

Once they forded the river and Dickens easily kept up with Fancy, Piper sat easier in the saddle. She'd never ridden in moonlight. Under the trees, the going was dim, but when they came out into a creek, shadows shimmered in the water sliding along over the rocks. The whole world seemed to have a certain glow while the whippoorwills added music.

When a screech owl sounded overhead, Dickens tossed his head. Then a different owl hooted.

"Keep a good hold on those reins, Pippay." Nurse Robbins looked over at her as they splashed along in the creek. "If an old hoot owl swoops down out of the trees, even the steadiest horse might take a fright."

Piper tightened her grip on the reins. "But it is beautiful out here."

"You're fortunate to have this nice moonlit June night. It's not so pleasant in January, with snow blowing in your face and the horses struggling to keep their footing on icy trails. Or when the rains pour down and little creeks like this one swoosh down the mountain, ready to take you with it. At times like that, you need a fine horse under you as you head to higher ground."

"Sounds like you've had some scary times."

"There have been moments, but the good Lord must watch over us nurse midwives. He knows we mean good." Nurse Robbins glanced over at Piper. "That doesn't mean he doesn't let us see some storms. I'm sure you'll get the pleasure of riding in a few while you're here. I can handle the wind and rain, but I don't like it when the lightning starts cracking. Nothing for it but to keep going. Babies do love to come when the skies are thundering."

"My mother says I came during a snowstorm."

"Yes, babies love those too." She stretched up in her saddle to peer on up the creek. "Mr. Whitton must have kicked his mule into a trot the whole way, but we'll just keep going along steady. Always the best way. Steady and sure. Don't want to stress my Fancy." She patted the mare's neck. "She always gets me there in time."

"You never have to hurry?"

"My dear girl, we are hurrying. Didn't you note how quickly we were ready and on our way? But no need galloping our horses up the mountain and risking their legs and our heads unless a life is hanging in the balance. I have no doubt Mrs. Whitton's baby will wait until we get there. Probably will wait all night after we get there. That's another thing about babies. They take their time."

"How long have you been a nurse midwife?" Nurse Robbins always seemed so poised and in control.

"I've been here in the mountains for two years. But I delivered my fair share of babies in the home country before Mrs. Breckinridge talked me into coming to Kentucky. That woman is a charmer." She shook her head a little.

132

"Were you sorry you came?"

"The place was a bit of a surprise when I got here. More wild than I expected." The woman flashed a smile over at Piper.

"Wild?"

"The landscape, I suppose, and then the men with their guns. I've treated my share of gunshot wounds. Nearly always an accident, according to my patients, even when the only thing accidental was that somebody didn't die. But that's not for me to judge. I merely try to stop the bleeding and patch them up."

"Does that happen often?"

"Often enough." She looked over at Piper and laughed. "No need to worry. The mountain men treat all of us with the utmost courtesy and go out of their way to help us. They help their neighbors the same."

"When they aren't shooting at one another?"

"Not usually at neighbors." Nurse Robbins laughed again. "But sometimes feelings run high. Especially when revenuers come into the picture. We stay out of that. No talking about religion, politics, or moonshine."

"I know. Miss Aileen made sure I understood that." They rode a little way in silence before Piper asked, "So why did you decide to come to America?"

"You should have heard Mrs. Breckinridge talk about it." Nurse Robbins sighed a little. "Made the place sound like a veritable paradise where I'd have my own horse, my own dog, and could save children's lives. All true. Except she failed to mention a few problems in paradise. The poverty. The snakes. The briars if a person loses the trail. The ice and snow in the winter. The heat in the summer. The lack of anything close to conveniences in most of the houses where I go to bring babies into the world."

"But you stayed."

"Paradise won out. The mountains speak to me." Nurse Robbins glanced at Piper. "What about you, Pippay? Why are you here?"

Piper hesitated before she answered. The owl hooted again and a dog howled in the distance. Finally she said, "I guess because I heard Mrs. Breckinridge talk too."

"She can spin a great picture of the mountains and the people here. She admires their strength and pioneer spirit. As anyone should, though you can see some things not to admire as well. But the mothers, they are the heart of the mountains."

"What a lovely thought." Piper looked around. There was a feel of paradise here.

Fancy put her head down to drink and Nurse Robbins didn't goad her forward. "Let Dickens drink too. We have to head up the hill now. Almost there."

While the horses drank, the nurse studied Piper. "I always wonder about you girls. You come from a life of ease to do our bidding and that of Mrs. Breckinridge. Wait until you must make tea to satisfy that woman. She's more English than me when it comes to her tea."

"Suze has warned me."

"Suze was as green as you last summer, but she knows why she's here this summer." Nurse Robbins tipped her head to the side as she watched Piper. "But I'm not sure you know why you're here. Perhaps simply a charitable spirit. Then again, you wouldn't be running away from something, would you?"

When Piper started to deny that, the nurse held a hand up to stop her. "Don't bother your head to come up with an answer, because unless I miss my guess, you don't know the answer. Nurse midwives get very good at reading people." She tightened Fancy's reins and turned her out of the creek. "Besides, dear Mrs. Whitton is having a baby, and Mr. Whitton has, no doubt, lost his mind by now."

She smiled back at Piper. "Worry not about what I said. You will figure it out. The mountains give you time to ponder."

Piper followed the nurse up the hill. Why was she here? Had she really simply wanted an adventure or could Nurse Robbins be right? Could she be running away from all the expectations? Marriage. Children. Society must-dos. What was the matter with her that she wasn't sure she wanted that? No, she did want to marry and have children. Of course, she did.

I'm ready to pick a wife. Braxton Crandall's words circled in her head. She wasn't an apple to pick off a tree. A debutante tree. She swallowed down a giggle as she imagined all the pretty girls in their white dresses perched on the branches of a giant tree.

She pictured herself climbing down from that tree. If any picking got done, she wanted to do the choosing. She thought of the tree again, but this time the guys in their dark suits, straddling the branches. Braxton was on a low branch easy to pick, but Jamie was on a top branch.

Piper squeezed her eyes shut and mentally erased the image before she could imagine a blonde climbing up through those limbs faster than she could.

They came out into a little clearing where dogs ran down off a cabin's porch to bark at them. The man waited in front of the cabin.

"I was fretting you'd lost your way up the hill." He stepped up to take Fancy's reins. "I'll tend to your horses. You tend to my woman."

CHAPTER
SEVENTEEN

A dog lying right in front of the door raised his head and growled when they stepped up on the porch. Piper stopped in her tracks, but Nurse Robbins wasn't bothered.

"Now see here, Blackie, we're not having any of that. It's good you're guarding your family, but you know me. And this other one is quite harmless as well, I assure you."

The dog's tail came up and went down with a whack on the wooden porch.

"That's about the best you get with Blackie. His welcome signal. We can step over him and go in now."

"Can't you just make him move?" Piper eyed the dog.

"He didn't sound in the mood to move. Come on, Pippay. The old fellow is harmless. About all he has left is his growl, so you can't blame him for using it now and again." She pushed open the door and stepped over the dog, then looked back at Piper. "Keep the noise down. Mrs. Whitton's little ones are probably asleep. But if they get up, you might have to corral them and keep them away from their mummy."

"What else will I need to do?"

"I'll let you know. Just remember Suze's advice about breathing and not fainting."

An oil lamp flickered on the table, but the moonlight through the window was brighter. Heat from a small stove in the kitchen area had the room extra warm. A big kettle sat on the stove top.

"I hope that's hot water," Nurse Robbins said.

"Should I check?"

"Later. First we need to talk to our mother."

In the corner of the room, a woman pushed up on her elbows in her bed to a near sitting position. "Nurse Robbins, you're a fine sight for sore eyes. This one appears extra eager to be born. I was feared I'd have the babe before you got here. My other two didn't come on so fast."

Piper trailed after Nurse Robbins over to the bed. The woman was young, maybe not much older than Piper but with weariness stamped on her face. Strands of dark hair had pulled loose from her long braid.

"If this one's in a hurry, then you'll be glad to soon have the laboring over with and the little fellow in your arms, won't you, Mrs. Whitton?" Nurse Robbins kept her voice cheery.

"I ain't arguing against that." The woman fell back on her pillow. "Babies are powerful sweet but can't say I enjoy getting them here."

"But you'll do fine." Nurse Robbins pulled Piper up beside her. "This is Pippay. She's new, just down from the city." She looked from Mrs. Whitton to Piper. "If dear Mrs. Whitton felt able to get out of bed, you'd see she's tall and lanky the same as us, Pippay. You find many that match us up here in the mountains."

"Not so lanky right now." The woman cradled her baby belly with her hands.

"But lanky again very soon, my dear. How are the pains?" The nurse scooted a chair close to the bed and draped her saddlebags across it, but she didn't open them up.

With a shake of her head, the woman's lips tightened in a grim line as her body went tense. Nurse Robbins laid her hand on top of the cover over the woman's belly. "That is a strong one. Try to breathe in and out, Mrs. Whitton. You know how this goes. You've done it before." The nurse looked over her shoulder at Piper. "Pippay, you must remember to breathe too."

Piper had pulled in her breath and held it along with Mrs. Whitton. Embarrassed, she let it out.

Nurse Robbins laughed, and as the woman in the bed relaxed, she smiled too. "A first time to be along with the midwife, honey?" she asked.

Piper nodded.

"Surely at your age you've seen babies born," the woman said.

"Well, no," Piper said. "I have a little brother, but they took me to my grandmother's before he was born."

"Smart. To get the young'uns out of the way." Mrs. Whitton nodded. "My pains came on so fast I didn't have time to send my ma word. The girls are abed now anyhow. I'm hoping they have a baby brother before sunrise wakes them."

"How close are the pains, dear?" Nurse Robbins asked.

"I ain't for sure. I don't have a timepiece, and I didn't think to ask Alvin for his pocket watch afore he took off for you." The woman pulled in a breath. "I tried to count, but I kept losing my counting spot around two hundred."

"Never mind. I'll get washed up and we'll check things out." She patted the woman's arm. "Come along, Pippay. You'll have to wash the trail dirt off you too. But first get some wood for the stove. We need plenty of hot water."

"I knowed that from last time, Nurse, so's I had Alvin bring some from the spring and put it on the stove, but I ain't fed the fire for a while. It mighta gone out." She started to sit up. "I can fix it, if you want."

Nurse Robbins pushed her back down. "No getting up unless you need the pot. Pippay will see to the fire."

"You're a gift, sure enough, Nurse." She looked at Piper. "There's some wood in the box just outside the back door."

Piper waited until they were in the kitchen area to say, "I don't know how to fix a fire."

"It's not hard." Nurse Robbins held her hand over the stove. "The fire hasn't gone out. So you just shove the wood in on top of the coals." She pointed to an empty bucket. "We'll need Mr. Whitton to fetch more water if he hasn't gone off."

"Gone off?" Piper said. "He surely won't go anywhere."

"Maybe not, but some of these fathers get so anxious about a baby coming, they can't stay still. They have to be off doing something." She poured some water out of the kettle on the stove into a wash pan and lathered her hands with soap from her saddlebags. "I'll leave the soap here for you after you tend to the fire."

When Piper headed for the door, Nurse Robbins added, "If you hear a rattling sound, take a close look before you pick up anything. Wouldn't want to have to treat you for snakebite."

Whether she was serious or merely teasing, Piper's ears were on high alert as she reached into the box. Nothing rattled, so she grabbed a few pieces of wood and hurried back inside.

Nurse Robbins looked up from laying out her instruments. "Open up that little door and use the poker to rake the coals together. Then shove in the wood." She turned to Mrs. Whitton. "Girl's never fixed a fire before."

"Well, imagine that. Not having to keep a fire going." The woman looked toward Piper. "Don't burn yourself, honey."

"I won't." Piper felt inordinately pleased when the wood started popping.

When she headed outside with the bucket, the dog gave no notice to her stepping over him and off the porch. "Mr. Whitton," she called.

"The babe here already?" He spoke right behind her.

Startled, Piper jerked in a breath and then let it out slowly. If nothing else, she was learning to breathe. "No baby yet, but we need more water."

"I brung water earlier. Filled the kettle to the brim."

"I know, but Nurse Robbins says we need more."

"Then I reckon I better fetch some." With a sigh, he took the bucket. "You wouldn't think a body would need to drain a spring dry to birth a baby."

No handy way to get water around here. Every drop had to be carried in from somewhere. Even on the hottest summer days, fires were needed to heat that water. Nothing was easy. But that didn't mean there wasn't joy in the struggle. Piper stood still a moment, listening. She never had reason to step outside in the city to hear the night sing.

She shook herself a little and headed back inside. No time for listening to the night right now. Nurse Robbins might need something.

A few minutes later, the man set the bucket inside the door and peered across the room at his wife. "How are you, Rosalinda?"

"Fine, Alvin. Just doing what has to be done."

"You'll get me a boy, won't you, Nurse?" The man looked at Nurse Robbins.

"I can't be promising that." Nurse Robbins smiled at him. "I help bring them into the world, but I don't make them boys or girls."

"I reckon that's up to the good Lord." The man ducked out of sight and shut the door.

"I'm prayin' the good Lord seen fit to make this one a boy for my Alvin. He is gonna be some disappointed if I push out another girl," Mrs. Whitton said.

"Come now," Nurse Robbins said. "Girl babies are a gift and a pleasure. Just look at the three of us. All girl babies once upon a time."

"True enough," Mrs. Whitton said. "But my pa lacked some

being happy each time a girl got added to the family. Ended up six girls to three boys when Ma quit having babies. I was the fourth girl. Good thing the one before me was a boy or Pa might have pitched me out with the bathwater."

The woman's laugh was cut short when another pain pushed through her. She pulled in a breath and let it out slowly.

"That's the way, Mother." Nurse Robbins murmured encouragement as she massaged the woman's belly. She looked at Piper. "Dampen a cloth to bathe Mrs. Whitton's face."

Piper did as the nurse said and gently wiped the perspiration off the woman's face.

With the pain receding, Mrs. Whitton managed a smile. "Thank you, honey. What was it the nurse called you?"

"Pippay, but my name is Piper." Piper made a face. "Sort of a weird name, isn't it?"

"Don't know that I ever heerd of anybody else called that."

"Your name, Rosalinda, is pretty," Piper said.

"I've always favored it. My ma named me, but then she called me Rosie. But Alvin and me, we decided to use the names we was given on those first breaths and not shorten 'em down." The woman shrugged. "So I give my own babies shorter names to begin with. Linda's four and Faye, the baby, is nigh on two."

"Not the baby much longer. She'll have to move over for this new one," Nurse Robbins said.

"Do you have a name picked out for the baby?" Piper asked. "For his or her first breaths."

"Some folks take a while to name their little ones, but I like having a name in mind. Be easy if it's the boy Alvin wants. Then it's Alvin Junior. Not sure what we'll call him though. Maybe all of Alvin Junior."

"And if it's a girl?" Piper asked.

"I'm thinking Robin. Like the bird." The woman gave Nurse Robbins a shy look. "And after Nurse Robbins here." Her voice caught as another contraction grabbed her, followed by a second one right on its heels.

"Now you have me hoping for a girl instead of Mr. Whitton's boy, but either way, let's get this done." Nurse Robbins made a tent with the sheet and positioned Mrs. Whitton's legs.

Labor pains took control of Mrs. Whitton's body. She clutched the bedposts, but she didn't cry out. Nurse Robbins kept up a steady stream of encouragement. Push. Wait. Breathe. Push.

Nurse Robbins told Piper to get a soft towel ready. "The baby's wee head is crowning. Come see. It's a marvel you shouldn't miss."

Piper found the towel, took a deep breath, and stepped to the end of the bed. Mrs. Whitton grunted as the head emerged.

"You're doing lovely, dearie. Another push and then it will be easy sailing," Nurse Robbins said.

The nurse gently guided the baby's shoulders out. The dark hair was plastered to its head and blood and fluids streaked the baby's face, but Piper didn't think she'd ever seen anything more beautiful.

Another push and the baby was in Nurse Robbins's hands. She laughed. "Your Alvin is going to be a happy daddy. You have a boy."

With efficient movements, Nurse Robbins tied off the umbilical cord, cut it, and then wiped out the baby's mouth. He screwed up his face with a cry of protest. "That's the way, young Alvin. Let your daddy know you're here."

Mrs. Whitton made a sound between a sob and a laugh as she lifted her head to see the baby. "Is he good?"

"He has all his toes and fingers and looks to be about eight pounds. I'm thinking he's very good, Mother." Nurse Robbins took the towel Piper held and wrapped the baby up. "Bath time is coming, but first you need to meet your mother face-to-face. Here, Pippay, show our mother her new son." She handed the baby to Piper. "Support his head and hold him gentle."

"He's beautiful," Piper said as she placed the baby in Mrs. Whitton's arms. The baby's tongue quivered in his wide-open mouth as he kept up his warbling cry.

The woman's face seemed to melt with love as she stroked her new son's cheek. "Hush, little baby. You're in your mama's arms now."

Nurse Robbins watched for a moment. "He is a fine boy, but time to finish what we started here. Pippay, cuddle our little man and keep him warm while we do what needs doing."

Piper picked up the baby and held him close. When she swayed a little to rock him, he blinked and stopped crying for a few seconds as if trying to figure out what was happening.

When Nurse Robbins had taken care of Mrs. Whitton, she looked at Piper. "Look, Mrs. Whitton. I think Pippay is in love."

Piper grinned. "Who wouldn't be with such a sweet little guy?"

Mrs. Whitton scooted up in the bed. "Does it make you want to be a midwife, Piper?"

"Not a midwife. A mother."

"That's a dream you can make come true," Mrs. Whitton said. "Babies are easy to make."

"If you have the right man to help you with the job," Nurse Robbins said. "Pippay, do you have a fellow back in the city ready to make babies with you?"

"Maybe. But I'm not sure I'm ready to make babies with him."

"Ain't no room for doubting there," Mrs. Whitton said.

"That's for sure," Nurse Robbins said, "but enough romance advice for our Pippay. Time to get baby and mother cleaned up."

Piper placed the baby on the bed beside Mrs. Whitton and went to get a pan of water for Nurse Robbins. But Mrs. Whitton's words echoed in her mind. *No room for doubting.*

CHAPTER
EIGHTEEN

Dear Jamie,

How are you? I guess you're surprised to get this letter since it's been a while since we've seen each other, but I hope we can continue to be friends although we both have stepped out on new paths with new people this year.

Jamie stared at those words. *New paths. New people.* Whatever did she mean by that? Had to be Crandall, but there was that word "both."

His heart had been pounding in his ears ever since his mother handed him the envelope. He knew Piper's writing at once.

His mother recognized her writing too. After all, they had exchanged letters for years, up until he had quit writing after his father died. It hadn't seemed right to hang on to hope with Piper when he had nothing to offer. But now somehow hope had been reborn in him that he did have something to offer Piper. Love. He might be a foolish romantic, but he wanted to believe love trumped money.

Simon's words echoed in his head. *Not when you don't have a roof over your head or food on the table.*

He had a job, a position he'd taken solely to convince Piper's father that he could buy food and take care of Piper, but her father wasn't impressed. He had picked another man to provide for Piper.

Crandall could do that. In style. But did Piper love Crandall? Did Piper love him—Jamie? Those were the questions. New paths didn't sound like the answer he wanted.

After his mother gave him the letter, he had casually stuffed it in his pocket as though in no hurry to read it.

His mother knew better, but she merely said, "I hope Piper is well."

He forced himself to walk up the steps and not take them two at a time with the letter burning in his pocket. In his room, he tore open the envelope. Anxious to read what she wrote. Afraid to read what she wrote. And now in the very first lines were those words about new people, new paths.

He shut his eyes and wondered if it would be wrong to pray that the next lines didn't say she was marrying Crandall. *Please, Lord, not that.*

He'd been going to church with Uncle Wyatt. Not that he hadn't always gone to church. He had. Practically every Sunday of his life. Out of habit. Duty perhaps. Appearances for sure. But that wasn't why Uncle Wyatt went. He believed. Truly believed. Said he didn't know how a doctor who continually saw life and death could not believe.

That was where Jamie had found new hope. From being with Uncle Wyatt. There was such peace in this house. The kind he'd never known in his parents' house, with the continual struggle to gather more money and rise in society.

He opened his eyes to read more. If Piper had written to say she was marrying Crandall, it wouldn't change the words for him to cowardly fold the letter and put it in his pocket.

I've certainly found some new paths to walk here in Leslie County with the Frontier Nursing Service. I love it. You probably think that's funny. I have to work. I mean really work. Cleaning out stalls. Currying horses. Delivering medicines and messages. Sometimes walking miles to the hospital when Miss Aileen, that's our supervisor, decides I should walk instead of ride. On top of all that, I've been planting gardens and learning what's a weed and what's a bean plant. I know you're laughing at that, since I always insisted daisies should not be called weeds.

Jamie smiled as he remembered picking Piper daisies and claiming they were weeds. His heartbeat had slowed. This wasn't a Dear John letter. Not that she would have to write him that kind of letter. They weren't engaged. No promises between them. But oh, how he wished there were. That was his fault. Totally his fault.

I thought of you the other day when I went across a swinging bridge. You should have seen me when I first stepped out on it. A person should expect a swinging bridge to swing, but I was hanging on for dear life. Then I thought of you and how you would probably run across the bridge. Maybe jump on it to make me shriek. Do you remember all the fun we used to have?

Did he ever. At least she remembered too.

But I had the best adventure yet yesterday. I went with one of the nurse midwives to deliver a baby. Well, I didn't deliver the baby, but I watched. Didn't faint, either. Wow! That's all I can say. I don't have words for how great that was—to see a new baby come into the world. He was so precious.

*I've probably written too much. Bored you silly. I wish
you happiness on your new paths and hope we can still be
friends.*

Your pal,
Piper

*P.S. You'll laugh at this. Down here they call me Danny.
Except for the midwife I was with yesterday. She calls me
Pippay. They say everybody has to have a nickname. I'm
afraid to tell Truda. She claims Piper is a fine name.*

Pal? Nothing remotely romantic about that. Had they always
only been friends? But there were those few kisses stolen now and
again at dances or in the meadows when they gave their horses a rest.
Thinking about that started his heart pounding like crazy again.

He read the letter over again, wishing it ended with *Love, Piper*
instead of *Your pal, Piper.* At least his prayer had been answered.
She hadn't said she was marrying Braxton Crandall. Not yet anyway. Her new path was this adventure in the mountains. But why
had she said he was on a new path?

Perhaps her father had told her about his teaching job, but he
couldn't imagine that being true. Mr. Danson wanted Jamie to
disappear from Piper's life completely. To go teach school in Cali-
fornia or on the moon. How about in the Appalachian Mountains?
Maybe they had summer school down there. He could always
volunteer for something. Like Piper had.

He'd found out about those frontier nurses Della said Piper had
talked about from Cal Rogers, the local newspaper's editor who
knew about the Frontier Nursing Service that Mary Breckinridge
had started in Hyden, Kentucky. He said his wife had donated baby
clothes for the midwives to give new mothers there.

Jamie liked Cal. The man tried to act the part of an irascible newspaper man expecting nothing but bad news, but the editor was happiest when some local kid did something good he could put in the paper.

"Sells papers," Cal claimed, but it was more than selling papers for him. He wanted to make his town look good.

Cal had taken Jamie under his wing after he showed up with an article about how people at Centre College still celebrated their upset football victory over Harvard that had happened almost fifteen years before.

After motioning Jamie toward a chair in his cluttered office, Cal read through Jamie's article. When he finished, he threw the piece down on a pile of papers and leaned back in his chair to study Jamie. "Writers are durn fools. You realize that, don't you?"

Jamie didn't know whether to nod or admit that no, he didn't know that. He decided to be honest. "I guess not."

"That's because kids like you are ignorant to how things really are. You come out of college thinking the world is going to welcome you with open arms, and instead it clips you behind the knees and then kicks you when you fall."

"Nothing much has been easy for my family for a while."

"So your pop was one of them that lost everything in the crash. What's he doing now? Licking his wounds or drowning his sorrows in booze?"

"He died." Jamie stood up and held out his hand for his story. "I appreciate you reading my article. If you'll hand it back, I'll quit wasting your time."

Cal leaned forward and planted an elbow on Jamie's story. "Don't be in such an all-fired rush. If you want to be a writer, you've got to toughen up. So sit down. We're not through here yet."

Jamie sat back down. The man wanted tough. He could be tough.

The editor picked up his story again. "This isn't half bad.

Trouble is, this story's done been told about five hundred times in this very paper."

Jamie didn't say anything. What was there to say? He was simply going to have to wait until the man was ready to hand him back his story.

Cal peered at the page again. "You got a little fancy with the adverbs. You need to let verbs do the work." He looked back at Jamie. "But tell you what. We're coming up on the fifteenth anniversary of that crazy win, so if you're willing to let this be on file until October, maybe I'll print it then. Can't pay you much, but I could use another pair of feet to cover what's happening. Nothing full-time, you understand. But a story now and again. Get you a few bucks."

"Something I come up with or something you assign?" Jamie asked.

"Could be both. To start off and see how things go, the little woman has this garden club. She expects me to go poetic on it every time they meet. Flowers make me sneeze. But if you go to that meeting and write up something interesting enough that maybe five people besides the garden club members are willing to read it, then we'll be in business."

"Do I get a byline?" Jamie asked.

The editor shrugged. "Sure. Why not?"

"Then I like flowers."

"Good. You're my man." Without standing up, Cal had stretched his hand across the desk for Jamie to shake.

The arrangement had worked out. Jamie didn't make much money. Not enough to keep food on the table for a family, for sure. That was why he took the teacher job. The job he wanted to resign before school started.

But the few dollars here and there for the stories Cal published bolstered Jamie's hope that someday, with enough fortitude, he might make money with his words. Not just by writing news articles, but fiction too. Somebody was going to write the next great American novel. He could dream that might be him.

Maybe that novel should be set in the Appalachian Mountains. A writer needed to do research. Plus, Cal was interested in a Frontier Nursing Service story.

"That would be a great human-interest piece. Nurses on horses. Babies born in cabins. You write it, I'll run it," Cal had said. "Who knows? A story like that might get some syndicates interested. Think about it, kid. I nickel and dime you for your stories, but those syndicates, that's where the money is."

Syndicates buying something he wrote had sounded good. Better than good. Now Jamie stared at the address on the back of the envelope he held. Wendover, Kentucky. Maybe it was time he wrote that story.

When he stuck the letter in a desk drawer, his eye caught on a picture of Piper and him. He picked it up. Jamie had his arm around Piper and they were both laughing. Seemed like then, they were always laughing.

A finger of sadness poked him as he put the picture back in the drawer and slid it shut. How long had it been since they had laughed together like that? Too long. Much too long.

Last week's paper lay on the desk folded open to his yawn of an article about the safest way to can vegetables. Useful, but boring. Still, the "by Jamie Russell" was good to see.

He picked up his composition book, turned to a blank page, and wrote *Frontier Nursing Service—Wendover, Kentucky*. He stared at the words a long time. He'd have to come up with money for a train ticket. Going would be a leap of faith. In his ability to gather a story. To take the right pictures. To convince Mary Breckinridge to give him an interview.

Get Piper to laugh with him again. *Your pal*. He wanted to be more than pals. Much more than pals.

CHAPTER
NINETEEN

"'Bout the only way a body is ever gonna get ahead of the chick-weed is to die and go to heaven, where I'm nigh on certain the Lord won't let in any chickweed seeds."

Delora Miller knelt down beside the bean row in the garden at Wendover. Piper squatted down across from her to help pick the early beans, but Mrs. Miller said they might as well get rid of any weeds while they were at it.

"You ever pick beans before, Danny?"

"Can't say that I have." That seemed a bad thing to admit here in the mountains where everybody had gardens, or sass patches as they called them.

"That's city life for you." The woman took off her straw hat and fanned herself.

Her gray hair was tucked into a bun on the back of her head, and she wore a green-checked apron over a cotton dress so faded the flowery print had lost its color. But it looked cool.

Piper was ready to chop off her jeans at the knees, but Miss Aileen wouldn't go for that. The couriers had to dress right. Jeans for dirty work in the barn and gardens or chicken yard. Riding trousers, boots, and white shirts when they went to Hyden or out into the districts.

Piper stood up and stretched her back before she bent over to rustle through the bean leaves for more pods. "Have you always grown your own food, Mrs. Miller?"

"We'd have gone hungry if we didn't. That's for sure. Most folks around here depend on sass patches. That's why things can get lean when the rains don't come." Mrs. Miller put her hat back on and watched Piper pick a handful of beans. "Careful with the vines there. This is the first picking, but it won't be the last."

"Yes, ma'am." Mrs. Miller had shown her how to hold the vine and pull off the bean pod. The leaves made her arms itch, but that wasn't worth complaining about. No need in fussing about the heat either.

"I hoped starting early we'd get done before the sun started cooking us. It's a hot one for June." Mrs. Miller pulled a handkerchief out of her apron pocket and wiped the sweat off her forehead. "But the weather is whatever the good Lord sends our way." She looked up at the sky. "And I'm thinking he might be sending us a storm later, with how the air is feeling. That will get the nurses busy. Babies like coming on in a storm."

"Why is that?" Piper asked.

"It don't really matter why. It's good just to know what is. Full moons bring them on too, but with that said, the Lord's truth is that babies are born every day of the year with or without storms or full moons." She bent down to start picking again.

"Do you have children?"

"Lawsy, yes. Eight of them. Don't think a one of them came in a storm, but seems like little Robert showed up on a moonlit night."

"Did the nurses deliver your babies?"

"They all was born way before Mrs. Breckinridge came to these parts. Now, some of my grandbabies have found their way into the world with the help of her nurses. A granny midwife was my help.

That's all we had back in the day. Granny Em caught my babies, every one without a lick of trouble."

She dropped some beans in her basket before she went on. "But it's better with the nurses. Whilst I was healthy and so were my babies, that's not so for everybody up here in the hills. The nurses' way of watching over mothers is a good thing. Hardly ever hear of them losing a baby unless'n it's something that couldn't be helped. The Lord's will."

Piper wasn't supposed to talk religion, politics, or moonshine with the local people. Mrs. Breckinridge's orders. But ever since she talked to Maxine Crutcher on the train, questions about what Piper truly believed poked her now and again.

She'd gone to chapel at the Big House on Sundays, but a person could quietly listen to Scripture and bend one's head in prayer without letting anything change inside. She did say her prayers every night when she wasn't too tired, but had she ever considered the Lord's will in her life? Was it his will that she be here in the mountains beside this woman who knew what to weed out and what to let grow? Would it be too wrong to ask her how she knew what was the Lord's will and what wasn't?

"You look to be puzzling something out, Danny," Mrs. Miller said. "Are you wishing you was back in your city with somebody else picking the beans for your plate?"

"Oh no. I'm glad to be here. Picking beans or whatever."

Mrs. Miller eyed Piper a minute. "But I'm thinking you have something worrying you. Questions don't bother me. Just so you know."

Piper kept her gaze on the beans. "When you mentioned the Lord's will a while ago, that made me wonder how to know what is the Lord's will and what isn't. I know Mrs. Breckinridge doesn't want us talking religion, but—"

Mrs. Miller waved her hand. "Don't let that worry you, girl. You maybe shouldn't be talking with everybody about such things, but you can me. Not that I'm a preacher what can explain it all. But I do believe in the good Lord and that his will ought to be done."

"But how do you know if you're doing what the Lord intends?"

"There's a verse somewhere in Proverbs that tells us to trust in the Lord and not lean on our own understanding." Mrs. Miller reached across the beans to touch Piper's cheek. Her hand was work roughened, but her words were gentle. "That does take some trusting. Sort of like stepping out on a swinging bridge. You done that yet?"

"I have."

"Well, maybe when you first looked at it, you wondered about it holding you up on account of how it was trembling there in the wind. But then you stepped out on it and found it did hold you up. That can be how faith in the Lord is. You might feel a little trembly when you take that first step of trusting your ways to him, but once you do, you can always depend on that firm foundation of the Lord's love. Way firmer than that swinging bridge to be sure." Mrs. Miller smiled. "Fact is, it's not impossible to fall through one of those bridges, so see that you step lightly and hold tightly."

"Thank you, Mrs. Miller. Something about being here has me wondering about things I've never thought about before."

"It's the stars."

"The stars?"

"You look up at the heavens here in the mountains, and the stars spill out across the sky. Somehow that makes you ponder things that go deeper than whether we get to eat these beans come dinnertime." She picked up her basket and moved it a little farther down the row. "But one thing for sure, we won't be eating them if we don't get them picked."

They were almost to the end of the row when Miss Aileen walked over from the Garden House.

Mrs. Miller looked up at the sun. "It's a mite early for lunchtime. She must have something for you to do. She keeps you girls hopping."

"We're here to help," Piper said.

"I do appreciate your help this day. I fancy talking to you girls and getting to know what you're about."

"Sometimes I'm not sure what I'm about," Piper said.

That made Mrs. Miller laugh. She had a good laugh, the kind that made Piper ready to join in. "You'll figure it out, Danny girl. Just remember that first step on the bridge of faith."

Miss Aileen was close enough to hear her last words. "You haven't been preaching to Danny, have you, Delora?"

"Now, Aileen, a granny like me can't keep from talking a little faith now and again." Mrs. Miller swept her arm around to take in the garden and the flowers blooming on the hillside. "Takes a powerful lot of faith to grow what we grow here on this hillside."

"You do have a green thumb," Miss Aileen said. "I hear Mrs. Breckinridge is bringing home a rosebush from Illinois."

"Is that so?" Mrs. Miller said. "Then I'll think on where it might have the best chance of blooming and get a hole dug."

Miss Aileen looked around. "I wouldn't mind digging my fingers down in some dirt myself."

"Then why don't you?" Mrs. Miller said.

"Too much to do back in the office." Miss Aileen sighed. "Papers to fill out. Letters to write. Books to balance."

"Sounds like a right smart chore. This one here did good at bean picking, but she'd probably be a fine hand at letter writing too. Right, Danny?" Mrs. Miller smiled over at Piper.

"I can write letters." Piper thought of the letter she'd finally written to Braxton. A "how are you? I'm fine" boring missive. Then there was that letter to Jamie she probably shouldn't have mailed. But mailed it she had. One pal to another.

"Another time maybe, but right now, I've got something else for you to do," Miss Aileen said. "Dr. Jack called from the hospital.

Seems there's a patient they want you to take home. Can't for the life of me figure out why he asked for you, but he did. And what Dr. Jack asks, we try to do."

"That's great. It must mean Billy is getting to go home."

"Billy?" Miss Aileen raised her eyebrows in question.

"This little boy over at the hospital. He got in his head it would be neat to show up back at his house on a frontier nurse horse." When Miss Aileen frowned, Piper rushed on. "I told him I probably wouldn't be around when he was ready to go home. So he wouldn't count on it."

Every time Piper was at the hospital, she took Billy a treat. Some candy or a book. Maybe that had encouraged him to continue to hope she'd be there to take him home.

"Well, perhaps you should have been clearer."

"He's just six," Piper said.

"Looks like Danny's got a feller." Mrs. Miller smiled. "No need to be cranky about it, Aileen. Think how happy the little feller is going to be, and Dr. Jack too."

"Foolishness, but I guess you're right, Delora." Miss Aileen looked at Piper. "You'll have to change and grab a bite to eat in the kitchen."

As they started away from the garden, Mrs. Miller called after them. "You take care, Danny, if that storm comes up."

Miss Aileen looked up. "There's not a cloud in the sky, Delora."

"That may be, but my knees are aching. I'm thinking a storm could be coming." Mrs. Miller headed toward the Big House with the beans. She called back over her shoulder. "My rheumatism never lies, so you be careful, girl."

Miss Aileen watched the other woman walk away. "I hate to admit it, but Delora is generally right about the weather. So pick a gentle horse to go on. Don't want you getting thrown with a little boy riding with you."

"Which horse, then?" Piper asked.

"How do I know?" Miss Aileen sounded exasperated. "You couriers handle the horses. You should know, or ask Kermit if he's out at the barn. He knows them all. Of course there's Puddin, but I guess he's still nursing that leg."

"Yes." Piper was relieved she wouldn't have to creep up into the hills on Puddin. She'd never get Billy home, wherever home was.

"I don't know what Dr. Jack is thinking, asking this." Miss Aileen made a face. "But I don't suppose it will hurt anything. Since you're going up that way, you can take some supplies to Wilder Ridge Center. Just spend the night there but come on back tomorrow. Mrs. Breckinridge is bringing a visitor and she wants you to show whoever it is around." Miss Aileen gave Piper another look. "You must be the popular girl right now."

"I guess," Piper said. "Where do I get the supplies for Wilder Ridge?"

"Nurse Thompson will have them ready." Miss Aileen made a shooing motion with her hands. "Now, go. Don't keep Dr. Jack waiting."

CHAPTER TWENTY

At the barn, Kermit told Piper to take Bella. "She's a steady ride with a sure step. Bella won't run off with you, even if she hears a rattler."

"I might want her to run off if she hears a rattler." Piper shivered.

"Aww, snakes can't get you up on a horse." Kermit laughed. "You just have to make sure you don't fall off."

He was a big man with a head of bushy brown hair that he kept corralled under a hat. He could jerk down a horse that was cutting up and convince it to change its ways.

"In that case, I'll try to keep my seat." Piper put the saddle on Bella and tightened the cinch. "Do you think it's going to storm? Mrs. Miller said it might later today."

"Did she now?" Kermit went to the end of the barn and peered out. "Don't see no clouds gathering, but if Delora says it's gonna rain, then I wouldn't say it won't. But I don't think you'll have to worry about any tides."

Piper knew that meant a flood. "Do you get floods, er, tides often up here?"

"It can happen quick in a gullywasher. The hills funnel the water down into the creeks. If'n you haven't seen that happen, it's hard to wrap your mind around how fast the creeks can rise." He came back to smooth his hand across Bella's rump. "You'll be fine with Bella. She's steady as Puddin but a sight quicker at picking up her feet and getting somewhere."

"I'm glad to hear that." Piper led Bella out of the barn, where she mounted her. She waved at Kermit and headed out.

By the time Piper got to the hospital, a few clouds were building in the west, but the sun was still bright. Nothing to worry about. She would trust Kermit on that.

When Billy saw Piper, his face lit up like he'd just won the biggest prize of the year. Dr. Jack was smiling almost as much and so was Nurse Thompson when she stepped over from one of the other beds.

"Here she is, Billy," Dr. Jack said. "So, are you ready to go home?"

The little boy was dressed in pants with the cuffs rolled up and a new-looking shirt. His shoes didn't have a scuff on them.

"Wow. You're looking spiffy, Billy," Piper said.

"I got new stuff. Nurse said I'd been here so long I'd probably outgrown my old clothes. I've got the car you give me in one of my pockets." He stuck his hand in his pants pocket and pulled out a red metal car.

Dr. Jack laughed. "He's run that thing five hundred miles here on this bed." The doctor looked at Billy. "Now, you'll have to share that with your brother and sister when you get home. Along with this sucking candy I got for you." He pulled a bag out of his pocket. "Can you remember to share?"

"Yes, sir." Billy grinned as he reached for the candy.

"The nurse will check on you in a few days. You remember to wash your leg after you're outside playing or if you are in the creek."

Billy frowned. "Can't I just wash it in the creek?"

"No. Put some warm water in a wash pan and use plenty of soap. Understand?" Dr. Jack said.

"Do I have to use soap forever?"

"Soap is a good thing to be on speaking terms with," Nurse Thompson said. "Always."

"Yes, ma'am." Billy hung his head.

Nurse Thompson laughed and tousled his hair. "None of that. Time to be happy. You're going home."

"Indeed." Dr. Jack smiled up at Piper. "Danny has a horse and she's ready to ride. Right, Danny?"

"The horse is waiting."

Nurse Thompson held out her hand to Billy. "Come on, Billy. Let's go tell everybody goodbye while Dr. Jack talks with Danny."

Piper looked at Dr. Jack. "Do you have directions or a map?"

"Nurse Thompson will get you directions. It's not far from Wilder Ridge Center."

"I have been there."

"Then you'll be fine. You'll need to tell the nurses up there that Billy is home so they'll know to look in on him."

"But he is okay? That looked like a bad burn."

"It was, but Billy's a tough kid. We thought for a while we might have to send him out to Cincinnati for treatment, but I'm glad we didn't. He was homesick enough here." Dr. Jack smiled then. "You helped with that."

"I like coming here." Piper waved at a toddler named Opal standing in her crib, babbling at her. Piper had rocked her to sleep one day.

"You have a caring touch. Are you interested in nursing?" Dr. Jack asked.

"Me? A nurse?" Piper shook her head. "No, I don't think so. I couldn't do what they have to do."

"It takes training. And fortitude. Especially up here in the mountains." The doctor seemed uneasy as he fingered the stethoscope hanging around his neck. Why, Piper couldn't imagine.

Piper turned toward the door. "I better go find Billy so we can get started."

"He'll come back in here to get his poke when he's ready."

"Poke?"

"Bundle of things. Country talk." The doctor motioned toward a cloth bag on the bed, then hesitated before he said, "I've been thinking about you. And your aunt."

"Truda?"

He looked everywhere but at Piper. "Meeting you has stirred up my curiosity. Made me wonder about her after all these years."

"How many years?" Now Piper was curious.

"Oh gee." He massaged his forehead with his fingers as though to help him think. "I was just out of medical school and about to start my residency. That was over twenty years ago."

"She must have made quite an impression on you."

He looked straight at Piper. "She did. I do hope she's had a happy life."

"I think she has. She never married but is a bookkeeper in the bank my grandfather founded. She has a gift for numbers."

"She appeared to have many gifts when I met her." Again he hesitated before he asked, "Why didn't she ever marry? I'm sure she had opportunities."

"She claims the right man never came along for her and she wasn't willing to compromise."

"Admirable."

"My father would say lonely."

"That could be," Dr. Jack said. "But a person can be lonely at a table surrounded by others, if not the right people."

"How long did you know her?"

"Not nearly long enough." The doctor pulled in a breath and let it out. "No indeed, not nearly long enough. But time for me to get back to my patients. Thank you again for taking Billy home. The little guy has talked and talked about it. Said you promised to take him if you were here when he got to go home. So I decided to make sure you were here."

"And here I am."

"It's good to make other people happy when we can. Billy's got a good family, but they struggle to get by. I hear their mule died. That's a hard blow and probably why they haven't been down to get him."

Before Dr. Jack went out of the room, he looked back at Piper. "Tell your aunt hello for me if you happen to write her."

"Oh, I will."

The door shut behind him.

"You can count on that," Piper said under her breath.

CHAPTER
TWENTY-ONE

A local woman who worked at the hospital gave Piper directions.

"It's a good ways up there." The slim little woman shoved her gray hair away from her face and studied Piper's map. A frown deepened the wrinkles around her eyes. "You could go to Wilder Ridge and then on up, but you and the little one would be better off sliding to the east away from Middle Fork to follow Greasy Creek a mile or two and then go up Lower Bad Creek." The woman pointed at a spot on the map.

Piper must have looked lost, because the woman smiled. "It ain't so hard. Once you get to Lower Bad Creek, Billy is likely to know where he is. He probably ran all over that hillside afore he got hurt."

"Thank you." Piper folded the map and stuffed it in her pocket.

The woman patted her arm. "If'n you get a little addled on your directions, you can ask anybody you meet. Folks will be glad to point the way. But be careful about that quicksand in the river coming back from Wilder Ridge. That can give a horse some trouble."

"Quicksand?" Suze hadn't told Piper anything about quicksand.

"I reckon it's not like you've maybe read about in jungle stories where it swallows people up, but it can bog down a horse."

"How will I know where it is in the river?"

"Just trust your horse. They generally step ginger-like if they feel the river bottom sucking at them."

Rattlesnakes. Quicksand in the river crossings. Piper shook away her worries. Bella was a good horse. Things would be fine. Even if the clouds in the west were darker when they went outside.

"I'm a little hungry," Billy said as he watched her tie on his poke. "You think it would be okay if I ate a piece of Dr. Jack's candy?"

"It's your candy now to eat if you want."

"But Dr. Jack told me to share."

"Maybe you can sample one piece." Piper untied his sack of stuff and pulled out the candy.

"I could put it in my pocket." Billy clutched the bag of candy.

"You might lose it on the trail. I better put it in your poke." Piper held out her hand and the little boy reluctantly handed it over.

"You could have a piece if'n you wanted to."

"That's okay. I'm not hungry right now." Piper smiled and adjusted the packs again. "Now go stand on that rock. After I get on Bella, I'll help you aboard."

Billy giggled when she pulled him up in front of her on the saddle. "I ain't never been on a horse before. Just Pa's mule when he's plowing. Pa says I make Spec pay attention to what he's supposed to be doing, but my brother says Pa's just getting me out of the house so Ma don't have to keep an eye on me."

"Do you need an eye kept on you?" Piper headed the mare down the hill toward the river.

Billy sighed. "Most all the time. Pa says I could hurt myself sitting in the middle of a featherbed. That I'm an accident waiting to happen. Guess I proved that spilling lye on me."

"That had to hurt."

"Dr. Jack said Ma did the right thing to douse me in the rain barrel, but mighta ruined the water. Sometimes I ain't nothing but trouble."

"Accidents happen." Piper kept her arms loose around him as she held the reins. "So you've got a brother. Any sisters?"

"One brother older than me and a sister younger than me. Ma was thinking on a new baby. Don't know if the nurses have brought her one yet."

"Oh." Suze had told Piper how the mountain children thought the nurses brought babies in their saddlebags. "So you think a nurse might have visited your house with a baby while you were at the hospital?"

"Could be. Seems like they bring babies pretty regular. Ma says they catch babies, but that sounds kinda funny. Babies can't do no running, so I can't see why they'd have to chase them down to catch them."

Piper didn't laugh. "I'm like you. I've never seen babies running."

Billy thought a minute. "You think maybe they fall out of the sky? Ma says the Lord sends her babies, so I reckon maybe God might pitch them down to the nurses. Careful like."

Piper did have to smile then. "That's an idea. Your mother and father will tell you more about that when you get older. Now rest back against me. We've got a ways to go."

"I don't want to nod off. I ain't wanting to miss nothing." The little boy did lean back against Piper. "The clouds are getting kinda dark. We're liable to get wet."

"Maybe they'll blow over." But Billy was right. Dark clouds had spread ominously across the sky to cover the sun as the wind picked up. "Maybe we'll get there before the rain hits."

"Ain't no problem for me. I've been wet before."

Piper should have listened to Mrs. Miller's warning that morning and brought her rain slicker. But no going back for it now. They would just have to weather the storm. A rumble of thunder sounded in the distance, and Piper tried to think how long it would take to get Billy home. Too long, from the looks of the clouds.

Lightning stabbed the sky to the west. They should find shelter, but she didn't see anything but trees. Nothing to do but keep going.

The trees above the trail began shaking their heads as if letting her know her thinking was faulty, but what else could she do? They had gone too far to head back to the hospital. They were already to Greasy Creek, and Bella didn't seem bothered by the thunder or the wind. She just kept walking.

As they left Greasy Creek behind and started up Lower Bad Creek, Piper asked, "Do you recognize where we are, Billy? Are we on the right trail?"

He peered around. "Hard to tell with the wind blowing things around. Besides, I ain't been here for a while. I been in the hospital since forever."

Piper took that to mean the boy had no idea. They started climbing uphill. The branches swayed overhead as leaves shook loose and spun around them. Twilight was hours away, but the day went gray as though night was falling.

Lightning lit up the woods around them, and a second later a thunder boom seemed to shake the creek bed. Piper jumped and Bella danced to the side.

Billy twisted around in front of Piper to bury his face against her chest. "I don't like thunder, Danny."

"Me either." Piper kept a strong hold on the reins. She didn't like thunder, but lightning was what was really scary. Especially under these trees. As though somebody had opened the floodgates, rain dashed down on them in sheets. Could this be one of Kermit's gullywashers?

Lightning flashed again, with an immediate cracking noise followed by another thunder boom. The lightning must have hit a tree.

"We need to find cover, Billy." Piper leaned down to talk into Billy's ear. "I think I see a house up the way there. Maybe a barn."

Billy raised his head and peered the way she pointed. "That looks like Old Mann Taylor's place. Pa told me never to go 'round about there. Old Mann Taylor don't like nobody bothering him."

"I don't think he will mind us taking shelter in his barn until the storm passes." Piper turned Bella out of the creek toward the house she could barely see through the rain. She shook her wet hair out of her face and bent her head to keep the water from hitting her eyes.

Billy clutched her tighter. This ride home wasn't turning out the way he had hoped. With his face against her, she could barely hear him when he said, "He might shoot us."

"He won't shoot us." She tried to sound very sure, but a tremble ran through her hands and arms that had nothing to do with the cold rain.

She rode straight to the barn. If the man was in the house, he might not even know they were there. Besides, Billy could be wrong about whose house this was, or his father could have simply been trying to keep Billy from worrying the neighbors. Then again, Old Mann Taylor might be a moonshiner who didn't want anyone around his place. That could include a frontier nurse courier who was supposed to be safe up in the mountains, as long as said courier had the FNS patch on her sleeve. Piper resisted the urge to feel for the letters.

Piper rode Bella straight under the roof of an open shed on the side of the barn. The lightning flashed again outside and thunder cracked. Piper was very glad to be in the barn.

"It's all right, Billy. As soon as the storm lets up, we'll head on to your house. If you're right and this is Mr. Taylor's house, then you should know how much farther to your house."

"I don't know." He sounded as though he might be crying.

Piper put her hand under his chin and lifted his face up. "I'm sorry this ride isn't going the way you imagined, but we're having an adventure."

The poor kid looked terrified.

She smoothed his wet hair back away from his face. "Thunder and lightning can be scary."

"So can Old Mann Taylor," he mumbled. "He shot Pa's dog. Dog still can't run right. Ain't no use for hunting no more."

"Oh." Piper was ready to say they could move on, look for a different barn, but lightning cracked again, hitting something so close that debris hit the barn roof.

Piper patted Bella's neck, but the mare was standing like a rock, not bothered by the fury of the storm. So Piper tucked the reins under her leg, tightened her arms around Billy, and bent her head closer to him. "Someday you'll tell this story to your children and laugh about being stuck with a city girl in a barn on the side of the mountain during a storm."

She reached behind her for his sack of belongings. "Maybe another piece of Dr. Jack's candy will make you feel better." She dug out the candy sack and handed it to him.

He looked almost ready to smile, but the scared look came back as he pointed out the end of the barn. A man was striding toward them. Lightning flashed, but the man kept his steady pace as though he hardly noticed the thunder or the rain beating down on his hat. A rifle was looped over his arm.

Piper pulled in a breath. A lot of the mountain men carried guns, but that didn't mean they were ready to use them. At least she hoped not, as she tightened her arms around Billy. It could be they had exchanged one storm for another.

CHAPTER
TWENTY-TWO

Piper resisted the urge to spur Bella out of the barn past the man. She pulled in a shaky breath and kept her arms around Billy. The little boy was stiff against her as he clutched his sack of candy.

She forced her arms to relax. "It's okay, Billy. He just wants to see who we are."

"And shoot us."

"No, he won't do that." At least she was almost certain he wouldn't.

The man stepped into the barn and stared at them without saying anything, while rainwater dripped off his hat.

"Hello, sir," Piper said. "I hope you don't mind us taking shelter in your barn."

The man stared at her so long she started to repeat what she'd said, thinking he must not have heard her over the rain beating down on the roof.

"I heared you." He held up his free hand, the one not holding the gun, to stop her. "Did the storm skeer you?" He didn't wait for her to answer. "Or is that terrified look on your face on account of me?"

"The lightning made us a little nervous." Piper managed a smile. Billy was still twisted around with his face hidden against her. She was about to say they'd leave, when lightning cracked and thunder shook the barn. This time Bella danced a little to the side.

"You better gather up those reins or your horse is liable to make a run for it. Horses can act like they ain't got good sense if'n they get jumpy."

She did as he said. Not because she thought Bella was going to bolt, but so that they could if need be. "Yes, sir."

"Sir, is it?" The man stepped closer. He shifted the gun in his arm as though it was part of him. "The name is Taylor. Mann Taylor. I 'spect you know yours."

Piper wasn't sure if that meant he wanted to know hers or not, but it seemed rude not to tell him. "Danny Danson."

"Danny. Funny name for a girl." He stared up at her. "You must be one of them gals with that Breckinridge woman."

"I'm working with the frontier nurses." She shifted her shoulders slightly to make sure he could see the Frontier Nursing Service initials on her sleeve.

"You kin quit looking so skeered. I ain't about to shoot you." He pointed the gun down. "As long as that boy there don't pull no gun out on me." The man almost smiled. He stepped closer and poked Billy's leg. "Are you that ornery West kid what's been laying up down there in Hyden whilst your brother and pa been doing all the work?"

Billy was still trembling a little, but the words must have rankled. He raised his head and turned to stare at the man. "I wanted to come home, but them nurses said I couldn't go walking up the hill with how my leg was. And Pa didn't come get me."

"Reckon he couldn't, boy. Not after his old mule died."

That made Billy forget being afraid. "Spec died?"

"'Fraid so."

Billy sat up straight. "Did you shoot him?"

"Billy." Piper put her hand on his shoulder.

"Now why would you accuse me of that?" The lines on the man's face deepened as he stared at Billy. "I wouldn't kill a man's mule. The man maybe, but not his mule."

"Billy, tell Mr. Taylor you're sorry."

Billy lifted up his chin defiantly. "I ain't gonna. He shot Pa's dog."

"That's enough, Billy." She tried to sound stern.

"Aww, let him talk, girl. Fact is, I did happen to shoot the dog. It was down here messing with my hens. I admit to aiming over the critter's head, but it run up the hill faster than I thought it might. Ran right into my bullet, but, boy, you can be sure if I'd aimed to shoot your pa's dog dead, he'd been naught but a skeleton now 'stead of just crippled a bit." The man's eyes narrowed until they were mere slits.

Billy relaxed a little against Piper. "I reckon Pa says nobody can abide a chicken-killing dog."

"Your pa's a smart man. Better listen to him and not be accusing folks of things when you don't know the whole story. Especially when you're in that feller's barn."

"Sounds as though the storm is letting up." Piper tightened the reins a bit. Rain was still peppering down, but the thunder was only a rumble in the distance. "We can probably move on now. Thank you, Mr. Taylor, for letting us shelter here."

"Don't reckon I let you. Seemed like you just took the spot on your own."

"Yes, but you didn't chase us away." Piper gave him her nicest smile.

"Or shoot you. There is that." Again the corners of his lips almost turned up, but instead he screwed up his mouth and spit on the ground.

"I'm glad of that too." Billy's hand only shook a little as he held out the bag of candy. "Want a piece of sucking candy? The doctor give it to me."

"Don't mind if I do." The man dug a piece out of the bag and popped it in his mouth. He wallowed it around a minute before he went on. "Generous of you, boy. When you get on up the hill, you tell your pa if'n he needs to borrow my mule to come on down and get him."

"That's nice of you, Mr. Taylor," Piper said.

"Don't know how things are where you come from, Danny girl, but around here neighbors help neighbors." The man settled his eyes on Billy. "But you best keep your chicken-killin' dog at home."

"I'll aim to." Billy stuffed his bag of candy into his pocket instead of handing it to Piper.

She pretended not to notice. They weren't far from his house. When they went out of the barn, the rain was only a gentle shower.

The man called after her. "Stay clear of the creek, girl. That rain was mite near a gullywasher. A horse can go down in rushing water and break a leg. I had to shoot a broken-legged horse once. Not something I ever want to have to do agin."

Piper looked back with a nod, but Bella kept going, not bothered by the rain or the wet ground.

"We're almost there, Danny." Billy stretched up as tall as he could in front of Piper. "I hope Ma has some cornbread. Them down at the hospital couldn't make it like Ma. Can't nobody make it like Ma. Pa says so."

The little boy's eagerness was contagious, and Piper shared his excitement when they came out into a little clearing and saw his home. A dog barked and came to meet them with its tail flapping, one leg held up. The dog Mr. Taylor said he hadn't aimed to shoot.

As they rode toward the cabin, the sun came out and turned the raindrops clinging to the leaves and dripping off the roof into sparkling diamonds.

A little girl came out on the porch. "Ma! Billy's home," she shouted. "On a horse!"

Billy giggled. "I knew they'd think me showing up on a horse was something."

A woman rushed out the door, no baby in her arms, but from the looks of the bulge under her apron, the nurses would be catching a baby here soon. Piper helped Billy slide down off Bella and did some giggling herself as the little boy ran into his mother's arms.

The woman went down on her knees in front of the porch and pulled Billy close. "Are you good as new, my Billy boy?" She leaned back to look him in the face.

"Good as new, Ma."

"That ain't so, dear heart. You're better than new." She pulled him close in another hug. "Your ma has missed you."

Piper got off Bella and pushed her wet hair back from her face. A few tears mixed in with the leftover raindrops on her cheeks.

The woman looked over Billy's head toward Piper. "And who's this you've brung with you? Or I reckon she brung you. And through that storm. The two of you look like drowned chickens. Here, Billy boy, help your ma up."

She put her hands on Billy's shoulders and pushed to her feet. Not an easy task with the baby weight pulling on her. Her skirt had mud splotches where she'd knelt on the ground.

Piper kept hold of Bella's reins and stepped toward the woman. "I'm Piper Danson. Danny to Billy. I'm sorry to bring him home so wet, but the storm came up on us after we were on the way."

"Don't you worry none about that. A feller has to get wet now and again. Storms can come up quick and lightning can shake a body's nerves. Hope you found some shelter from that."

Billy pulled on her sleeve to get her attention. "We waited out the storm in Old Mann Taylor's barn. He didn't shoot us, but he said Spec was dead. Was he just fooling?"

"No, son. Sorry to say he wasn't. Spec started hanging his head a couple of weeks ago. Your pa did all he could, but I reckon it was just Spec's time." The woman rubbed her hand up and down Billy's back. Behind her, the little girl looked ready to cry. "I know that's a hard blow for you, seeing as how you favored the old mule. We all did. In time, your pa will get another one."

Billy's mother was obviously trying to keep Billy from being upset, but her own worry over losing the mule came through.

"Billy, tell your mother what Mr. Taylor said."

"He said Pa could borrow his mule if'n he needed one." Billy pulled the sack of candy out of his pocket. "I give him a piece of the candy Dr. Jack sent home with me. You want a piece?"

"Well, if that ain't a treat. I hope you told the doctor thank ye. I'll get me a piece later, but you can give your little sissy a piece. I'm guessing her mouth is watering by now." She gave Billy a pat on the head before he went over to the little girl.

Mrs. West moved closer to Piper. "Won't you come sit awhile on the porch, missy? Or stay to supper. I put some beans on a while ago. Not fancy but filling. I can stir up some cornbread to go with it."

"Billy will be glad to hear that. He was telling me how you make the best cornbread. Way better than what he's had at the hospital."

"Billy's always been my good eater." Mrs. West smiled.

"But while it would be nice to visit, I need to get back down the hill to the Wilder Ridge Center before dark." Piper looked at the sky that was thankfully clearing.

"Are you a new nurse there? The one that's been coming up to see me is Nurse Freeman. She's a treasure." The woman cradled her abdomen with that inward-looking smile Piper had seen on other expectant mothers.

"I'm not a nurse. I'm one of the couriers, just here for the summer to help out."

"It's right fine to meet you. You want me to send Billy after a towel for you to dry off?"

Piper ran her hands through her wet hair. "I'll dry out on the ride to the center unless it starts raining again. You think it will?"

Mrs. West looked up. "The storm looks to have moved on. But you be careful going down the hill. Wet ground can be slippery."

"Bella is a surefooted horse." Piper stroked the mare's neck. "But I appreciate your concern."

The woman looked over her shoulder toward where Billy's little sister was hugging him. "Ellie has missed him. My older boy is off with his pa all the time. Ellie is anxious about this new one coming and hoping the nurses bring us a girl." She laughed a little. "The young'uns think the nurses bring babies in their saddlebags. Don't know what they think about their mamas' big bellies."

"That is something to wonder." Piper laughed too. "Billy was telling me about the nurses catching babies. He thought maybe the Lord dropped them down out of heaven."

"That's a sweet thought with some truth to it. The Lord has blessed me with my babies." Her smile disappeared before she went on. "But what was that about Billy saying Mann Taylor didn't shoot you? Seemed contrary to what he said later about the mule."

"Billy didn't want to stop there. Said his father told him never to go around Mr. Taylor's place, but lightning was striking all around us. So when I saw the barn, I headed for it to wait out the storm. Mr. Taylor must have seen us and came out to the barn with a gun."

"I don't know that I ever seen Mann without a gun in reach." She frowned a little. "But he didn't threaten you in any way?"

"No, ma'am. We were fine."

"That's good to know. Neighbors can get crosswise with one another at times, but if Mann said that about the mule, maybe we can go back to being regular neighbors."

"Good." Piper didn't know what else to say. "Dr. Jack said a nurse will come check on Billy."

"Nurse Freeman will be up here to see me anyhow. But it's

good to have my boy home." She looked back at him again with a soft smile on her face. "I felt like a part of me was down there in Hyden, and I hated that the rest of me couldn't be down there with him. But I had the other young'uns to see to."

"The nurses took good care of him." Piper untied Billy's bag from Bella's saddle and held it out toward him.

He ran back to get it. "Will you come see me again? Now that you know how to get here."

"Maybe I'll just do that sometime if I'm over this way." Piper reached out her hand to shake his, but he pushed past it to give her a hug.

"I won't forget about our adventure."

When Billy's mother looked puzzled by that, Piper smiled. "I told him that someday he'd tell his children about riding through a storm with some city girl."

Piper waved at Billy, who watched her leave from the edge of the porch. Then she was into the trees, with raindrops showering down whenever she brushed against a branch. Once after a rainstorm, she and Jamie had chased ahead of one another to be the first to a tree with low branches along their riding path. Then they lay in wait for the other one. They both ended up as soaked as she was now.

Piper laughed, glad to be in the middle of the woods with raindrops sliding down the neck of her shirt. Birds sang again now that the storm was past. The canopy of leaves split the sunshine into rays that divided the shadows.

She felt a million miles away from Louisville. Nothing here was anything like back in the city. Not the trees surrounding her or the muddy trail Bella was following. Even the sky didn't look the same here. She stopped Bella in a cleared spot where the trees had been felled. Perhaps for a cabin.

Bella dropped her head down to snatch some grass while Piper soaked up the sun. From deep inside her, a song rose. A hymn. She softly sang the first line. "'For the beauty of the earth . . .'" She couldn't remember the next words. So instead she looked up and whispered, "Thank you, Lord, for bringing me here."

What had Suze told her a few days ago? That nobody came to the Frontier Nursing Service by accident. Not nurse midwives. And not couriers.

CHAPTER
TWENTY-THREE

When Truda got out of the taxi at the train station, she stood on the platform for a moment, reveling in the absolute freedom she suddenly felt. No numbers to write down in ledgers for at least a week. Maybe two. Erwin's disapproving frown faded from her thoughts. It didn't matter what Erwin thought. It didn't matter what anyone thought. She only had to please herself. And on the grander scale of things, the Lord.

This is the day the Lord hath made; we will rejoice and be glad in it. She'd heard that verse from the Psalms many times when sitting in a church pew on a Sunday morning and had considered the message of joy in it on other days. But never on a day quite like this. A perfect June day with a slight breeze whispering through her hair like the gentle breath of those palm-leaf fans lazily turning overhead.

But it was more than the perfect weather. Truda had experienced many beautiful days. She hadn't had to spend every sunshine day between marble walls. No, the weather had little to do with this giddy schoolgirl feeling. She was very glad she would have a long train ride to talk some sense into her own head.

She had never been foolish. Ever. Not even as a child. Everyone always said what a sensible girl she was. Then a mature young woman. And now a woman who knew how to make the best of life, to be satisfied with what she had. She was. Her life was good.

But at the same time, she didn't have to act as though that life were set in concrete. *This is the day*. Each day the sun rose to the possibility of new experiences. New joys. *Rejoice in it*.

How long had it been since she had thrown open the door of her house to walk out with so much expectation? Too long. She liked her position at the bank. Enjoyed seeing behind the numbers to the possibilities money offered. But she did know, especially now, that many things were more important than the balance in her bank account. Some of those things she had. Some she simply did not have.

It was time to shake up her life a little.

She looked around for Mary Breckinridge. Truda had contacted Wendover to schedule her visit. The person she spoke with indicated Mary Breckinridge was headed back to Wendover and might be catching the same train out of Louisville. But Truda didn't see her.

Instead, a younger woman with two children in tow was making a direct path toward Truda. The little boy, who was maybe three or four, had to rush his steps to keep up with the woman's determined progress. The older child trotted along with no problem. Oddly enough, the woman's eyes were locked on Truda as she clutched the children's hands.

Truda looked over her shoulder to see who might be behind her, but no one was there.

"Miss Danson, we've been watching for you." The woman, a bit out of breath, stopped in front of Truda. "Mrs. Breckinridge has been delayed and won't make it back to Wendover until tomorrow. But she wanted me to assure you that you are expected."

"Thank you for letting me know." Truda smiled at the two

children staring up at her. "I'm sorry you had to bring your children out so early in the day to tell me."

"My children?" The woman looked surprised. "Oh no. These aren't mine. I'm just delivering them to you."

"Me?" Now Truda was definitely surprised. "I don't understand."

"The children have been in the hospital here getting special treatment and now they are ready to go home." She smiled down at the girl and the little boy. "Aren't you, children?"

The two nodded solemnly, with their eyes wide as they watched Truda. "So you are taking them back to the mountains?"

"Mrs. Breckinridge must have been unable to contact you, but I'm not taking the children home. You are. My instructions were to hand them over to you so you could watch out for them on their return trip to the mountains. Mrs. Breckinridge was certain you would be glad to help out."

The woman must have seen Truda's complete astonishment, because she hurried on. "Forgive me. I haven't introduced myself." She pulled her hand away from the girl's and held it out to Truda. "I'm Carol Fisher, a member of the Frontier Nursing Committee here in Louisville. I did so want to attend the tea you had for Mrs. Breckinridge in May, but I was out of town. I heard from others how delightful everything was. Mrs. Breckinridge was very pleased."

"Nice to meet you." Truda took her hand. "But I don't know anything about children." Guilt stabbed her at the stricken look on the girl's face. The little boy didn't seem to know what was happening as he looked around. The woman kept his hand in her grip.

"You'll do fine," Mrs. Fisher said. "They are delightful children and will do whatever you tell them. Won't you, darlings?"

The girl nodded. The little boy kicked at some gravel on the platform.

The woman nodded toward the girl. "This is Bonnie and the

little guy is Thomas. All you have to do is take them on the train and then to the hospital at Hyden. Somebody will be there to get them."

The little girl tugged on the woman's arm and then tiptoed up to whisper in her ear.

"You're right, Bonnie." Carol Fisher looked back at Truda. "Bonnie reminded me that Thomas is to get off at the stop before you get to Hazard. Then she will go on to Hyden with you. They should have written these instructions down for us, but the nurse who dropped them off at my house was in a terrible hurry to get back to wherever. We're lucky we have Bonnie to keep us on track." When she smiled down at Bonnie, the girl gave her a shy smile in return. "Thank you, Bonnie."

"Very well." What other choice did Truda have, with the train nearly ready to leave and the girl giving her a pleading look? She reached for Bonnie's hand. "Come on, Bonnie. You too, Thomas." The little boy looked a little unsure, but he let her take his hand. "We don't want to miss our train."

"Oh, thank you so much. Mrs. Breckinridge will be pleased." After Mrs. Fisher handed Truda two tickets, she pointed toward two cloth bags behind them. "Their things. Bonnie, run get them." The child did as she was told. "The girl's a sweetheart. She can carry their things aboard while you manage your case. But you will need to keep hold of Thomas's hand. His attention has a way of wandering and sometimes his feet follow along."

And just like that, Truda was tugging the little guy onto the train, with the girl practically stepping on her heels to stay close. Truda felt a little as though she had been run over by a bus, but there was nothing for it except to carry on.

When they found seats, Truda put the little boy between her and Bonnie. He didn't make a sound as tears rolled down his cheeks.

"It's all right, Thomas." Bonnie patted his head and then looked over at Truda. "He doesn't like changing people. Scares him some."

"Changing people?"

"We had people bringing us down here, and then the nurses at the hospital, and last night, the nurse who took us to Mrs. Fisher's house, and now you." Bonnie looked straight at Truda. "I ain't scared, but Thomas, he's little."

"So what can I do?" Truda's heart hurt as she watched the boy cry.

"Might help if you was to hold him in your lap."

Truda pulled the child into her lap and held him close. He settled against her as if he'd known her forever. His little body was warm and somehow welcome against her chest. At least this way he couldn't wander off.

She couldn't imagine children being sent off to hospitals with no family member accompanying them. Then they had to give that child over to a virtual stranger for the trip home. She'd always heard the saying that the rich were different, but the poor must be every bit as different. The thought shamed her a little. Money gave the rich many choices. The lack of money gave the poor few and sometimes none.

"Are you glad to be going home, Bonnie?" Truda softly rubbed her hand up and down the little boy's back.

"Oh yes, ma'am. I can't wait to see my ma and my little sister and brother. That Mrs. Fisher, she give me new shirts and shoes to take to both of them. I know they'll be tickled."

"Will they be at the hospital to pick you up?"

"Don't rightly know. But if'n they aren't, somebody will be heading up our way to get me close enough to walk on home."

"You're very self-sufficient." When Bonnie looked puzzled, Truda explained. "That means you can take care of yourself."

"Well, I reckon so." She smoothed her skirt down over her knees. "I'm seven years old. That's plenty old enough to know something."

"So it is," Truda agreed. "But you look tired. Why don't you lean against my shoulder and take a nap. We've got a ways to go."

"If'n you're sure you don't mind." The girl's eyelids were droop-ing. "Hard to sleep there in that hospital. It was either noisy with trucks and trains. Clanks and clacks. Or as quiet as rocks on a path. No noise was the most worrisome. Especially in the middle of the night. I'm used to crickets and whippoorwills."

"That does sound better."

"You ever heard sech?" Bonnie peered up at her.

"Crickets are everywhere. Sometimes in my broom closet. I'm never happy to hear them chirp there, but my grandmother always told me it was bad luck to kill a cricket."

"Them I know don't think it's bad luck to use a cricket as bait for fishing. Except I reckon that could be bad luck for the cricket and the fish." Bonnie grinned.

"True enough." Truda smiled back at the girl. "But as for whip-poorwills, I can't hear them where I live."

"A whippoorwill is too smart to go to the city. It knows where it wants to be." Bonnie got a dreamy smile on her face. "The city has nice things. Water that don't have to be packed in the house. Comes right out of a faucet, and the outhouse is in a room indoors. Seemed funny doing my business in the house, but I got used to it. There weren't no fires to stoke. Things was some easier, but it weren't home."

"Home," Truda echoed. "That is a place we want to be. Right, Thomas?"

Bonnie leaned over to peek at him. "He's off to sleepyland."

"Might make the trip go faster if we both took a nap."

"Yes'm." The girl obediently leaned against Truda's arm and shut her eyes.

Truda closed her eyes too. She hadn't expected to have the com-pany of two children on this trip, but she had set out to see a differ-ent world. Her face relaxed in a smile. No need to play games with herself. While she did want to visit the Frontier Nursing Service, seeing the nurse midwives wasn't what made her pulse speed up when she thought about getting there. Foolish or not, that was the idea of seeing Dr. Jackson Booker.

It was foolish. Worse than foolish. Insane. She'd seen this man a total of three, maybe four hours out of her entire life. Twenty-five years ago. She had not set eyes on him since. No letters had exchanged hands. And yet she could not wait to see Jackson.

She wondered if he would recognize her. She was older, yes. Gray streaked her brown hair. But she had kept her figure, and some said she didn't look her age. Truda always wondered what they meant by that. As if forty-five was ancient. What was wrong with looking one's age anyway?

Still, she hadn't completely conquered vanity. She was happy to have aged well. Better than some of her fellow debutantes who had been touted as beautiful at their debuts. Truda's features were strong. Some said she was a handsome woman. Handsome was a compliment for those who wore trousers.

But that no longer bothered Truda. She had no argument with the face that stared back at her from a mirror and was grateful for the mind the Lord had given her so that she could make her way in life. While she had no children of her own, she was blessed to be a dear aunt to Erwin's children. But with this little boy sleeping in her lap and the girl leaning against her, she did wonder what she'd missed by never mothering a child.

Perhaps she wasn't so old that she couldn't do something during the rest of the years the Lord gave her to help children like these. Open her house to them as that Mrs. Fisher had. Open her heart to them too when they were in need.

She had the feeling this train was taking her to a new start in life that had nothing to do with the destination of Hazard.

TWENTY-FOUR

At the last stop before Hazard, Jamie stood up and walked down to the door to stretch his legs. They'd made multiple stops since Louisville, but generally the train was fast to empty out the people for the stop and pick up new passengers. This time they seemed to be delayed.

Jamie swung down off the train. He would have time to get back on when the conductor called "All aboard." Right now the conductor was talking to a woman on the platform. Her back was to Jamie, but something about her made him think of Truda Danson. Except two children were clinging to this woman's skirt. Truda didn't have children.

"Are you sure this is the last stop before Hazard?" The woman had the little boy's hand clutched in hers. She not only sounded very concerned, she sounded exactly like Truda Danson.

"Yes, ma'am. No more stops until Hazard."

"Do you think you could be wrong about where Thomas is supposed to meet his family, Bonnie?" The woman looked down at the girl beside her.

Jamie had heard that everybody had a double somewhere, but this was more than a double. This was Truda Danson.

The little girl nodded. "They put a paper with it writ on it in his bag."

Truda pulled something out of a bag the girl was holding and showed it to the conductor. "Is this where we are?"

"This is the place. Right as rain." The man handed the paper back to Truda and looked around. "He's where he's supposed to be, but his people aren't where they're supposed to be. And sorry as I am about it, we can't hold up the train any longer. We have a schedule to keep."

"I'm very aware of that." Truda's voice rose. "But I can hardly leave a four-year-old child here alone, now, can I?"

"Then you'll have to wait here with him or take him back on the train to wherever you are going." The conductor matched Truda's irritation.

"But I can't stay here. This other child is expected in Hyden."

Now Truda sounded near tears. Jamie couldn't imagine the Truda Danson he knew ever dissolving in tears. Piper was the same way. Ready to fight. Never ready to cry.

He stepped over to them. "Miss Danson, is that really you?"

A mixture of surprise and relief flooded her face. "Jamie Russell, what in the world are you doing here?"

"I might ask you the same thing, but I'm on the way to interview Mary Breckinridge for a newspaper story."

Her eyes narrowed on him. "Is that the only reason?"

He didn't shy away from her look. "That's the reason I'm giving, but seems you might need some help. How about I stay here with the boy until his family shows up? I can catch a train tomorrow." He looked over at the conductor. "Will my ticket still be good?"

"If you help us out of this dilemma, I'll see to it." The man seemed relieved. "I don't want the little fellow to miss his folks. Or the girl either."

The boy hid his face against Truda's skirt. "Stay with you," he said.

Truda looked stricken. "Bonnie says Thomas doesn't like changing people. Poor boy has been pitched between several on his way home."

Jamie squatted down in front of the kid. "Hey, Tommy, I bet your folks will be here to get you soon, but before they get here, maybe we can go find us a candy bar. Do you like candy?"

The boy eased around to peek at Jamie with tear-streaked cheeks.

Jamie reached out to the boy. "Come on, Tommy. I'll give you a ride up on my shoulders."

The little boy took Jamie's hand but still held on to Truda's skirt with his other hand.

She leaned down. "I've heard Jamie tells great stories. I wouldn't be surprised if he knows one about a dog. Do you have a dog back at your house?"

Thomas nodded and let go of Truda's skirt. "Bo. Pa says he's crazy 'cause he chases his tail." The kid's smile was shaky, but it was there.

"Well, I want to hear more about this crazy dog." Jamie grinned at the kid. "Wait here while I get my bag off the train."

He had to be as crazy as the kid's dog to be doing this. What if the kid's folks never showed up? What then? He shoved aside his worries as he ran to fetch his bag. He was traveling light. A change of clothes, a composition book, and his camera. He was light on money too. He wouldn't starve, but he might have to skip some meals.

Sometimes a person had to forget the obstacles and jump into the moment. Piper's aunt needed help. Wendover wouldn't disappear overnight and neither would Piper.

Truda was waiting with the two children when he climbed down from the train. The conductor was there too, ready to get the train rolling.

Jamie picked up the little boy. "Ready to have some fun, Tommy?"

The little fellow's lips trembled a bit, but he wrapped his arms around Jamie's neck.

"Thank you for this, Jamie. The Lord must have put you on the same train to watch over these children." Truda stuffed a dollar bill into Jamie's shirt pocket and waved away his protests. "Just in case you need something while you wait. Does Piper know you're coming?"

"No." Jamie should have written back to Piper, but too late for that now.

"She doesn't know I'm coming either." Truda laughed. "Things may get interesting for my favorite niece." She put her fingers to her lips and then touched the little boy's cheek. "Goodbye, Thomas."

After she climbed up the steps onto the train, the boy waved. "Bye bye, nice lady."

The kid seemed resigned to his fate. At least no new tears were coursing down his cheeks.

"Let's go find that candy bar." Jamie grinned at the kid. "You want to take that ride on my shoulders so you can point the way?"

When the boy nodded, Jamie hefted him up on his shoulders. "You hang on up there. Grab my hair if you need to, just don't yank it out. I need my curls. And my ears too. I'd be grateful if you leave them in place. Wouldn't want to lose them."

"You're funnin' me." The kid giggled. "Ears don't come off."

"You never know." Jamie flipped his ear with his finger. "They do wobble a little. And if I lost an ear, the girls might not think I was worth looking at, and fact is, I'm hunting for a girl."

At the store, Jamie splurged on a candy bar and a soda for both of them. He was surprised when he pulled Truda's money out of his pocket to see that the bill was a five spot and not a one. Maybe he wouldn't have to skip any meals after all.

They sat on the edge of the train platform and ate their candy. Thomas giggled when he tipped the bottle up to drink. "It tickles my nose," he said.

"The fizz is what makes it good."

The kid had chocolate on his chin and orange lips from the soda. Jamie pulled his camera out of his bag. With the money Truda had given him, he could buy more film, and this was a picture wanting to happen, even if the orange lips wouldn't show. He'd read about color photographs, but the equipment was far beyond his means.

Jamie stepped back and sighted in on the boy. When Thomas took a sip from his soda bottle, Jamie snapped the shutter. He took a second picture after the kid set the bottle down on the platform. If the pictures turned out good, maybe he could sell them.

Jamie sat back down beside Thomas. "You ready for that story now? About your dog, Bo?"

The boy nodded as he licked the candy wrapper.

"Then here goes. The adventures of Bo and Tommy." Jamie started a story where the boy got lost and the dog had to find him. He had them splashing through creeks more than once and fighting off wildcats. For fun, he threw in a talking crow.

He was winding down the adventure when Thomas jumped up and shouted, "Pa!"

Jamie stood too as the man came toward them on a horse. The man got off his horse and glared at Jamie. "What are you doing with my boy?"

"Just keeping him company until you got here." Jamie met the man's stare straight on. Cal Rogers had said some mountain people didn't like outsiders and warned him to watch his back. There was no ignoring the gun hanging by the man's saddle.

"You one of those government men?" The man's frown got darker. When Thomas pulled on his hand and tried to say something, the man hushed him with a look.

"Not me." Jamie tried another smile. "The lady who brought Thomas here on the train was somebody I knew. So when the train had to leave and she couldn't stay with your boy, I volunteered to wait with him."

Thomas grabbed his father's hand again. "Wanna go home. See Ma."

The man's face softened as he looked down at the boy. "She wants to see you too, son."

"Here are your things, Tommy." Jamie handed the boy his bag. "Give Bo a pat on the head for me when you see him."

When he turned to leave, the man stopped him. "I reckon I owe you for seeing to my boy till I could get down here."

"No, no. Glad to do it. Tommy's a great kid."

The man sat Thomas up on the horse and then climbed up behind him. "You still look like one of those government men. What's your business here?"

"I'm headed to Wendover to talk to Mary Breckinridge about the frontier nurses."

The man's face relaxed. "She's the one that seen to it my boy got fixed up at that city hospital. I hear she brings in all kinds over there."

He tightened the reins and turned his horse away. The kid leaned around him to wave as they rode off. Jamie breathed a little sigh of relief. Did he look like a government man? If so, that obviously wasn't good. But he was stuck here until the next train came through. Could be he should keep a low profile.

The ticket agent came out of the depot. "You got someplace to go tonight, young man?"

"Not really. Would it be all right if I just hang around here until the next train?"

"If you're headed on to Hazard, that won't be until tomorrow. You sort of got stuck with that boy and didn't look like his pa was the first bit grateful. That's Clem Baker for you, but the boy's ma is as sweet as his pa is sour. Not that Baker don't care for his young'uns. He does that. He just doesn't cotton to strangers."

"He didn't shoot me."

The agent laughed. "Folks come down here they're always thinking they're gonna get shot. Trust me, son, it doesn't happen that often."

"Glad to hear that."

"Tell you what. I appreciate you helping out with that boy. I wouldn't have wanted to try to watch him myself. That age takes both eyes on them. I'm closing down for the night. No more trains coming through till morning. But a cot's inside there where I take a rest now and again that you're welcome to use." The man pointed back toward the depot. "Door's not locked. No need in it." He winked. "In spite of how we shoot strangers."

"That's comforting," Jamie said.

The man clapped him on the back. "You'll be fine. The cot isn't fancy, but it beats a hard bench."

And it did. Jamie settled down on the cot after he went back to the store to get some crackers and cheese to ward off hunger. As night fell, he considered how different his life was from a few years ago. Then he'd be sitting at a fancy dining table with his family or perhaps at a dinner party with servants setting the dishes in front of him. Now here he was in the near darkness on a cot with a blanket that smelled of coal dust in a town where he knew absolutely no one, if he didn't count Tommy.

Very alone. Except for his thoughts of Piper. As different as everything else was, that was the same. Those thoughts of Piper. He did hope she'd smile when she saw him.

CHAPTER
TWENTY-FIVE

Nurse Freeman, the nurse midwife at the Wilder Ridge Center, came out on the porch with a big smile when Piper rode up.

"It's your lucky day, Danny. We've got a whole list of things that need doing. I hope you brought a change of clothes."

"I did." Piper lifted the saddlebags off Bella.

"Come on inside and let me find the list before you tend to your horse." The nurse kept talking as Piper followed her inside. "Things are so busy out here right now that it's hard to keep up with everything."

"What do you need?"

Piper and Marlie had stopped at this center when they made the rounds a few weeks ago. The front room was cozy, with a rag rug and rocking chairs around an iron stove. Two big windows gave a view of the hillside running down to a creek. Through a doorway, she glimpsed the clinic area as she trailed the woman into a kitchen with a cookstove, a white cabinet, and a table with three chairs.

"Plenty." Nurse Freeman was shorter than Piper, with a tough leanness about her. She rummaged through some papers on the table.

"Now where did Janet put that list? Janet—Nurse Hankins—is out on a call. Been gone all the day. I'm guessing Mrs. Jefferson's baby is being a slow comer. Fact is, I could be called out tomorrow, but tonight should be peaceful if nobody shoots themselves in the foot, gets snakebit, or falls off a cliff. The way people can injure themselves around here, you just wouldn't believe."

She looked up at Piper. "How long did you say you've been here in the mountains?"

"I came the last of May."

"So about a month. Have you had the privilege of being with one of us on a delivery?"

"I went with Nurse Robbins once and got to watch her deliver a little boy."

"Ahh, Robbie. She's a good one for sure. Been here for years. Loves the mountains." She shuffled through another pile of papers. "Janet and I could use some better organization. Maybe you can do that while you're here. But back to Robbie and the mountains. These hills do pull you in. Do you feel that, Danny?"

"I did as I rode down the mountain after the rain."

"They are a sight to behold. I fancy the early morning with mist rising up out of the valleys. Of course, it's not so nice when fog blankets the place, and you have the dreadful feeling that your horse might take a wrong step and you'll end up in a hollow. Maybe with the both of you having a broken leg. At least they don't shoot nurses who break their legs. Horses, poor things, are a different matter."

"Bella didn't have any problems."

"I've ridden Bella. She's a good one. Lady I have now is a fine mare but reluctant when the creeks run high. Then again, I'm reluctant when the creeks run high. Not that much rain today. Thank the heavens."

"Yes." Piper waited, not sure what she might be expected to do. She did hope it wasn't cooking. She could clean out the barn.

Weed the garden. Take the horses to the creek, but if it was cooking, they were all in trouble.

"Oh, I give up." Nurse Freeman pushed the papers back into the semblance of a pile. "I remember the things we needed most, anyway. One of the boys came around the end of last week and took care of weeding the garden. And weeded around the center too. So that got done. Praise the saints. Weeds give snakes too good a place to hide to sneak out on our steps. Trust me, it is not pleasant to step on a snake as one is rushing out on a call." The nurse peered over at Piper. "Are you afraid of snakes?"

"Not my favorite of God's creatures."

"Nor mine. But wait until you meet Nurse Hankins. She's amazing. Not that she likes snakes, but she's not afraid of them. She killed this big rattlesnake. Don't ask me how. I intend to never get that close to one. But she did, and then skinned it to make a belt. Can you imagine?"

"I'd rather not."

"Right. Just having that snakeskin around gave me the shivers." The nurse gave a little shake.

"Does she have a snakeskin belt now?"

Nurse Freeman laughed. "That's the thing. Her dog found it and chewed it up. Good boy, I say."

Piper laughed too.

"But don't tell her I said that. She was rather put out with Bandit."

"Do you have a dog? I didn't see one when I came in."

"I had one, but poor girl got sick and died. So very sad. Miss her." Nurse Freeman brushed away a tear. "Silly to weep over a dog, but she was great company, night or day."

"I'm sorry. But if you decide you want another dog, Ginger had her pups at Wendover."

A smile replaced the nurse's tears. "I heard that. Do they look like Ginger?"

"They do. Round little balls of golden sunshine."

"I'll put in an order for one, although pups can be a trial the way they like to chew up things. Things besides rattlesnake skins. But back to business." She pointed at a paint can on the floor. "The doors and woodwork here in the center need painting in the worst way. Have you ever done any painting?"

Piper gave the can a dubious look. "Nothing except a watercolor picture when I was a kid."

"Not exactly the same." The nurse looked amused as she shook her head. "Well, it's not hard. You dip the brush in the can and smear it on. You'll do fine. You can start in the morning. I've got an old shirt you can wear. Now you need to see to the horses."

She handed Piper a basket. "Take that to get the eggs on the way back in. But watch out for the rooster. He'll try to spur you in a second if you turn your back on him. I keep telling Janet we should have chicken soup. Anyway, you can find corn in a barrel out in the barn. The rascal behaves if you feed him. Meanwhile, I'll see what I can find for us to eat. Might have to be eggs. Oh, and if I get called out tonight, you can go with me."

Piper's head was spinning as she picked up the basket and started outside.

"I don't suppose you could milk the cow," the nurse called after her.

Piper looked around at the nurse. "I have no idea how to milk a cow."

"No time like the present to learn." The woman must have noted Piper's complete astonishment at the thought of milking a cow. She waved her hand at Piper. "Never mind. I'll milk the old girl. I'm guessing you've never seen anybody milk a cow."

"Actually, no."

"I was the same way when I came to the mountains, but you learn pretty quickly how to do things around here. But me mentioning milking has you looking about ready to hightail it back to Wendover. Even in the dark. Night does fall fast here in the mountains, so hurry on about the chores." She nodded toward the door. "I'll be out to milk old Clara in a bit."

Piper rubbed down Bella and then fed and watered her and the nurse's mare. With a watchful eye on the rooster, she fed the chickens and went in the chicken house to hunt for eggs. The light was so dim she couldn't see into the nests. She wished for her flashlight that was back at the Garden House. She cringed each time she reached into a dark nest. She was relieved to find some eggs while no unseen critter nipped her fingers.

When she came out of the chicken house, Nurse Freeman called to her from the barn. "Come on, Danny. I'll give you a milking lesson. It's something you can brag about when you go back home."

Piper sighed. Nothing for it but to go back to the barn and get way closer to a cow than she'd ever expected to be. Nurse Freeman obviously wasn't someone to be refused.

With her head secured in a wooden stanchion, the yellow-brown cow munched on feed. She swished her tail to brush away flies.

"She's a gentle soul." Nurse Freeman sat down on a short stool by the cow's flank and washed her udder. "She might hit you with that tail, which isn't pleasant, but she won't kick you. At least she hasn't me." She grinned up at Piper. "I'm careful not to pinch her."

She squeezed out a stream of milk from each teat into a small can and handed it to Piper. "Pour this in that pan over there for the cat. Jinx will be looking for it later." She positioned the bucket under the cow's udder and looked to be sure Piper was watching. "First you wrap your thumb and index finger around the top of the teat and squeeze it gently. Then slowly work your way down the teat by adding one finger at a time to make the milk squirt into the bucket." Two streams of milk hit the metal bucket. She kept working her fingers until no more milk came out.

She eased up off the stool, holding the bucket. "Don't want to spill the milk we have." She motioned to Piper. "Now, you give it a try."

Piper pulled in a breath. "You're sure she won't kick?"

"Not Clara." The nurse patted the cow's rump. "We ought to hire her out to people who want to learn to milk."

Piper started to say she wasn't one of those people, but instead she sat down on the stool and put the bucket Nurse Freeman handed her back under the cow. The odor of the milk and cow along with some hints of manure was earthy. Different from a horse's smell, but not totally unpleasant.

"Don't try both hands at once until you figure it out," Nurse Freeman said. "Pick one of the teats I didn't strip."

Piper did as she said. Nothing happened. The cow shifted a little to the side as though to get away from Piper.

"Don't be so tense. You're making the poor girl wonder. Try again." Nurse Freeman leaned down to watch Piper's hand as she repeated the directions. "Don't forget to point the teat toward the bucket."

Piper took a breath and relaxed her shoulders as she positioned her thumb and index finger and gently squeezed the top of the cow's teat that felt somehow both soft and firm in her hand. She squeezed her other fingers slowly one at a time along the teat. A stream of milk squirted out into the pail. A giggle tickled Piper's throat as she repeated the squeeze again and more milk came out.

"How do I know when I'm through?" Piper asked.

"You can tell. The teat will feel empty."

Piper could tell and she stripped the milk out of the other teat too. She was feeling pretty good, with her forehead almost touching the cow's belly.

"Watch out." Nurse Freeman reached around her to grab the bucket away from under the cow just as Clara let loose a stream of urine.

Piper tried to jump back but tripped on the stool and fell on her backside. The cow's pee hit the hard dirt and splattered on Piper.

Nurse Freeman was bent over laughing. Not exactly rolling-on-the-ground laughing. That was Piper. Rolling on the ground but not laughing.

The nurse caught her breath and gasped. "Better scramble up, Danny. The next thing she lets out could be worse."

Piper didn't have to be told twice.

With her laughter subsiding into chuckles, Nurse Freeman released the cow from the stanchion and smacked her on the rump to get her out of the barn and back into the field.

"I'm sorry about that, Danny. But when you're milking, you've got to be ready for any eventuality." She pulled in a breath. "I guess that's true for about everything here in the mountains. We never know what to expect next. But you can be pretty sure when a cow lifts her tail, it's time to scoot out of range."

"Now you tell me." Piper rubbed her face off on the underside of her shirttail.

"Come on, girl. There's a teakettle on the stove. You can wash up and give your clothes a rinse too." She gave Piper a pat on the shoulder. "But think of it. You milked your first cow. I like a game girl. Those kind do better here in the mountains."

Piper picked up the basket of eggs and followed the nurse through the twilight to the house. She was the one who smelled earthy now, but that was okay. She had done things today she never dreamed of doing two months ago. She'd ridden through a storm with a young charge and discovered that the scariest-looking mountain man wasn't necessarily all bad. She'd seen a mother welcome her son home and ridden through a rain-washed forest. And now she'd gathered eggs out of dark nests, managed to keep from being spurred by a belligerent rooster, and milked a cow. Tomorrow she would dip a brush in paint and spruce up the Wilder Ridge Center.

She had come to the mountains because she wanted to do something different, and for sure, she had. Very different. She could only imagine what Braxton Crandall would think of her now with her earthy smell. Actually, she couldn't imagine. She didn't know him well enough, but she could definitely imagine Jamie Russell leaning over, hands on his knees, laughing at her the way Nurse Freeman had. Then he would have helped her up and they could have laughed together.

It was funny. When Piper thought of how she must have looked sprawled on the barn floor, trying to scoot away from the cow's splattering pee, a smile turned up her lips that turned into a laugh.

Nurse Freeman looked around at her. "What's funny?"

"Everything." Piper threw out her hand that wasn't holding the basket of eggs. "Me. Old Clara. Pee splatters. Probably paint splatters tomorrow. Life."

"That's the attitude, Danny girl. Enjoy life. We all have some bumps and bruises along the way, but the old world keeps turning. Even in the darkest hour, a smile can bring some light."

Nurse Freeman stopped and looked up at the sky where one lone star had appeared. "I sometimes imagine our Lord in the midst of his agony may have smiled when he looked down at his weeping mother at the foot of the cross and told her to count John her son from that time on."

Piper looked up at the sky too. She didn't know what she should say, so she stayed silent.

After a moment, the nurse went on. "And then come that Sunday morning when the grave couldn't hold him, smiles burst out all around. What a wonder that must have been."

"Are you religious?"

"Religious?" Nurse Freeman glanced over at Piper. "That's an interesting word. Rather makes one think of nuns and priests, doesn't it?" She looked back up at the sky. "I'm certainly not that. In fact, I rarely thought of such things back in England before I came here to the mountains. But there's something about these hills. Something about being so close to the stars and helping babies come into the world. So I'm not sure I'm pious, but I do believe. How can one not believe here in this place?"

Silence fell around them then as more stars came into view. Piper's heart seemed to soften as a thankful prayer rose within her that she was here on this hillside considering her blessings.

"Come, Danny. We've got to get this milk strained and you cleaned up. Then we can fry up some eggs for supper. We have some bread we can warm in the skillet and a jar of strawberry jam. Life is good."

CHAPTER
TWENTY-SIX

After his unplanned layover in Helmer, Jamie was more than ready to board the train to Hazard the next day. Not that he'd had any problems waiting. No one else had accused him of being a government man. And little wonder, as rumpled as he felt. He had managed to shave in the little washroom at the depot. So at least he wouldn't show up with a bristly beard.

He had to laugh at himself. He was acting as if Piper would fly into his arms and kiss him. While that wasn't likely to happen, his heart sped up a little at the thought.

The ticket agent had brought him breakfast. Biscuits and sausage. "It's not much, but it might tide you over till you get wherever you're going."

"This is great. Thank you." Jamie's stomach had been growling.

"I should have took you home with me for supper last night. The wife said so when I told her about you."

"I did fine here." Jamie took a bite of the biscuit and sausage. "You tell her I'm grateful for these. You've been more than kind to a stranger passing through."

"Well, I didn't want you to think all of us here in Helmer are like that Clem Baker. That man is so mean, poison ivy is scared to break out on him."

"That's pretty mean." Jamie had to smile as his fingers itched to grab a pencil and write the man's description down in his notebook. "He might have been extra unfriendly because he thought I was a government man."

"That could be." The man stepped back and gave Jamie a considering look. "Are you?"

Jamie wrapped his hand around the other biscuit and sausage, not at all sure the agent might not take it back. "Not me. I'm headed to Wendover to interview Mary Breckinridge for the newspaper back in Danville."

The man's face eased back into a smile. "That ought to be a story and a half. That Mary Breckinridge come down here and the same as moved a few mountains to get going over there in Hyden. She got them to build a hospital. You'd told me ten years ago that Hyden would have a hospital up there on Thousandsticks Mountain, I'd have said you were crazy in the head."

"She sounds like quite a woman."

"I reckon so. In spite of her being an outsider, folks up here generally favor her. My wife's sister over that way might have died having her baby if it hadn't been for Breckinridge's brought-in midwives."

"Brought-in?"

"Those that come down here to the mountains from somewhere else. Something like you." The man nodded toward Jamie. "But these nurse midwives come from way farther than you. Some all the way from England. Imagine that?" He shook his head. "You'd think they would have been plenty busy with babies over there."

"If I get the chance, I'll ask them why they came."

"You do that, and if you get that piece written, you send a copy down here to Josh Brandon. That's me. I'll get it printed in our paper too. The editor, he's a friend of mine and he's always after something to fill his pages."

While Jamie simply used writing about the Frontier Nursing Service as an excuse to chase after Piper, the story possibilities were beginning to excite him.

Uncle Wyatt had tried to get him to see that when he'd given Jamie a little money for his trip, along with some advice. "I know you're heading down there to see that girl, but pay attention to what other doors the good Lord might open up for you. Sometimes we find blessings where we least expect them."

When Jamie climbed aboard the train, a woman stood up and beckoned him toward her. When he hesitated, thinking he was surely mistaken, she called to him. "I've saved you a seat, Jamie Russell."

He had no idea how she knew his name, but one seat was the same as the next. She looked familiar. Perhaps one of his mother's friends. She appeared to be about the same age as his mother. Not very tall, and thick through the waist. Gray was salted through her brown hair that was bobbed short, as though the woman had better things to do than mess with her hair. A sensible-looking woman.

Not until he got close enough to see her intense blue eyes did he realize this had to be Mary Breckinridge. He'd seen pictures, but people always looked a little different in person.

She sat down and patted the seat beside her. "I'm so happy you got on this car. The Lord must have been watching out for me." She gave him a look. "And for you."

Jamie dropped down in the seat. "You're Mary Breckinridge." He couldn't believe his good fortune to be sitting beside the very woman he had come to interview.

"I am indeed. Was that just a lucky guess or have we met before?"

"I've seen pictures of you."

"And where would a young man like you see my picture? Not only see it, but remember it. I must say I am complimented by that." The woman smiled.

He figured he might as well be out with it. Even if she turned him down flat, he could still go on to Wendover to see Piper.

"I work for a newspaper and I'm hoping to interview you about how you started the Frontier Nursing Service and how it works for the people here in the mountains."

"I see."

He noted that she didn't agree. But at least she didn't say no straight out either. "I'm excited about the story possibilities." A little enthusiasm never hurt.

"Are you now?" Her eyes danced with amusement. That surely wasn't all bad. "After meeting me?"

"Oh yes, more than ever. Nurses on horseback are a compelling story. The ticket agent there in Helmer told me about how his sister-in-law had trouble having her baby, but the nurses brought her through okay. The baby too."

"The baby too." Mary Breckinridge looked down at her hands folded in her lap.

Too late Jamie remembered the background he'd read about her and how she'd lost two children. One of them only a few hours after birth. "I'm sorry if I brought up bad memories."

"Oh no. Not bad memories at all. I cherish the memories of my children, even my little Polly, who lived such a very short time. She was a beautiful baby." Mrs. Breckinridge breathed out a sigh and looked up at Jamie. "Sweet memories. I've never understood why some think a person dying means one can never mention their name again in the presence of those who are left behind. It shouldn't be that way at all."

Jamie nodded. He had noticed something the same after his father died.

"At any rate, losing those precious children set me on a different path in life. You are probably too young to know anything about such things. How life can change so quickly."

"I know a little. I lost my father last summer."

She gave him a considering look. "Well then, perhaps you do. Many have seen troubles in these last years." She brushed her hands across her lap as though sweeping away sad thoughts. "But now that we have decided why you knew my name, aren't you the least bit curious about how I knew yours?"

"More than a bit," Jamie said. "How did you know?"

"Telephones, dear boy. I spoke with my secretary at Wendover, who relayed the news that Truda Danson had arrived for a visit and safely delivered two children to their parents. Or so we assume, in the case of young Thomas." She looked over at him with raised eyebrows. "Since the boy is no longer with you, I can trust his father eventually showed up to claim him."

"Yes, ma'am."

"Clem Baker can be contrary at times, but he does care for his children. The people here in the mountains are the salt of the earth. Like these all around us right here on this train." She motioned toward the other seats. "Good people."

The man across the aisle looked over with a nod, as if he'd heard what she said.

She went on. "But we were talking about you, weren't we?" She didn't wait for him to answer. "Miss Danson relayed to my secretary how you volunteered to help with Thomas. I do think she was a bit overwhelmed caring for the two children, but we use those available to shepherd the children to and from the city hospitals when there is a need."

"I wasn't sure it could be Truda when I first saw her with two children."

"It's good for people to have a challenge now and again." She peered over at him again. "Don't you agree?"

"I like a challenge."

"Do you? And what challenge are you chasing down here to the mountains? Merely a story about the frontier nurses or something more?" She gave him a searching look. "I understand you are acquainted with Miss Danson. And her niece."

"I know the Dansons. Piper and I have been friends a long time, and it will be great to see her. But I do want to write a story about you if you will agree."

"Oh no. Not about me." She frowned and shook her head. "That will never do. But perhaps about my nurse midwives and how they help mothers have healthy babies here. That would be good. I do like getting the word out to potential donors."

"My editor says his wife sends baby clothes."

"Many do, and toys for the children at Christmas. People love Christmas. The first year after I built Wendover, I had a Christmas party for our families. Imagine my surprise when five hundred people showed up. We didn't have enough toys for all the children that year, but since then we've filled the attic with all sorts of things to be ready. Every little girl deserves to have a baby doll, don't you think?"

When he didn't answer right away, she laughed. "I suppose a young man like you has never given much thought to little girls having dolls. I should have said a bag of marbles or a toy truck." She touched his hand lightly. "I'm guessing you had lovely Christmas gifts as a boy."

"Those were good times."

"You sound as if they are past times."

"I'm not a kid any longer, and my family lost everything in the crash."

"Everything?" Mrs. Breckinridge peered over at him. "You appear to have your health. That's a very good thing. And your good humor. You speak of a family and friends. Not to mention your youth and perhaps the talent and fortitude to take advantage of opportunities that might come your way."

"All true." Jamie smiled. "Very true. And I'm hoping that first opportunity is writing about the Frontier Nursing Service. That's what I really want to do. Write. Perhaps a novel someday."

Jamie had shared that dream of writing a book with only one other person. Piper. But something about this woman next to him made it easy to say. Perhaps because she had worked for a dream too after things were hard for her.

"Then perhaps you will." She patted his hand. "Do you have a plan for when you get to Hazard? On how to get to Hyden? Where you might stay?"

"Can't say that I do. I'm sort of winging it."

"Winging it." She smiled. "That's how I've often felt in the past. With plans but depending on the Lord to open ways. Breckie—that was my son—I sometimes feel he sends me help from heaven. Do you ever feel that way about your father?"

"No."

"I sense bitterness there. My advice to you would be to turn that loose and let it slide right down the creek and out of your life."

"Yes, ma'am."

"No hesitation allowed. First creek you come to in the hills, you just throw all those things you can't change into the water and let them float away." She flung out her hands as though throwing something away.

"I'll try." He didn't know whether he could do it or not, but it sounded good.

"Young people." She shook her head, obviously sensing his doubt. "I suppose I might have been the same at your age. Sure I was right about so much. But I've learned a few things since then. That's because I watch."

She pointed to a young woman holding a baby in a seat up from them on the other side of the aisle. "Take that mother there. She's tired. Bone tired. You can tell by the droop of her shoulders, but she keeps trying to comfort her fussy little one." Mrs. Breckinridge stood up. "Excuse me a minute. I'll be right back and we can figure out what we're going to do with you."

Mrs. Breckinridge held on to the seats and stepped over to the mother. She slipped off her sweater and draped it around the young woman's shoulders. "You look like you might be chilled, dear."

Jamie couldn't hear the young woman's answer over the clatter of the train, but he could see her face with its look of appreciation. Mrs. Breckinridge sat down beside the young mother and reached for the child. She held the baby up to her shoulder, rubbed his back, and appeared to be cooing in his ear. After a few minutes, she returned the baby to his mother and made her way back to her seat beside Jamie.

"You didn't get your sweater back," Jamie said.

Mrs. Breckinridge waved her hand to indicate that was of no concern. "I don't need it. The sun is shining, but nursing babies can drain a woman of stamina and make her feel chilled even on a warm day like today."

"That was kind of you," Jamie said.

"Kindness often takes action. There's a place in the Bible— James, I think—where he says if your sister or brother is naked or hungry and you simply say depart and be warm and fed without doing anything to make that happen, then you have failed your calling."

"Do you feel you have a calling?"

"I certainly do. A calling to help mothers and children." She fastened her gaze on Jamie. "I think we all have a calling. Sometimes we live up to it and sometimes we don't. You lived up to a calling for kindness yesterday when you upset your schedule to help out young Thomas and your friend's aunt. An act of kindness, don't you think?"

"I didn't think about it being kind. Just that Miss Danson needed help."

"And perhaps you wouldn't have been moved to help if you

had not known Miss Danson, but whether that is true or not, the fact that you did has made me ready to help you. I will submit to an interview and send you out to see how my nurse midwives live and work in the centers we have established. You will have to find your own way to Wendover from Hazard, but once you do, I have a tent up in the attic that you can use while you are there. A week, perhaps? No more than two unless you find a way to make yourself useful besides writing a story."

"Again, kind of you and very appreciated."

"You look like a nice boy, but I know boys." Her gaze sharpened on him. "I don't believe you were completely honest with me about simply being friends with Piper Danson."

Jamie started to say something, but she held her hand up to stop him. "Don't bother denying or explaining. Just be absolutely certain that I will not stand for any unseemly behavior between the two of you. She is one of my couriers and, as such, is expected to live up to our rigid behavior standards. I'll tell her the same thing. Here in the mountains, you must truly be simply the casual friends you claim."

"Yes, ma'am." What else could he say? But again, he wasn't being completely honest. If Piper acted like she would welcome a kiss, he would remember Mary Breckinridge's words, but not abide by them. A kiss wouldn't feel like unseemly behavior to him.

CHAPTER
TWENTY-SEVEN

Painting wasn't hard. Keeping the paint only on the places that needed painting, that was the hard part. By the time Piper made the last swipe of paint on the porch posts, her hands and arms sported a multitude of white spots.

"You've got a little paint on your face, Danny." Nurse Hankins had shown up that morning after, as she said, catching a nine-pound, three-ounce boy for Mrs. Jefferson. "There's a mirror in my room if you want to clean up."

"I have paint on my face too?" Piper touched her cheek.

"You are a bit speckled." Nurse Freeman laughed. She'd just come in from checking on some of her patients. "Not to mention the streaks of white in your hair." She glanced at the other nurse. "She's looking something like you, Janet."

"I've earned every bit of frosting I have." Nurse Hankins ran her hand through her short hair that did sport a fair amount of gray, but no paint as far as Piper could tell, in spite of the fact the nurse had found a smaller brush and painted the window facings. She didn't get the first spot of paint on the window glass.

Nurse Freeman held up the old shirt she let Piper borrow. "You did know you were to use the brush and not dip the shirt in the paint, didn't you?"

"Sorry. Do you want me to wash it?" Piper picked at a spot of paint on her hand. It was already the middle of the afternoon, and if she was going to get to Wendover before dark, she needed to get started. "I did clean up any paint I got on the floor."

"Now, now, Alice. Give the girl some credit." Nurse Hankins covered a yawn with her hand. "Mercy. I do hope no baby wants to discover the world this night."

"You should have taken a nap," Nurse Freeman said.

"And leave poor Danny working alone? My mum taught me better than that." Nurse Hankins grinned over at Piper. "Plus, I do like our view out the windows. Didn't want us to have a blind cabin."

When Piper looked puzzled, Nurse Freeman explained. "A cabin without windows. I suppose Nurse Hankins worried you might paint the window white." She shook her head and smiled. "And from the looks of this shirt, that appears to have been a possibility."

"Guess I was pretty messy." Piper looked down at her bare feet. She'd been smart to take off her riding boots.

"That you were," Nurse Freeman said. "But the doors and the porch posts look great. So white and clean. No need to concern yourself over a few paint splatters."

"My mum used to say it would all come out in the wash," Nurse Hankins said. "If not right away, then eventually."

"That word 'eventually' is a good one to remember," Nurse Freeman said. "It could be you'll need some kerosene to get that paint off. We have some if you want to give it a try."

"I think I'll head to Wendover and do the paint removal there," Piper said. "If I douse myself in kerosene, I'll need a bath."

"A bath." Nurse Freeman sighed. "Maybe I should visit Wendover and take my turn in that bathtub of Mrs. Breckinridge's. I do miss soaking in a hot-water bath."

"Can't be riding off now, Alice," Nurse Hankins said. "We have babies to catch."

Piper saddled Bella and waved goodbye to the nurses as she rode past the center. With a sigh, she relaxed as Bella headed down the trail. She was tired, but it was a good tired. Neat or not, she had done what the nurses asked. Painted every wood surface in sight. Milked Clara. Eaten wild raspberries off a bush near the barn and made friends with Nurse Hankins's dog, Bandit. When Piper asked what breed the short-haired black-and-brown dog might be, Nurse Hankins laughed and said mountain dog was as close as she could come.

By the time Piper forded the Middle Fork River and started up to Wendover, deep shadows were falling over the hills. It felt like coming home. That surprised Piper. She was miles from her home in Louisville, but she liked the feeling of belonging here in this place, at least for a summer. Rusty ran to meet her with his tail wagging, and Ginger came out of the barn, followed by a couple of her more adventuresome pups.

Kermit walked down Pig Alley toward Piper as she slid off Bella. "Pushing it kinda late, aren't you, Danny? Mrs. Breckinridge don't like you girls being out by yourself after dark."

"I know. I had to finish the painting they wanted done at Wilder Ridge Center." Piper led Bella toward the barn.

"Good to know you were painting. I was feared you might have broke out in the white-spotted measles." Kermit chuckled and reached for Bella's reins. "Don't expect this ever again, but I'll take care of your horse. Everybody on the place has been looking for you. Including Mrs. Breckinridge."

"She's here?"

"Got here middle of the day. Asked where you were straightaway. Well, after she fed her chickens and geese. Hardly anything comes before that when she gets back here. But could be you should head on up to the Big House. Mrs. Breckinridge wants something done, she generally wants it done yesterday."

"Am I in trouble?" Piper asked.

"More likely you'd know that better than me, wouldn't you?" Kermit looked over his shoulder as he started into the barn. "If'n you are, it won't get no better dragging your feet out here."

Ginger licked Piper's hand while Rusty jumped up for a pat and the pups started play fighting. "He's just pulling my leg, isn't he?" Piper ruffled Rusty's ears and stroked Ginger's back. "I brought Bella back in fine shape and found the way to Billy's house and nobody got shot. I even milked a cow. That ought to get me a medal. Not trouble."

"Piper." Marlie ran down the road from the Garden House. She didn't use Piper's nickname. That made her more nervous.

Marlie skidded to a stop in front of her. "Good. You're back. We were worried you might stay at Wilder Ridge another night." She gave Piper a better look. "What in the world? Is that goose doo-doo all over you?"

That made paint not sound as bad. "I've been painting."

"Oh. Well, Mrs. Breckinridge told me to watch for you and make sure you went to the Big House right away."

"Maybe I should clean up first."

"You don't know Mrs. Breckinridge. She wants to see you now. Paint and all."

Worry jumped up in Piper that Mrs. Breckinridge might have brought bad news from home. Had something happened to Leona or the baby? When Piper thought about Leona struggling to have her baby the way Mrs. Whitton had, her heart started beating faster. That didn't seem like anything Leona could survive.

"Don't look so tragic," Marlie said. "It's not bad news. Your aunt is here and—"

"Truda?"

Of course, it was Truda. Piper didn't wait to hear more. She whirled and ran toward the Big House. She wondered if Truda had been there long enough to go see Dr. Jack. Or if she even wanted to see Dr. Jack. Truda had not once mentioned him in her letters after Piper wrote that she'd met the doctor. No *How does he look? What is he doing?* Nothing. But Piper knew she had to be curious.

In the dining room, the supper dishes had been cleared away and account books and papers were spread out in front of Truda and Miss Aileen. A pencil was stuck behind one of Truda's ears and her reading glasses were propped on her nose. She looked the way she did whenever Piper visited her at the bank. She could almost see numbers circling around her head.

"Piper." Truda pushed back from the table and held out her arms.

Miss Aileen stood up too and frowned at Piper. "Good gracious, Danny, did you fall into a flour bin?"

That was better than goose doo. "It's paint. But it's dry. It won't rub off on anything." Piper gave Truda a hug. "You should have let me know you were coming."

"Why? Were you going to bake a cake?" Truda smiled.

"Who knows? Maybe I could. I've been doing plenty of other things I've never done before." Piper laughed. "But I'm so glad to see you. Are Mother and Father all right? Has Leona had her baby?" She didn't wait for answers but rushed on. "I saw a baby being born last week. It was amazing."

"Everybody at home is fine. The doctor says another month at least for Leona. She's not happy. Poor child. Your mother has been over there every day. Wanda Mae can hardly contain her excitement. In fact, she's so wrapped up in helping Leona get the nursery ready that I think she's almost glad you decided to forgo your debut season."

"Not half as glad as I am. It's an adventure a minute down here. I actually milked a cow."

"And painted something besides your face, I hope." Truda touched a spot on Piper's cheek.

Miss Aileen spoke up. "You should have cleaned up."

"I was afraid it would get dark before I got back if I did that, and you did say I should stay one night."

"One night. Two." Miss Aileen waved her hands as if it was no matter. "You do whatever the nurse midwives need when you go out on district."

"Yes, ma'am. But I got Billy home and finished the painting." Piper would wait to tell her about the standoff with Mann Taylor. No need worrying Truda. "I can go clean up now, but Marlie said Mrs. Breckinridge wanted to see me. Was it just because Truda is here?" Piper smiled over at her aunt. "I'm so glad to see you. Have you been to the hospital?"

"Not yet. I was waiting for you to give me the grand tour. Meanwhile, I've been helping Miss Aileen with her books."

"I do appreciate your help." Miss Aileen sighed as she looked down at the table. "We need to find a way to stretch our dollars. This is a difficult time for everyone." Then she seemed to remember Piper. "But Mrs. Breckinridge does want to speak to you, Danny. Right away. She's upstairs in her bedroom, resting. So off with you." Another wave of her hands dismissed Piper.

"More surprises await." Truda raised her eyebrows in a look that Piper couldn't quite interpret.

Piper started to ask again if she was in trouble, but she bit back the words and headed for the stairs. "Which room?" She hadn't been upstairs in the Big House.

"Trust me." Miss Aileen sounded irritated. "You won't need a map."

Miss Aileen was right. If she could find Billy West's house up in the hills, then she could surely find Mrs. Breckinridge's bedroom in what might be called the Big House but was hardly castle size.

She looked up as she went down the hallway. Someone was walking around overhead in the attic. Suze said all sorts of things were stored there.

The glow of an oil lamp came from the far bedroom where

someone was talking. Piper hesitated in the hallway, but Mrs. Breckinridge must have heard her coming.

"Come on in, child."

"I didn't want to disturb you." Piper looked around, but nobody was in the room except Mrs. Breckinridge, who was propped up on pillows in the bed.

"I was just telling Breckie about my trip. Breckie was my son, you know. He died when he was four, but I imagine him wise beyond his years in heaven. Anytime I have lost a baby or little child I was treating, and praise be, there haven't been many, I was sure my Breckie would be waiting to usher them into paradise." She blinked and blew out a breath before she sat up straighter to peer at Piper. "My word, child, did you get any paint on the walls?"

At least Mrs. Breckinridge knew it was paint. "Not on the walls, but on the doors and porch posts." Piper rubbed a spot off her hand. "Nurse Freeman and Nurse Hankins were pleased."

"Good girls, both of them, and the place did look in need of sprucing up last time I was by there. Any babies being born out that way?"

"Nurse Hankins delivered a little boy for a Mrs. Jefferson. And Mrs. West looked not far from her delivery date."

"Ah yes, Billy's mother. Aileen told me you took him home. Such a sweet little fellow. Aileen thought it highly irregular, but then she likes all her ducks in a row." Mrs. Breckinridge's gaze was sharp on Piper. "And you girls are her ducks. Don't forget that."

"Yes, ma'am."

"Also keep in mind that I expect the highest standard of behavior from you." She pointed a finger at Piper. "If I hear any different, you'll pack up and be out of here."

"Yes, ma'am." Piper shifted on her feet. "Have I done something wrong? Dr. Jack asked me to take Billy home."

"No, no. That was fine. A treat for the child. Heaven knows, the children around here get few of those. But they are such dear little ones." A smile flashed across her face and was gone as once again her eyes were intense on Piper. "I simply want to make sure you understand the behavior expected from my couriers." She shook her finger at Piper. "Absolutely no hanky-panky."

"I don't know what you mean." Piper frowned a little. "Not much chance for anything like hanky-panky around here."

"So it would seem. But sometimes unsettling opportunities can sprout up like weeds in a bean patch." The woman leaned to look past Piper out into the hallway. "Come in here, young man."

Piper couldn't imagine what young man could have Mrs. Breckinridge concerned about hanky-panky. The only man who was always around Wendover was Kermit, and he was old enough to be Piper's grandfather. Truda was the one who had come to the mountains with the idea of seeing a man from her past. That thought made Piper smile as she turned to see whomever Mrs. Breckinridge had beckoned into the room.

Piper's heart dropped, then bounced back up and started beating like mad. She shut her eyes and opened them again. That couldn't be Jamie Russell in the doorway. She had to be dreaming.

He smiled his Jamie smile. "Hello, Piper."

The sure knowledge of Mrs. Breckinridge's eyes boring into Piper was absolutely the only thing that kept her from running to grab Jamie's hands and dance in a circle like they were still kids. Instead, with the talk of hanky-panky behavior fresh in her mind, she stayed rooted to her spot.

"Jamie." She hated that she sounded breathless. She pulled in some air and went on. "What are you doing here?"

CHAPTER
TWENTY-EIGHT

Piper Danson was absolutely the most beautiful sight Jamie had ever seen. Even in her riding clothes with paint spattered on her face and streaking her windblown hair. She must have just ridden in. She never worried about her hair when she was on a horse.

He loved how she looked, hair combed or not, but more, he loved her spirit and heart. Their match had surely been written in the stars from the first time they met as children. At least that's how he felt. He could only pray she felt the same.

That afternoon when he'd finally made it to Wendover after a crazy ride from Hazard to Hyden in an old big-band limousine converted to a bus and then a four-mile hike, he could hardly contain his disappointment when Piper wasn't here. He wanted to grab a horse and go find her.

But he'd looked at the river and the trees climbing up the hills on all sides and faced reality. Horse or no horse, he had no idea how to find Piper. So instead he had talked to Mrs. Breckinridge again and to Aileen Simpson, who had not smiled once at him, but at least hadn't ordered him gone. Instead she had screwed her mouth up in a tight circle while Mrs. Breckinridge told Jamie to look in the attic for the tent she'd told him about on the train.

"My nephew and I slept in it one summer when the house here got overcrowded with patients. That was before we built the hospital." She had looked at Miss Simpson. "And before you came, Aileen. Thank the saints for that hospital now."

"Yes." Miss Simpson's face still registered disapproval. "Are we expected to feed him as well?" She gave Jamie a hard look that wasn't softened a bit by the best smile Jamie could summon up.

"Come, come, child." Mrs. Breckinridge gave Miss Simpson's arm a little shake. Miss Simpson was much younger than her and slight of size. "We can't let the boy starve. That wouldn't be very hospitable."

"It could be he shouldn't have come without the resources to see to his own needs." Miss Simpson sent him another narrowed-eye look.

"But resources are hard to come by in this present time of difficulty. I know you are aware of that."

"Very aware." The woman's frown got darker.

"But you have to admire this young man's moxie in finding a way to follow his heart to Wendover."

Jamie looked at her. His heart for writing or his heart for Piper?

Without the first glance at him, she kept talking to the other woman. "You know what our nurse midwives are fond of saying. No one comes to these mountains by accident." Mrs. Breckinridge smiled over at Jamie. A bland smile that gave nothing away. "That can be true for our visitors as well, and we have never let our visitors or staff go hungry. We won't start now."

"I suppose you're right," Miss Simpson said.

"Of course I'm right. Besides, the young man is going to help us with some publicity. Free of charge, I might add."

"Except for those meals," Miss Simpson muttered.

"True. Might be good to let Rayma know we're feeding a young man for a week or two." Mrs. Breckinridge laughed as she looked over at Jamie. "But the boy will earn his keep. Perhaps he can assist me in penning something for one of the ladies' magazines."

"That would be great," Jamie said. "I'm looking forward to talking to you about the Frontier Nursing Service and what the nurses do here in the mountains."

"We will get to that eventually. After I get caught up on things. Until then, Aileen can find ways to keep you busy. Or our handyman, Kermit, might need help with something."

"Sure. I'm glad to help however I can." As long as he got to hang around.

Almost as if she read his mind, she turned back to Miss Simpson. "It appears he not only knows our guest, Truda Danson, but is well acquainted with our new courier, Piper Danson."

"Danny?"

"Is that what you're calling her?" Mrs. Breckinridge smiled again. "Fits nicely. I thought you might go with Pip."

"That was suggested. Poor girl shivered. However, Nurse Robbins does call her Pippay."

"The French coming out in Robbie, I suppose. But then she's from England, isn't she?" Mrs. Breckinridge waved her hand to dismiss the question. "Matters not. France is just across the channel. Is she working out well? Our Danny?"

"She's very willing to do whatever we ask. But it wasn't my asking that she take that little boy to his house. That was all Dr. Jack's idea. Seemed most irregular." Miss Simpson was frowning again.

"We do want to keep Jackson happy, and if he wanted it done, then you were right to let her go." Mrs. Breckinridge ran her hand along the mantel above the fireplace. "It is so good to be home. I'm going up to my room to rest a bit. My back is complaining." She started up the stairs. "Point the boy in the direction of the attic so he can get that tent."

That had left Jamie alone with Miss Simpson. She glanced

toward the long table in the dining area where she and Truda Danson appeared to be going through account books. With evident reluctance, she led the way up the staircase behind Mrs. Breckinridge.

At the top, she pointed toward a door. "Through there. A tent should be easy enough to find. Step lightly and don't bother anything else up there."

"Thank you." Jamie tried out his smile on the woman again, but she gave him a sour look in return that said more than words before she headed back down the stairs.

The attic was packed with boxes and trunks. A tent should be, as Miss Simpson had said, easy to find, but the light was dim. Not only was it near sundown, the two small windows obviously hadn't been washed for a long time. Maybe that could be one of his extra jobs to pay for the meals Miss Simpson appeared to begrudge him.

He needed a flashlight. He started at one end of the attic and worked his way through stacks of everything imaginable. Chairs. Crates full of dolls. Trunks of clothes. Christmas decorations. Books. A cradle. Finally a canvas bag clanked when he nudged it with his toe. The metal poles of the tent.

He picked it up and made his way back toward the attic steps. The muted sound of voices came up through the floor, but he couldn't make out words. On the way out, he grabbed a couple of wool blankets and then spied what might be a camping cot, folded up and tied in a bundle. He added that to his collection. Surely Miss Simpson wouldn't mind him borrowing a little comfort. As long as he didn't eat too much.

When he came out in the upstairs hallway, Mrs. Breckinridge called him. He had laid his finds down and followed her voice to the bedroom. And there was Piper. What in the world had been wrong with him that he had stayed away from her so long?

He kept his feet rooted to the floor in the doorway, when what he wanted to do was throw caution to the wind and grab Piper in his arms.

"What are you doing here?" Surprise froze her smile.

Surely she knew she was the reason he was there. Plain and simple. But that wasn't what he'd told the woman propped up on pillows in her bed. So he kept up the farce.

"The editor of the Danville newspaper sent me down here to write a piece about the frontier nurses." That was mostly true.

"And the couriers. Mustn't leave out the couriers." Mrs. Breckinridge sounded amused. "They are very important to our operation here."

"That's great." Piper's smile looked more polite than genuine. "Surprises all over the place today. First Truda and now you. I knew Truda might be coming, but I haven't heard from you in months." She stared at him a moment and repeated, "Months."

"I'm not much of a letter writer."

Again Mrs. Breckinridge spoke up. "That's not a very good admission for an aspiring writer. But a man of action isn't a bad thing, Piper. A woman of action either. Sometimes you have to grab the bull by the horns." The woman frowned. "I've always thought that's such a silly saying. Not particularly wise to grab a bull by the horns. But be that as it may, it does appear the two of you know each other. And I have gotten promises from both of you that I will not have to worry about any but the most proper behavior between friends. Correct, Piper?"

"We are friends," Piper said. "Have been since we were kids."

"You're not children any longer. So do I have your word, Mr. Russell?"

"I would never do anything to hurt Piper," Jamie said.

"Hmph," Mrs. Breckinridge said. "If I can read faces, and I can, it appears that what you say and what has transpired in the past may not be completely factual."

When Jamie started to say something, the woman waved her

hand at him. "Off with you both. You need to set up a tent, young writer. And dear Piper—or rather Danny here at Wendover—needs to do some paint removal." She peered at Piper. "You did take care of your horse?"

"Kermit offered to do it," Piper said. "He told me I shouldn't keep you waiting."

"Put the fear of God into you, did he?" Mrs. Breckinridge laughed. "That Kermit. But I'll warn you. He will find a way to get that favor repaid. I'm guessing you have some tack cleaning in your future."

"I can clean tack," Piper said.

"I can help," Jamie said.

"I love a willing helper." Mrs. Breckinridge looked between Jamie and Piper. "But tomorrow, Piper, you will need to squire your aunt around. Take her to the hospital and then to Red Bird Center or back to Wilder Ridge or wherever Aileen tells you. She'll know if any supplies need to be delivered. With your aunt along, perhaps young writer can go with you to see the hospital." Mrs. Breckinridge peered at Jamie. "You can ride a horse, I assume."

"I can ride," Jamie said.

"Then it's settled. Now go. Go." She waved them toward the door.

Jamie stepped to the side to let Piper go ahead of him. She didn't even look over at him. He hoped she was merely giving him the cold shoulder because Mrs. Breckinridge was watching. He hoped. It could be he should have been a better letter writer.

When they reached the pile of things he'd brought down from the attic, he touched her shoulder. "Hey, Piper, think you could help me with some of this?"

He could carry it all, but if she helped, she'd have to go outside with him where they could talk without other ears listening.

"I suppose so. Since I'm going that way anyway." She didn't sound thrilled.

He handed her the two blankets. "It's really nice of Mrs. Breckinridge to let me use her tent."

"You must have given her that smile that knocks over all the women."

Jamie picked up the cot and tent and hefted them up on his shoulder. "Didn't work on Miss Simpson. She would like me to disappear."

When Piper started down the steps without saying anything, he whispered, "Do you want me to disappear too?"

"I thought you already had." She glanced back at him. "Disappeared."

"Here I am."

"So you are. But the question is why." This time she didn't look around but led the way through the sitting room and into the dining area, where Truda and Miss Simpson looked up from their ledgers.

"I see you found the tent." Miss Simpson frowned at him. "And more."

"I saw the blankets and the cot and hoped you wouldn't mind." Jamie didn't bother trying his smile on her.

Miss Simpson sighed. "You do need something to sleep on besides the ground, I suppose. Since it seems you're staying."

Truda looked at her and then winked at Jamie. "Tell you what, Aileen. Let me sponsor him for a little stay here the way I'm sponsoring Piper. He was so very helpful to me yesterday with little Thomas. I don't know what I would have done if Jamie hadn't come to the rescue."

"Rescue? What rescue?" Piper asked.

"I'll explain it later, dear," Truda said. "It's a long story and one that you'll find hard to believe, I'm sure. Aileen says you will be showing me around tomorrow and we'll have more than enough time to talk. But right now we're in the middle of all these figures and you still have paint speckles everywhere. So I'll see you in the morning."

"Mrs. Breckinridge says Jamie can go to the hospital with us," Piper said.

"Oh, that's wonderful. Jamie can tell me all about what happened with Thomas. We'll have a grand time catching up on everything."

"And with everybody." Piper smiled at her aunt as if the two of them were sharing a secret.

"Behave, Piper." Her aunt tried to look stern, but it didn't quite work.

Piper actually laughed. "Oh, I will. Never fear. I do not plan to do anything to jeopardize the rest of my summer here."

When she headed on out the door, Jamie told the two women good night and followed her. Once outside, he said, "I get the feeling you're mad at me."

"Mad at you?" Piper sounded as if that was the farthest thing from her mind, but Jamie could see past her words. "Why in the world would I be mad at you? You have a perfect right to do whatever you want. To not write me. To forget we were ever friends. To see other people."

Other people? He didn't know where that came from. She was the one seeing other people. But now wasn't the time to bring up Braxton Crandall. He hoped never to bring up Braxton Crandall. "I'm sorry."

"I am too." She blew out a long breath. "But let's forget all that and be the friends we told Mrs. Breckinridge we were."

"That might be easier if you weren't angry with me."

"I'm not angry." But she didn't sound happy as she moved down the pathway. "So where are you setting up the tent?"

"I don't know. I'll hunt a level place somewhere." He gestured toward the hill behind the house with his free hand.

"Level? On that hill?"

Her smile gave his heart hope. "If Mrs. Breckinridge could pitch the tent on this hill, then I can."

"Good luck with that. Think you can carry the blankets now?"

"Sure. Can you tuck them under my arm?" She came enticingly close as she did as he asked.

She stepped back quickly. "I need to go scrub off some paint."

"I don't know. You look cute with white freckles."

She didn't look back at him as she headed on down the path, but she laughed. That was even better than a smile.

He climbed up the hill and dropped the tent on a fairly level spot. With night falling, he hurried to get the tent set up. The cot just fit inside. He hoped it wouldn't slide down the hill with him on it.

Stars were appearing in the sky as he walked down to get his bag from where he'd stashed it on Mrs. Breckinridge's porch. He looked up at the stars and whispered a thank-you prayer. So what if his stomach was growling because it had been hours since he ate something in Hazard? Miss Simpson wasn't likely to show him to the kitchen, but he had the promise of breakfast come sunrise.

With Piper in sight.

CHAPTER
TWENTY-NINE

"Who is he? And why is he here?" Marlie pounced on Piper as soon as she went into their room to get a towel and clean clothes.

Even Suze watched Piper with unconcealed curiosity.

"Just an old friend who happens to be here to write an article about the Frontier Nursing Service for his paper back home."

"Uh-huh," Marlie said. "And I'm going to do the jitterbug on the moon. We saw his face when he got here and asked where Piper Danson might be. Right, Suze?"

"Well." Suze ran her hand down the crease of her jeans. "We might be able to believe the 'old friends' story and that it's just a coincidence you both happen to be here at Wendover at the same time except for the look on his face when we told him you weren't here." Suze grinned.

"Yeah, except for that." Marlie snorted a laugh. "You'd have thought somebody stole all his chickens." She shook her head. "I've been in the mountains too long. Talking about chickens. I don't even like chickens. Always trying to peck your shoelaces."

"Chickens aren't so bad," Piper said. "At least they won't mash your toe if they step on it like a cow will. Do you believe it, girls? I milked a cow last night."

"Don't try to change the subject. We want to know about that good-looking guy out there." Marlie pointed toward the door. "That dreamboat with a smile to stop your heart who followed you to the mountains." She sighed.

"He doesn't have a roadster," Piper teased, since Marlie was always talking about riding off with somebody in a roadster.

"Or a horse, but if he'd had a horse, he would have been riding up in the mountains looking for this girl we know." Suze lifted her eyebrows. "I'm surprised Mrs. Breckinridge didn't send him packing. No girl-boy adventures allowed around here."

"She made that very plain," Piper said. "Look, he's a friend. That's all. And I've been ordered by the boss to get this paint off my face and arms."

"You are somewhat spotted," Suze said.

"Just a friend." Marlie smiled. "We should all have friends like that."

"I'll tell you all about him," Piper said. "Tomorrow. Now I've been painting doors and porch posts all day and I'm exhausted. And starving."

"Your friend is probably hungry too. He didn't get here in time to eat with us," Suze said. "Where is he anyway? Did Miss Aileen run him off?"

"She wanted to," Marlie said.

"Mrs. Breckinridge told him he could set up a tent and sleep out there on the hill," Piper said.

"You have got to be kidding," Suze said. "A tent!"

"Don't ask me. I'm the new girl on the block." Piper grabbed her towel and clothes. "And I'm going to scrub off some paint."

Piper turned on the shower long enough to get wet and then turned it off while she lathered up. They had limited water and everybody was expected to conserve it. It didn't matter if she was covered with paint spots. Or white freckles.

Jamie did have a way with words. And that smile. What was he doing here? And what about that pretty blonde in Louisville? But Piper had written to him with a claim of old friendship. She could stand by that. They were friends. But somehow she'd have to keep her heart in check. It had wanted to jump clear out of her chest when she saw that smile. Oh, Jamie.

Piper finished her shower, but she couldn't tell if she still had paint spots or not. She hadn't brought a lamp to the bathroom with her, and very little light was left in the day to filter through the high window. The hallway was even dimmer, but every step was familiar. She knew which planks squeaked, which doors to tiptoe past because the person who slept there was early to bed. Miss Aileen was usually one of those, but tonight she might still be poring over books with Truda.

In her own room, the lamp was still lit. Suze was gone and Marlie was in bed with the sheet pulled up over her head. She roused enough to say, "We expect a better story tomorrow, Danny girl." She turned over and went back to sleep.

Piper's stomach growled as she combed out her hair. It seemed like forever since she'd eaten a jam sandwich with Nurse Hankins at Wilder Ridge. They had carried the sandwiches outside where they sat on the front steps and listened to the birds while they ate. Then they'd gone back to painting.

As quietly as possible she reached into her stash of snacks. She still had several candy bars from her last trip to Hyden. That made her remember Suze saying Jamie didn't have supper either. His stomach would be growling too.

Would it be improper to take him a candy bar? As one friend to another.

She picked up three of the bars and put out the lamp before she slipped out into the hallway to tiptoe over to tap on Suze's door. She nearly always stayed up late making her drawings of plant life.

When Suze opened the door, she kept her voice low. "You don't look as speckled." She pulled the door wider. "Want to come in?"

"No, I wanted to see if you'd go with me to take Jamie a candy bar. I don't know whether Mrs. Breckinridge would consider that improper or not, but he's probably hungry."

Suze gave her a look. "Two's company and three's a crowd."

"Exactly."

"Sure then, why not? I didn't really get to talk to him earlier. Marlie was the one filling him in on your absence. I was working on Puddin's leg."

"Is it better?"

"I don't know. Kermit shook his head when he looked at it. Not a good sign." She went back to blow out her lamp. No one ever left a lamp or candle burning in an empty room. Miss Aileen impressed on them the danger of fires.

"He's such a sweet horse. Slow as a snail, but sweet."

"Nobody ever falls off him." Suze led the way down the hallway. She looked back to whisper at Piper. "We better tiptoe past Miss Aileen's room."

"She was still at the Big House looking over account books when I was there a little bit ago."

"Then we'd better run to get out of sight before she sees us," Suze said. "Three's a crowd or not, she might not be happy with us having a rendezvous with your young man."

"He's not my young man. Simply a friend."

"But you want him to be your young man."

"You're the one saying that. Not me. My father has the same as promised me to Braxton Crandall. And Jamie has a girlfriend. I think friends will have to do."

"Don't you think it should be your promises that matter? And you must be wrong about that other girlfriend."

Piper didn't answer for a moment as they climbed the hill toward where the shape of the tent was visible. Stars spilled across the sky, more appearing every second. The waning moon had yet to come up. Finally Piper said, "My father wants what's best for me. And I like Braxton okay. As my mother once told me, love can grow."

"If you say so. Actually, Braxton is a great guy, but I'm not sure you will be doing him any favors if you marry him when you're carrying a torch for some other guy."

"I told you. Jamie is a friend. That's all. Besides, it's not like Braxton is in love with me. He barely knows me. When I talked to him, he sounded as though he'd made a business decision. Time to have a wife." Piper deepened her voice as though talking for Braxton. "Hmm, that Piper Danson's father didn't lose his money in the crash. She may do."

"A business deal. That sounds awful." Suze covered her mouth to muffle her laugh. "But at the same time, I know what you mean, except one has to wonder what makes a proper wife. Do you think there is such a creature? "

"My mother is a proper wife."

"Not mine. She's always telling my father what's what. She's the new generation of women. One that most of us will be running along behind, because anyone who's paying attention can see that things are changing now that women have the vote. And about time too."

"My mother was a suffragette before she married."

"See. You have female rebel blood. You don't have to let your father push you into this niche he thinks you should fit. You can burst out of those confines. Design your own life. If you want to."

"Sometimes I don't know what I want. That's why I like it here so much. Totally free of romance and decisions about men."

"At least before today and you started worrying about this man's empty stomach."

"My *friend's* empty stomach. I'd be just as worried if you hadn't had anything to eat."

"I would hope so. You did grab a candy bar for me too, didn't you?" Suze looked over to where all was quiet at Jamie's tent. "What do you do when you visit someone in a tent? Knock on the tent flap?"

"No need to knock." Jamie stuck his head out through the flap. "I heard you and hoped you were coming my way." He crawled out and stood up to greet them.

"Hope we didn't wake you," Piper said.

"Sleep? With all this racket going on?"

"Racket," Suze spoke up. "We weren't that noisy."

"Not you." Jamie looked at Suze. "The frogs. An owl out there somewhere. Dogs barking. And birds singing. Are birds even supposed to sing at night?"

"The whippoorwill," Piper said.

"Yes, now that you mention it, that is what it said."

Piper couldn't see Suze's face very well, but she knew she'd be frowning at Jamie's complaints. "He really loves it, Suze. Don't you, Jamie?"

He laughed. "Actually, I do. It's been a while since I camped out under the stars. I think God must have added a few million since then." He put his hands on his hips and stared up. "This place is amazing."

"That's good to hear," Suze said. "I was about to turn Danny around and head back down the hill. With your candy bar."

"Candy bar?" Jamie's teeth flashed in a smile. "That changes everything. I'd ask you inside, but the stars up above and the music from the trees are better out here anyway. Besides, I doubt we'd all fit. Do you think Mrs. Breckinridge really slept in this tent out here on this hillside? Really?"

"If she said she did, then she did," Suze said. "They say she just rode by this place and fell in love with the spot and that's why she built her house here."

"I should be taking notes."

"Too dark for that." Piper was beginning to feel like she was the third wheel instead of Suze. Except Jamie did keep sneaking looks over at her. Her eyes had adjusted to the night enough that she could see his face. But she wasn't out here to make a conquest, merely to give a friend a candy bar to allay his hunger.

"Yeah. I'm going to wish I'd stumbled over a flashlight up there in that attic."

"I think I have an extra you can borrow. I'll give it to you tomorrow." Suze held out her hand toward Jamie. "I'm Susan Tipton. Suze here in the mountains. I don't think we were ever properly introduced this afternoon."

"Glad to meet you, Suze." He shook her hand. "I'm Jamie Russell, wannabe journalist and friend to the lovely Piper Danson."

"Danny to us." Suze poked Piper. "She's the one with the candy in her pocket, but it appears she may let us starve before she shares it."

"Oh, sorry." Piper handed them each a candy bar. "Hunger must be making me forgetful." Or it could be standing close to Jamie Russell was making her heart pound so hard it was shaking her brain too much to think.

"That can do it." Jamie sat down on the ground. "Won't you lovely ladies join me for a late-night repast here on the front stoop of my abode?"

"You sound more like a poet than a journalist." Suze sat down.

"Do you think we should?" Piper hesitated to join them, remembering Mrs. Breckinridge's orders, while knowing how very much she did want to sit down next to Jamie and lean her head against his shoulder.

"Sure, you should." Jamie patted the ground beside him, the very place Piper wanted to sit. Suze was on his other side.

"We'll get chiggers." Piper sat down, but she made sure to leave space between her and Jamie.

"Won't be the first time." Suze tore open her candy wrapper.

"But it's not every day we can go to a dinner party under the stars where they serve our favorite food. Chocolate."

"You're a lifesaver, Piper." Jamie took a bite of his candy. "I was feeling kind of lean."

"You should have bought some supplies in the town." Piper didn't like how she kept sounding like somebody's mother. But the memory of the blonde girl in Louisville kept poking her. It was best she keep thinking like a mother. Or at least a sister.

"I guess so, but you know me. Sometimes I forget to think ahead," Jamie said. "Besides, I had no idea where I might land when I got here."

"Probably didn't think it would be on a hillside in a tent," Suze said as she tore the rest of the wrapper off her candy bar.

"You're right about that. I feel far from home here," Jamie said. "Although it's not really that far in miles."

"Suze is the one far from home," Piper said. "She's from New York City."

"Really?" Jamie looked at Suze. "And what brings you all the way down here to this spot on a mountainside?"

"I wanted to try something different," Suze said. "At least that's how I felt last summer. This year, I couldn't wait to get back. I love it here where I'm doing something that matters." She looked around Jamie toward Piper. "Is that how you feel too, Danny?"

"I'm not an old hand the way you are," Piper said. "But yes, it is."

"Okay, your turn, Mr. Russell," Suze said. "Why are you here?"

"Do you want the truth, Miss Tipton?" Jamie asked, but he wasn't looking at Suze. He was looking at Piper.

"Of course. Is there anything else?" Suze said.

"I could tell you many things. That I want to write a story. That like you and Piper, I seek adventure and purpose. Both of those could be true, but not the real reason why I'm sitting here on a hill in the Appalachian Mountains under the stars." Jamie didn't reach out and touch Piper, but his voice wrapped around her.

"So are you going to give us the real reason, Mr. Russell, or leave us to wonder?" Piper almost whispered the words.

"Perhaps wondering is best."

"Perhaps. If the truth is too hard to say." Piper turned her eyes away from Jamie to stare up at the sky. In the silence that followed her words, she wasn't sure she couldn't hear the stars twinkling.

Suze yawned and got to her feet. "One truth is that, though the stars still shine, the candy is gone. Soon the morning sun will bring a new day with work to do for couriers who won't have time to ponder why they are here. So good night, Mr. Russell."

"So glad you came to dinner, Miss Tipton." Jamie scrambled to his feet too and reached down a hand to help Piper up. "Thank you for the candy, Piper."

His hand felt strong and right in hers. How many times had he helped her up just like this? She pulled her hand free, and in silence, she and Suze made their way down to the Garden House.

When they got inside, Suze stopped at the door to her room and looked at Piper. "You are the reason he's here. You know that, don't you?"

"I saw him with another girl."

"No other girl is here now. He loves you."

"How do you know?" Piper whispered.

Suze touched Piper's cheek. "I saw it written in the stars. Good night, Miss Danson, you lucky girl."

CHAPTER
THIRTY

"The first giggle I hear in regard to my riding ability, I'll write you out of my will," Truda warned as she clambered aboard a horse they called Dickens. She just hoped it wasn't named that because the animal was in the habit of scaring the dickens out of his riders.

Piper and Jamie were already aboard their horses. *Aboard* wasn't the right word. Were Truda to say that, both youngsters would laugh so hard they'd fall off their horses. Mounted. That was the word. But aboard seemed more correct for Truda, who felt a little at sea. Not only had it been a while since she was on a horse, she had never sat easy in any saddle.

People always assumed she would be a fine horsewoman, but she only rode a four-legged creature if she had absolutely no other choice. She'd never warmed up to horses. At least not riding them. She loved stroking their velvet noses and feeding them apples. That was fine. So was riding in a carriage pulled by a spirited team of horses, although she much preferred the horseless carriages of modern times.

Cars with wheels. That was the thing. Except here in these mountains, cars with wheels lacked accessible roads up into the hills. Piper said the creeks were often used as roads. As if that made any sense at all, but Piper claimed Truda would understand once she saw the terrain.

She saw cars in Hyden. Trucks too. She'd ridden from Hazard to Hyden in a kind of bus made out of a long car. But Suze, one of the couriers, had met her in Hyden with a horse for the ride to Wendover. Suze had been wonderful, not hurrying Truda, and when they forded the river, she'd taken Truda's reins and led the horse across. All Truda had to do was not fall off in the river. She did manage to keep her seat then. She wasn't sure she'd manage it again, but nothing for it except to try.

Were she to actually be unseated in the river or anywhere along the way, she would be sure to hear laughter as long as she didn't seem injured. Perhaps she should practice some pitiful moans, just in case. Either that or laugh first. That was generally a good way to keep the psyche from being wounded by others' smiles.

Not that she wasn't happy to see the smiles this morning. Bright as the sun coming up over the hills. This place was as beautiful as Piper had said in her letters. Trees and flowers. A blue sky with white clouds that seemed near enough to touch. The cows and pigs wandering around wherever added to the lovely country feel while making it necessary to watch one's step even in the yard to what they called the Big House.

Mrs. Breckinridge hadn't been at breakfast. Aileen said she could be still recuperating from her trip, since travel was so hard for her due to fracturing her back the year before. Or that she might be out feeding her geese.

"If you see those geese, avoid them at all cost," Aileen cautioned. "They're mean as snakes, but Mrs. Breckinridge does love her Jack and Jill goose and gander."

Breakfast was delightful with the couriers there, along with the rest of the staff. Lively talk of the day's plans filled the air around the long table. Good food too. The mountain air did give one an appetite. Jamie Russell found a place at the far end of the table, probably to avoid Aileen's evident displeasure at him being there at all. A good-looking young man in the midst of her courier girls spelled trouble to her, and with the way the girls were sliding their eyes toward Jamie, she could be right. The only girl who studiously considered the food on her plate and didn't take one glance toward Jamie was Piper. To Truda, that proved Jamie's face was where Piper most wanted to linger her gaze.

Jamie, on the other hand, was watching Piper every time Truda looked his way. The boy had it bad, but he wasn't so lovesick that he had lost his appetite. He had finished off every biscuit, and a good thing. He was entirely too thin, but young people were like that. Could eat a horse without gaining the first ounce.

She stroked Dickens's neck. "Not you," she muttered under her breath. Around here, nobody would ever consider eating a horse. They were necessary partners with the nurse midwives to get care to the mountain people.

"Being able to work with the horses is especially important for our couriers," Aileen had told Truda. "Your niece is well accomplished in that area. While I am in charge of the couriers and thus the horses as well, I have to depend on the girls to tell me what's needed. And Kermit, our hired man. I can ride, but only if I have to, and I certainly have no desire to hammer loose horseshoe nails back into a hoof or comb burrs out of horses' tails. I'm continually amazed at how eager these girls are to do whatever is needed. Sometimes they volunteer to stay with the horses in their stalls overnight when one is ill. Your niece did just that a week ago."

"I'm not surprised. She has always loved horses," Truda said.

"I suppose that does help, but some of the tasks with horses are less than pleasant. However, as odd as it may sound, I do think what the girls dread most is Mrs. Breckinridge's afternoon teas." Aileen made a face. "I understand. I seem to lack proper tea-making skills myself. Very difficult to get it exactly right for

Mrs. Breckinridge. Not only that, but when we have guests, she expects the girls to remember how they like their tea after they are served once. Sugar, no sugar, cream, no cream, and so on."

"That must test their memory," Truda said.

"Indeed. But the girls are generally up to the challenge of whatever they are asked to do, although some are like I was when I first came. A bit overwhelmed. Oftentimes I still am. *Can't* is not a word Mrs. Breckinridge ever wants to hear from any of her staff or nurses. She is somewhat more understanding with the couriers." Aileen smiled. "But in spite of the difficulties we face here, we all feel privileged to be part of this service. Especially the couriers, I think."

As Piper led the way down to the river, she did look very happy to be at Wendover, but Truda suspected some of this morning's glow had to do with the young man riding with them. If Erwin's plan to match Piper with Braxton Crandall had ever had a chance, it could be slipping away.

Seeing Piper acting as though the sunshine was a gift sent particularly for her this day made Truda smile. She supposed she should consider the comfortable life Piper might be passing up.

But then, at times comfort could be overrated. Just look at her. While she was far from comfortable on this horse as he stepped into the river, at the same time this was exactly where she wanted to be. Even if the whole trip turned out to be an old woman's foolishness.

She wasn't that old, she amended. She was in good health. At forty-five she surely had many more good years ahead of her. Nobody ever said a middle-aged woman couldn't fall in love. Or act a fool by thinking she might be in love with a man she hadn't seen for twenty-plus years. A man she'd only seen for one brief evening.

When she thought about it in the clear light of day, she realized she was being an absolute idiot, but every person should be allowed one idiotic dream in her lifetime. She wasn't going with the expectation that she and Jackson would do more than exchange a few pleasantries and perhaps wonder how the other one had gotten so old. She blushed when she remembered how long she'd spent in front of a mirror that morning, trying to decide how old she did look. When she twisted to the side and peered at her rear in the mirror, she had smiled. At least she hadn't put on weight. She looked the same as she had years ago, except, of course, for the aging.

Right. Except for those wrinkles beginning around her eyes and gray hairs sneaking in among the dark brown tresses. As water splashed up around her, she could almost feel the waves she'd worked so hard to crimp in her hair wilting in midstream.

Midstream. That's where she was in her life. While she was absolutely out of her mind with this fixation on a man she'd built up in her imagination, that didn't mean she couldn't change her life. She didn't have to stay at her father's bank as though he were still pulling all her strings. She was an independent woman with the wherewithal to take care of herself.

She could quit her job and take her turn serving food to the hungry in a soup kitchen. She could set up an easel in a park and paint landscapes. She'd always wanted to do that. The landscapes around her now, as she followed after Piper, were nice. She could set up that easel right here at Wendover. Maybe volunteer to help Aileen with the books or do some sort of fundraising work for Mrs. Breckinridge. It might be interesting to live in the hills for a while. Sometimes one should go with the current and try something new. When they were midstream. When they had the means to do so.

Poor young Russell trailing behind her had no means if the gossip about his family was to be believed, and Truda supposed it was. But he seemed to have plenty of spirit and he was so very young. Opportunities would come his way. She did hope Piper would see that and not let Erwin bully her into doing something she'd regret.

Truda really must have a talk with her brother. Another talk. But perhaps she should simply telephone him. Let him yell at her over the phone line instead of in her parlor. For sure, Erwin wouldn't be pleased to know Jamie Russell was here in the mountains.

Dickens plodded along behind Piper's horse as if he knew the trail so well he didn't need to keep his eyes open. But Truda's eyes were open, and when she saw Hyden Hospital up the hill, her heart did a funny little stutter beat.

"I hope Dr. Jack is here," Piper called back over her shoulder.

Not once since receiving Piper's letter saying she'd met Jackson had Truda considered him not being here if she came to Hyden. As though he would be at the hospital watching out the window for her to show up. Truda almost laughed out loud. All this wondering and preparing and then he might not be there. He could have picked this week to go on a European tour or be attending a medical convention somewhere. Perhaps in Louisville. Wouldn't that be a joke on her? Serve her right for building up this meeting as though it was going to mean something, when actually it meant nothing at all.

She sat up a little straighter on Dickens as they started up the hill toward the hospital. Time to change her thinking. She was here to tour this hospital built by a woman who did not know the word *can't*. That was it.

They rode up to the front entrance and dismounted. Piper took Truda's horse. "Wait here, Truda, while I find the horses some water and a place in the shade." She peered over at Jamie. "You can wait here too if you want."

"What if all three of your horses try to run in different directions?" Jamie said.

"They won't." Piper reached for his reins, but he didn't give them up.

"Just in case, I better come along. If Truda doesn't need me to keep her company." Jamie looked at her.

241

"Go." Truda waved them off. "We wouldn't want a stampede down the mountain, now would we?"

Piper rolled her eyes at Truda before she led the two horses away. Jamie trailed along behind her. Truda smiled as they disappeared around the building. A nice little breeze was blowing, but the sun was very warm. She should have worn a hat, but not only was she afraid of losing it on the ride over, she had her carefully coiffed hair to consider. Crossing the river had taken care of that. She pushed some sweaty strands back from her face. More reason that a hat would be nice now.

She moved up onto the hospital porch out of the sun. Aileen might not be happy that she'd let Piper and Jamie go off alone, but Truda trusted Piper's good sense. After all, she did take after Truda. Then again, on this day Truda seemed to have lost her good sense, acting like a besotted schoolgirl.

The hospital door flew open and a man came outside. "Truda Danson! Is that really you?"

Truda turned toward him. "Jackson?"

He came toward her, his hands out to take hers. He was older. Of course he was, but at the same time, she would have recognized him anywhere. Just as he must have recognized her—unless Aileen had let the hospital know she was coming. She took his hands in hers and the years fell away as she looked into those blue eyes that had watched her so intently that night they met.

"In the flesh." A smile lit up his face.

He wore a doctor's white coat with a stethoscope looped around his neck. His dark blond hair was thinner, with gray at the temples, and just as she had noted wrinkles on her face that morning in her mirror, he had his fair share. Smile wrinkles. Nothing bad about that.

"I'm surprised you recognized me after all this time," she said.

"Why wouldn't I?" His smile got wider. "You haven't changed a bit. Still the same lovely girl I met by happenstance at a dance when we were both too young to know what life meant."

"Oh, I don't know. If I remember correctly, we managed to cover some life topics that night." He still had her hands and she saw no reason to pull away.

"So we did. But at the same time, we had no idea, did we?"

"I suppose not."

His eyes seemed to delve into the depths of hers. "I've always regretted not coming back through Louisville after I finished my residency in Chicago."

"It's too late for regrets."

"So it is. Have you had a good life, Truda?"

"I have." She smiled as she added, "So far."

He laughed and squeezed her hands before turning them loose, and then as if it was the most natural thing in the world, he put his arm around her shoulders to turn her toward the door. "We can hope for a few more years, can't we? Come, let me show you around."

"I'm supposed to wait for my niece."

"Danny? A fine girl. I've been hoping you'd come visit ever since she said you were her aunt." He continued to walk Truda toward the door. "But come along. The hospital isn't so big that she won't find us." He stopped then. "Unless you'd rather wait."

Truda smiled. "She'll figure it out. I'd love to have the doctor show me around."

Some things were simply meant to be. Even if decades had to pass in between.

CHAPTER
THIRTY-ONE

Jamie wanted to break out in song, maybe dance, from the sheer joy of breathing the same air as Piper Danson.

If only she felt the same, but she hadn't really looked straight at him all morning. Instead she slid her gaze over him quickly, as though afraid simply looking at him would be breaking Mrs. Breckinridge's rules. Maybe it would.

Rules or no rules, he couldn't keep his eyes off her. He had to make up for lost time when he'd been wallowing in a trough of self-pity that kept him away from her.

They led the horses around the hospital to a pump with a bucket hanging on it. Jamie worked the pump while Piper held the horses. When he set the bucket down for the first horse, he said, "Are you going to be mad at me forever?"

Her eyes flew up to his then. "Mad at you? I'm not mad at you."

"Are you sure?" Jamie didn't bother hiding his doubt.

"Why would I be mad at you? We both have our own lives to live. I certainly can't blame you for going on with yours nor can you blame me for going on with mine. We haven't seen each other for months."

"I know. That's my fault, but you did write to me."

"So, a friend can't write a friend a letter?" She didn't wait for him to answer. "I suppose some friends can't write some friends letters." She handed him the bucket.

"You are mad." He pumped out another bucket of water.

"That's silly. If I was mad at you, would I have climbed up that hill in the dark last night to bring you a candy bar?"

"I suppose not. So you're not mad at me and we can be friends as long as we aren't hand-holding friends." He set the water down in front of another horse, then grinned at her. "You remember that, don't you? When you were seven and you asked your mother if we could be hand-holding friends."

She twisted her mouth to the side to hide her smile. "I guess I was always afraid of breaking the rules. Do you remember what Mother said?"

"I do. She looked at us very seriously and said as long as hand holding is all we did." He reached over and took her hand. "We held hands every time we were together for weeks."

"Until you stopped." Piper pulled her hand away to pick up the bucket to give back to him.

"Simon made fun of me. Said I was acting like a silly girl." Jamie shrugged. "I always paid too much attention to Simon." He pumped more water into the bucket for the last horse.

"I cried." Piper stared down at the ground.

"You did? But you told me you didn't care. That you were tired of holding hands anyway."

"A girl has her pride. Even at seven." She looked up with a grin.

"I guess a guy does too. Even at twenty-one."

"I'm not sure what you mean by that." Her smile disappeared as she studied his face.

"I don't know. Maybe I'm not saying it right. But I'd lost so much that I was afraid to risk more loss. More rejection. So I closed off to everything."

"You didn't give me much credit if you couldn't trust our friend-ship."

"No, I didn't." He looked straight at her, and this time she didn't turn her eyes away. "Will you forgive me?"

For a few seconds, he thought she might reach for his hand, but then she looked away. She picked up the bucket, dumped out the rest of the water, and handed it back to him to hang on the pump. "I told you. There's nothing to forgive. Life goes on."

He tried to block the image of Piper and Braxton Crandall on the balcony of the hotel the night of her debut. Close together. Perhaps Jamie was wrong to believe Piper had once wanted a future with him, that she might still want that. He was ready to throw caution to the wind and tell her he loved her, but she moved away with the horses toward some shade beside the hospital.

"Truda will wonder where we are," she said.

The moment was lost, but there would be other opportunities. A time that was right for giving his heart to Piper. No, that was wrong. She already had his heart. If only he had hers in return.

Piper should have asked about the blonde. Just been out with it. *Are you in love with another girl?* Suze said Jamie loved her, but Jamie had never said it. Ever. Then again, she had never said those three words to him either, although it was a wonder she hadn't when they had those hand-holding weeks. Thinking about that now made her smile, but she kept her face away from Jamie. Things were easier that way.

He was here to do a job. Write a story. She was here to do a job. Take care of horses and do whatever Miss Aileen said. Piper smiled again, thinking about Miss Aileen and how Jamie had fi-nally found a woman his smile couldn't win over. She wouldn't be happy if she found out Piper let Jamie take her hand in his. She would be even unhappier if she knew how much Piper wanted to keep holding hands.

But Piper had stepped away. Her task today was showing Truda how the Frontier Nursing Service operated. If they ran into Dr. Jack in the process, so much the better. Piper couldn't wait to witness that meeting. Earlier when Piper had mentioned the doctor's name, an extra sparkle lit up Truda's eyes. The same kind of sparkle Piper had seen in Dr. Jack's eyes when he talked about meeting Truda years ago.

When they got back to the front of the building, Truda was nowhere in sight. "She's not here."

"It's hot. She probably went inside out of the sun." Jamie looked at the building. "It's not very big for a hospital."

"I guess not, but it's pretty amazing they have a hospital at all. You'll have to ask Mrs. Breckinridge how she got it built so you can add it to your story."

"If she decides she has time to talk to me. Not that I'm complaining. I'm happy in my present company." Jamie gave her that smile she loved. It would be easy to forget Mrs. Breckinridge's rules.

She didn't allow herself to smile back. "Are you a good writer?"

"I've sold a few pieces. But you should know. You used to read what I wrote. Remember?"

"Those were made-up stories. Not articles for a newspaper."

"True, but you claimed they were good. Were you pretending?"

"I was just a kid. What did I know about writing?" She did remember sitting in the shade in her front yard, reading his stories. He'd bring a page a day. Said it was like a serial story in the newspaper. She had waited so eagerly for the next page. What was his next page going to say now? Or hers?

"Do you remember those stories?" His smile was back.

This time she couldn't keep from smiling as she started toward the hospital entrance. "You mean those stories about a boy named Skip and a girl named Sally." She laughed. "Sally, of all names."

"You picked it."

"I know. I so wanted something ordinary. I was tired of people looking at me as though I was from outer space when I told them my name."

"Yeah, that's why you told me to call you P.J. that time."

"And you did, until Mother threatened to make you stop coming over if you couldn't call me by my real name. I liked P.J. I should have suggested that when they were thinking up a nickname for me." She pulled open the door and went inside

"Danny isn't so bad. Sort of fits a girl who rides horses up into the hills."

"Danny the courier." She looked down the hallway. Truda was nowhere in sight. "The courier who lost her aunt."

"Truda can take care of herself."

"She never did tell me how you came to her rescue the other day."

Jamie shrugged. "It was nothing. I just took charge of this kid she had with her until his father came to get him over in the next town. Meant I had to sleep in the depot, but the guy there brought me breakfast."

Piper frowned. "She had a kid with her?"

"I was surprised about that too. I wasn't sure it was really her at first. But she said Mrs. Breckinridge had sent someone to hand over the kids to her in Louisville so she could bring them on down here. So she was making a delivery. A kid delivery."

"Interesting," Piper said. "I made a kid delivery the other day. Took a boy named Billy home from the hospital."

"The kid I had was Thomas, but I called him Tommy. He liked my stories."

"Of course he did. You probably had him fighting dragons to save a damsel in distress."

"No, it was wildcats, and he had a dog, not a girl." Jamie laughed.

"Danny." Nurse Thompson hurried down the hall toward them.

"Did you get Billy safely home? I worried after the thunderstorm came up."

"We took shelter in a neighbor's barn through the worst of it." Piper glanced around. Still no sign of Truda.

"Who's this with you?" The nurse looked from Piper to Jamie.

"Oh, sorry. Nurse Thompson, this is Jamie Russell. He's here to write a story about the Frontier Nursing Service for his paper back home." Piper looked over at Jamie. "Jamie, Nurse Thompson."

"Nice to meet you." Jamie gave her his winning smile that appeared to work better on the nurse than it had on Miss Aileen.

"Miss Aileen called to say you were coming. All three of you." Nurse Thompson looked over at Piper. "If you're looking for your aunt, no worries. Dr. Jack has her in hand. But when the two of you are ready to leave, Miss Aileen says to take your aunt to the Wilder Ridge Center. I know you were just up there, but Nurse Freeman needs some medicine."

"What about Jamie?" Piper asked.

"Ah, yes. Jamie." Nurse Thompson looked back at him. "Miss Aileen says you have volunteered to do whatever to help until Mrs. Breckinridge has time to give you that interview. So, since our housekeeper didn't make it in today, how are you with sweeping and mopping?"

"Not much experience with either, but point me toward the broom. How hard can it be?" Jamie didn't lose his smile, but he didn't look exactly happy about the turn of events.

"Good. Danny is to take your horse on to Wilder Ridge, where one of theirs came up lame yesterday. Nurse Freeman desperately needs a sound horse, with several babies due in her district." The nurse looked at Piper. "Then you're to bring her horse to Wendover, where you girls can coddle the animal for a while. Miss Aileen says you may need to spend the night at Wilder Ridge." Nurse Thompson blew out a little breath. "There. I think I've covered it all."

"All right. So where's my aunt?"

"Down the hall." The nurse pointed. She touched Jamie's arm. "And you, young man, come with me and I'll show you where to start."

Jamie looked over his shoulder at Piper. "See you later, P.J."

"P.J.? I thought they decided on Danny," Nurse Thompson said.

"That girl has many names," he said.

"Don't believe everything he tells you," Piper called after them. "He's a storyteller."

"A storyteller?" Nurse Thompson sounded interested. "Then he'll fit right in around here. These mountains are full of story-tellers."

Piper shook her head a little and headed down the hall to find Truda, who obviously had wasted no time finding Dr. Jack.

Or to have a good time. Piper followed the sound of Truda's laughter to a small office. Truda sat with her back to the open door while Dr. Jack perched on the edge of his desk, a cup of coffee in his hand, with his gaze locked on the woman in front of him. Piper couldn't see Truda's smile, but she could Dr. Jack's.

When the doctor noticed her there, he motioned to her. "Danny, come on in. We're swapping stories."

Truda looked around, an easy smile on her face. "Yes. Jackson was just telling me how one morning the nurses noticed a bed oc-cupied that had been empty the night before. It seems one of the local women came into the hospital in the middle of the night, found an empty bed, and crawled into it."

"That she did." Dr. Jack picked up the story. "She told the nurse she had appendicitis and turned out she was right. Luckily for her, we were able to operate before the appendix ruptured."

"Why didn't she tell somebody when she came in?" Truda asked. "She had to be in pain."

"Oh, definitely. But that's simply how people are here. Stoic but resourceful." Dr. Jack looked over at Piper. "Have you found that to be true with those you've met, Danny?"

Piper nodded. "Not only the mountain people but also the nurse midwives and the couriers."

"Perhaps it's something about the mountains," Truda said.

"What do you mean?" Dr. Jack asked.

"That Bible verse. The one about looking unto the hills from whence cometh my help. Perhaps just having the mountains rise up around you gives you a different kind of strength than when you see nothing but bricks and pavement. Here, you feel the earth beneath your feet. You see things growing." Truda's cheeks suddenly flushed and she looked down at her hands folded in her lap. "Oh dear, I didn't mean to get carried away."

"Preach on." Dr. Jack laughed. "I agree with you completely. These hills are an excellent place to feel the nearness of God. Agree, Danny?"

"I've heard the whippoorwill and seen the stars." Piper wasn't sure where that answer came from, but it was what spilled out. But not only did Truda and Dr. Jack not laugh, they both nodded as though her answer made perfect sense. And perhaps it did. She felt her spirit swell each time she looked up at the multitude of stars and heard the birds sing.

What made her feel just as happy inside was how these two in front of her kept looking at each other as though they'd been waiting to meet again all their lives.

Truda stood up. "It's been so good to see you again, Jackson." She looked over at Piper. "What's next on the agenda? And have you lost Jamie?" She looked back at Dr. Jack. "Jamie Russell is a young man who rode over with us from Wendover. He's here to write a story about the frontier nurses."

Piper shrugged. "Miss Aileen told Nurse Thompson to put him to work sweeping. Seems the housekeeper didn't make it in today."

"That Aileen." Truda laughed. "She's trying to make it hard on the poor boy. So what does Aileen have planned for us?"

"A nurse at the Wilder Ridge Center needs some medicine. Something I didn't take them the other day. And a horse."

"Then I guess you should go," Dr. Jack said. "I need to get back to work too. Did you get young Billy safely home, Danny?"

"I did. His mother was very glad to see him."

Dr. Jack caught Truda's arm as she stepped past him. "And I am very glad to see you, Truda. I'd be very pleased if you'd have dinner with me tomorrow."

"Are there restaurants here?" Truda asked.

"Some, but nothing fancy. However, I'm a fair cook." When Truda hesitated, he went on. "Bring Danny with you, if you want."

"That sounds delightful, but I don't know where you live and have no way to get there if I did. Except by horse, and I have to admit that I'm not an accomplished horsewoman. I'd be sure to fall in the river in the middle of the night and drown."

He laughed. "I'll come get you."

"By horse?"

"I have a truck that can make it to Wendover if the river isn't up. And it doesn't look like rain. Of course, that's barring an emergency here at the hospital."

"So if it doesn't rain, the river doesn't rise, and nobody needs your services here at the hospital, I'd be delighted to have dinner with you. But I'm sure Piper will have other duties, won't you, dear?"

"Oh yes." Piper bit the inside of her lip to keep from smiling. "You know how Miss Aileen is. She's sure to have something for me to do."

CHAPTER
THIRTY-TWO

Piper and Truda chatted about everything except what was on both their minds. They pointed out this or that tree or flower. Talked about the rough road. Swatted at horseflies. They had left Hyden behind and were riding side by side on a broad stretch of trail while Piper towed General behind her before Truda finally mentioned Dr. Jack.

"Do you like him, Piper?"

Piper played dumb. "Who? Jamie?"

"Don't be obtuse." Truda sounded irritated. "I don't have to ask if you like Jamie. That's plain as day. And I'm glad to see it. But don't tell your father I said that. He has made it very clear your friendship with Jamie is not to be encouraged. Told me that in no uncertain terms after Jamie showed up in Louisville the day you left."

"Oh?" Piper saw no reason to tell Truda she'd seen Jamie at the depot. With that blonde. "Do you know why he was in Louisville?"

"You, of course." Truda gave her a look. "To formally court you, it seems, since he went to your father's office to ask permission to call upon you."

"He didn't need permission for that." Piper gripped the reins so tightly Bella stutter-stepped, not sure what Piper wanted, and General bumped against Bella's rump. Piper pulled in a slow breath to relax.

Truda didn't seem to notice. "I agree, but he did ask anyway."

"I'm sure that went well." Piper could only imagine what her father might have said to Jamie. None of it good.

"You will be glad to know your young man didn't take no for an answer and made his way out to your house. Regretfully, you left that morning for here. Della says when she told him you weren't there, Jamie looked like he'd just found out the last piece of cake was gone." Truda laughed. "It's all about food with Della, but I might look sad too if I found out somebody else got the last piece of her strawberry supreme cake. That woman can cook."

"You're making my mouth water." *And my heart race*, but Piper wasn't about to admit that. Even to Truda. The blonde on the train platform was fading away. Perhaps no one special after all.

"But I'm not talking about Jamie and you know it. I'm asking about the doctor."

"Oh, Dr. Jack." Piper kept a straight face as she glanced over at Truda. "I've only talked to him a few times, but he seems very nice. I hear he's a fine doctor. Why? Are you feeling ill?"

Truda stripped some leaves off a trail-hugging bush and threw them at Piper. "You know very well why I'm asking, and it has nothing to do with my health. Or maybe it does. I have to admit my heart skipped a couple of beats when he came out of the hospital and called me by name. He remembered me from all those years ago."

Piper picked a leaf out of her hair. "And you remembered him."

"I did. And look at me acting like a silly teenager." Truda blew out a breath. "But it was so odd. Or maybe that's not the right word. Not odd at all. Rather remarkable or—"

"Incredible? Amazing?"

"Very incredibly amazing. We started talking as if all those years since I met him simply melted away." A smile lit up her face. "You're not going to believe this."

"It's already a little unbelievable, but let's hear it." Piper slowed Bella to an easy walk. She wanted to see Truda's face.

"I think I'm in love." Truda's eyes widened in astonishment. "With a man I've met twice. Obviously, the mountain air has made me lose my senses."

"Could be you should slow down your runaway heart."

"Slow down? Heavens, no. I love it. I love being in love." Truda laughed. "At my age you don't want to ponder too long if you have a chance for love. Of course, I have no idea if Jackson is feeling anything at all the same as I."

"He did invite you to dinner."

"So he did. And should he invite me to a church chapel to say I do, I might be ready for that too."

"Whoa, Truda. Don't you think you should have at least three or four meetings first?"

"Tomorrow will be three. But of course, you're right. I've gone crazy." Her smile faded as she peered over at Piper. "It might be better if you could embrace a little more craziness. And that boy Jamie too. The two of you tiptoe around each other as though you're on the edge of a great precipice and if you fall, you'll be swallowed up in a bottomless abyss."

"Swallowed up," Piper echoed.

"Exactly," Truda said. "Actually that might not be so bad. Swallowed up by love. If you aren't too afraid to trust the feeling." Truda gave Piper another look. "And I promise you, should Jackson and I move forward along this path, I'm not going to be afraid to embrace the feeling."

"I'm not afraid," Piper said.

"Then what are you?"

"A courier who purposely planned not to think about guys all summer while at Wendover. I never expected Jamie to show up."

"And I never expected to see Jackson again. Life is full of the unexpected."

As if to prove her words, a snake slithered across their path. Truda gasped and Dickens did a few fast steps to the side. Piper kept a firm hold on Bella's reins and those of the horse she was leading.

"Just a harmless cowsucker. Not a rattler," Piper said.

"That's a relief. I guess. But I have to admit, I'm not fond of snakes. Whatever kind."

"Suze says snakes are plentiful up here. She'll happily tell you all about them and how good they are for the ecology. She should be a biology teacher."

"I hear your Jamie has a position as a schoolteacher next year. At least, that's what your father said."

"How did Father know?"

"I suppose Jamie told him."

"I'm glad he's telling everybody else something," Piper muttered under her breath. The trail narrowed and she moved out in front of Dickens, towing General behind her.

Just because Truda was going off half-cocked, ready to believe she was in love with a man she hardly knew—actually didn't know at all—that didn't mean Piper had to follow suit. But then, her father wanted her to marry a man who was practically a stranger, and she had agreed to consider such a match. At least Truda thought she was in love. Piper knew she was in love. Just not with Braxton Crandall.

Nurse Freeman came out on the porch when they rode up. "Danny, I didn't expect to see you again so soon. But I'm glad to see you if you've brought the medicine I need for a patient tomorrow. And very glad to see you bring me a horse!" She peered around Piper toward General.

"I do have a package for you from Nurse Thompson." Piper slid off Bella to pull General forward. "And Miss Aileen sent you General."

"Wonderful." The nurse looked from the horse to Truda, still on Dickens. "Forgive my manners. I shouldn't have welcomed General before you, ma'am, but I am desperate for a horse with my Lady going lame. I have some babies threatening to come anytime now." She smiled. "But it's always a pleasure to entertain one of Mrs. Breckinridge's friends."

"This is my aunt, Truda Danson, as well as Mrs. Breckinridge's guest," Piper said. "Truda, Nurse Freeman."

Truda groaned as she dismounted. "It feels good to have my boots on terra firma again. I'm not the horsewoman my niece is." She stepped over to shake Nurse Freeman's hand. "But very nice to meet you, Nurse Freeman. I'm anxious to hear about your work here in the mountains."

"Wonderful," Nurse Freeman said. "Come in and I'll make some tea while Danny sees to the horses. Nurse Hankins is caring for a sick child in her district. And I must call on an expectant mother later today. She has some weeks to go, but we keep a watch on our mothers. Perhaps you'd like to ride along after the horses rest a bit."

"That sounds great." Truda handed her reins to Piper. "Can you handle all three horses?"

Nurse Freeman answered for Piper. "Don't worry about Danny. I've found these courier girls can do almost anything you ask of them. Your niece milked her first cow here the other day, and then painted our woodwork and porch posts. I daresay three horses will be no problem at all for her."

Piper hoped they would save her some tea, but the nurse was right. The horses came before pleasure. Always.

At the barn, poor Lady was standing light on one of her back hooves. After Piper rubbed down the other horses and watered and fed them, she lifted Lady's leg to check her hoof, but the shoe looked okay. She did feel some heat around her fetlock. The mare might have stepped wrong on a rock or in a hole. Kermit would know how to treat it back at Wendover.

She was heading to the house when the nurse and Truda came outside. Nurse Freeman said, "I should have had you leave the saddles on two of the horses. We're going to make that visit now, but the cabin is just down the way. Not far." She looked over at Truda. "An easy trail, I assure you."

"If you think your patient won't mind all of us barging in on her," Truda said.

"Most of our mountainfolk like meeting brought-in people." Nurse Freeman smiled. "At least that's what they call those of us who come from beyond the mountains. As curious as you might be about them, they're every bit as curious about you. And it will only be two of us. Danny can stay here and fix supper for us. Do you think fried chicken sounds good?"

Piper spoke up. "I don't know how to fry chicken."

Nurse Freeman waved her hand to dismiss Piper's concerns. "It's easy. You heat some grease in a frying pan, coat the chicken pieces in flour, and fry it up. And you can peel some potatoes and boil them."

That didn't sound terribly hard. "All right. Is the chicken in the refrigerator?"

Nurse Freeman laughed. "My dear girl, you forget where you are. No ice boxes or those fine new electric refrigerators up on this mountain, although I've heard some of the centers may get a kerosene-powered cold box. That would be amazing." She looked at Truda as if hoping she'd offer to donate one on the spot. "But no, the chicken is right out there." She pointed to some chickens pecking in a side yard. "They hatched out this spring and are a perfect size for frying. Pick a rooster. We keep the pullets for laying."

Piper was too astounded to speak.

The nurse went on. "One of the mountain women wrote down directions for me about how to prepare a fryer. When I came, I was as green as you, but if you want to eat up here, you have to learn some things. The instructions are on the kitchen table under the butcher knife." She moved past Piper toward the barn. "And some tea and a cookie for you too."

"I can't kill a chicken." Piper stared at the nurse. Milking a cow was one thing, but killing a chicken?

"Certainly you can. We're counting on you. But go enjoy your tea first. I'll saddle the horses." She ignored Piper's protests. "I'm not sure when Nurse Hankins will be back. According to how sick she finds the child. She might have to take her to the hospital."

There went the hope Nurse Hankins would show up to help her.

With a sympathetic look, Truda leaned close to Piper to whisper, "When in the mountains, do as the mountaineers do." Then she followed Nurse Freeman toward the barn.

Piper stared after them. The nurse couldn't really expect her to slaughter a chicken. But then she had expected her to milk a cow after Piper said she couldn't. Milking a cow was one thing. Killing a chicken was something else.

No need arguing with Nurse Freeman about it though. Piper headed to the house. She was thirsty. She needed that tea. Sans ice, of course. No ice. No ice boxes. She was foolish to ask about refrigerators. Her parents had only replaced their ice box in the kitchen with an electric refrigerator a few years before. At the time, Della had been jubilant.

If only Della were here with her now, to deal with this challenge. But hadn't Piper come to the mountains in search of something to test her comfortable life? But killing a chicken?

On the way inside, she admired the nice white doors and porch posts. A week ago she'd never painted doors. And now painting seemed an easy enough task. She ignored the paper folded under the butcher knife as she poured her tea and munched on a thick sugar cookie.

She stepped out on the back porch when Nurse Freeman and Truda rode past. As always, Truda sat too stiff in the saddle. After the sound of the horses faded away, the only noise was a breeze ruffling through the leaves and the chirp of a bird. Piper caught a flash of red among the branches. A cardinal. In the distance, a dog barked. Closer at hand, the chickens carried on a clucking conversation. Perhaps about which one of them was destined to be supper.

Shoving that thought aside, she considered the novelty of being alone with no one near enough to call on for help. Just her and the mountain. But she wasn't concerned. She smiled, thinking how different her summer had turned out to be than what she'd expected to endure. A round of debutante parties and events. Perhaps dates with Braxton Crandall as her father pushed her into marriage. But instead, here she stood, the mountain breeze on her face while Maxine's words on the train echoed in her mind. *"You get up high on those hills and the Lord just seems nearer."*

Standing on this porch with the birdsong in her ears, she did feel the Lord was near. That somehow he knew her lacks and could bolster her courage. She was happy to be sipping tea here on his mountain instead of seated in a parlor somewhere with an iced tea in a crystal goblet. Although the ice would be nice.

The thought of ice brought her back to the task at hand. She gave the chickens another wary look. At least she did know the roosters from the pullets. With a sigh, she went inside to slip the note out from under the thick handle of the big knife and stare at the concise directions.

Chop off the chicken head. Let it flop for a spell.
Douse it in a bucket of hot water.
Pluck off feathers.
Slit the underside and pull out the innards. Save the gizzard and the liver.

Piper looked up. What did a gizzard look like? She'd seen them fried crusty, but never before they were cooked. She shook her head.

Figuring out the gizzard was the least of her worries. Killing the chicken was the big worry. She stared at the butcher knife.

Maybe there wasn't any hot water. She couldn't do it if there wasn't any hot water, but a big kettle was simmering on the cookstove. Nurse Freeman must have left it there to be ready for whichever courier showed up to dress a chicken. Or rather undress it of feathers. A bucket sat by the stove too, ready for her, and a skillet was on the table next to the butcher knife.

She thought of Billy just up the hill from here. His mother had probably killed and cooked dozens of chickens. If only she could carry one of the doomed roosters up to their house and let them do what needed doing.

But no. It was her task. With a deep breath and much trepidation, she picked up the knife.

CHAPTER
THIRTY-THREE

Jamie could hardly believe he was riding up into the hills. He'd been resigned to janitor duty at the hospital. It wasn't so bad. Anybody could use a broom, and he liked talking to the patients.

One, a sweet little lady who looked to be pushing a hundred, said she'd make him some molasses cookies. She claimed a person hadn't lived until they had a molasses cookie. He was still talking to her when Nurse Thompson came to find him.

"You should have had the whole hospital swept by now," she said.

"Don't you fuss at the boy." The woman sat up in bed and shook a finger at Nurse Thompson. "I'm tellin' him about how eatin' a 'lasses cookie can make a feller smile."

"That's for sure, Miss Virgie, if it's one of yours." The nurse adjusted the woman's pillows. "But settle back and relax. We don't want to get your heart all in a twirl again, now do we? Fact is, I've got another job for Jamie."

Miss Virgie sank back against the pillows. "You watch her, son. She'll have you digging holes jer the fun of it."

"That's not true. I'd make him plant flowers or something."

Nurse Thompson gave the woman a mock frown before she turned back to Jamie. "But no shovels or brooms needed for this. We didn't give Danny one of the medicines they need up at Wilder Ridge tomorrow. So Miss Aileen says to let you take it."

"Walking?" Jamie asked.

"Good gracious," Miss Virgie said. "You'd be walking in moonlight 'fore you got there. Best take a horse or a mule."

"Good idea, but I seem to be lacking either of those."

"We've got that taken care of," Nurse Thompson said. "Dr. Jack keeps a horse stabled close by in case he gets a call to a place he can't get to in his truck."

"Plenty of places like that," Miss Virgie said. "They had to carry me down here on a bed. Good thing I've got me some strong grandsons. They'll do anything to get me better so's I can make them my 'lasses cookies." She chuckled.

"What if Dr. Jack needs it?" Jamie asked Nurse Thompson.

"We can always find a horse for emergencies." The nurse pointed him toward the door.

Miss Virgie called after Jamie. "You come on back anytime, young feller. I'll tell you about my honey cornbread next time. I could use some of that right now. Maybe I'll go on down to the kitchen and stir me some up."

"You stay right there in bed and behave," Nurse Thompson ordered. "You want to get well enough to cook for those grandsons again."

"I could adopt that one there." Miss Virgie pointed toward Jamie. "Can't never have too many grandsons."

"I'll remember that, Granny Virgie, and look forward to that molasses cookie," Jamie said.

That made every wrinkle in the old lady's face smile as she sank back down on her pillows.

Out in the hallway, the nurse said, "You are a charmer, aren't you?"

"I like people."

He did like people, he thought now, as he rode Sid, Dr. Jack's horse along the trail. He had the map one of the nurses drew for him memorized. Past three oaks standing like soldiers guarding the trail. Around a couple of boulders and then into the creek for a ways. Not a typical map, but then this wasn't typical country. At least none that Jamie had ever traversed even on the few trail rides he'd taken out west. Before the crash.

Jamie brushed that thought aside. He had to stop thinking about the crash. The family money was gone, but he had his strength and God-given abilities. Would that be enough? Especially for Piper, who was accustomed to so much more.

But he was here. He wasn't going to shy away from her answer, whatever that might be. If she said no, he'd pack up, resign the teaching job before he started, and head out west to write stories of new places. He was crazy to even think about asking Piper to share that dream. Women liked houses and families and stability. Didn't they?

He turned the horse out of the creek up the hill. The gelding was a spirited animal that stepped lively along the mountain trail.

Jamie felt the same energy. He was happy to be riding through the trees to where Piper would be. He should be close, but then the trail changed. Where it had looked plain enough coming out of the creek, now it was no more than a trace nearly covered over with bushes. The trail to the center shouldn't be petering out. They were bound to have plenty of visitors to keep the path beaten down.

He stopped and pulled the map out to study it. He must have turned out of the creek too soon. Nothing for it but to backtrack and give it another try.

"Don't make no sudden moves." A man stepped out of the bushes with a rifle pointed straight at Jamie.

He didn't look like Clem Baker, but it was plain there were similarities.

"I'm sorry if I'm trespassing. I lost my trail," Jamie said. "I'm headed to Wilder Ridge Center."

"Likely story. I'm thinkin' you're one of those feds out here poking around where you ain't got no business bein'." The man's gun stayed steady on Jamie.

He was thin and hard looking, with a felt hat pulled down low on his forehead to almost hide his eyes, but Jamie could see the grim line of his mouth.

Smiles weren't going to work on this man. Jamie sat stone still with his hands in clear view. "You've got me all wrong. I'm taking some medicine up to the center. They sent me from the hospital."

"They use girls for that," the man said. "But government men are all city-looking fellers like you."

"You're right about the girls, but one of the nurses needed this and I happened to be there handy."

"Handy to be hunting moonshine stills. Well, there ain't none around here to be found."

"I don't know anything about stills." Jamie tried to keep his voice strong, but he was trembling inside. This man meant business. "If you'll point me toward the center, I'll just ride on over there."

"I could do that." The man pushed back his hat brim with the gun barrel before he leveled it at Jamie again. "Or I could just shoot you and let the buzzards have you. I could use a good horse."

"It's Dr. Jack's horse. People would know that. Might get you in trouble." Jamie acted like shooting him wouldn't be the trouble, and he wasn't sure it would be if people thought he was a revenuer. He needed to change whatever was making him appear to be a government man, and fast. If he lived long enough.

The man stepped closer to look at Sid. "I reckon you're right about this being the doc's horse. But I ain't got no way of knowing you didn't steal it."

"If you'll go with me over to the Wilder Ridge Center, they'll vouch for me there."

"Matter of fact, I need to go over there anyhow to get something for my old woman." The man's eyes narrowed on him. "But if you ain't telling the truth, I'll shoot you there. Them nurses wouldn't turn me in. Not over a blamed revenuer." He shook the gun barrel at Jamie. "You get down off'n the horse. I'll ride. You can hoof it."

Jamie got down and smoothed the gelding's neck when he danced to the side.

"You like horses?" The man motioned Jamie away from Sid.

"I like horses."

"You ever had one of your own without having to steal the doc's?"

"I used to have a horse, and I didn't steal this one. They let me ride him."

"I ain't never had no fancy-riding horse. Just mules. They's better for hill country, anyhow." The man swung up on Sid.

Jamie considered making a run for it while the man didn't have the gun pointed at him, but the man was probably a crack shot and would get Jamie before he got out of sight.

Jamie walked in front of the horse back to the creek. He noticed every leaf, every squirrel chattering in the treetops, every breath as he wondered if it might be his last. He did hope he got to tell Piper he loved her before he died.

The man probably wouldn't shoot Jamie, but he obviously enjoyed scaring him. He'd done that well enough. A verse from Psalm 23 ran through Jamie's head. *Yea, though I walk through the valley of the shadow of death, I will fear no evil; for thou art with me.*

Somehow he didn't think the man behind him was evil. That was a funny thing to think, with a gun pointed toward his back. Not evil. Just mean. Ornery mean. Those were good words to describe him. Jamie almost smiled. With his insides quivering with fear, he was still thinking of how to write about this someday.

The trail out of the creek was plain as day. If he had found it, he'd be at the center by now. Maybe talking to Piper. Maybe telling her he loved her. Not maybe. He would tell her. Before he died.

When they got to the center, Piper was in the yard, chasing some chickens that were squawking and flapping away from her. With all the commotion, she didn't notice them.

"What's the girl doing?" the man muttered.

"Looks like she's trying to catch a chicken," Jamie said.

"Then I'm reckoning she ain't noticed that rattler curled up by the gate. Get down, boy, so's I can get a clear shot."

Jamie wasted no time dropping to the ground.

———

Catching a chicken wasn't all that easy. They squawked and scattered to all sides as if they knew exactly what Piper intended to do once she caught them. She finally cornered one of the young roosters beside the gate and grabbed it.

She had the chicken clutched under her arm when a rattling noise froze her in place. Slowly, she turned her head. By the gate post, a coiled snake rattled its tail. Slitted eyes stared at her from its raised head while its tongue slithered in and out.

Piper's mouth went dry as she tried to remember what Suze said to do if she happened across a rattlesnake. No sudden movements to make the snake strike. Ease away from it very slowly. Don't forget to breathe. While that last one had been what Suze told her about helping Nurse Robbins catch babies, it seemed good to remember now too.

Just as she started to inch back from the snake, a man yelled, "Don't move."

She froze again. A gunshot boomed. Piper couldn't keep from

jumping then, but it didn't matter, since the bullet hit the snake's head. The chicken squawked and tried to fight free, but Piper held on.

"Stick the blame chicken's head under its wing," the man said. "The stupid thing will think night's come."

Piper did as he said and the rooster went limp in her hands. She turned to look at the man.

"Mr. Taylor." Mann Taylor was astride a horse and Jamie was pushing up off the ground. "Jamie." She didn't know which of them she was the most surprised to see.

"You know him?" They both spoke almost in unison.

"I do. Know both of you." She looked from Jamie's amazed face to Mr. Taylor. "And I thank you, Mr. Taylor, for shooting the snake."

"You need to keep a better watch on what's around you, girl," Mr. Taylor said. "Else you're liable to get snakebit. Such might not kill you, but take my word for it. It ain't pleasant." He looked around. "Is the nurses here?"

"Nurse Freeman will be back soon." She looked at Jamie. "What are you doing here, Jamie? And how'd you get here? You couldn't have walked here that fast."

"I rode Dr. Jack's horse." Jamie nodded toward the horse Mr. Taylor was riding.

"And a fine horse it is." Mr. Taylor swung down off the horse, never losing his grip on the gun. He handed the reins over to Jamie. "If the girl knows you, I reckon as how I won't shoot you. This time. But I'm warning you. Don't go poking around in bushy thickets where you ain't got no business."

"Yes, sir."

Mr. Taylor made a crusty sound that might have been a laugh. He lowered the gun to point toward the ground. "You city folk get polite as all get-out when you're scared, but you can ease down. I ain't shooting nothing else today."

Piper moved away from the snake. Even dead, it made her shiver. Mr. Taylor strode across the yard toward it. "If you don't want the creature, I'll fetch it home." He picked the snake up by the tail and held it out toward Piper. It was almost as long as she was tall. "Less'n you want it for supper."

"No, no." Piper backed away. "I'm supposed to kill this poor chicken for supper." She kept its head under its wing as she stroked the chicken's feathers.

"Best think of it as food instead of petting it like a fool cat." He held out the snake again. "If'n you're too squeamish to kill the bird, snakes taste something like chicken."

"I'm too squeamish to cook a snake for sure," Piper admitted.

That made the man laugh again. "I ain't never figured out how brought-in people the likes of you two survive. Don't you ever eat meat?"

"Nothing we have to kill ourselves," Piper said. "We go to the butcher shop."

His eyes narrowed on her. "I'm doubtin' you ever set foot in a butcher shop." He looked over at Jamie, who seemed more than anxious to give the man room. "Or that feller who looks like a government man either. So you vouch for him?"

"He's here to help the frontier nurses for a while." Piper smiled at Jamie, who gave her a relieved look.

"Hmm. Then maybe he can kill that chicken for you." He jerked his head to the side to motion Jamie toward them. "Come on over here. I done told you I ain't gonna shoot you this time."

Jamie looped the horse's reins around the fence and stepped closer.

Mr. Taylor studied him a second. "You ever kill anything, boy?"

"Never anything I planned to eat except fish."

"Fish don't count. So now's your chance. Hand that chicken over and let the boy jerk off its head. He surely ain't as squeamish as you."

269

Piper held the chicken out toward Jamie, who looked every bit as squeamish as she felt.

"Jerk off its head?" Jamie gave the chicken a dubious look.

"I can get a knife," Piper offered.

Mr. Taylor let out a sigh. "Lord a' mercy, if you two ain't past useless. Here, boy, hold my snake." He held it out and Jamie took it, though gingerly. "Now give me that chicken."

Piper handed it over.

"Women's work," the man muttered as he gave the chicken's neck a twist and yanked off its head. He dropped the flopping chicken on the ground. "I ain't plucking no feathers. You can't figure that out, you'll have to eat feathers and all." He flung the head to the side.

Piper stared at the chicken. "Nurse Freeman left me directions."

"I reckon it had you chopping off the head. Some think that's more civilized, but the chicken is dead either way." Mr. Taylor's lips twisted in a sideways grin as he took back his snake and draped it around his neck. He motioned toward the chicken that had stopped flopping. "Boy, grab that up before the hens go to pecking at it. Blood messes with them. Sometimes the fool things will peck a wounded one to death. They's tasty, but not smart."

Jamie grabbed the dead chicken by the feet and held it up. He didn't look much happier holding the chicken than the snake.

"I'll get some hot water." Piper started toward the house.

Mr. Taylor called after her. "Whilst you're in there, look for something the nurse left for me. She generally leaves it on the table by the door with my old woman's name on it."

Piper found the bottle just where the man said. She ran back out with it before she got the hot water. When she handed it to him, he said, "Thank ye."

"Thank you. For . . ." She hesitated.

"For killing the chicken?" He raised one eyebrow as he stared at her. "Jest don't count on me doing it ever again. That's women's work."

270

She called after him when he started off. "Why aren't you riding your mule?"

"You're a nosy thing." He turned to scowl at her. "Don't know as how it's any of your business, but that little West boy's pa needed to do some plowing." He pointed toward the chicken Jamie was holding. "I'd advise you to get at it if'n you aim to have that bird for supper."

CHAPTER
THIRTY-FOUR

Jamie was glad to see the last of Mr. Taylor. He wouldn't mind seeing the last of this chicken too. "What are you going to do with this?" he asked Piper.

She made a face and shrugged a little. "I'm supposed to fry it." She smiled at him. "Want to stay for supper?"

"That might be the safest thing. For some reason, I keep getting mistaken for a revenuer. Those guys are not popular around here."

"So Mann Taylor was worried you'd find his still and turn him in?"

"How do you know he has a still? And how do you know him anyway?" Jamie asked.

"A wild guess on the still, but I ran into Mr. Taylor the other day when I was up here. Do you think his name is actually Mann? Or that they just call him 'man' the way he called you 'boy'?"

"I don't care what he's called. I'm just glad he didn't shoot me."

"Did you think he would? I mean, really?"

"He talked about letting the buzzards have me. So yeah. Really."

"He scared my socks off when he shot that snake. Not that I wasn't glad he did."

"Wonder if he'll eat it." The snake had been heavier than he'd expected when the man handed it to him.

"I don't know." Piper shrugged. "But at least we don't have to get rid of it." She gave the chicken another look. "We better de-feather this bird."

"We?" Jamie held it out toward her. "I don't know anything about dressing out chickens."

"You think I do?" She gave him a sweet look. "But you will help me, won't you? Mrs. Breckinridge would want you to. Nurse Thompson would tell you to. Come to think of it, how come you're up here anyway, instead of sweeping floors at the hospital?"

She started toward the house and he walked with her, still holding the chicken. "The nurses up here needed some medicine by tomorrow. Something they forgot to give you. So, they let me borrow Dr. Jack's horse to bring it. Sid over there might be the only reason I'm still breathing."

"Why's that?"

"Your Mr. Taylor was ready to shoot me and keep Sid, but I told him everybody would know the doctor's horse."

"People here do know the horses and mules the same as they know one another."

Jamie looked over at Sid. "I better take care of him."

"Not yet. You're holding the chicken." She smiled at him as she went up the porch steps. "I'll get some hot water. That's what they say to do next. Dunk it in hot water."

The water sloshed out of the bucket when she set it down on the porch and nodded at Jamie. "Go ahead. Put it in there."

Jamie did as he was told. "How long?"

She pulled a paper out of her pocket. "It doesn't say." She wrinkled her nose. "Eww. It stinks."

"Like wet feathers." He pulled the chicken back out of the water and yanked on some feathers. They came out. "Are we supposed to save them?"

"Save what?"

"The feathers."

"Why?"

"To put in pillows."

"Oh." Piper looked at her paper again. "It doesn't say anything about that. Just to pluck them off."

"Then pluck we will."

They set to work pulling off feathers.

"I'm glad Mann Taylor didn't shoot you."

"Yeah. So am I." He wasn't sure that sitting on porch steps while plucking a chicken was the greatest place to admit he loved her, but he wanted it out in the air between them before something else unexpected happened. "Piper."

"Yes?" She looked over at him.

Yes was a good word. He pulled the last feathers off the underside of the chicken and rinsed off his hands in the bucket. "When I thought maybe he was going to shoot me, I kept thinking how much I wanted to see you at least one more time before I died."

She placed the plucked chicken in the pan she'd brought out and put her fingers over his lips. A feather tickled his chin.

"Shh," she said. "I can't bear to think about you getting shot."

He captured her hand in his. "I so regretted how I'd put off saying something to you I should have said a long time ago." He looked straight into her eyes. "I love you, Piper Danson."

———

Piper pulled in a breath. Had Jamie really said the words she had so long dreamed of hearing him say? *I love you.*

He was smiling. Somewhat tentatively. Unsure. How could he be unsure?

Above them, a bird sang a joyous chorus of tweets and chirps.

She didn't need to see it to know it was a mockingbird. She was becoming a bird expert. But why was she thinking about birds when Jamie had just told her he loved her? Maybe because her heart was singing like the bird. Or maybe because of the plucked chicken between them. She looked down at the chicken. She still had to clean out its innards and save the gizzard.

Laughter bubbled up inside her. "You know how to pick a romantic moment."

"That's not what you're supposed to say." But he started laughing too. Then as suddenly, his laughter died away. "I don't know why I've never told you I love you. I've loved you since way back before I knew what saying I love you even meant."

"What does it mean?" Her laughter was gone too as she looked up at him. His eyes were waiting, and she knew he'd never looked away from her.

"It means I can hardly breathe when I look at you. It means I want to be with you forever." He tightened his hold on her hand. A couple of little white feathers drifted off in the breeze. "I know I don't have much to offer you. Nothing but my love."

"What more could I want?" She leaned toward him across the chicken between them. Their lips met. A chaste kiss, but that didn't keep her heart from feeling ready to explode.

He stood and pulled her to her feet. She was more than eager to step around the chicken into his arms.

"Halloo."

The boy's voice jerked them both around.

"Halloo. Nurse Freeman." Billy West ran into the yard.

Piper brushed another feather off her hand and called out. "Back here, Billy."

"Oh, hello, Danny." He smiled when he saw her. His smile turned shyer when he looked over at Jamie. "Where's Nurse Freeman?"

"Is something wrong?"

"Ma sent me after the nurse. The baby's coming. Pa's plowing out in the back field, so she sent me to fetch the nurse. Figured that would be faster than me going for Pa." The boy frowned as he looked around. "Said for me to tell the nurse to hurry."

"Nurse Freeman is out on a call and the other nurse is gone too."

The little boy's face fell. "But Ma needs her."

"She didn't think she'd be gone long."

"Ma can't wait." Billy's mouth tightened with determination. "Did you reckon which way she went so's I can chase after her?"

"She went down that way." Piper pointed. When Billy turned to leave, she stopped him. "Wait, Billy. Jamie's horse is saddled and ready. He can take you to find the nurse."

"Sure, but I better give Sid a drink first." He looked over at Piper. "You still going to finish with the chicken?"

Piper sighed. "I guess I should or all that effort will go to waste."

After Jamie led the horse away to get water, Piper stared down at the chicken. No need putting it off. She took the knife and slit open the soft underside of the carcass. Billy watched her pull out the guts.

"You wouldn't know what a gizzard looks like, would you?" she asked him.

Billy gave her a funny look. "You don't know what a gizzard looks like?"

Piper made a face as she dumped what she'd pulled out of the chicken carcass on the pan. "Not a clue."

Billy peered down at the mess. "Maybe you can just cook the rest of the chicken. You do have to cut off those feet." He pointed.

Piper stared at the three toes on each foot that had been scratching in the dirt only a little while ago. Her stomach turned over. A bowl of beans sounded better and better. But Nurse Freeman said to fry the chicken. Like it was the easiest thing in the world to do. Sort of like milking the cow the other night.

She'd eaten fried chicken. That someone else had butchered

and someone else cooked. But someone else wasn't here. She held up the knife.

"Careful you don't cut off your fingers." Jamie led Sid across the yard toward them. "I like those fingers."

Her heart took a flutter beat as his smile had her remembering his arms around her.

Billy ran over to Jamie. "Can we go? Ma told me to be in a right smart hurry getting the nurse."

"Then come on," Jamie said. "But I don't know how we'll know where to go."

"Danny said they went thataway." Billy pointed. "Ain't but a few houses down that trail."

"Maybe you'll meet her coming back." Piper wished the nurse and Truda were riding up to the center. Not only would that get Nurse Freeman on the way to help Billy's mother, Truda might know how to cut up a chicken. How hard could that be?

How hard indeed. After Jamie pulled Billy up on the horse, they cantered off, with Jamie looking back at her, seeming as uncertain about his what-next as she was with the chicken. But he was moving. Time for her to be moving too. With the knife.

Cutting off the feet was easier than she expected. When she had the legs, thighs, and wings severed and resting in the pan, she felt a surge of accomplishment. She eyed the remaining carcass and then knifed it into two pieces. She cut the back apart where it had some give and then split the breast. Her arms were trembling as though she'd done some kind of extreme manual labor.

Extreme or not, perfect or not, she did it. She carried the chicken inside to figure out the next step. As she washed the chicken pieces, she thought of Jamie's words of love. Why hadn't she answered by confessing her own feelings for him?

I love you, Piper Danson. His words danced in her ears. He was right about not having anything to offer but his love. That was enough. More than enough. Her father's frowning face popped into her mind. She could almost hear him saying love was fine for those who could afford it. But it was hardly legal tender to buy a house or food for a pantry. In his mind, security was more to be desired than love. Love would grow as it had for her parents.

She didn't need love to grow afresh. Love had long ago taken root inside her and, like a trailing vine, entwined her heart and mind. Just not for the man her father had chosen for her.

CHAPTER
THIRTY-FIVE

The iron skillet was heavier than Piper expected when she picked it up to set it on the stove. Then she rummaged around until she found lard, some flour, and salt. Nurse Freeman had said to coat the chicken pieces in flour. She hadn't mentioned salt, but everything needed salt.

Piper poked some wood into the stove. Thanks to Nurse Robbins, she did at least know how to make the fire hotter. A few minutes later she was immeasurably proud when she dropped floured chicken pieces into the melted lard in the skillet and they started sizzling.

After she had all the chicken pieces situated in the skillet, she stared at them and wondered how long to cook them. At the sound of horses outside, she nearly cheered out loud. Help was on the way.

Nurse Freeman stepped into the kitchen. "I'm amazed. I smell chicken frying." She looked surprised. "I didn't think you could do it."

"You told me to."

"So I did, but I'm afraid we don't have time to eat it." She pulled the skillet off the stove.

"I know you have to go see about Mrs. West, but I could still finish cooking it. Truda can help me." Piper peered around the nurse. "Where is she?"

"We've had some complications. I'm afraid your aunt took an unfortunate fall."

"Is she all right?" Piper forgot about the chicken as she started for the door.

"Not entirely." She caught Piper's arm to stop her. "She has a fractured wrist that needs attention. Take a breath, girl, and slow down. You don't want to startle the horses. Your aunt will be fine."

Out the front window, Piper could see Truda on her horse by the front porch. Jamie was on Sid, close beside her, holding Dickens's reins. "Shouldn't you do something for her?"

"I've wrapped it up, but she needs to head down to the hospital for an x-ray." Nurse Freeman let go of Piper and turned to rummage in a cabinet. "Besides, I need to attend to Mrs. West. Billy said his mother asked me to hurry. Makes me think something might be amiss."

"Where is Billy?" Piper didn't see the boy anywhere.

"He went on up the hill to assure his mother we were on the way."

Piper looked at Truda again. She was clinging to the saddle with her uninjured hand as though her life depended on it. "Truda can't ride like that." Piper shook her head. "She'll fall off again."

"I didn't say she fell off a horse, Danny. She did have an encounter with an energetic dog and took a pitch off some steps. But your aunt's a trouper. Sat right up and patted that dog on the head."

"That's Truda." Piper took that deep breath the nurse recommended and headed outside to not only see Truda but also Jamie.

She shouldn't be thinking about Jamie and his words of love right then. Not with Truda white-faced and obviously in pain. A wide cloth bound her arm to her chest. "Are you all right?"

Nurse Freeman followed her outside. "Please, Miss Danson, tell the girl you'll live so we can get on with things."

"I've been better, but I'll be okay." Truda grimaced a little before she managed a smile. "Who'd have thought I'd be taken out by a dog instead of a horse."

"I'll ride with you down to the hospital."

"No." Nurse Freeman spoke up. "I need you to go with me. Young Russell can escort Miss Danson to the hospital."

"But—"

"No buts. You're here. I might need you. Patients come first."

"Truda is a patient."

"Then babies first." The nurse didn't hide her irritation. "As I said, young Russell will take care of Miss Danson. Very opportune that he is here to be of help." Her irritation seemed to dissolve as she smiled at him.

It was useless to protest. Nurse Freeman would not be swayed.

"Indeed, babies first," Truda said. "Jamie will get me to the hospital, won't you, Jamie?"

"We'll go slow and easy, Miss Danson." He looked down at Piper. "I promise."

His eyes seemed to promise more than taking care of Truda. Piper's heart did a little dance. "I got the chicken cut up and in the skillet."

"I'm not surprised. You can do anything." He looked as though he really believed that.

"You're kidding." Truda stared at Piper, her eyes wide. "You actually chopped off a chicken's head?"

"No, a neighbor, Mr. Taylor, did it for me."

Now Nurse Freeman looked surprised as she glanced up from packing the new supplies into her saddlebags. "Mann Taylor killed that chicken for you?" When Piper nodded, she went on. "You are a wonder, Danny. Mann Taylor is not generally so neighborly. Did he get his wife's medicine?"

"He did."

"Good." The nurse fastened her saddlebags and mounted in one graceful movement. She gave orders. "Go back and put a top on that skillet. Nurse Hankins might be here in time to finish cooking it. Then saddle up and follow me to the West house." She looked up at the sun. "Don't worry about milking Clara. It's too early now. One of the neighbor girls will come milk her later if we're not back."

It had never once entered Piper's mind to milk the cow.

Nurse Freeman turned her attention to Truda and Jamie. "You do know the way back to Hyden? Down to the creek, follow it a ways, ford the river and you're home free." A frown wrinkled her brow as she studied Truda. "The river isn't too high right now, but perhaps you should wait here, Miss Danson, until I get back. Then I can recruit some help to carry you out."

"No need. I can ride." Truda said the words, but she sounded less than sure.

"Yes, well . . ." The nurse hesitated as she looked up at the sun again. "You should make it by the edge of dark."

"The edge of dark?" Truda frowned.

"Sorry. Mountain talk for twilight," Nurse Freeman said. "Do whatever you think best, but I must head up to see about Mrs. West." She looked back at Piper. "Don't tarry, Danny." She turned her horse away from the house.

Piper watched her ride out of sight, then looked at Truda. "I think I should go with you."

"And I think you should do what Nurse Freeman says." There was no doubt in Truda's voice now. "That's why you're here."

"But . . ."

"I'll take care of her," Jamie said.

Piper blew out a breath and looked at Jamie. "You won't get lost again?"

"A fellow gets lost once and people lose all trust in him." Jamie grinned at her. "But I know the way now. I could find the trail in the dark." He looked up at the sun. "Which I may have to do if we don't get started."

"So go." Piper waved him away.

"You won't forget what I said."

Piper met his gaze. "How could I ever forget that?"

His smile embraced her, and she wanted to whisper those same love words back at him.

Piper reluctantly pulled her gaze away from Jamie to look at her aunt. "You will be careful."

"A little late for that." Truda attempted another smile. "No need you fretting. I'll be fine with Jamie."

Piper watched as Jamie led Truda's horse away from the center. Before he went out of sight, he turned to give her a long, lingering look that was almost as good as a caress.

"I love you," Piper whispered into the wind, then rushed inside to put a lid on the skillet. She smiled at the thought of someday telling their children how their first words of love had been while plucking a chicken. If only they had had a few more private moments together. But that would have to wait. Babies didn't wait. Time to do as Nurse Freeman said and follow her to the West house.

Dogs barking and the sound of wailing greeted Piper as she rode up to the cabin. Not a newborn's cries, but those of a child. It wouldn't be Billy. Not crying like that. Instead, his little sister was sitting in the open door to the cabin, loudly weeping.

Piper leaned down to her. "What's wrong, sweetie?"

The little girl just cried louder. Nurse Freeman called from inside the house. "Thank goodness you're here. See if you can quiet that child, but get this bird out of here first. Came right in the open door."

"A bird in the house means death." Mrs. West spoke up from the bed. Her face was haggard and her eyes sunk back into her head.

"No talk like that." Nurse Freeman draped a sheet over the woman's legs. "This guy is coming hard, but we haven't lost him yet."

"I was thinking more of me," the woman said weakly.

"Shh." Nurse Freeman moved to caress the woman's face. "You can do this. We can do this."

The woman's lips turned up in a very small smile. "I'll pray you can, but the bird is a bad omen."

Piper grabbed a broom and shooed the bird toward the door. She had to make two passes at it, but finally the bird saw the open space and was gone in a flash of black wings. "It's gone."

"Then shut that door before it flies back in here," Nurse Freeman said.

Piper gently scooted the little girl back and pushed the door closed. Her wails changed to pitiful sobs. She looked to be three or four.

"Bring my little Ellie over here to me," Mrs. West said.

When Nurse Freeman nodded, Piper picked up the child, who didn't protest. "Where's Billy?"

"I sent him after his father. Ellie wanted to go too and that's why she's raising the roof." Nurse Freeman smiled at the little girl, then turned a concerned look back to Mrs. West, who grimaced and tensed as a pain attacked her. She took her hand. "Try to relax, dearie."

Mrs. West gave her a look as though that was a crazy thing to tell her, but she did blow out a slow breath and pull in another. Piper wanted to ask if something was wrong with the woman's labor, but she kept quiet. Instead she waited until it looked as if the pain had passed before she put Ellie down beside her mother.

The woman's face softened as the little girl snuggled against her. Mrs. West wiped the little girl's tears away with her fingertips.

"Now you listen to me, young missy, and you listen good. You have to be brave for your ma. Whatever happens, remember that the Lord loves you and intends good for you."

"You too, Ma?"

"For me too. Whatever happens." Her body began tightening up as a new pain came over her. She was a little breathless as she went on. "Now, you go wait on the porch for your pa while I get you a new baby brother or sister."

"I want a sister." Ellie's bottom lip came out in a pout.

Mrs. West couldn't answer as the contraction grabbed her. Nurse Freeman set Ellie off the bed and shooed her toward the door. "Go watch for your pa and we'll try to get that little sister for you." The nurse gave Piper a look. "See that she gets outside and close the door." She lowered her voice as Piper moved past her. "Don't want any more birds in here. Then wash up, Danny. Use lots of soap. I could need your help." Piper barely heard her whisper as she went on. "This one is coming hard."

The nurse was right. Piper helped brace Mrs. West's legs as the strong contractions twisted her body. She groaned but never screamed out. While Mrs. Whitton had suffered strong contractions, her birthing labor had been nothing like this.

Nurse Freeman kept up a chatter of encouragement and instructions. "Breathe in a moment of rest. You're doing great." She muttered under her breath, more to herself than to Piper. "The baby didn't turn." She raised her voice with no sign of the worry that had been in her muttered words. "Your baby is breech."

"Feet first?" the woman gasped. "Or butt?"

"Feet. We need to move you down on the bed. Help me, Danny. Now stuff those pillows behind her."

Once the nurse had Mrs. West positioned as she wanted, she said, "All right, dearie. We're going to help hold you here and we'll soon see if Ellie has that little sister she wants. I see toes." The nurse sounded almost cheerful before she lowered her voice to a bare whisper. "Pray I see fingers. Stand steady, Danny, and keep our mother in this position. We have to make sure the baby comes out exactly right."

Piper did as the nurse said, ignoring the strain on her back as she supported the woman's weight. She concentrated on breathing in and out slowly. No time to feel faint now.

Sweat ran down Nurse Freeman's face as she guided the emerging baby. "Ellie has her sister. Praise the Lord, we have fingers. We've almost got this baby here, dearie. You're being a champ for sure." Her words came out in a calming rhythm with none of the worry that showed on her face.

Another push and the baby was in the nurse's hands. "Reach that blanket behind you," the nurse told Piper as she cut the cord and cleaned out the baby's mouth. No warbling cry followed.

The cabin was silent except for Mrs. West's heavy breathing. "She's dead, ain't she?" When Nurse Freeman didn't answer, the woman went on. "And me not far behind her."

"Nonsense," Nurse Freeman said. "You hang in here with me, Ella West. Danny is going to help you scoot back a bit in the bed now. Then you keep in mind all those who love you and need you. Asa and Asa Junior. Billy, Ellie. Now this little one here."

"She ain't doing no crying," Mrs. West said as Piper helped her move back in the bed.

The silence was heartrending as the baby lay still in the nurse's hands. Piper wanted to breathe for the newborn as a desperate prayer without words rose within her.

Nurse Freeman looked grim as she massaged the baby's back, but she kept her voice calm. "Come take our baby, Danny, while I make sure mother is all right."

Nurse Freeman handed the limp baby to Piper. "Wrap her in that blanket, Danny, and keep rubbing her back and arms."

"Is she . . . ?" Piper let her words die away.

Nurse Freeman had an answer. "Yes, she is beautiful." She softened her voice. "We're not giving up yet, but for sure, I don't want to lose both of them." She raised her voice again. "Let's get you squared away, Mrs. West. That's a trouper, dearie. You'll be up fixing supper for us in a minute if we don't watch you."

Piper couldn't stand the silence, so she began softly crooning to the newborn as she stroked her arms and back. She cleaned the baby's face with the blanket edge. So beautiful. Piper's heart hurt, but she followed Nurse Freeman's example, pulled in a deep breath, and blinked away the threat of tears.

"Don't be so gentle." Nurse Freeman suddenly looked around and gave one of the baby's feet a firm thump. "Massage her like you might rub a newborn colt. Make her know she's out of her mama's cocoon."

Piper turned the baby sideways on her lap and did as the nurse said.

"My baby." Mrs. West's wail tore a hole through the air.

The cabin door opened and a man stepped in. "Ella?"

Nurse Freeman looked back at him. "Come, comfort your wife, but leave the children outside." She took the baby from Piper and cleared out the newborn's mouth again. She laid the baby belly down in her lap and dropped one knee so the baby's head was lowered as she firmly patted the baby's back.

The man knelt by his wife's bed and stroked her face. "It's as the Lord wills, Ella."

Mrs. West quietly wept. Piper held her breath. Nurse Freeman hadn't given up, so Piper wouldn't either as she prayed the Lord would give this baby breath.

Nurse Freeman muttered under her breath. "Come on, baby. Breathe for us."

"Please," Piper whispered. "Please."

All at once the baby made an odd little gurgle. The next moment she let out a pitiful little cry that got stronger with the next one.

"Sweet baby girl." Nurse Freeman lifted the baby up and kissed her head.

Laughter bubbled up inside Piper. She didn't know when she'd ever heard a sweeter sound.

The father smiled and wiped the tears from Mrs. West's cheeks with a corner of the sheet. "See there, Ella. The Lord willed her alive to us. We best take extra good care of this one here. The Lord must have something good planned for her."

CHAPTER
THIRTY-SIX

Truda wasn't nearly as sure about keeping her seat as she'd said before Jamie led her horse away from the center. But she couldn't let people carry her down off the mountain. She wasn't that helpless. At least she hoped not. However, the Bible did say pride goeth before a fall. At least that was how people generally quoted the Proverbs verse. She had looked it up once and found the pride went before destruction and a haughty spirit before a fall.

Wasn't that just like people? To shorten and leave out parts when it came to Scripture. She was as guilty as the next person, but she didn't want to think she had a haughty spirit. That sounded even worse than being prideful.

She did dread showing up at the hospital with evidence of her clumsiness. She didn't want to be Jackson's patient. She wasn't sure what she wanted to be to Jackson, but the very thought of him made her heart beat a little faster. Or perhaps it was the pain shooting up her arm. That wretched dog. No, that wasn't fair. The dog hadn't intended to send her flying off the steps. He'd simply been overly friendly.

Was that what she was being with Jackson? Overly friendly? And apt to experience another fall, albeit a different sort of tumble. One that might hurt worse than this broken wrist. Fractured, the nurse had said. A heart could be broken or fractured too.

To keep from thinking about that or how her arm throbbed, she studied Jamie leading her horse. He sat on his horse as though born to a saddle.

That look he'd given Piper before they left the center was enough to melt Truda's heart. If not for her unfortunate accident, the two young people might be sitting on the porch, doing some spooning. That sounded like a country word. When in Rome and all.

But it could be the young man was headed for disappointment. Oh, Truda had no doubt Piper was as taken with Jamie as the boy was with her, but sometimes romance wasn't so simple. Truda could attest to that. A chance meeting with a young man years ago had perhaps raised her romance expectations too high, and now she had the impossible dream of recapturing that feeling.

Why did her thoughts keep circling back to Jackson Booker? She did hope he was a good doctor. Maybe that was all she should hope.

"Are you all right, Miss Danson?" Jamie looked back at her.

"Just peachy." Jamie flinched, and Truda was sorry for how the words sounded.

"Sorry. I guess that was a dumb question."

"No, really. I'm okay. Just wishing we were there already." The light was fading among the trees and nothing looked familiar. Not that she'd paid much attention on the way up to the center. She'd just followed along. But shouldn't she at least see something she remembered? The problem was, trees had a way of looking alike. "It's getting dark."

"I know." Jamie slowed the horses. "It shouldn't be much farther. I think I hear the river."

Truda held her breath and listened. "I'm not sure about the river, but I am sure someone's coming toward us through the woods."

———

Miss Danson was right. Someone was coming. Jamie fought the urge to take off in a gallop rather than face another mountain man. But Miss Danson could barely keep her seat moving at a snail's pace. Nothing for it but to hope they weren't about to meet up with another Clem Baker or Mann Taylor.

When Miss Danson suddenly called out a hello, Jamie jumped and his horse took a side step.

"Easy, Sid." Jamie gathered the reins. He'd hardly needed to use them since the horse appeared to know his way.

He looked around at Miss Danson, who shrugged a little. "I thought we could ask whoever it is if we are on the right path."

"Whoever it is might not be friendly."

Miss Danson frowned. "Why wouldn't they be friendly? Everybody I've met since I got here has been friendly."

She hadn't met Mann Taylor, and he hoped she wouldn't or anyone like him. A man on a mule came around a bend in the trail. At least no guns were in sight.

"Evening, ma'am." The man stopped his mule beside them and tipped his hat at Miss Danson before his eyes tightened as he stared at Jamie. "This fellow giving you trouble?" The big man had a bushy red beard streaked with gray.

"Oh no," Miss Danson said. "He's helping me down the mountain to the hospital. I fell and broke my wrist. I hoped you could assure us we are on the right path since night is falling and we are strangers to this place."

"What you two doing up here anyhow?" The man sounded a little less friendly.

"I'm a friend of Mrs. Breckinridge. We were visiting the Wilder Ridge Center."

The man visibly relaxed at the mention of Mrs. Breckinridge. "I shoulda guessed you were one of her ladies, but generally one of those girls is escorting 'em instead of a feller."

Jamie spoke up. "I'm just helping out. Running errands and such."

"Is that so?" He studied Jamie a moment. "I reckon I'll take your word for it, but others might not. Could be you oughta watch your step in these parts. You don't look like you belong, and some get worried about them that look like they don't belong."

"Yes, sir. I've found that out."

The man actually chuckled. "So who'd you run afoul of up here? Benny White or Mann Taylor?"

"Mr. Taylor pointed me toward the Wilder Ridge Center." No need saying how he pointed him.

"Well, you don't have to worry none about Malcom Jenkins. I'll be glad to help you get on down to the hospital. The lady here looks plumb tuckered out, but my old mule, he's steady as a rock. I'll ride alongside her through the river to make sure she don't fall in."

"I'd be grateful." Miss Danson did seem to be wobbling a bit in the saddle.

"Don't you worry about a thing. Dr. Jack, he's a good bonesetter. Took care of my boy when he fell out of a tree and broke his leg. Fixed him right up."

Mr. Jenkins kept talking all the way down the hill. At the river, he guided them to the shallow ford, something Jamie might not have found in the near darkness.

When they splashed into the water, Jamie stored up the sight and sounds in his mind. Someday he might write a story with a river crossing. Perhaps an adventure story. Perhaps a love story with a happy ending.

He so wanted a happy ending to his own love story. He and Piper living happily ever after made his heart sing along with the sound of the water flowing downstream.

Once out of the river, Mr. Jenkins said, "Just head on up Thousandsticks Mountain. I need to get on home. The old woman will be fretting over me."

"Thank you so much, Mr. Jenkins. You've been such a help," Miss Danson said. "The Lord must have sent you to make sure we found our way."

"My pleasure, ma'am. You ever need any more help, you just give a shout out for Malcolm Jenkins." He splashed back into the river.

At the hospital, Jamie dismounted beside a shiny black Ford roadster parked near the entrance. "Now that's the way to travel," Jamie said as he helped Miss Danson off her horse.

"Looks like something that should be on Louisville streets, not here," Miss Danson said.

His stomach growled as he walked her into the hospital.

"Feeling a little lank?" she asked.

"I could go for a piece of that chicken Piper was frying."

Miss Danson shook her head. "I can still barely believe Piper actually plucked a chicken."

"As Nurse Freeman said, Piper's a wonder."

"That she is," Miss Danson said.

A man in the hospital lobby turned toward them. "Did you say Piper?"

Braxton Crandall. The last man Jamie wanted to see. And now he was smiling at them, ready to steal Piper away from Jamie. Or perhaps simply step back into his place as her intended. Her father's intended for her anyway. And why not? That slick roadster out in front of the hospital was just the tip of the iceberg of things Braxton Crandall could give Piper. Jamie didn't have so much as a horse to call his own.

The man came toward them, concern on his face. "Miss Danson, you appear to be injured. I do hope nothing too serious."

Miss Danson looked down at her arm. "A broken bone, I fear."

She smiled at Braxton before glancing over at Jamie. "Jamie helped me down the mountain. Jamie, have you met Braxton? Braxton Crandall."

Jamie rubbed his hand off on his trousers and held it out for Braxton to grasp in a handshake. But what he wanted to do was sock the man in the jaw and tell him to drive that fancy car of his back to Louisville.

"Jamie?" Braxton gave him a questioning look. "Ah yes, Simon Russell's little brother. I've been talking to Simon about his venture into radio set manufacturing."

"Simon thinks everybody wants a radio, hard times or not." Jamie pushed something he hoped resembled a smile out on his face.

"Indeed. He's a progressive thinker. I'm sure you're excited about his plans."

"Yes." Jamie didn't bother explaining the only plans he was excited about were plans with Piper. If he had any chance for plans with her, now that Braxton Crandall was in Hyden. He turned to Miss Danson. "We need to find someone to help you."

As if she heard him, a nurse came down the hall to take Miss Danson in hand and lead her away.

"I'll check on you after I see to the horses," Jamie called after her.

Miss Danson smiled over her shoulder at him. A smile that included Braxton Crandall. Jamie shifted on his feet. He was suddenly tired as the good memory of Piper's lips on his drained away in the presence of this man.

"Horses? Do you have a horse?" Braxton Crandall asked. "They tell me I will need one to get to this Wendover place to see Piper."

"Right. But the horses I need to take care of aren't mine."

"Whose are they? I could buy one of them."

"Neither of these is for sale."

"I get the feeling you don't want me to make it to Wendover." Braxton frowned a little.

"Not at all." It wasn't much of a lie. Jamie knew Piper wasn't there, but she would be the next day. "Have someone here call Wendover. Somebody will bring a horse to escort you over. Especially if you say you want to talk to Mrs. Breckinridge about contributing to the Frontier Nursing Service."

Braxton's frown turned to a smile. "Actually, my mother is very interested in being a sponsor. She hopes to visit later in the year. I volunteered to come first to see the lay of the land."

"And see Piper," Jamie said.

"Yes. We're going to be married after she gets this insane desire to do something different out of her system."

Jamie's throat felt tight, but he wouldn't let this man see how his words upset him. "Getting married would be different."

The man's smile got wider. "So it would."

"Do you love her?" Jamie shouldn't have spoken that question out loud.

Braxton gave him a look. "I'm not sure why that matters to you."

"Piper and I are old friends. I want her to be happy."

"Oh, I see." And he did appear to understand more than Jamie wanted him to. "Well, Jamie, let me assure you that I will love Piper. We might not have known each other long, the way you and Piper have, but love will grow between us."

"That's good to know." Jamie managed to almost smile as he choked out the words.

Without bothering with a "nice to meet you" or to say that Piper was up in the hills and not at Wendover, Jamie headed outside to take care of the horses. Braxton Crandall would have to find Piper on his own.

But what would happen when he did? She might send him away. An uncomfortable feeling scratched around inside Jamie. What kind of life could he offer Piper when Crandall could provide for her every need, perhaps even love, if it had a chance to grow? He wanted to kick the side of the roadster as he passed by it, but all that would do was bruise his foot. He could almost hear Simon telling him it was time to grow up and face facts. Dreams didn't always come true, and love didn't always conquer all.

CHAPTER
THIRTY-SEVEN

Truda hated leaving Jamie alone with Braxton Crandall. She'd seen the look on his face. A mixture of jealousy and despair. But her wrist needed tending. She fervently hoped it was merely sprained instead of fractured, the way Nurse Freeman thought. Painful either way, but at least then this nice nurse might be able to treat her without bothering Jackson.

Not that she wouldn't like to see Jackson. She would, but not in her current disarray after riding down a mountain, through a river, and back up another mountain. She smoothed down her hair with her uninjured hand and plucked out a twig. She did know how to mess things up. Now instead of going to dinner with him in her nicest outfit after curling her hair, she was going to look a wreck.

"We'll get an x-ray before Dr. Jack gets here." When Truda flinched at the mention of Jackson, the nurse assumed she was concerned about the x-ray. "Don't worry. X-rays don't hurt."

"I know. I just hate for you to have to call the doctor in this late," Truda said.

"Dr. Jack is used to coming in when we have an emergency."

"Is this an emergency?"

"Outcomes are better when injuries are treated as soon as possible." The nurse unwrapped Truda's arm. "I'll try to be gentle, but this might hurt a little."

Truda bit her lip to keep from crying out as the nurse positioned her arm on the machine.

"Don't move." The nurse adjusted some dials and hit something that made a light flash. She moved Truda's arm a little and did it again. "These take a while to develop, so let's get you settled in an examining room."

Truda wished she could just disappear back to Louisville for a few weeks and then make a return trip to Hyden. Maybe she should have asked Braxton Crandall to drive her there in his roadster. That would have solved two problems. Her having to let Jackson see her in such a shambles and Braxton being in Leslie County to convince Piper marriage to him was the only sensible course of action.

Dear Jamie didn't have many prospects. Much like Jackson when she met him years ago. But Jackson had made his way. In time, Jamie would do the same, but first he might have some bumpy years.

Perhaps Erwin was right to push Piper toward Braxton. He seemed a nice enough young man. She felt a pang for Jamie with the thought. But it wasn't her decision. Nor Erwin's, although he thought it should be. Piper had a good head on her shoulders. She'd do the right thing. That thought made Truda feel even worse. The right thing, the sensible thing might not be, probably would not be, to follow her heart. Just as the sensible thing for Truda to do would be to find a ride to Hazard and buy a train ticket home. But for once in her life, she wasn't feeling sensible. Not sensible at all.

Nor was she happy when the nurse, whose name she'd forgotten, told her she'd have to take off her riding shirt.

"I'd rather not." Truda wasn't concerned about the shirt, but surely she wasn't expected to sit here in nothing but her brassiere for the doctor to treat her. Not any doctor, but Jackson.

"I'm afraid you don't have a choice, Miss Danson. The doctor will need to examine your whole arm." She held up a cotton gown with big sleeve openings. "So off with the shirt and on with this. You can leave on your brassiere unless you have to have surgery."

"Surgery?" Truda frowned.

"To mend your arm, but that may not be necessary. If it's a clean break."

Truda sighed. In a hospital a person had no chance for dignity or little choice about anything when needing medical care. She started working one of her buttons loose with her right hand. It was devilishly unhandy doing things with one hand.

"Here, let me."

The nurse unbuttoned the shirt quickly and pulled it off Truda's right arm, then gently eased the sleeve over her injured arm. She helped Truda slip on the hospital gown that felt like it had been starched. Why would anybody starch a hospital gown?

Truda felt completely out of sorts, ready to grumble about anything. She wasn't normally a grumbler. She was a fixer, but a person couldn't fix anything in a hospital gown with her arm propped on an examining table. She was the one who needed to be fixed. It was not a spot she liked being in.

The nurse gave her something in a glass. For pain, she said. Truda didn't ask what it was, just swallowed the vile-tasting liquid.

"That may make the doctor's examination less painful."

"Thank you." She tried to mean it, but Truda was glad when the nurse left her alone.

Truda knew how to be alone. The Lord had given her a good life. Work she was capable of. Erwin's children to love, especially Piper. But now when she thought about returning to that life, her heart constricted. Perhaps she could get a dog for company. One of those adorable Golden pups at Wendover. As soon as her wrist healed.

That was crazy thinking. A dog is what got her in this shape.

She couldn't have a dog. She couldn't have a husband. But she could have a broken wrist.

The door opened and Jackson rushed in. "Truda, what happened?" He had on a sport shirt instead of the doctor coat he'd worn earlier.

"I tripped over a dog or a dog tripped over me. I'm not sure which, but we both ended up in a heap. The dog seemed to come out the better of the two of us."

Jackson sat down on a stool in front of her. "Good you can smile about it."

"I'm sorry about this, making you come back to the hospital after you were through for the day."

"Happens all the time. At least it wasn't to head up in the hills, but wasn't that where you were going? Up to Wilder Ridge?"

"Yes. I met the dog on some cabin steps near there."

"How did you get here? Does somebody up there have a truck now?" He gently probed her arm.

"I wouldn't know about that, but I got here the same way I got up there. On a horse."

"You have to be kidding. Riding down a mountain with a fractured wrist." He smiled up at her. "My Truda. One of a kind."

Her heart did a crazy leap. *My Truda.* She was glad he hadn't felt the need to use his stethoscope. He might think she had heart trouble. Maybe she did.

"Before I sound too much like a brave heroine in a storybook, I have to admit that I had help. Jamie, the young man you met this morning, led my horse, and then a man named Malcolm Jenkins helped me through the river. I told him he was heaven sent."

"Probably the only time Malcolm has ever been accused of that." Jackson stopped examining her arm and scooted back on his stool to study her.

When he didn't say anything right away, Truda asked, "Well, Doctor, am I going to live?"

"A long and happy life, I do hope. I looked at the x-rays before I came in here. You have a crack in the scaphoid bone in your wrist, but fortunately, the fracture has not displaced the bone. That's the bone right here." Jackson turned his hand palm up and then ran a finger along the base of his thumb to show the location of the break. "Nurse Freeman wrapping it up so quickly may have helped keep your hand stabilized so the break isn't any worse than it is."

"So I can just go about my business?"

"Afraid not. You'll need to be in a cast six weeks for the bone to heal properly. Wrists at times can be difficult." He leaned forward to touch her hand again. Not as a doctor examining it but as a friend giving comfort.

"But I'll be able to go back to my position at the bank?"

"I'd like to tell you that you shouldn't travel with your wrist in a cast." He looked her straight in the eyes. "But it wouldn't be true. Still, it might be good for you to consider staying here in Hyden for a few weeks? That way we can keep an eye on how the bone is healing by doing more x-rays."

"They have x-ray machines in Louisville." His eyes on her made her more than a little breathless.

"True enough." He stared down at his hand on hers for a moment before he brought his gaze back up to her face. "Have you ever wanted to ask something completely outlandish?"

"I don't know. Maybe I've never been brave enough to think outlandishly."

His lips turned up in a little smile. "I don't believe that. I imagine you are very brave. Perhaps just not outlandish."

"I've not always done the expected. Never married, for example."

"Nor have I. Ever married. Which brings me back to the outlandish request."

Truda's heart was beating so hard, she was surprised it wasn't shaking the hospital gown. "What is so outlandish?"

"I want you to stay here in the mountains. Not because of getting treatment for your wrist. No need pretending that you couldn't find able doctors in Louisville. Better ones than me, I'm sure." He reached and took her other hand in his. "But I do so wish for time to get to know you better." He paused a few seconds before he went on. "For you to get to know me. To see if we can be more than simply ships passing in the night."

"That doesn't sound so outlandish. It sounds nice." Truda almost whispered the words. He had such beautiful eyes that seemed to read her every thought and dream.

"It does, doesn't it? But I'm tiptoeing around the outlandish part."

"Oh?"

"Yes. So outlandish that, right here this minute, I can imagine dropping to one knee and asking you to marry me." His gaze on her didn't waver.

Truda didn't blink. If he could be outlandish, then so could she. "I can imagine saying yes."

His hand tightened his hold on her uninjured hand, and for a few heart-stopping seconds, she was sure he was going to kiss her. She couldn't remember the last time she'd been kissed, except for a peck on the cheek by a family member. But as he leaned nearer, he jostled her left hand and she couldn't hold back a gasp.

That seemed to bring them both back to earth. His cheeks reddened. "I'm not acting very professionally here. Time to be a doctor instead of a love-blinded swain." He let go of her hand and stood up. "Let me get Nurse Randall to help with the cast."

"Wait." Truda stopped him. "We can't leave it at this. Not my wrist, but our imaginations."

He looked down at her. "How should we leave it?"

"We aren't foolhardy youngsters. We know about life. And missed chances." She took a breath and went on. "So perhaps we should postpone the outlandish and embrace a more measured approach."

"Yes?" His gaze on her was intense. "In what way?"

"I can find a place to stay here while my wrist heals. Perhaps volunteer my services to Mrs. Breckinridge at Wendover or here at the hospital for a few weeks. I seem to have a talent for numbers that makes me a capable bookkeeper. Luckily, I'm right-handed." She held up her uninjured hand.

He grasped it and pulled it to his lips. "Luckily, my sister has a nice house with a spare room she rents on occasion. This will be a very good occasion."

Truda laughed in spite of the pain shooting up her left arm. "Then plans made and bargain sealed."

"Not exactly sealed yet." Jackson let go of her hand, put one hand on each side of her face, then bent to kiss her forehead.

Truda shut her eyes and absorbed the feel of his hands and lips. When he stepped back, she said, "Thank you, Jackson."

"For what? Letting you sit here and suffer with a broken wrist while I made outlandish statements?"

"No. For making those outlandish statements."

Jamie came into the room, followed by the nurse. He stayed just inside the door while the nurse shifted past him and began getting supplies out of a cabinet.

"Are you all right, Miss Danson?" Jamie asked.

"Just peachy." Truda smiled to let Jamie know that this time she meant it.

CHAPTER THIRTY-EIGHT

Jamie didn't have to spend the night in the stable as he thought he might. Nurse Randall took pity on him and let him sleep on a couch in the nurses' gathering room. At daybreak, a couple of nurses were surprised to find him there, but then laughed and brought him breakfast. They even pointed him toward the shower, but since he didn't have a razor, he still looked rough when he went to see Miss Danson.

Nurse Thompson, back on duty, let him peek in on Piper's aunt, who was sleeping with her casted arm on a pillow.

"She's doing fine. We'll let her sleep." She pulled Jamie back out into the hallway. "Mrs. Breckinridge called to see where you were. Seems she's ready to let you interview her for your paper."

"So no sweeping today?"

"You only halfway cleaned two rooms yesterday." Nurse Thompson let out an exaggerated sigh.

"You sent me off to the mountains."

"So I did. Where it seems you decided to take on a mountain look with those whiskers."

"No razor." He rubbed the bristles on his cheek.

"I'll find you one. Mrs. Breckinridge likes her people to look neat."

"I'm not exactly her people."

"Are you sure about that? You're here, running errands for us. Sleeping at Wendover."

"In a tent."

Nurse Thompson cocked one eyebrow at him. "Mrs. Breckinridge's tent, I'm told."

Jamie gave in. "You're right. I should shave before I see Mrs. Breckinridge."

The roadster was no longer parked in front of the hospital when Jamie, freshly shaven, went outside. He hoped that meant Braxton Crandall had gone back to Louisville, but that was surely an empty hope.

The same as expecting Piper to choose him over Braxton was a vain hope. Braxton wanted to marry her. Love would grow, the man said. In comfort. Better than comfort. Luxury. Piper would never lack for anything. How could Jamie deny her?

He pushed aside those thoughts. He was here to get a story. Maybe not the love story he'd hoped for, but a story about the frontier nurses. He should have taken pictures at Wilder Ridge. Maybe one of Mann Taylor with the snake draped around his neck. Or of Nurse Freeman riding away to attend a birth or Piper holding that plucked chicken. Before she kissed him.

But things had happened too fast for picture taking. He had his camera now, with time to focus in on the hospital building. He considered sneaking back inside to get a picture of Miss Virgie, but no time for that. Nurse Thompson said not to be slow about heading to Wendover, that Mrs. Breckinridge was not a patient woman. When she was ready for something to be done, she was ready for it to be done now.

At Wendover, he unsaddled and brushed down Dickens. A

couple of the pups came out and grabbed his pants legs. He pushed them back. "Hey, guys. Don't tear my pants."

"Got to whack them harder than that to get them to pay you some mind." Kermit looked up from repairing the stirrup on a saddle. "These pups are a plain aggravation. Be glad when they're gone from here. Thinking Ginger there is feeling the same." He nodded toward the mother dog, going out of the barn while several pups kept trying to nurse her. "Sometimes a body just wants to be done with something."

"Surely not a mother with her pups."

"Yep. All kinds of mothers get wore out with kids before they move on." Kermit laughed. "My ma would chase us outside and bar the door. 'Course there was fifteen of us. I reckon you city folks don't have the same boatload of kids."

"Only three of us." Jamie finished with Dickens and pushed one of the more determined pups away from his leg again. "You want me to put him in a stall?"

"Naw, he's earned a day off. He can go out to the pasture field today." Kermit spit on his fingers to smooth the end of the lacing he was winding through the stirrup. "Less'n that city feller decides he needs a ride back to Hyden."

Jamie looked out the barn door. "Oh? Braxton Crandall's here?"

"Nobody told me no name, but Suze brung him over last night. Said Mrs. Breckinridge would be glad to see him. I figure he must have loaded-down pockets."

"Family owns some railroads." Jamie gave up on getting the pup to leave his pants alone and picked him up. The pup wriggled up to lick Jamie's face.

"Is that right?" Kermit shook his head. "Mrs. Breckinridge brings them all in. That Mrs. Ford whose husband makes them cars comes down now and again too." The man looked up at Jamie. "Ain't no telling what that dog's been eatin'. Pups ain't too particular."

"He probably thinks the same thing about me." Jamie laughed and rubbed the pup's ears.

"Well, long as you ain't too particular either." Kermit stood up and put the saddle on a rack. "You into railroads too?"

"No loaded-down pockets here." Jamie put the pup down. When it tried to climb up his leg, he squatted to pet it. "Are you married, Kermit?"

"Nope."

"Ever been married or wanted to be married?"

"Did want to once." Kermit blew out a breath and stuck his hands in his pockets as he stared out the barn door. "I woulda swum a river for that girl."

"What happened? Didn't she love you back?" Jamie looked up at the man.

"I'm thinking she did have some caring for me in her heart, but she went off with a man from the next county what had fuller pockets than me. Later on he went broke and they had some struggles."

"Guess it served her right."

"Naw, I never took no joy in their misfortune. I wanted her to have a good life. She couldn't have known that I'd land this here job with Mrs. Breckinridge and be the one better off. Last I heard, she and her husband were living with one of her daughters. Husband went to work in the mines and got the lung trouble."

Jamie stood up. "You could have married somebody else." The pup finally ran off to find the others.

"I guess I coulda." Kermit shrugged. "My ma always used to say coulda, shoulda, woulda never got you nowheres."

"Sounds like your ma knew." Jamie picked up the lead rope on Dickens and started out of the barn.

Kermit spoke behind him. "You're sweet on that Danny girl, I'm told. Known her long?"

Jamie looked over his shoulder at Kermit. "Forever. But she's promised to somebody else."

"That guy with deep pockets, I reckon."

"Afraid so."

"Well, deep pockets ain't everything and promises ain't necessarily permanent if'n you aren't speaking them in front of a preacher." Kermit put his fists on his hips. "Remember that coulda and shoulda, then maybe somebody woulda."

"I'll keep it in mind."

"Oh, and when you see that Danny, tell her to come down to see Puddin. The poor old thing got that sore leg hung up somehow. I'm feared it's broke. Mrs. Breckinridge was down here looking at him earlier. Said we might have to put him down." Kermit's face darkened. "Ain't something I'm wanting to do."

"Sorry to hear that. I'll tell her." He'd noticed the horse hanging his head when he went by his stall earlier.

Jamie turned Dickens into the pasture. He kicked up his heels and trotted across to two other horses under a tree, as if he had plenty to tell and he knew the other horses would be happy to hear it. Jamie leaned on the gate and thought about Kermit's coulda, shoulda words. He could try to step between Piper and Braxton Crandall, but the question was, should he.

Not a question he was ready to answer today. Instead he was supposed to be getting answers from Mrs. Breckinridge. He found her in the rose garden in front of her house.

"Ah, there you are," she said. "I had about given up on you."

"I had to take care of the horse I brought back."

"Of course. Horses more than earn their place around here." She clipped off a cherry-colored rose and held it to her nose. "So lovely, but this one never has the scent you might wish for it. Do you appreciate roses, Mr. Russell?"

"Appreciate? I'm not sure what you mean." When she just

kept giving him that quizzical look, he went on. "But yeah, I guess so."

She put the cut rose into a basket and moved to clip off a white bloom. "This one lacks the vibrant colors of the last one." She gave it a sniff. "But it smells heavenly." She put it in the basket too and then looked out at the other bushes lining a rock walkway. "Many of these roses have been developed with grafting."

"Oh?"

"Yes, but the thing to remember is that whatever man does develop, he does so with the materials and intelligence the Lord supplies. That's what I've tried to do here at Wendover. Develop something to help these people with the gifts the Lord has given me. I've invited many along to help make this successful, and it is working. Mothers are not dying in childbirth. Our babies are healthier."

"Why did you decide to build here?"

"You mean here on this hillside?" She looked back at the log house behind them. "Or do you mean why did I pick Leslie County for my grand experiment with midwifery services?"

"Both." Jamie pulled a little notebook and a pencil stub out of his pocket. He was relieved the pencil showed lead.

"I like a reporter who lets me talk without telling me what he expects me to say." She picked up her basket. "Come walk with me down Pig Alley."

"Pig Alley?"

She laughed. "You have been here a short time if you don't know the road past the barn and the Garden House is Pig Alley. And before you ask, it got that name from Stella, a very bossy sow we had a few years ago, who wandered up and down Pig Alley looking for dogs or people to terrorize. We eventually had to get rid of her, but she left behind enough progeny to continue the chance of finding a pig in your path. Looks as though the way is clear today and we can take these roses to Aileen. She does love a rose on her desk."

"So your animals have free range?"

"Not all of them. The geese, dear things, and Matilda, our pet cow. Along with the pigs. Even the dogs know not to bother Matilda or the Stellas of now. And of course, they all make wide circles around the geese." She chuckled. "I've heard our girls make wide circles around them too. The horses have to stay contained to be ready, should someone need to go to Hyden or out into the districts."

"I've been told you traveled by horseback on all these trails before you started the Frontier Nursing Service here."

"Oh, I didn't answer your earlier question, did I?" She shook her head a little. "Pig Alley distracted me. But yes, I did interview every granny healer I could locate and talked to the local people too about the need for proper healthcare. That was before I had my fall from Traveler and broke my back. Since then, riding is more difficult. I do still ride, but I can't stay in the saddle for the hours and days I did at that time."

"I'm sorry."

"So am I, but the good Lord did allow me to get things up and running here before my accident. That was a blessing." She looked around. "And this place. Another blessing. I rode past here, and it was as though the sun shone brighter on this hillside. I simply knew this would be the place for the headquarters of my midwifery service."

She started walking again. "The mountain people helped build my house. They have been so welcoming, appreciative of our service bringing their babies into the world. And they are blessed with many babies." She sighed. "As you know I was not. I had two babies of my own. Dear Polly did not live out the day after her birth, and my cherished Breckie died not long after his fourth birthday. A sudden illness. Heartbreaking. But he was so brave. How could I be any different?"

She blinked back tears. "His dear little cousin said my Breckie always said he was a bird and could fly. He might fall down, but he thought he could fly. I want other children to have that same feeling. That they can fly as well as fall. That is why I started the Frontier Nursing Service."

"He must have been a special little boy," Jamie said.

"Oh yes." She smiled. "Breckie has been with me through all my endeavors, and whenever I have had the misfortune to lose a baby at birth or to illness, I know Breckie is there waiting to usher them into paradise. Not that it happens often."

She pointed toward his notebook. "Make sure you note that. We have a wonderful healthy-baby rate here due to our prenatal care and midwifery training."

"That's great for an area like this with so much poverty."

Her look hardened on him. "No. For any area, no matter the family income. You can check the records. Our midwives have a better mother-baby survival rate than anywhere in the country. Be sure you put that in your story. And I don't want to read any nonsense about our people here. These are good people. The men love their families, and the women are strong and resourceful. And the children, who wouldn't love these children?"

"Yes, ma'am."

She smiled then, as the hard look slipped away. "I told you about our Christmas party, didn't I? On the train?"

Jamie nodded. "I saw all the toys stored in the attic when I got the tent."

"Yes, we get donations all year long. Not only toys but layettes, so our babies can have soft new clothes. Then we're always happy to get shoes for the children. We do all we can to keep our people healthy. Early on, we began an inoculation program for diseases like typhoid and diphtheria, but when we first came to the mountains, deaths from such were common." She looked sad. "So common in fact that we treated one little boy at the hospital who begged us not to send him home because he said everybody died there. He was sure if he went home, he would succumb too. Fortunately, he is doing fine. I see him now and again."

Jamie scribbled notes as fast as he could.

"The hospital has been such a blessing. People were so kind to send donations and now we have a good place for those who need extra care our nurse midwives can't supply in the patients' homes." She pointed up the hill to the tent Jamie had set up. "I told you, didn't I, that I slept in that tent awhile. Before we had the hospital, Wendover was the hospital, and sometimes things would get very crowded. My nephew was one of the first couriers, and the two of us slept in the tent to free up room at the house. Not the most comfortable bedroom, as I'm sure you have discovered." She laughed.

"Are all your midwives from England?"

"Trained in England. There's no midwifery school in America. I trained as a midwife in England, and so did a Texas girl who is working with us now. You may have met her at Wilder Ridge. Nurse Hankins."

"No. The other nurse, Nurse Freeman, said Nurse Hankins was away taking care of a sick girl."

Mrs. Breckinridge chuckled again. "Oh, Alice. That young'un is tough. She can handle anything."

"She had Piper plucking a chicken."

"Good for her. Your Piper needs to learn some survival skills. My courier girls come here having been served all their lives. Here they learn to serve others." She gave him a sideways look. "She is your Piper, isn't she?"

He blew out a breath. "I would like to say yes, but she's been promised to another."

"Oh yes, that Braxton Crandall. I met him at breakfast. A nice young man. Says his mother is quite interested in our work here." She shook her head. "I don't believe I've ever had a girl here that had two fellows chase after her to the mountains. That is why you're here, isn't it?"

"Partly." He knew better than to lie to this woman. "But I do want to write this story. Is it all right if I take some pictures before I leave?"

"Are you leaving soon?"

"I should." That made Jamie think of Kermit's mother's coulda, shoulda, woulda advice again.

"Should you?" Her lips turned up in a little smile. "I don't think you've interviewed enough people to get the full story. You should talk to Danny about how it feels to be a courier. That would add to your story. Young society girls coming down and working with horses and running errands. Oh, and plucking chickens."

"Piper is still up at Wilder Ridge."

"Then talk to Suze. This is her second time here. She's a wealth of information." Mrs. Breckinridge waved her hand toward the barn. "She's been showing young Crandall around. Seems their families are connected through business somehow."

"All right. Anybody else I should talk to?"

"Mrs. Miller, who helps me with my flowers, can tell you more about the mountains. And I'm sure you've already talked to Kermit." She looked toward the barn again. "Dear Kermit. I fear he's facing a difficult task with Puddin. Poor horse, but worse, poor Kermit. Perhaps you can help him dig the horse's grave before you leave."

"I'd be glad to help however I'm needed."

She reached over and patted his cheek. "Why don't you stay

out the summer? Be a courier like the girls. My first two were my nephew and his friend. They were such help in those early months. You could follow their tradition."

"I'll think about it."

"You do that. And think about other things as well. I note you said your Piper was promised. Not that she had promised." She turned toward the Garden House door. "Something to consider."

CHAPTER
THIRTY-NINE

Piper rode back to Hyden the next day with a light heart. Witnessing a miracle of life made everything look brighter, fresher, greener. A bird up in the treetops sang, "Cheery, cheery." Then on down the trail another bird picked up the refrain. What a beautiful day.

That morning after she milked Clara, they had fried chicken for breakfast. Nurse Freeman had determined frying it that morning made it fine to eat. One of the chicken legs was wrapped in brown paper and stuffed in her saddlebags. Jamie deserved a taste of their chicken.

Perhaps Mann Taylor did as well, but she had no desire to cross his path on this day. Or any day. She was grateful he'd killed the snake before it bit her, but the blast of that gun had nearly made her heart stop.

Then Jamie's kiss had more than started it racing. Along with those beautiful words, *I love you*. She should have said them right back. Let him know she had loved him forever and would continue to love him forever.

Yesterday had been a day of miracles. She hadn't killed a chicken, but she had plucked it. She had kissed Jamie. A baby started breathing when it seemed she wouldn't. Piper laughed at herself when she realized how she had listed what she counted miracles. Backwards for sure. The baby was the real miracle. That sweet infant taking a breath. Prayers answered.

Nurse Freeman had been quiet on their ride down from the West cabin late in the night after Mrs. West and the baby were nicely settled. Mrs. West's mother had shown up at the cabin, alerted to the birth by the mountain grapevine that seemed to spread news faster than a string of telephones.

Piper smiled again, thinking of the grandmother rocking the new baby while Billy and little Ellie stood on either side of her. Everything was making her smile today. And she had weeks more here in the mountains before she had to return to Louisville and face her father.

That thought did wipe her smile away. He might disown her for refusing Braxton Crandall and choosing Jamie instead. But how could she do differently? She'd have to write Braxton. Tell him her decision not to become Mrs. Crandall. He didn't love her. How could he? They barely knew each other. He had simply determined that she fit his specifications for a wife. No romance there. An arrangement was all.

Love will grow. Her mother's words echoed in her mind. Perhaps that might be true if her heart wasn't already so full of love for another. Whatever the consequences of her choice, she would have to live with it.

Life. Here on this hillside on this day astride a trusty mare and leading along another they could nurse back to health was a day to rejoice and be glad. Her heart sang along with the birds. "Cheery. Cheery." Being in the mountains had awakened her to the wonder and beauty of God's world. Just as Maxine Crutcher had promised it would.

Piper felt so good that she didn't let it bother her that much when the sky suddenly darkened and raindrops splattered down through the leaves. Lightly at first and then pounding through to drench her. The horses were resigned to walking on through rain or shine. She might as well be too. No drying out until she got to Wendover.

Even in the pouring rain her heart had a song. That was what rejoicing in the miracle of life and love could do.

———

Digging a grave for a horse wasn't easy. Jamie and Kermit had been at it for a couple of hours, with Kermit looking more and more gloomy. Two other men had shown up to help. Jamie only got first names. Butch and Zeke.

Jamie had his own reason for gloom that had nothing to do with the poor horse that Kermit and Mrs. Breckinridge had determined to put down.

"Only thing to do," Kermit said when they headed down to the horse graveyard. Puddin wasn't the first horse to be buried here. Mrs. Breckinridge didn't allow the buzzards to feast on her horses. "A horse ain't a creature that can make it on three legs. I've seen three-legged dogs that make out fine, but not a horse. Just can't be done."

"Right."

"But it's a fretful thing."

Jamie didn't say anything.

"A sorrowful, fretful, awful thing." Kermit muttered the words as he attacked the ground with his pickax to lay out the lines of the grave.

Now as the hole got deeper, Butch and Zeke seemed happy to have a job, whatever it was, while Kermit and Jamie wallowed in their gloom. Jamie should have left. Just taken the pictures of Mrs. Breckinridge, her log house, and the barn, and gone. But she'd said to talk to Suze. And Mrs. Miller, the garden lady he hadn't yet met.

Mrs. Breckinridge was right. Talking to others would make

for a better story. So he'd tracked down Suze, who was drinking lemonade on the porch with Braxton Crandall.

"Russell, I see you made it here to Wendover too," Braxton had said. "Thank you for suggesting I get someone to come get me last night. Susan was kind enough to bring a horse and lead me through the wilderness and across the river." He smiled at Suze, whose cheeks pinked.

Jamie had talked to Suze several times, and she had never shown the first hint of uneasiness or embarrassment. She had seemed to be something like Mrs. Breckinridge, sure of her place and glad to be here.

"Susan?" Jamie said. Her cheeks flamed a little brighter.

"That's my name," she said. "Braxton and I were acquaintances in New York."

"Acquaintances?" Braxton broke in with a smile. "I would hope you'd say we are old friends." The smile slid off his face when he looked at Jamie. "Old friends like you and Piper. The Piper who wasn't here when I made that late-night ride to get here. I think you knew that would be the case."

Suze spoke up before Jamie could say anything. "She'll be back this afternoon if the nurses don't have things they need her to do."

"Is that the case? Is she going to be occupied there for a while?" Braxton asked Jamie.

"I have no idea," Jamie said. "When I left Wilder Ridge to bring Miss Danson to the hospital, Piper and the nurse were headed off to deliver a baby."

"Sounds busy." Braxton kept his gaze on Jamie. "Susan says you're writing a story about Mrs. Breckinridge. That you work for a newspaper. I was under the impression you were going to join your brother in his new endeavors."

Jamie took a couple of breaths. He refused to let the man get under his skin. It could be he was merely making conversation, and Jamie needed to remember Simon's need for investment money.

"No, I'm afraid I'm not cut out for that kind of work. I have a teaching position this fall, but right now I'm writing stories for the Danville paper."

"Not a very big operation, is it?"

"The people there like it."

"Small towns do enjoy their local news. Tell you what. If you get the story written, have the editor send me a copy. I'll show it to one of my friends in the newspaper business. Might be just the kind of human interest piece they might like in the city."

Braxton didn't say which city and Jamie didn't ask. No need thinking too far ahead. He had to write the story first. "I'll tell him that."

"That would be wonderful." Suze's smile included them both.

Jamie looked at Suze. "Mrs. Breckinridge said I should talk to you to get some insight on why young women like you volunteer to come here."

"I wouldn't mind knowing that myself," Braxton said. "Might help me understand why Piper was so eager to run off down here this summer instead of staying in town so we could get better acquainted. That would seem to be a priority before we get married this fall."

"Oh." Suze's eyes widened a bit. "You're getting married this fall?"

"That is the plan. Didn't Piper tell you?"

"No, I don't think she did." An odd look crossed Suze's face. She reached for her glass of lemonade on a table between their chairs and knocked it over. She did catch the glass, but lemonade went everywhere. She jumped up. "Oh dear. I'd better get some water to wash that off the porch or we'll have ants." She gave Jamie a little smile. "But I'll be glad to talk to you later about being a courier. Maybe Danny will be back by then and you can get her impressions too."

After Suze went inside, Braxton shook his head. "Danny. I can't believe Piper lets them call her Danny."

"Piper said Danny was better than Pip."

"I can understand that, but not what she's doing here in the first place. Or Susan either." He nodded toward the screen door Suze had disappeared through. "Both girls with everything going for them. And they actually volunteered to come down here to clean horse stalls. That doesn't make sense."

When Jamie didn't say anything, Braxton went on. "Look, I realize you and Piper maybe had a romance going before her debut. I'm sorry to break that up for you, but if you truly care for Piper, then don't you think it would be best for all of us if you step out of the picture? I assure you I will do everything in my power to give Piper the life she deserves. Not one of struggle."

Not one of struggle. Those words were the reason for Jamie's gloom as he helped Kermit dig this huge hole to put poor Puddin in. The problem was, he couldn't deny the truth of Braxton's words. With him, life could very well be a struggle, at least nothing like the life Piper was accustomed to. Besides that, he couldn't even dislike the man. He gave every indication of being a good guy. Suze obviously liked him. Maybe had hoped for more, before Braxton said he and Piper were getting married. Poor Suze. Left out in the cold the same as Jamie.

Not that he was cold digging this hole. Definitely not. Jamie stopped to wipe sweat off his face before he put his foot on the shovel to push it in the ground. The blade clanked against another rock.

Butch looked over at him. "Your shovel must be a rock magnet." He laughed. "Grab that digger over there to prize it out. We keep digging, maybe we'll strike gold. That black gold anyhow. Coal. Ain't that right, Kermit?"

Without looking up, Kermit mumbled something that was no doubt better unheard and kept digging in the other corner of the hole.

Butch shoved the long iron digger's point down beside the rock and then motioned to Jamie. "Come on, boy, let's see what you got. Heft that rock up where we can get hold of it."

Zeke laughed. "That boy ain't got the muscles to move that rock."

"I think he can do it." Butch grinned at Jamie. "Give it a try, kid, but don't break nothing."

"Don't break the iron digger?" Jamie took hold of the digger. Both men laughed this time. "You ain't breakin' that," Zeke said. "Butch was meaning don't break nothing on you. Like your back."

Jamie put his weight into pushing down on the top end of the digger to lift up the rock, but it didn't budge.

"Or maybe your head from straining too hard," Butch said.

Kermit threw down his shovel. "You two jackals stop raggin' on the boy. He ain't never had to move rocks before." He pushed Jamie away and pulled the digger out of the dirt to pound it down beside the rock in several places. "Sometimes you got to loosen it first." He handed the digger back to Jamie. "Now give it a try."

Jamie dropped the sharp end of the iron digger into the ground beside the rock again, and this time when he pulled down on it, the rock moved. He shoved the digger deeper under the rock and had it out of the dirt on the next try.

Butch slapped Jamie on the back and then helped him heft the rock out of the hole.

Could be Jamie didn't need to grow a beard to fit in with the mountain men. Maybe he just needed to get dirty working alongside them. He was doing that and getting blisters from digging, but doing something hard felt good. Piper would like him helping Kermit, although she wouldn't be happy about Puddin.

Jamie looked toward the hills where just yesterday he had told her he loved her, and now it might be that if he loved her enough, he should walk away. Wish her the happiest life possible. Not one of struggle. Just walk away.

The first raindrops to hit his face were cooling and welcome. But then the rain got harder, turning the dirt into sticky mud and making the shovels of dirt heavy to throw out of the deep hole.

"Good thing it's 'bout deep enough," Zeke said.

They dug another foot down, with water pooling around their feet, before Kermit leaned on his shovel. "I reckon we need to get on with it afore the hole fills up with water." His face was grim, with water dripping from the bill of his hat. "I was aiming to wait until dinnertime when all the girls would be in the house and not paying no mind to what was happening out here."

"Won't they want to know?" Jamie asked.

"They'll know. But they won't want to see. Ain't nobody wanting to see this."

"You want me to do it?" All the earlier joviality was gone from Butch's voice.

"I reckon not. It's the least I can do for the old feller. Be his friend to the end." Kermit sighed and pitched his shovel out of the hole and climbed out after it.

The others followed suit.

"We'll stick around and cover him over for you." Zeke threw a wet arm around Jamie's shoulders. "The boy here will stay and see it through too, won't you, Russ?"

See it through. He could do that. He should do that, but then what would he do when Piper got back to Wendover and found Braxton Crandall waiting to see her? Was he brave enough to see that through? To see her promised to another man?

FORTY

"You look like a drowned kitten," Truda told Piper when she found her at the hospital.

"And you look like a cat with a broken paw."

Truda sighed. "A small fracture. Nothing too serious, but Jackson says I'll need a cast for weeks." She held up her injured arm.

"I'm glad he could fix it here and didn't have to send you to Louisville or somewhere."

"Oh no, Jackson is a very capable doctor."

Piper raised her eyebrows. "With a wonderful bedside manner too?"

"Indeed." Truda wasn't bothered by Piper's teasing. "An excellent bedside manner."

"So what are you going to do? Go home? Riding to Wendover might be difficult with that cast."

"True." Truda folded her sheet over into pleats with her good hand. "I suppose I could go home." She smoothed out the folds and looked up at Piper. "But I'm not. I'm staying here. In Hyden. Jackson's sister has a room she lets. I may stay all summer. Maybe longer. According to how things go."

"But what about your job at the bank?"

"I'm not the only person who can add up a column of figures." She stared at Piper, as though daring her to dispute that.

"I suppose not."

Truda touched Piper's arm. "I've always intuitively recognized risks and taken steps to avoid them. But not this time. This time I'm flinging caution to the winds."

"Father will be upset." Her poor father. He would be even more upset with Piper not accepting Braxton Crandall's proposal. If that talk of needing a wife and thinking she might fit the bill could count as an actual proposal.

"I'm sure he will, but he should have realized long ago that I make my own decisions." Truda narrowed her eyes on Piper. "As can you."

"I can't marry Braxton Crandall."

"Of course not. You're in love with that Russell boy. It's never a good fit when you love one man and marry another. That's why I'm a spinster."

"Did you love Dr. Jack even back then?"

"I don't think I can say that, but I did compare every potential suitor to this man I dreamed of meeting again. And now we have met again and we plan to give ourselves that chance we missed out on years ago." She tightened her fingers on Piper's arm. "Don't you miss out. No matter what your father says."

"Well, I don't guess he can say anything until the end of the summer." Piper smiled.

"That might not be true."

"Father's here?" Piper was astounded.

"No." Truda hesitated before she said, "But Braxton Crandall is."

Braxton Crandall here in the mountains. Piper still couldn't quite believe that as she headed to Wendover. First Jamie had shown up and now Braxton. Piper's plan to put aside all thoughts of men for a summer here in the mountains was shot. She almost hoped Mrs. Breckinridge would order them both to leave. The couriers were to put aside their personal life while they were volunteering their time here.

Piper had intended to do just that. Not think about her future until the end of summer, but she couldn't stop thinking about Jamie. She didn't want him gone. Not until she had time to echo his words *I love you.*

She did love him and not Braxton, but then Braxton hadn't expected her to love him. Only marry him and then wait for love to grow. But wasn't it better for love to already be sprouted in the garden of your life before vows were spoken? It definitely wouldn't be good to need to root out love for a different person from her marital garden.

Like Truda, she had her heart set on one man. She could no longer consider Braxton's marriage arrangement. She wouldn't call it a proposal.

As she slowly led Lady up the hill to Pig Alley through the drizzling rain, she hoped she wouldn't see Braxton until she had time to find dry clothes, although if he saw her looking like a drowned kitten, as Truda said, he might ride away in search of a more appealing bride. Problem solved. She didn't worry about Jamie seeing her wet and wilted. They'd been caught out in the rain together in the past. Besides, he'd seen her plucking a chicken.

Ginger's pups started yipping when she went in the barn. Locked in a stall, they jumped up on the bottom half-door when she peeked in at them.

"What's going on, guys?" She looked around. "Kermit?"

No answer. She'd have to wait to see why the pups were fastened up. She unsaddled Bella and rubbed down both horses. Poor Lady was hardly putting her sore leg down.

Piper stroked the mare's neck. "We'll get you fixed up. I promise."

That made her think of Puddin. The poor horse had been hanging his head when she checked on him before leaving the day before. She glanced over at his stall. Empty.

She ran out of the barn. Still nobody around. The rain must have everyone inside. Plus, it was dinnertime. They'd be sitting around the table at the Big House. Her heart gave a little lurch as she imagined Jamie sitting across the table from Braxton Crandall. Maybe comparing himself to Braxton. Maybe thinking he came up short.

She'd let him know that wasn't true, but first she had to find out where Puddin was and why the pups were locked away. Ginger wasn't anywhere in sight, and Rusty hadn't come to meet her the way he usually did. The rain could account for that. Dogs had the sense to get out of the rain. Unlike her.

No dogs, but Kermit was headed up Pig Alley toward her, carrying his rifle. With his hat pulled low, he didn't act as though he saw her. She grabbed his arm.

"Kermit, where's Puddin?"

"Gone." He pulled away from her to walk on toward the barn, with no notice of the rain coming down harder and getting his gun wet.

Rifle. The empty stall. Gone.

Down in the field, three men were shoveling a big mound of dirt into a large hole. Puddin gone. Their nursing hadn't saved the horse. Tears mixed with raindrops on her face. There was nothing she could do. She should turn around and go clean up. But instead she kept walking toward where they were surely burying Puddin. Ginger appeared beside her to nudge her hand with her nose. That dog always seemed to know when somebody needed her.

"Oh, Ginger." Piper knelt down and buried her face in the dog's wet fur. "I hope you told Puddin goodbye for me."

"I don't know if she did, but I did." When Jamie had seen Piper coming, he stuck his shovel in the ground and told Butch and Zeke he'd be right back to finish helping them cover the horse.

Piper looked up from the dog. "Jamie."

He knew her face was wet from more than raindrops. When she stood up, he wanted to pull her to him in a hug, but he was covered with mud. "I'm sorry, Piper."

"Kermit shot him?"

"Said it was the last thing he could do for the horse, but he was grim. A hard thing." Jamie flinched at the memory of the man's face as he pulled the trigger. "I'd hug you, but I'm filthy."

"I don't care." She stepped into his embrace then, and they stood like that in the rain, sharing the sorrow over a good horse. "Puddin was slow, but he was such an agreeable horse."

He kissed her wet forehead. "You should go in out of the rain. I've got to help the guys down there finish up."

"Right." She sniffed and backed away from him. "Thank you, Jamie."

"For what?"

"For being here. For helping." She motioned toward the horse's grave.

"I've got blisters to show for it." He hesitated and then went on. "Braxton Crandall is here."

"I know."

"You've seen him already?"

"No. I stopped at the hospital. Truda told me he was here."

Jamie couldn't read her face. Was she glad? He ran his fingers down her cheek, leaving a streak of mud. "I love you. No matter what happens, I will always love you."

She looked ready to say something when Butch yelled, "Hey, Russ. This hole ain't gonna fill itself."

Were there more tears on her face or just the rain? He pointed her toward the Garden House. "Go before you get soaked."

"I'm already soaked."

"Then before you dissolve." He used to tell her that when they were kids. That she was sugar and he was salt and both of them might melt away in the rain.

"Don't be silly," she said, but she had a little smile. She started to turn away, then looked back. "I brought you a chicken leg."

"From your chicken?" When she nodded, he asked, "Is it good?"

She shrugged. "We ate it and I'm not throwing up. So I guess so."

"As Nurse Freeman said, you're a wonder, Piper Danson."

She actually laughed then, before running toward the Garden House and perhaps out of his life forever. He'd had time to think while digging and then witnessing the poor horse being put down. Her father was right. Braxton Crandall was right. The best way to show how much he loved her was to go back to Danville, pack up, and head west. Search out new stories to write.

He could find odd jobs. Maybe sell something he wrote now and again. Take a leap of faith into his future and not ruin Piper's future. She'd have a good life with Braxton Crandall.

Once upon a time there was a beautiful girl who married a prince and lived happily ever after. They used to play filling in the details of the story. Piper would always argue the girl would be happier marrying the stable boy. Jamie would counter that the poor girl would have to live in a stable, and Piper would say, as long as there were horses. But now Jamie couldn't promise her so much as one horse. But Braxton Crandall could give her a stable full and a fine house besides.

He watched Piper until she went into the Garden House. Then he turned back to help Butch and Zeke finish filling in Puddin's grave. He was glad it was raining to hide the tears rolling down his cheeks.

CHAPTER
FORTY-ONE

Although still sad, Piper felt better after getting on dry clothes. Puddin wasn't the first horse she'd lost. Her riding mare had died suddenly when Piper was twelve. The mare's time, the stable owner said. That could be true for Puddin too, except that wasn't what Kermit said. His one word had been *gone*.

She wished she could say that about Braxton. She didn't want him gone like Puddin. Of course not. But gone from Wendover. She looked out toward the Big House. With night falling, the glow of lamps lit up the windows. She should go see him. She should, but morning seemed soon enough.

Except she was hungry. Breakfast was but a faint memory. The box that held their stash of candy bars was empty. Marlie, on rounds to the centers again, must have taken whatever was left. So starve till morning or face Braxton Crandall tonight in order to rummage something to eat in the kitchen.

A dog barked outside, and the next minute somebody knocked on her door. "Danny, you in there?" Suze called.

Piper opened the door. "I hope you brought food."

"If you're hungry, why didn't you come get something?" Suze gave her a long look.

"I was a mess after riding in the rain." Ginger followed Suze into the room and sat down next to Piper's leg. The dog whined and licked her hand.

"I guess it makes sense you wouldn't want to see your fiancé until you cleaned up."

"My fiancé?" Piper stared at Suze.

"Braxton Crandall. Didn't you know he was here? I fetched him from Hyden last night. He drove down in his roadster."

"He told you he was my fiancé?"

"Isn't he?" Suze frowned. "He said you were getting married after the summer."

"My father did make an arrangement of some sort with him, but I haven't made any promises to Braxton. Other than to consider his offer." Piper shook her head. "I have considered, and if Braxton wants a wife—and he seems very ready to find one—he'll have to look elsewhere."

"Are you sure?" Suze studied Piper the way she did when she was trying to identify a new flower. "He's a super nice guy."

"That's right. You did say you knew him." Piper suddenly smiled. "Am I detecting some interest in our Suze in applying for the open position of wife?"

"No, no. A man like Braxton would never look at a girl like me." Suze put her hands up to hide the flush climbing into her cheeks.

"Don't sell yourself short." Piper pulled Suze's hands away from her face. "I see an attractive, intelligent future Mrs. Crandall."

"That might be moving a bit too quickly."

"Trust me. Braxton Crandall isn't a man slow on his feet. He believes in moving fast."

"He did say we were friends." A hopeful tone crept into Suze's voice.

"That's more than the two of us could say when my parents

330

chose him as my debut escort." Piper shook her head. "My debut. When I think about that now, it's like I was a whole different girl then."

"Didn't have muddy boots then, eh? Or blisters from handling pitchforks."

Ginger went to the door. The dog looked back at them and whined again.

"What's the matter with her?" Suze asked.

"Her pups!" Piper smacked her forehead. "Somebody locked them in one of the stalls and I guess Kermit didn't let them out."

"Come on. We can go by there on the way to the Big House." Suze headed for the door. "You still need to see Braxton after he came all this way."

"I know." Piper sighed. "Is Jamie there getting something to eat? He missed supper helping the men down there."

"I haven't seen him since before . . ." Her voice trailed off and tears popped up in Suze's eyes. "Poor Puddin."

"Shh. Let's just think about Ginger and the pups right now." Piper snuffed out her oil lamp and grabbed her flashlight.

"And Braxton and Jamie. He's really why you're turning Braxton down."

A little smile curled up Piper's lips and a warm feeling settled in her heart. "I've been in love with Jamie since forever."

"Mrs. Breckinridge is not going to be happy with all this romantic stuff going on." Suze laughed and squeezed Piper's arm.

Ginger raced ahead of them to the barn, where the pups set up howls that turned to happy yips when Piper opened the stall to let them tumble out.

As rain began peppering down again, Suze and Piper ran to the house, the stone steps as familiar as the steps at home to Piper now. In the sitting room, Miss Aileen looked uneasy as she fingered the pages of an open book in her lap. Braxton stood at the front windows, looking as if he'd rather be anywhere but there.

When he heard them, he turned from the windows with a genuine smile. "If it isn't the elusive Piper Danson."

Piper smiled back. "Not elusive. Just busy. I certainly didn't expect you to be here."

"I'm glad to know you didn't invite him." Miss Aileen closed her book with a snap and stood up. "That wouldn't be acceptable at all. I expect my girls to have behavior above reproach."

"Yes, ma'am," Piper and Suze said almost in unison.

Braxton's smile got broader.

"Now, now, young'un, don't give the girls a hard time." Mrs. Breckinridge stopped halfway down the stairway. "Our girls, pretty young women that they are, have done nothing wrong. Bees are drawn to flowers." She laughed softly. "And it's working out. Mr. Crandall and I have discussed his mother's interest, and I'm sure he's anxious to give her a full report." She looked at Braxton.

"I do need to return to Louisville soon," Braxton said.

"Soon is very good." She turned her gaze back to Miss Aileen. "And young Mr. Russell has his story and may be ready to be on his way too. Although I did invite him to stay awhile. You know our first two couriers were young men. My nephew and his friend."

"Yes, but if I remember correctly, you had no girls then. Only the boys. Mixing the two would not be a good idea," Miss Aileen said. "Not at all."

"Perhaps not. At least not him staying in that tent up on the hill. I wouldn't be surprised if that thing leaks after years in the attic. If he should decide to stay, we'll find him a place in Hyden. Nurse Thompson reports he has a wonderful way with the patients. She was quite taken with him, and you know our Tommy. Not taken with many."

Miss Aileen looked ready to protest more but clamped her lips together when Mrs. Breckinridge raised her eyebrows. "Danny and young Mr. Russell have promised proper behavior."

Braxton looked at Piper. "Is there something I don't know here?"

"Jamie and I have known each other forever." Piper felt her face turning red. She hadn't planned on sending Braxton away in front of witnesses.

"Come now, Danny. Don't tiptoe around the truth." Mrs. Breckinridge came down another step. "If there's one thing I've learned in my years, it's that honesty is always not only the best policy but what causes the fewest unpleasant repercussions. I happened to be watching out the window when you came home earlier and went down to see them burying poor Puddin." She shook her head sadly. "Dear horse. Actually, that's why I came down to speak to you, young'un." She looked back at Miss Aileen. "You need to send the girls to find Kermit and bring him back here before he does harm to himself."

"Harm?" Piper said.

"Miss Aileen will explain what's needed. This weather is difficult for me and I'm afraid my back is demanding I lie down." Mrs. Breckinridge smiled at Braxton. "It has been a sincere pleasure meeting you, Mr. Crandall, and I do hope your mother will visit soon. Be sure to let us know so we can welcome her properly."

They were silent as they listened to her make her way back up the stairs and down the hallway to her bedroom.

Then Braxton surprised Piper by laughing. "I think I've just been nicely told here's your hat, what's your hurry."

Suze and Miss Aileen both started to say something, but Braxton held up his hand to stop them. "Don't concern yourselves. Susan has been a great hostess today and I did plan to leave tomorrow anyway. As soon as I saw Piper. And here she is." He fastened his gaze on her. "Tell me, Piper, are you handing me my hat and showing me the door too?"

"I never gave you any promises, Braxton. My father is the one who perhaps made you think I would, but . . ." Piper let her voice die away.

"But Russell owns your heart." Braxton didn't seem upset.

"I'm sorry." Piper met his eyes.

"And your father will be sorrier, but I happen to agree with Mrs. Breckinridge that it's better to be out with the truth than to dance around it." He looked almost cheery. No broken heart for certain. "Some deals just don't work out. I'll tell your father that."

Miss Aileen cleared her throat. "The two of you can figure this out later, but now, Danny, you and Suze need to go find Kermit and bring him back here. I'll put on some coffee."

"Coffee? Isn't it late for coffee?" Piper's head was spinning.

"Yes, well, poor Kermit struggles when he has to do the task laid out for him this afternoon. He does love the horses, and at times like these, he tends to imbibe a bit too much." Miss Aileen fluttered her hands. "We try to bring him back here where we know he won't stumble off a cliff or get into who knows what trouble."

"Oh," Suze said. "But how will we find him?"

"In the dark," Piper added.

"You have flashlights." Miss Aileen looked uncomfortable again. "Down the way is a cabin where Kermit probably found the comfort he was seeking."

"I think I know the place." Suze leaned close to Piper and whispered, "Moonshiner."

"No need naming it." Miss Aileen shushed her. "He'll let you bring him home. Poor man."

"Perhaps I should accompany the ladies," Braxton said.

"I think not." Miss Aileen was quick with the refusal. "Our girls are safe enough wherever they go, but you might be mistaken for a government man. That would not be good at all."

"Rejected again. Seems everyone is rejecting me." His smile didn't waver.

"Not me." Suze shyly looked up at him.

Braxton's smile warmed on Suze. "That's good to know, Susan. Perhaps I will have time tomorrow before I am sent on my way to look at those flower illustrations you mentioned earlier."

"I'd like that," Suze said.

"Oh dear heavens. Not more romance." Miss Aileen waved her hands in a shooing motion at Piper and Suze. "Off with the two of you. And good night to you, Mr. Crandall."

"And now I've been told to go to my room." Braxton maintained his good humor. "I'll expect to hear all about it in the morning, girls."

Outside the rain had stopped and stars peeked through the clouds. As Suze led the way down the hill, she warned, "Be careful. It's slippery."

"Should we take horses?"

"It's not far. Maybe a mile. I think."

"You think? I thought you knew where it was."

"I do. Sort of. In the daylight."

Fog was rising up from the river. "We might really get lost in this fog." Piper slowed her steps.

"Courage, Danny. We've been given a task and a courier always completes her tasks."

"Always?"

"Always."

"You won't mind if I ask a little guidance from above? I saw a miracle birth last night and we may need a different kind of miracle tonight."

"No shortage of miracles among the frontier nurses," Suze said. "Could be another miracle on the morrow if Braxton really does want to look at my flower illustrations."

Piper had to laugh at that while at the same time sending up a silent prayer they would find Kermit without stumbling over a cliff in the fog.

"Go tell Aunt Rhody. The old gray goose is dead." A man's raspy voice snaked through the fog. "And her old horse is too."

"That has to be Kermit," Piper said.

When he saw their flashlights, he stumbled, then stopped walking. "Well, if it ain't two of Aileen's girls. Out here hunting trouble." He swayed on his feet and grabbed a limb hanging over the path to steady himself.

"Not trouble. Hunting you." Suze got on one side of him and Piper on the other. "Want us to help you sing about telling Aunt Rhody?"

"I ain't wanting to tell her." Kermit sounded weepy. "I done killed her horse. Killed him dead, I did. 'Twas an awful thing to do."

"No, no, Kermit. You just sent him on to pastures where he can run and run," Piper said.

"You think so?"

"We know so," Suze said.

It was late by the time they got coffee down him and took him on to his cabin down the hill. He sprawled across his bed and was snoring before they got his boots off.

Suze put her hands on her hips. "Task accomplished. Time for us to turn in and do some snoring too."

Back in her room, Piper was almost too tired to take her own boots off. But she did feel as though her mission was accomplished. Braxton Crandall knew she wasn't going to marry him. And come morning, she would climb up to Jamie's tent and let him know she returned his love. She'd worry about telling her parents later. One task at a time.

CHAPTER
FORTY-TWO

Sun sneaking in her window woke Piper. She jumped out of bed and pulled on her jeans. She didn't want to miss another meal. She had found a leftover biscuit and ham the night before while they were getting coffee down Kermit. Poor man would probably have a brutal headache this morning.

But she didn't. She felt great. Braxton Crandall was looking in new directions for a wife, and Suze was standing in line, waiting to see if their friendship might blossom. Truda was making eyes at Dr. Jack. Love was in the air, along with the scent of honeysuckle. A glance at her clock said she might still get the horses fed and watered in time to make breakfast at the Big House. Best of all, Jamie had told her he loved her. Twice.

She felt like bursting out in song. But not "Go Tell Aunt Rhody." A happier song, even as she did feel a tremor of sorrow for Puddin. She would think about the sweet horse the way she'd told Kermit. Running through a field of clover. Happy. As happy as Piper was. She ran a comb through her hair and jerked on her shoes. The day was waiting.

Not until she opened her door into the hallway did she notice the folded paper on the floor. She made herself pick it up. Nobody slipped good news under doors.

Her heart sank when she saw Jamie's handwriting. She shut her eyes a moment and wished fervently for nothing more than a sweet love note, but she knew better. Her fingers trembled as she unfolded the note.

Dearest Piper. I do love you. More than you can imagine, and that is why I'm leaving. I cannot stand in the way of your happy future with Braxton Crandall. You will have everything you ever dreamed of having. And more. Things I could never give you.

"But what about the most important thing?" Piper muttered as though the paper could hear and transfer her words to Jamie's ears.

He told me you were promised to him and promises should be kept.

"I never promised him anything." Her voice was louder this time. Angry.

Please promise me that you will be happy.

"Not without you." Tears slid down her cheeks. "Not without you."

Love always, Jamie.

"But you didn't let me tell you I love you." She was whispering now.

"Are you talking to yourself?" Suze came out of her room and over to Piper. Her smile disappeared. "Hey, you're crying. What's wrong?"

"He's gone."

"Who? Braxton?" Suze frowned.

"No. Jamie." She shook the letter at Suze. "Left me this and went without saying goodbye. Says Braxton told him we were getting married."

"Braxton did tell him that. Yesterday." Suze took the letter and read it. She looked up. "You'll just have to tell him differently."

"I can't. He left." She pushed past Suze to look outside. The tent was gone.

Suze grabbed her and turned her around. "Think, Danny. The man doesn't have a horse. He doesn't have a car."

Piper stared at Suze, barely taking in her words. "He shouldn't have left without talking to me. Maybe he wanted to go."

Now Suze shook the letter at her. "Does this sound like he wanted to go?"

"But he went."

"Go after him."

"Miss Aileen won't like it."

"Probably not. So you'll be in the doghouse for a while. That's better than letting your heart break into a million pieces. And I don't think Mrs. Breckinridge will send you home. She likes you. Better, she likes Jamie. You heard what she said last night." Suze smiled and pushed Piper back toward her room. "Go put on your riding boots. I'll saddle Dickens."

Keep walking. If you truly love her, keep walking.

Every step, Jamie wanted to turn around. To go back. Talk her out of marrying Braxton Crandall. But that would be wrong. He wanted her to have a good life. The kind of life Crandall could give her.

The river was up after the downpours the day before. He might have crossed it if he'd had a horse, but what he really needed was a boat. So he slung his pack over his shoulder and headed for the swinging bridge. Once he got to the hospital, he might find a ride to Hazard, where he could catch the train.

He liked the swinging bridge. Maybe someday he'd write a story about a man and woman meeting on such a bridge. Loving the feeling of being suspended in the air. Loving each other. He pushed the thought away as he stepped off the bridge. Not a good time to think about writing romantic stories. Better to consider a western guy chasing bandits through some canyons. With a dog barking to show him the way.

But the barking wasn't only in his imagination. He looked back and saw a pup in the middle of the bridge. Poor little guy must have followed Jamie onto the bridge and then lost courage. He was crouched on his belly, whining now as he looked at Jamie.

Nothing for it but to go back out on the bridge and rescue the pup. His tail almost wagged off when Jamie picked him up. "Scamp. That's what they should name you. And now what to do? Take you back to the barn or on to the hospital and see if somebody there will take you home."

The pup squirmed up to lick Jamie's face.

"No telling what trouble you could cause at the hospital. Granny Virgie would like you, but I'm thinking Nurse Thompson wouldn't." Jamie sighed. "Okay. I'll get you back across the bridge. Then you'll have to find your own way home."

But when he put the pup down on firm ground again and tried to shoo him away, the pup sat down and swept the grass with his tail.

"I think he likes you and wants you to stay."

Jamie looked around. "Piper."

She dismounted and led her horse toward the bridge. "I saw you from the river."

"What are you doing here?"

"I might ask you the same thing."

"Didn't you get my note?" The pup looked up at him and barked before he put his head down with a huff of breath.

"I got it. I didn't like it. You could have at least said goodbye." She glared at him.

"You're right. I took the coward's way out. I didn't think I could bear telling you goodbye in person."

"Oh?" She tied her horse to one of the braces of the bridge and moved past Jamie to step out on the bridge. "The first time I came here, I wished you were with me. I wrote you about it, remember? How you would probably run across the bridge and have it shaking so much I'd scream."

"Come on. What kind of guy do you think I am?" He stepped back on the bridge beside her.

"I don't know. What kind of guy are you?" She didn't wait for him to answer. "A guy who says he loves me and then runs away, like those words meant nothing?"

"It's because I love you that I left. Crandall can give you the moon. With me, you'd have nothing."

"No, Jamie. Braxton can give me things." She reached to take his hand. "You're the one who can give me the moon. And the stars. And every dream we can dream."

"I might not be able to make those dreams come true."

"Then we'll dream new dreams." She stepped nearer him. "I'm not going to marry Braxton Crandall. I'm going to marry you."

He twisted his lips to keep from smiling. "But I haven't asked you yet."

"You will."

"Oh yes." He started to go down on one knee right there on the bridge.

"Not yet." She stopped him. "I have more time here as a courier, and we did promise Mrs. Breckinridge to be circumspect. No romantic behavior allowed."

"True." His smile matched hers. "But Mrs. Breckinridge is

nowhere to be seen, and the only witnesses we have right now are one pup that should be named Scamp and one horse named Dickens. They won't tell on us."

"I think you're right." She stepped into his embrace, slid her arms around his neck, and lifted her face up to him. "Let's try a kiss without a plucked chicken between us. It has to be better."

Indeed it was. So fine that he knew if he ever did write about a man and woman meeting on a swinging bridge, the story would be sure to have a happy ending.

CHAPTER
FORTY-THREE

THREE MONTHS LATER

"Can you believe this?"

Piper peered over Truda's shoulder as she stared into the dresser mirror in an upstairs bedroom at Wendover. "I believe you look gorgeous."

"Okay. Gorgeous maybe." Truda laughed. "But me in a wedding dress? A wedding dress!"

Truda wore a satiny ivory dress with flowing sleeves and straight slim lines that made her look ten years younger. Or maybe her radiance was what made her look younger. Piper had never seen her so happy.

"You're glowing. Dr. Jack is one lucky man to be downstairs awaiting such a beautiful bride." Piper squeezed her shoulder. "Are you nervous?"

"No. Yes." Truda shook her head. "No. I'm too old to be nervous." She stepped to the side to let Piper—wearing a similar dress, only in a soft green shade—see her reflection in the mirror. "And you're too young to be nervous. We make a pair, don't we?"

Piper smiled. "We do."

"That's *I* do, my dear. We need to get our lines straight." Truda gave her a mock frown. "Are you sorry you didn't go with traditional white?"

"Not at all. You were right when you told me at my debutante ball that white wasn't my most flattering color. Although I suppose I could have worn that dress and saved some money."

"It was my money and I'm very happy to spend it on these gowns." Truda had found a local woman to make the dresses for them. She touched Piper's cheek. "I am so glad we are sharing this day and do appreciate your mother letting us have these few moments alone."

Piper's mother had just kissed both Piper and Truda and gone back down the stairs to join Piper's father and brother in Mrs. Breckinridge's sitting room. Piper's sister, Leona, had not come since her baby, Thomas Harper the Third, was considered too young to make the trip. Piper had no idea how her mother had talked her father into coming to Wendover for the wedding. The weddings. Perhaps he thought he owed it to his sister to be present. Perhaps Piper's mother had worked some kind of miracle.

Miracles did not seem so rare here in the mountains. She had seen the miracle of birth again and again. She had seen love blossom between Truda and Dr. Jack. Then, wonder of wonder, Jamie's story about the frontier nurses had spread from paper to paper until he had been commissioned to write more articles about the mountains. And now she was about to realize the desire of her heart by stepping to the marriage altar to vow her love to Jamie forever.

"Your mother gave me a gift when you were born. I've told you I was there and named you Piper. That name has no doubt been a burden at times, as has mine."

"Just call me Danny." Piper laughed.

"I do hope the preacher doesn't do so." Truda's eyebrows went up. "But your mother allowed me to give you that name, and I owe

344

her much gratitude for letting me be part of your life. Although I doubt if Erwin will ever forgive me for encouraging you to wed your young man."

"Father is here."

"May wonders never cease."

"Mother is the wonder."

"Indeed."

"If you two don't come down"—Mrs. Breckinridge called up the stairs—"we are going to eat the cake Rayma baked without you."

"Mrs. Breckinridge summons, and what Mrs. Breckinridge says must be done. Miss Aileen made sure all us couriers knew that." Piper pointed toward the hallway. "You first."

Piper followed Truda down the stairs, where Dr. Jack and Jamie waited with Dr. Jack's minister, Reverend Combs. Jamie's uncle Wyatt stood with him. Mrs. Breckinridge stood with Dr. Jack, and Piper's mother stood with both Truda and Piper. Piper would have asked Suze or Marlie, but they'd gone back to their homes. Marlie to Ray, her young man in Chicago, and Suze to New York, where Braxton Crandall was helping her find a publisher for her flower and plant drawings. New couriers were feeding the horses and cleaning the stalls now.

The preacher had them repeat the vows one at a time.

"For better. For worse."

With Jamie's gaze on her face, everything felt better, but if worse came, they would deal with it together.

"For richer. For poorer."

Poorer might be their beginning if one counted the money in their pockets, but she could count so many better things. They were rich in love. That was the best way to be richer.

"In sickness and in health."

A promise made, whatever came.

"To love and to cherish till death do us part."

The vows said. The kiss shared. A new life begun.

Piper started the summer wanting to do something different. She was ending the summer the same way. Tomorrow she and Jamie would climb on a different kind of horse, the motorcycle his uncle had given them as a wedding present, and go wherever their wanderlust led them to search out new stories. Adventure awaited as they began living their own happily-ever-after story.

Loved this story?

Read on for the first chapter of another
historical romance in the mountains
of Appalachia from Ann Gabhart.

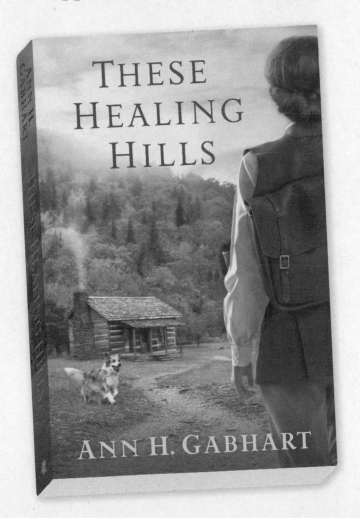

CHAPTER
ONE

May 15, 1945

Francine Howard stepped off the bus into another world. She should have been prepared. She'd studied the Frontier Nursing information until she almost knew it by heart. That should have given her a glimpse into this place.

Hyden was in the Appalachian Mountains, but it was still Kentucky. While she lived in Cincinnati, she had spent many summer weeks on her Grandma Howard's farm in northern Kentucky. But somehow the train from Lexington to Hazard and then the bus from Hazard to here had transported her away from everything she thought she knew about Kentucky and dumped her out in a place that looked as foreign to her as the moon.

But wasn't that what she wanted? To be in a new place long before Seth Miller brought his English bride home from the war. That might not be long. The war in Europe was over. Now, with all the firepower of the Allies focused on the Pacific, surely an end to the terrible war was in sight.

When the news flashed through the country last week that Germany had surrendered, Francine celebrated along with everybody else. How could she not be happy to think about the boys coming home, even if Seth's last letter had changed everything? Seth might finally be on the way home, but not to her.

The news of his betrayal hadn't taken long to circulate through Francine's neighborhood. Not from Francine. Seth's little sister took care of spreading the news. Alice had shown everybody the picture Seth sent home of him with his arm around this English woman. She'd even shown Francine.

"I know you and Seth used to date when you were in high school, but he didn't give you a ring or anything, did he?" Alice must have seen the stricken look on Francine's face, because she pulled the picture back quickly and shoved it in her pocketbook.

"No, no ring." Francine managed to push a smile out on her face and salvage a little pride.

Alice fingered the clasp on her purse. "You want to see the picture again? I jerked it away pretty fast."

"I saw it. She's very pretty."

She'd seen enough to know that. The woman had barely come up to Seth's shoulder. Petite with curly blonde hair and a dimpled smile. Nothing at all like Francine with her plain brown hair and hazel eyes. Just looking at the woman's picture had made her feel tall and gawky. In heels, Francine was nearly as tall as Seth.

Built strong, Grandma Howard used to say. Her grandmother told Francine she was pretty enough, but a person didn't want to be only for pretty like a crystal bowl set on a shelf folks were afraid to use. Better to be a useful vessel ready to be filled with the work the Lord intended for her. Back in her neighborhood, Francine had felt like a cracked bowl somebody had pitched aside.

People sent pitying looks her way. Poor Francine Howard. Going to end up just like Miss Ruby at church, who cried every Mother's Day. No husband. No children. No chances.

But where one door closed, another opened. If not a door, a window somewhere. Another thing Grandma Howard used to say. The Lord had opened a way for Francine to escape the pity trailing after her back home. The Frontier Nursing Service. She had a nursing degree and she could ride a horse. She needed an adventure to forget her bruised heart.

An adventure. That was what the woman had offered when she came to the hospital last November to recruit nurses to train as midwives at the Frontier Nursing Service in Leslie County, Kentucky. The need was great. The people in the Appalachian Mountains didn't have ready access to doctors the way they did in Cincinnati.

At the time, Francine imagined it might be thrilling to ride a horse up into the hills to deliver babies in cabins, but she gave it little consideration. Seth would be home from the war, and she planned to have her own babies after they got married. Babies she might already have if not for the war or if she hadn't let her mother talk her out of marrying Seth before he went overseas. Then everything might be different.

Everything was different now as she stood in front of the drugstore, where the bus driver told her she needed to get off. She had no idea what to do next. The people on the street were giving her the eye but staying well away, as though her foreignness might be catching. She squared her shoulders and clutched her small suitcase in front of her, the larger bag on the walkway beside her. She tried a smile, but it bounced back to her like a rock off a stone wall. Somebody was supposed to meet her, but nobody stepped forward to greet her.

She blinked to clear her eyes that were suddenly too watery. Francine wasn't one to dissolve into tears when things went wrong. She hadn't even cried when she read Seth's letter. What good would tears do? Prayers were better. But right at that moment, Francine didn't know whether to pray for someone to show up from the Frontier Nursing Service or for a train ticket back to Cincinnati.

"She must be one of those brought-in women."

The man was behind her, but she didn't need to see him to know he was talking about her. She was a stranger. Somebody who didn't belong. At least not yet.

First things first. If nobody was there to get her, she'd find her own way to the hospital. All she needed was somebody to point the way.

A man came out of the drugstore straight toward her. "You must be one of Mrs. Breckinridge's nurses."

"I'm here to go to the midwifery school." Francine smiled at the tall, slender man. "Somebody was supposed to meet me."

He didn't exactly smile back, but he didn't look unfriendly. "Been a lot of rain. The river's rolling. Probably kept them from making it to see to you. Do you know how to get to the hospital?"

Francine looked around. "Is it down the street a ways?"

"It's a ways, all right. Up there." He pointed toward the mountain looming over the town.

Francine peered toward where he was pointing. High above them was a building on the side of the mountain.

"There's a road, but since you're walking, the path up the mountain is shorter." The man gave her a dubious look. "You think you can make it?"

Francine stared at what appeared to be steps chiseled in the side of the mountain. "I'm sure I can." She tried to sound more confident than she felt.

"The path is plain as day. Don't hardly see how you could stray off'n it. But tell you what. Jeb over there is headed that way. He can take you on up."

The man he indicated with a nod of his head was the last person Francine would have considered following anywhere. In spite of the warm spring day, he wore a coat spilling cotton batting from several rips. A felt hat perched on top of a tangled mass of graying hair, and his beard didn't appear to have been trimmed for months. Maybe years. With a shotgun drooping from the crook of his arm, the man appeared anxious to be on his way and not at all happy to be saddled with a brought-in woman.

But what other choice did she have? She leaned over to pick up her other bag, but the man from the drugstore put his hand on it first.

"Don't bother with that. Somebody will bring it up to you later."

She left it, wondering if she'd ever lay eyes on it again as she fell in behind the man named Jeb. Back home, daylight would have a couple more hours, but here shadows were deepening as the sun slid out of sight behind one of the hills that towered around the town. Jeb gave her a hard look, then turned and started away without a word. Francine slung her purse strap over her shoulder, clutched her small suitcase, and hurried after him.

She had to be insane to follow this strange man away from town. He could be leading her to some godforsaken place to do no telling what to get rid of this interloper slowing him down. Not that he set a slower pace for her. She had to step double-quick to keep up. Nor did he offer to take her suitcase or even look back to see if she was still behind him. He didn't have to look back. He could surely hear her panting. Where were those horses the Frontier Nursing brochure promised?

When the path leveled out for a few paces, Francine caught up to the man whose pace didn't change whether the way was steep or level. She could at least try to be friendly. "My name is Francine Howard."

She wasn't certain, but she thought he might have grunted. She was certain he did not so much as glance back over his shoulder at her and that, in spite of the path taking a sharp upward turn, he began moving faster. His foot scooted on the trail and dislodged a rock that bounced down toward Francine. She tried to jump out the way, but she wasn't quick enough.

The rock landed on her toe. She bit her lip to keep from crying out. Mashed toes practically required a good yell. She set down her suitcase and rubbed her toe through her shoe. Her fingers were numb from clutching her suitcase handle and she could see nothing but trees. No wonder they called this place Thousandstick Mountain. This many trees had to make a lot of sticks.

She'd been totally mistaken thinking her visits to her grandmother's farm would prepare her for Leslie County. Everything wasn't straight uphill there. A person could walk those rolling hills without losing her breath. Trees didn't close in on you and make you wonder if you'd ever see sunshine again.

She gave up on her throbbing toe and massaged her fingers. She started to call for the man to wait, but she kept her mouth closed. The path was plain, and while the shadows were lengthening, it wasn't dark. How far could it be? People obviously traveled this way all the time, and the man's footprints were plain as day on the muddy pathway.

The Lord had pointed her to the Frontier Nursing Service. He wasn't going to abandon her on this mountain. Francine ignored the little niggling voice in the back of her mind that said the Lord had given her a guide. Her task was keeping up.

Too late for that now. The man was gone. Francine rotated her shoulders and picked up her suitcase. Time to carry on. Find her place on this mountain.

She started climbing again, slower now as she looked around. Thick green bushes pushed into the path with buds promising beauty. Rhododendron. She couldn't wait to see them burst into bloom. Delicate white flowers near the path tempted her to step into the trees for a better look, but the thought of snakes stopped her. Snakebit and alone on this mountain might not lead to a happy outcome.

At first, the man's footprints were easy to follow, but then the way got steeper and nothing but rocks. No sign of the man ahead of her. Worse, the path split in two directions. Even worse, the shadows were getting darker. It could be she should have run to keep up with silent Jeb after all.

Even standing on her tiptoes, she couldn't see the hospital up ahead as the trees and bushes crowded in on the path here. Both traces went up, so that was no help. She had no idea how high this mountain was. She might be climbing all night. But no, she'd seen the hospital from town. It couldn't be much farther.

Francine set her case down again and chocked it with her foot to keep it from sliding away from her. The word *steep* was taking on new meaning.

With her eyes wide open, she whispered, "Dear Lord, I know you haven't left me alone here on this mountain. So can you point the way?"

She stood silent then. She didn't want to miss a second answer if the Lord took pity on her after she'd foolishly trusted too much in her own abilities instead of scrambling after her mountain man guide.

Just when she was ready to give up on divine intervention and pick a path, she heard whistling. Not a bird, but a man. And the sound was coming closer. The Lord was sending her someone to point the way. Certainly not Jeb coming back for her. She couldn't imagine that stone-faced man whistling the merry tune coming to her ears.

"Hello," she called. She didn't want the whistler to pass her by without seeing her.

The whistling abruptly stopped. Francine called again. This time an echoing hello came back to her, and a gangly boy, maybe fourteen or fifteen, scrambled into view down the path to her left. His overalls were too short, showing a span of leg above well-worn shoes, but the best thing about him were his blue eyes that looked as friendly as a summer sky.

He skidded to a stop and stared down at her. "You lost?"

"A bit," Francine admitted. "Could you point me the way to the Hyden Hospital?"

"I reckon you're one of Mrs. Breckinridge's brought-in nurses." He gave her a curious look. "Do you catch babies?"

"I'm here to train to be a midwife." Francine smiled at the idea of catching babies. "At the hospital. Is it much farther?"

"Not all that far, but night might catch you. You best follow me." He came on down to her and started up the other path. "Weren't nobody down there in town to show you the way?"

"I was supposed to follow somebody named Jeb, but I didn't keep up."

The boy laughed. "That Jeb. And I reckon he never said word one. Jeb, he ain't much of a talker. Not like me. My brother used to tell me I jabbered as much as a jaybird that had been sipping out of a moonshine still. At least that's what he said before he went off to fight the Germans. That's been nigh on four years now, but I'm still a talker."

"I was very happy to hear you whistling a few minutes ago." Francine picked up her bag and followed the boy. "My name is Francine Howard. Do you have a name other than Jaybird?"

"Jaybird might be better than what folks call me. Woody. Woody Locke. Sort of sounds funny when you say it, but my pa was Woodrow. Woodrow Locke, that's a fine name. One I reckon I can take on after I get a little older." His voice softened, turned somber. "Now that Pa passed on last year."

"Oh, I'm sorry." Francine felt an answering wave of sympathy. Her own father had died two years ago.

"Ma says the Lord calls people home when he's ready for them, and we shouldn't look askance at the Lord's doing." The boy looked over his shoulder at her. "I get in trouble all the time asking too much about everything. Pa, he used to say I had a curious mind, but Ma gets worn out by my wonderings."

"That's how you learn things." Francine couldn't keep from panting a little as she climbed behind Woody.

The boy noticed. He looked stricken as he turned back to her.

"Give me that case. My ma would slap me silly if she saw me letting you lug that thing and me with two free hands."

"Thank you." Francine handed it to him. "But maybe you should just tell me the way now. You need to go on home before night falls so your mother won't worry."

"Ma don't worry none about me. She sent me up here to get some medicine for Sadie. That's my little sister and she's been punying around. The nurse over our way said she needed some ear drops she had run out of in her medicine bag. So I came on to fetch them. Sadie being the youngest and all, Ma babies her some. We all do. She ain't but four, nigh on five."

"But it will be dark soon."

"Dark don't fret me. I can find my way light or night. But Ma knowed I'd probably find a spot in town to spend the night 'fore I head on up the mountain come morning. Get me out of chores." He grinned at Francine and turned back up the path. "I oughta be shamed about that with Ma having to do them, but I laid in wood for her this morn and she milks the cow most every night herself anyhow. She'll have a list of chores a mile long to make up for me being late home, but she wouldn't want me not to help one of you nurses. No sir. I'd get in way more trouble if I didn't see that you made it to where you're going."

"You don't have any other brothers at home?" Walking uphill after him was easier without carrying the suitcase, but it didn't seem to slow Woody down at all.

"Nope. It's just me and Sadie now. Ruthie, she went north to work in one of the airplane factories and Becca got married and moved over to a mining camp in Harlan County. Ben, he's the oldest. He joined up with the army after Pearl Harbor. I been telling Ma I'm nigh old enough to go fight the Germans and the Japs too, but Ma don't like hearing that. Says she's busy enough praying that the Lord ain't ready for Ben to go home with Pa." He looked back at Francine again. "Ben's the one what says I jabber like a jaybird. Guess you can see why now."

"I always liked jaybirds." That made Woody laugh. "Where is your brother? In Europe or the Pacific?"

"Europe last we heard. We get letters now and again, but places where he might be are all cut out of them. He's a medic. Ma's right proud that he ain't just over there shooting people, but that he's doing some healing too."

"That does sound good. I'll add my prayers to your mother's for his safety and that he'll get home soon."

"That's neighborly of you. I'll tell my ma."

They stepped out of the trees to see the hospital on the side of the mountain. Not that big, but sturdy. Substantial and a little surprising. A road circled right up to its door. To the side was another building connected by a covered walkway. That must be where she'd be living for the next few months.

She'd loved working with the mothers and babies back in Cincinnati. And odd as it was here on this mountain with the long-legged boy beside her, she was looking forward to learning how to catch those babies, as he had said.

New life. And not just for the babies, but for her too. A new life in a new place. A window of opportunity for her to climb through. If only she could stop looking back at the door she had dreamed of walking through with Seth.

After she thanked the boy, she watched him disappear back down the hillside. Then she took a deep breath, squared her shoulders, and walked straight toward the hospital doors.

Acknowledgments

A story is not really complete until it has a reader or sometimes a listener. So thank you for being one of those who has allowed my story to come to life in your imagination through the magic of words. I've loved words and books ever since I can remember and dreamed of being a writer from a young age. I am blessed that my dream became reality.

But to have my stories end up in a beautiful book like the one you're holding right now takes a team. I owe much gratitude to my agent, Wendy Lawton, for always having an encouraging word and being ready to help with whatever I need. She's the best. My editor, Lonnie Hull DuPont, has been a gift to me ever since she liked *Scent of Lilacs* enough to take me into the Revell family. And thank you, Barb Barnes, for careful editing that irons out kinks in my writing. I appreciate the art department that comes up with fabulous covers. Thanks, Gayle Raymer, for your attention to detail. Karen Steele and Michele Misiak are always ready to answer questions and find ways to get my book out to readers. I appreciate you both so much, along with all those at Revell Books who do the things behind the scenes to make my stories into books. I visited Baker Publishing Group last year and saw smiles at every turn from those who work there.

I also thank my family for all the support through the years as I've followed my writing dream. My husband has been ever patient as I spend hours with imaginary people doing imaginary things. My children grew up to the sound of a typewriter, and now my grandchildren are reading my books. Blessings all around.

The Lord granted the desires of my heart by giving me stories to share with you. To God be the glory (Gal. 1:5).

Ann H. Gabhart is the bestselling author of over thirty novels, including *Angel Sister*, *The Refuge*, and *River to Redemption*, a Selah Award winner. Ann has been called a storyteller, not a bad thing for somebody who grew up dreaming of being a writer. Historical events inspire many of her stories, such as her popular Shaker stories set in her fictional Harmony Hill Shaker village or her Appalachian stories featuring the Frontier Nursing Service. She also writes about family life and love and sometimes mysteries set in small towns modeled after her hometown in Kentucky. She and her husband have three children and nine grandchildren and still enjoy country life on a farm near where she grew up. To learn more about Ann's books, visit www.annhgabhart.com.

Meet
Ann H. Gabhart

Find out more about Ann's newest releases, read blog posts, and follow her on social media at

AnnHGabhart.com